A FIRE IN THE HEART

Frozen, she watched him, her eyes dark with turmoil, her mouth full and red from his kiss.

Very slowly he took off his shirt.

Bonnie felt her knees grow weak. In the early hours of morning, awakened by her dreams, she had lain in bed and imagined what loving him would be like, but her imagination had never aroused these feelings inside her. They were unsettling, slowly stripping away rationality, possessing her body with uncomfortable yearnings. In truth, she didn't feel like Bonnie Eden. She felt as if some hot-blooded, restless animal had taken over her body . . .

Other Avon Books by
Katherine Sutcliffe

RENEGADE LOVE
WINDSTORM

A FIRE IN THE HEART

KATHERINE SUTCLIFFE

AVON BOOKS ◆ NEW YORK

A FIRE IN THE HEART is an original publication of Avon Books. This work has never before appeared in book form. This work is a novel. Any similarity to actual persons or events is purely coincidental.

AVON BOOKS
A division of
The Hearst Corporation
105 Madison Avenue
New York, New York 10016

Copyright © 1990 by Katherine Sutcliffe
Cover painting by Victor Gadino
Inside cover author photograph by Constance Ashley
Published by arrangement with the author
Library of Congress Catalog Card Number: 89-91916
ISBN: 0-380-75579-3

First Avon Books Printing: March 1990

AVON TRADEMARK REG. U.S. PAT. OFF. AND IN OTHER COUNTRIES, MARCA REGISTRADA, HECHO EN U.S.A.

Printed in the U.S.A.

RA 10 9 8 7 6 5 4 3 2 1

This book is dedicated to:

Neil, my own Lord Rogue, the "third Earl of Bradford."
My husband. My hero. My heart.

A very special thanks to those individuals who have done
what they can to help my career:

Harry Helm, of Waldenbooks,
Ron Hickman of FEC News in West Palm Beach, Florida,
Cessalee Hensley of Bookstop Bookstores, Austin, Texas,
Ric Williams of ET Distributing, Houston, Texas,
Jenny Jones of The Book Shelf, Grand Prairie, Texas.

And as always to:

Rebecca George, Jill Hunter, Amanda Jay,
and Phoebe Stell
For always being there for me.

And for Shelley Darmon, who never lost faith
in Damien's and Bonnie's story,
though occasionally I did.

PART ONE

Reputation, reputation, reputation! O, I have lost my reputation! I have lost the immortal part of myself, and what remains is bestial.

—WILLIAM SHAKESPEARE

One

Middleham, Yorkshire
Spring, 1861

The hounds' baying brought Bonnie Eden's head up, and though her mind was groggy and hazy with pain she was lucid enough to know that if she didn't move soon the animals would find her. She tried to rise, rocked back and forth on her knees, feeling the cold rain beat her back and the mire suck at her hands. Again the dogs. Their throaty howls filled the night wind like ghosts. Bonnie imagined she could hear their panting and slavering as the animals closed in for the kill.

No, she told herself. Birdie Smythe wouldn't allow them to kill her. He would do it himself. But first he would punish her. Lock her in that cold, black room and—

She stumbled to her feet, her fear of the horrible punishment far greater than that of being torn apart by the dogs. Keep moving. That was the only answer. Put Caldbergh Workhouse behind her as she should have done five years ago. But the pain. Her skin was on fire, and with each breath her lungs felt as if they were being torn apart.

Lightning ripped the sky, followed instantly by thunder. As Bonnie topped the rise, the sky brightened again, pouring light briefly over the towering ruins of Middleham Castle in the distance. Blinking the rain from her eyes, she stared at its shattered battlements, roofless, crumbling walls, and the black pit of water that surrounded it all. There was no safe haven among the decimated gray stones, so she turned and stumbled down the fell toward the river Cover, praying in some remote corner of her mind that the spring rains had not fallen long enough to make the river impossible to cross by foot.

She slipped on the dead bracken, fell flat on her back, feeling the scrubby scarlet brush scrape her face and neck. How long she lay there she could not guess. Only the driving, needle-sharp rain brought her to her senses again, and with her last will of survival she forced herself to stand, to stumble through the shin-high, frigid water to the opposite bank of the Cover.

Her mind tumbled back, experiencing again the evening of her father's murder. She'd run then, too. Forever it seemed, into the dark and cold, into the horrible nightmare that had haunted her every night since. In those recurring nightmares she was always fleeing, weeping as quietly as possible, expecting any moment to be discovered by her father's killer. Now she was escaping again—for real this time—and the danger advancing ever closer was no longer panting, howling dogs, but a devil on two legs, with cloven feet and bloodied hands. Her father's blood.

Oh, God, her father . . .

A fire had taken flame in her lungs now, consuming her with pain as she toiled up the final hill, her feverish mind denying defeat. Reaching the crest, she did her best to square her shoulders, feeling her body sway under the impact of the wind. A calmness came upon her, a peaceful acceptance as a glimpse of her mother's beautiful face flashed before her. How serene Mary Eden had looked when she had taken her final breath. Then she had simply given up the fight against consumption and slipped calmly over the precipice of life, leaving Bonnie and her father to suffer together over her death.

With the same detachment that her mother must have experienced in those last moments of life, Bonnie viewed the rain-soaked swell, the distant moor edge. Dark and bleak though the night was, she could distinguish between the marshes and pastures—the bogs being blacker than night, the pastures gray where heath choked the eroded soil along the hills. Then a light . . .

Her gaze swung back. The light sprang up again. Then another and another until they formed a steady yellow stream in the darkness. She stumbled forward, numb, exhausted, dazed. She fell. She rose and fell again. She heard the dogs and, gritting her teeth, regained her feet one last time, fixed her blurring vision on the beacons, and rallied forth.

Damien Warwick, Earl Warwick, Baron of Middleham, crushed out his cigar and left his chair.

He was hot and hard for the woman on the bed. He had been since her arrival at Braithwaite Hall. But then, she'd always had that effect on him, since the night they'd met at the Thamesburg soiree. He'd fallen a little in love with her that night. A little in love? Hell, he'd fallen a lot in love with her or at least as much as an eighteen-year-old boy who'd never had a woman could.

Lady Marianne Lyttleton stretched her exquisite white legs over the bed and smiled. "You've missed me, Damien," she teased in her husky, sensuous voice. "Don't try to hide it."

"I couldn't if I wanted to," he replied, then eased down on the bed.

"I was certain you'd forgotten me."

"Forget you? Impossible, sweetheart."

He brushed her temple with a kiss, lightly traced her delicate ear with the tip of his tongue. She purred in response, ran her long, bejeweled fingers up the length of his thigh. Damn, he'd forgotten how beautiful she was. Beautiful and treacherous. He was certainly glad he wasn't her cuckolded husband. He wouldn't be as uncaring as Harry. But then, he wasn't *turned* like Harry, preferring men instead of women.

"When you stopped writing I thought, perhaps, that you'd married," she said.

He shook his head, concentrating on the soft nest of hair he could see beneath the filmy triangle of material between her thighs. She'd been to Paris recently. He could tell. He could smell the perfumed steam of her earlier bath on her skin, one of those piercingly sweet floral scents that drove him crazy with desire. The lace-trimmed camisole came just to the top of her thighs and beneath it her breasts were full and naked, the nipples jutting and dark pink. Her red hair hung in a dark shadow around her shoulders and looked like night fire across the white pillows beneath her head.

Marianne threw her head back, laughing as his mouth followed the path of his fingers. "I always liked that about you, Damien. You were never one to dawdle."

He caught the brief covering on her hips and swiftly pulled it down. "Did you come here to chat," he responded, tossing the silk to the floor. "Or did you come here to—" Thunder crashed over the house, shaking the walls and driving a sudden blast of wind and rain against the window. Damn storm, he thought. The dreary clouds had dumped rain on the countryside every day since his return to Yorkshire. He kissed the inside of one white thigh and slowly, slowly moved upward, nuzzling, licking, feeling her grow even hotter and wetter beneath his mouth.

"Did you miss me a little?" came her unsteady voice above him.

"Every night . . . open your legs a little more, sweetheart."

She did so and arched up against him.

The night wind howled over the moor, sounding like a banshee, wailing plaintively and eerily through the eaves of the ancient manor house. Marianne clutched the sheet beneath her, gasping, her groans drowned out by the wind's force and the rain lashing the window. Her hands clawed at Damien's shoulders as he slid his body over hers, into hers with a power that drove her to dig her nails into the slick, moist flesh on his back and to whimper. She was so good. So damn good. The best he'd ever had.

He closed his eyes and continued to move, to draw and thrust. There was no ceremony with Marianne, no coy displays. She enjoyed sex as much as any man and made no bones about it: She wanted it all—fast and furious. Fast—faster—his flesh burned. He was going to finish too soon, he thought, but though he tried to focus his thoughts on the pummeling rain, she seemed to sense it and took delight in taunting him beyond his limits. The blood pounded in his head and loins. The pressure mounted inside him, in the part of him buried in the deep, moist tunnel of her, and he gritted his teeth, fighting back the climax. He was losing control. Damn, damn, he was losing it . . .

"Milord!"

The words echoed in his consciousness and he fought them back.

"Milord! Come quickly, milord!"

I'm trying, he thought. *I'm doing my best.*

"Milord!" came the cry again, just outside the door. This time the voice registered, and he was snapped back to reality as Marianne tensed beneath him. He heard footsteps running up the corridor, heard the housekeeper Jewel wail one last time before she threw open the door. Her cry of "Milooorrr—" came to an abrupt silence as Damien threw himself off an hysterically laughing Marianne and grabbed for the counterpane. Glaring at the red-faced, ogling woman, he growled, "You'd better have a damned good reason for this."

Jewel, her cap slightly askew and her chubby, short-fingered hands twisted into her black skirt, bobbed a curtsy and nodded her head. "Beg pardon, milord, but there's a child—" Damien snapped the sheet taut over his hips. "—um, a wee lad, milord, and I do believe he's poorly. Come stumblin' through the front door, he did, wi'out a single knock. Spilled onto the floor soakin' wet and shiverin' like a newborn lamb. He's right feverish, I vow."

As Damien moved to leave the bed, Jewel bobbed again and dashed from the room. Angrily, he thrust his legs into his breeches, swept his white shirt from the back of a chair and pulled it on. As Marianne began to rise, he rounded on her, pointed one finger in her face, and ordered, "Stay right where you are." Then he turned on his heels and left the room.

By the time he'd descended the stairs and entered the marble-floored vestibule, every servant in the house had collected just inside the door, crowding around the child. Damien nudged his way through the circle until he looked down on the skinny, dripping wet boy. The lad's face was flushed with fever and his body shook, racked with tremors.

Damien forgot his irritation in an instant as he went to one knee and gently pressed his callused palm against the boy's smooth, hot face. Then the child's eyes opened, and Damien was struck by a flash of such intense blue he caught his breath.

"Help me," came the small voice. "Don't let 'em take me."

"Who?" Damien responded. "Who's after you, lad?"

"The keepers. D-don't let 'em do it. Not *that.*"

Damien ran his hands down the boy's thin arm. Across the back of the lad's hand were angry red welts.

Looking over his shoulder, he said to Jewel, "Get plenty of blankets and warm the mutton broth we had for dinner."

"Aye, milord," came the response, then Damien turned back to the boy and gently lifted him from the floor, cradling him in his arms as he turned for the stairs.

Marianne stood on the bottom step wrapped in a scarlet satin robe. Her eyes wide with worry, she gasped as the boy's arm swung limply to his side and his head rolled weakly against Damien's chest. The slender shoulders heaved as the boy coughed then struggled for his next breath.

"Dear God," Marianne whispered. "Damien, we should send for the doctor."

"Certainly. Will you see to it?"

"I'll send someone to Middleham immediately."

The boy was so light, hardly heavier than a feather. There was something so stirring about that tiny, capped head against his shoulder. Damien was moved by the helplessness, the innocence of the child gripping his open shirtfront in his muddied, trembling fingers. He found himself soothing him with words.

"You're safe now. No one is going to hurt you here."

A shiver was the boy's only response.

Damien took him directly to the bedroom that had once been his sister's. They passed through the richly appointed boudoir into the sleeping quarters. He called back to the attending servant to build a fire in the grate, for though spring was several weeks old, the house was yet damp and cold from the constant fog and rain. He waited until another servant had pulled back the bed covers before he placed the boy on the bed.

Marianne entered the room and came to his aid. She began removing the boy's shoes, dropping them to the floor while Damien unbuttoned his shirt. When his fingers brushed the muslin binding around the boy's chest, he paused and tugged the shirt open a little more before stepping back and attempting to come to grips with why the lad should be bound so. Was the boy injured in some way? A broken rib perhaps, or—

A soft gasp from Marianne brought his head around. Marianne, in the process of pulling down the boy's breeches, suddenly grabbed the sheet and threw it over the invalid's loins. "My God," she whispered.

He looked at the boy's face, the delicate nostrils, the high cheekbones, the sweep of coal-black lashes resting against fair skin. His lower lip was full and red, and the upper lip was shaped like a cupid's bow. A slow realization took hold of Damien's senses. He reached down and flipped off the boy's cap.

Bonnie forced open her eyes and looked up at the white-faced, raven-haired man staring down at her. Then there was another face—a woman's—whose tumbling red hair reminded her of fire. Perhaps it was the same fire burning her mind and lungs. The woman spoke.

"Why, Damien, he's a—a—"

"She," he supplied. The deep timbre of his voice felt like a knife through Bonnie's head. She groaned and closed her eyes again.

"Who are you?" came *his* voice once more, agitating her pain. "Young woman, you will have to—"

"G-go away," she whispered. "Leave me alone." The effort of forcing out the words caused her to cough then gasp for breath. God, if she were going to die she hoped— prayed— it would be now and it would be over with. She was just too damn tired to care any longer. "Leave me alone," she finally managed, "and let me die."

"My dear child," said the woman, "we have no intention of letting you die. Do we, Damien?"

Damien. Odd name, Bonnie thought. Odd man. Odd green eyes. She imagined that snakes might have green eyes. Forcing open her own, she looked at him and said, "Bloody snake."

His lip curled in an unfriendly manner, and when he looked down at the woman at his side his black hair spilled in a wave over his brow, nearly to his eyes. He raked it to one side before saying, "She's hallucinating."

"Poor child. Her fever is high. I'll have Jewel bring more blankets."

Bonnie rolled her head in protest. Don't touch me. Please

don't touch me, she groaned inwardly. One more blanket and she'd suffocate with pain.

In that moment another voice intruded, slightly shrill and highly excited. "Milord, there be a pack o' men and dogs at our door! You'd best come quick or they'll be stormin' the house, I vow!"

Bonnie sat upright in bed, instinctively grabbing for the man's arm. She missed and raked her fingers down the front of his chest before he snapped her wrists back so sharply that she momentarily forgot her fear of Birdie Smythe, forgot even the confusion and discomfort of her illness. She felt only the intense grip of his fingers around her wrists, heard his hiss of pain and his oath of anger as he shoved her roughly down on the bed. She landed in a cloud of her blue black hair and groaned.

"Milord!" came the servant's plea.

"Aye, I'm coming!" he barked. Then to the red-haired woman he commanded, "See that the filthy little urchin remains quiet while I'm gone."

"I'll do my best," the woman replied.

Damien exchanged a look of challenge with the frightened, feverish girl before he turned for the door, buttoning his shirt and tucking it into the waistband of his breeches. He followed Jewel into the hallway.

Jewel, bobbing up and down before him as they hurried down the hall, clicked her tongue before saying, "Can ye imagine? Wot's this world comin' to when a mere slip of a girl is forced to run about the countryside in weather such as this? And wearin' breeches, no less!"

The front door was open. Damien's butler stood like a sentinel on the threshold, refusing entrance to the group of hounds and men clustered outside in the rain.

"What the devil is going on here?" Damien asked.

Stanley raised one brow in his usual disapproving manner and squared his shoulders. "Milord, these . . . gentlemen would like a word with you. Something about a runaway from Caldbergh, I believe."

Caldbergh! Frowning, Damien stepped into the doorway and centered his attention on the stoop-shouldered man trying desperately to control a red-spotted hound. Damien disliked him immediately.

"Warwick?" the stranger asked, squinting his small eyes against the intrusion of light over Damien's shoulder.

"I am Warwick."

"We're trackin' a runaway, my lord."

"What has that to do with me?"

"We've tracked her here."

"Her?"

The rain fell harder, dripped off the little man's hat as he shifted uncomfortably and looked over his shoulder at the others. Finally turning back to Warwick, he said, "Perhaps if we stepped inside where it's dryer—"

"Not necessary." Damien cut him off. "There is no runaway from Caldbergh at Braithwaite."

"But me dogs—"

"Are not welcome inside either."

Ignoring Damien's sarcasm, the man stepped forward, lowered his voice, and said, "The gal's name is Bonnie and she's a real troublemaker. If ye've taken her in, my lord, ye'll be regrettin' it soon enough."

"*If* I had taken her in I would hardly expect anything different coming from Caldbergh. The house's reputation precedes you, Mr. . . . ?"

"Smythe, my lord. Birdie Smythe."

"Well, Mr. Smythe. Should your little troublemaker— Bonnie—show up here, I will hasten her back to Caldbergh as quickly as possible."

"She's a villain," Smythe hurried to add before Damien could close the door. "She took a knife to one of me assistants not long back. See fer yerself."

A weasel-faced man stepped forward into the light and turned his cheek so Damien could see the jagged red wound marring his flesh. Cutting his eyes back to Smythe, Damien raised one brow and said, "I can't imagine what he might have done to deserve that."

"She's a thief," Smythe told him. "She'll rob y' blind afore y' can blink yer two eyes."

"Good night, Mr. Smythe."

Slamming the door in the man's face, Damien stared down at the puddle of water on the floor, then at Stanley.

"Caldbergh, milord?" Stanley said.

Damien looked away before replying, "Aye."

Glancing toward the gleaming silver candle holders on a table against the wall, the gray-haired servant frowned. "Shall I—rearrange some of the fixtures, do you think, milord?"

"I think there's no cause to panic yet."

"Very well," the servant responded, but Damien noted Stanley could not help but take one last, worried glance toward the silver before quitting the room. Not that Damien himself wasn't distressed to learn the visitor upstairs was a runaway from Caldbergh. But she was only a child. How much trouble could such a wisp of a girl cause?

Bitterly Damien's mouth thinned at the thought. Remembering the events of six years before, his hands clenched until his knuckles shone white. Ah God, he'd once believed that a woman with an angel's face could do no wrong. As a young man of twenty-seven, how he had worshipped Louisa Thackeray, with her gold hair and a body that could turn a man's heart and loins to fire. The Warwicks and Thackerays had been the closest of friends. Older than Louisa by ten years, he had watched her grow from a child into the most beautiful creature he had ever known. He, the biggest womanizing rakehell in England, had become smitten by her pampered and sheltered innocence, had worshipped her for her unaffected ways and free-spirited charms. They had been friends, confidants, conspirators in dreams. Marriage between them had been happily agreed on by themselves and their families. But everyone, including Damien, had encouraged Louisa to take her Season in London.

Fool. He should have known how London would change her, how every man on two continents would vie for her attention. He'd been an arrogant ass to think her head wouldn't be turned by men far wealthier than he. In a season he'd watched her change from a shy, unsophisticated child into a jaded woman who cared for nothing but her own pleasures. Still, through it all, he had loved her, trusted her, refused to believe what his intuition whispered to him . . . until he had witnessed the sickening reality with his own eyes . . . and then it was too late.

Suddenly needing a drink, he entered the library, a massive walnut-paneled room down the gallery from the vestibule, where he was immediately surrounded by the pleasant scent of well-oiled furniture. For a moment Damien was swept with memories of hours spent before the marble fire-place, stretched out upon the Persian rug while his mother read aloud from one of the thousand or so books lining the shelves. Occasionally his older brother would read. It was Randolf's position in life, after all, that he should be the best educated, the best mannered, to follow in Joseph Warwick's footsteps, down to the part in his hair and the slight tick in his left eye when he became overexcited—his only show of emotion. Randolf had been ''cut from the cloth,'' to quote his father. And Damien . . . was trouble's own son: hot tempered, rebellious, and impatient. He never waited for disaster to find him. He went looking for it.

Yet, Damien had always sensed a certain pride and approval from his father over his minor rebellions. When Damien became older, he thought, though he could never be certain, that he detected a hint of envy in his father's eyes when he would come in from a hard day or night of carousing with ''the lads,'' as Damien called them. They were more like a pack. A half dozen young men who each stood second or third in line for his father's title. Each time they met they went to their knees, clasped hands, and prayed that their fathers and brothers lived to be a thousand.

Jerome Abernathy, however, had been fated for the yoke. At seventeen his father and older brother were killed in a coach accident, and suddenly skinny, freckle-faced Jerome was Lord Ravensworth, Earl of Burnsall. They called him Ravi, at least for a while, until he no longer showed up for their weekly sessions of pubbing and wenching. They held a mock funeral for him on the Middleham green, for their friend Jerry had died and been replaced by a stiff-lipped impersonator who *looked* like Jerry, but called himself Burnsall.

Damien poured himself a drink, splashing sherry over his hand and the top of the liquor cabinet. It seemed *he* was now destined for the yoke. His father had died five years ago, leaving Braithwaite to Randolf. Randolf had died last autumn in a hunting accident. Apparently he had accidentally shot himself with his own gun when his horse threw him. He'd somehow managed to live long enough to drag himself to the river Cover where he was found facedown in the water.

Staring into his drink, Damien wondered what, in the end,

had finally killed his brother. The bullet in his brain? Or had he drowned?

"Damien?"

He tossed back his drink before turning toward the door.

Marianne, looking lovelier than any woman had a right to, frowned at him with concern. "Are you all right?" she asked. "You look as if you've just seen a ghost."

He nodded, placing his glass on the table. "How's the girl?" he said.

"Resting. She's burning with fever, though. I suspect she's in for a tough time of it."

He poured another drink.

Marianne came to stand beside him, her cool fingers comforting upon his arm. "Something's wrong," she stated. Before he could lift the glass to his mouth, she gently took it from his fingers and pushed it aside. "Talk to me," she told him. "Friend to friend."

He touched her cheek. She *was* a friend. A very good friend. One of the best he'd ever had. She'd been there for him through it all: the humiliation, the pain. The only time in his manhood when he'd ever cried, it had been on her shoulder. With her hair and skin smelling like sweet flowers she'd soothed him, invited him to bed, and allowed him to take out his fury on her. She'd understood his anger, his not hating her but women in general, and she'd come away a little bruised and a lot sore. She'd remained at his side the next morning, along with his father and brother, and greeted each guest as they arrived at the church, explaining that the ceremony had been "postponed" to a later date. Though by nightfall the whole of London had known the truth. Earl Warwick's second-born son had found his fiancee—on the eve of their wedding—in bed with another man.

"Talk to me," Marianne said.

Damien lied. "I was wondering if Palmerston will persuade Parliament to see me."

She looked incredulous. He was amazed how she could always sense when he was lying.

Running one tapered fingernail over his lower lip, she smiled into his eyes. "I hope they keep you waiting forever, milord. It may keep you out of harm's way and here among the civilized where you belong." As he reached for his drink, she reached too, drawing his hand and the glass to her mouth. She ran her tongue lightly over the rim, over his fingertips, before saying, "I can't imagine what you find so appealing about toiling in Mississippi mud three thousand miles from where you were born."

"There are profits in that mud," he said. "It's called cotton. And it's made me very, *very* wealthy."

"You were already wealthy."

"Not so. My father was wealthy. My brother was wealthy."

"And now it's all yours. Forget Mississippi, Damien. Forget the war in America. Settle down at Braithwaite and set to producing heirs so you will have someone to pass all that wealth on to when you die. Otherwise, what's it all for?"

He glanced at the portrait over Marianne's shoulder, the one dominating the wall between two bay windows that overlooked the garden. His father's green eyes stared back at him, reflecting the firelight.

"Your life is here," Marianne continued. "Granted, you needed some time away. Enough time to put Louisa's betrayal behind you. You worked the anger out of your system, reestablished that you're a man. No one will question that, never fear, not if they have two eyes in their head."

He drew his gaze back to hers.

"Don't go back, darling. Forget Mississippi. Forget the War. If President Davis wants Parliament to address the issue of supporting the South by bombarding the Commons with a pair of frantic commissioners, let him arrange it. Braithwaite needs you. *I* need you, as a friend, a lover . . . hell, even the child up those stairs needs you at this very minute. You're too valuable to us to sacrifice your youth—dear God, your very life—on a war you don't believe in." As he quirked one eyebrow in surprise, she lifted her delicate, fine-boned chin and said, "Well, you told me yourself you don't believe in slavery."

"Whether or not I believe in slavery is not the issue. The fact is, if slavery is abolished the South as we know it will die."

"So will you if you go back."

He stood still for a long moment, contemplating her words. She was wrong, oh, so wrong. There was nothing for him here, while back in Vicksburg everything he held dear was on the verge of collapse. He'd driven himself hard over the last years to build a new life, a new empire, something *he* himself had constructed with his own sweat and blood. While here, over the centuries his ancestors had taken care of everything quite nicely, thank you. But for the few businesses on the side, which his uncle oversaw, there was naught to do but stand by and grow fat and senile with boredom.

Marianne seemed to read his thoughts. She knew him that well. Pressing her hips against his, she teased, "Settle down, Damien. Get married. Have children. You might be surprised how adequately a wife and children can take up your time."

Damien laughed. "All right. Divorce your fop of a husband and marry me."

"And have children? You aren't serious. I'm thirty-five years old, for God's sake. Besides, life with Harry is too . . . convenient. I knew what I was getting into when I agreed to marry him. I was aware of his preoccupation with Parisian gentlemen. It was a marriage of convenience, giving him the respectability he so desired and the freedom I felt was necessary for the pursuit of my own . . . pleasures."

"But if I was to marry someone else," he responded softly, "there would be no more *us*, sweetheart."

"Don't tell me you'll turn out to be one of those husbands who never cheat on their wives. I've heard they exist, but I'm not certain I've ever met one."

He tilted the glass to his mouth, just enough to wet his lips. Marianne stared at his mouth before moistening her own with her tongue.

In a huskier voice, she said, "You would be. Faithful, I mean." A ghost of pain washed over her features, and her face was suddenly pale. With a catch in her voice, she added, "I'll be envious as hell, Damien. Sometimes, when I think of us together the way we were before you became betrothed to Louisa . . . I wish I was younger, wish I had never compromised my youth and love for a man who isn't a man just so I could boast of a titled husband. I'll be envious of her— not because of the sex, but because of the love you'll give her. You see, I know you, Damien. I know that when you fall in love with a woman you'll love her with your body and soul. You won't give it up easily—not your heart. You didn't with Louisa. That's what made her betrayal all the more wretched for you. The next time will be worse. Far worse. The next time you fall, you'll fall so hard, so deep, you'll think you stepped off the edge of the world and went somersaulting through space. You'll be frightened because you won't trust it. You'll be afraid of the pain. And because you'll be more aware of your feelings, you'll love her all the more.''

Damien felt Marianne's breasts shudder against him, saw the glimmer of a tear start in her eye. He placed his drink aside, cupped her face in his hands, brushed the tiny lines at the corners of her eyes with his fingertips, then gently kissed her mouth. Her lips quivered beneath his, opened almost hesitantly at the urging of his tongue, and he felt the ache, the hungry, desperate need wash over him again.

It was going to be a long night.

Two

"Milord! Milord, come quickly, milord!"

"For Christ's sake." Damien rolled his head and looked at Marianne. She was sound asleep on her stomach, one strap of her camisole fallen off her shoulder and down her arm. She didn't even stir as Jewel banged on the door. "What the hell—" Damien roared.

"It's the lass, milord. Doctor says y' should come soon as possible!"

He closed his eyes, attempting to collect his thoughts. For an hour after the muddy little urchin—what had Smythe called her? Ah, yes, Bonnie—had barreled through Braithwaite's door and made a shambles of his love life, he had tried to explain to the help that just because the girl was from Cald-bergh Workhouse it wasn't necessary to call out the Queen's guards. For the next two hours he and Marianne had stood by helplessly while the physician had done his best to break the girl's fever. They'd retired to bed only after Bonnie had fallen into a troubled sleep, just two hours ago . . .

"Milord!" Jewel urged him.

"I'm coming," he snapped irritably.

He threw back the bed covers and slid on his red silk robe stenciled with green and gold Chinese dragons before answering Jewel's desperate plea. He followed her a little groggily down the corridor to his sister's room.

Damien heard the girl breathing even before he entered. It was torturous, the sound, rattling in and out of her lungs like dice in a cup. She was going to die, he thought, pausing outside the door. Possibly before the night was over.

Dr. Whitman, bending attentively over his patient, looked

up briefly as Damien stepped to the bed. "She's desperately ill, my lord. I fear you should contact whomever is responsible for her as soon as possible."

Thinking of Birdie Smythe, Damien shook his head. "There's no one, I'm afraid."

Damien stared down at the girl, pleased to note that Jewel had done a more than passable job of cleaning her up and redressing her in a nightgown. Her hands were pale and long fingered with thin blue veins just beneath her transparent skin. Her face was white and her hair . . .

He sat down in the nearby chair, lifted the hair in his hand, rubbed it between his fingers. He recalled the blue of her eyes and how they had challenged him. Caldbergh had no doubt done that to her. Made her angry, afraid. He could remember his mother speaking in whispers about the workhouse; whispered it so as not to hurt the sensibilities of her own children. "I dare say they starve those poor little creatures," his mother had told his father. His father had only pulled out his snuffbox and said, "There, there, dear, don't trouble yourself over it. Just praise the good Lord that our sons and daughter were born privileged, as were we."

Damien thought, by the looks of this one, they were starved. And beaten and God only knew what else.

Bonnie groaned, then turned her face toward Damien, and for a moment she appeared to smile. He found himself grinning back, until her lips opened in a gasp of pain and a struggle for air.

"This is not just something that's recently come on her," came the doctor's voice. "There's no telling how long the child has been ill."

"Is there nothing you can do?" Damien asked, still watching her face.

"I've done all I can."

Her lids were pale purple, her eyelashes like crow wings, coal black and thick. Her brows were heavy and black. And her hair . . .

It trailed off the bed like a wavy, coiling skein of spun silk, puddling on the lap of his robe like wet black ink.

"I understand she's from Caldbergh," the physician said.

Blinking, Damien nodded, sat back in his chair, and stretched out his legs.

"Could be trouble if she lives, my lord."

"Could be."

The doctor, warming his hands before the fire, stared at the Dresden figurine on the mantel with a thoughtful smile. "Your mother was actively aware of Caldbergh's conditions. She was continually rallying support among her friends to stop the mistreatment of the children."

"She would." Damien's eyes strayed briefly to the girl, then back to the doctor.

"I must admit, the conditions are wretched. Pneumonia is rampant, and usually by the time I'm summoned there to administer aid the child is so far gone there is little I can do. It is no wonder that the children who survive to adulthood have a warped opinion of society."

"No doubt."

"Something should be done," the doctor droned on, more to himself now than to Damien. But Damien knew how the doctor could talk all night about the atrocities of Caldbergh Workhouse, how he would write again to Her Majesty's officials, how he would personally consult with the house manager about the terrible conditions. But his involvement would go no farther than that. In truth, the doctor lived a comfortable life thanks to Caldbergh Workhouse. He was called there at least once a week, and Damien highly suspected that the good physician pocketed a high sum for his efforts and tolerance . . . and perhaps, silence.

As the girl on the bed stirred, Damien sat upright, left his chair, and stood at her side. Her cheeks were like bright torches and filmy with sweat. Her lips parted and she said: "Papa."

Her eyes opened, barely, then wider as she noticed Damien. He smiled and she smiled back.

"Oh, Da," she said. "You came. You finally came home."

He reached out and took her hand, soft and small and so very warm.

Her eyes fluttered closed again as, oh so slowly, her fingers curled like a baby's around his own. He stared at the small hand, the ragged nails that had been nibbled to the quick, and felt a shift in his heartbeat. He found himself closely watching the erratic rise and fall of her chest, noting how long it took between each breath; found himself coaxing each breath along until his own chest began to ache for lack of oxygen. How long he stood there, counting her breaths, he didn't know. But when he finally raised his head to look toward the doctor, he noted his neck and shoulders had grown stiff and his head had begun to throb.

"If she survives this," he said, "how soon can we get her out of here?"

The doctor looked surprised. "Recuperation may take some time. Considering her state of malnutrition . . ."

"How long?"

"Perhaps a month. Perhaps two."

Without looking at her face again, Damien peeled her fingers from his, then turned from the bed. Without looking back, he left the room. He really had no business in there anyway. He would supply the room and comforts, but it was up to the doctor to pull the urchin through, if he was capable.

Damien returned to the library, forcibly putting the image of the girl's sunken face from his mind. There simply was no place in his life for more baggage. He had enough problems to contend with without taking on Caldbergh Workhouse and one of its unfortunate orphans.

The tall case clock in the foyer chimed two as he dropped into his chair behind the desk. Briefly covering his face with his hands, he closed his eyes, thinking of Marianne, the smell of her skin and the huskiness of her laughter. He visualized her face, but the pleasant roundness of her cheeks gradually turned into those hollowed, haunting eyes of hunger and—

He shook his head, reached for a cigar, and lit it from the candle flame.

Outside, the storm had escalated. A brutal, icy wind blew south from Scotland, whipping its fury against Braithwaite Hall with all the force of a hurricane. He'd forgotten how bitterly cold spring could be in Yorkshire, how the wind driving over the moor could blister your skin and make your lungs ache as if someone had rammed a knife through them. There was never really a spring in Yorkshire, not when he compared it to that season in Vicksburg. By now the gentle folk in Mississippi would be lounging on the porches of their homes, sipping mint juleps and looking out over the oak and magnolia trees whose widespread branches dripped with Spanish moss. The planters would soon be opening the dog run through the middle of the house to cool and air out the rooms. They'd be watching the cotton closely, the skies just as carefully, praying for not too much rain so the tender plants didn't rot.

Damien stared down at the tip of his cigar, the ash glowing red and yellow in the dim light. He looked then to the letter that had arrived earlier from Vicksburg.

So, the war between the states was escalating, just as he'd feared. And just as Jefferson Davis had expected, the Union navy was rushing to blockade Southern ports, disrupting the exportation of cotton to England's textile mills. Damien supposed he should be honored that President Davis had asked him to approach parliament on the South's behalf, but he wasn't. He dreaded the effort like hell. Trying to convince his so-called peers into meeting with Commissioners Madison and Slidell would no doubt bring the roof of that noble house down around his ears. England had been embroiled in too many skirmishes to lightly enter another, especially one that could have such far-reaching consequences.

But something had to be done. And soon.

The South was short of money and arms. If the Southern ports were cut off from trade—as the Union navy appeared to be doing—it wouldn't matter if the heavens opened up and it rained for forty days and forty nights, rained until every tender plant was pounded into the mud. If there was no way to ship out that bumper crop of cotton come summer, it would sit on the docks and rot to hell. Or worse. If the Union men got their hands on it, it would all go up in a great ball of fire.

And what about his plantation, Bent Tree? He'd left his overseer in charge of the Vicksburg estate, believing his business in England would take only a matter of weeks. But Parliament's hesitation in speaking to him, however, made the prospect of returning to Mississippi soon look grim. John James, his overseer, was a competent man, but if war escalated before Damien's return . . . what then? There was already a call going out for men to enlist in the army. Three fourths of the men working his plantation were black freemen. Lines were being drawn and there would be little doubt whose side his workers would take.

And if that wasn't enough . . .

He reached for the ledger in the right-hand drawer, dropped it onto the desk, and flipped it open. Christ, what a bloody mess. What had Randolf been thinking to let Braithwaite get in such a financial upset? Half the mines were shut down, and the mills in Yorkshire and London had seen little—if any—profit in the last three years. Even if he wasn't forced to sit out half the war waiting for Parliament to make up its mind, he would spend the next six months trying to remedy Braithwaite's financial dilemma, because if it wasn't rectified . . . the ramifications could be staggering. And that was putting it mildly. In short, Braithwaite and the Warwick empire would cease to exist.

At first the haunting cry sounded more like a howling of the wind than a scream of pain. But as the tormented wail echoed again throughout the quiet chamber, Damien recognized it for what it was.

He jumped from his chair and ran from the library, took the long flight of stairs two at a time, and met a bleary-eyed Marianne at the top. They hurried to Bonnie's room where they found her thrashing in delirium on the bed. Dr. Whitman, his face white as he futilely attempted to quiet her, looked to Damien for help.

"Da!" Bonnie cried. "Don't leave me. Please don't leave!"

Bonnie's arms flailed helplessly, and her head rolled from side to side. Tears spilled from her eyes, adding moisture to her face that was already fever wet. Damien did his best to control her arms while the doctor grabbed her feet.

"Bonnie," Damien said. "Bonnie, you're all right, lass."

She threw back her head and screamed again, a long, eerie sound so full of grief and mourning that it made his flesh crawl.

"Da! Oh, Da, come back. It's gonna rain and y' don't have yer coat. *Pleeese* don't leave me here alone!"

"Bonnie. Bonnie, listen to me—"

"Nooo!" she cried. "He's killed him. Da, don't die. Don't leave me!" Her eyes flew open and fixed on Damien's face. With almost superhuman strength she wrenched her wrists from his hands and, before he could stop her, threw herself up against him, her frail arms wrapping around his neck, her face pressed into his chest while she sobbed so hard the bed shook.

"Y've come home," she wept. "Don't leave me. Please don't leave me."

Damien sank with her onto the bed, hesitantly wrapped his arms around her, and gripped her close while her body continued to shake with fear and fever against his. Soon the sweat from her body had penetrated his robe and he could feel the heat of her skin against his flesh. But his presence had somehow soothed her. So he continued to hold her, late into the morning, even as Marianne and the doctor napped fitfully in chairs near the bed. He held her until her body cooled and whatever nightmares had racked her dreams had ceased to haunt her. When he thought she slept peaceably at last, he attempted to pull his shoulder from beneath her head, but stopped as her lids fluttered open and he found himself under her watchful eye.

"Hello, Bonnie," he said softly.

"Hello," her lips formed almost silently. "Who are you?"

"A friend."

She lay her head back on his shoulder and stared at him with her wide blue eyes and her cherry-red lips quirked up in an odd smile. Finally she whispered, "I didn't realize I had any friends . . . especially any who look like you."

"Is that good or bad?"

She gazed at him a while longer, her eyes appearing to focus on his hair, his nose, his mouth before slowly coming back to his eyes. Her fingers came up and lightly touched his lips. "That's good," she whispered, then she drifted to sleep.

Bonnie felt the coolness of the cloth against her brow, and she opened her eyes slowly. Last time there had been a young woman, not much older than herself, she surmised, whose round eyes had widened in pleasure at Bonnie's waking. "Me name's Jewel, lass, and . . ." The words had faded.

The next time there had been the red-haired woman. Bonnie had studied her for several minutes before the woman had looked up from her book and smiled. "Hello, Bonnie," she'd said in a refined voice. "You're getting better. So much better. Damien will be so pleased . . ."

Who was Damien? Who were these people? They had all been strangers until now, and she'd hoped—oh, how she'd hoped—that she had managed to escape Birdie Smythe and Caldbergh Workhouse forever. But that hope was simply a silly dream, she realized. Feverish fantasies. For she recognized the man's face now. It was the surgeon Whitman. Somehow she was back at Caldbergh, sick, and Smythe had called in the old codger to finish her off.

How she managed to swing her fist with such force after tottering on the edge of death for the last week, she couldn't imagine. But she *did* manage, connecting with Whitman's jaw hard enough to send him flying off his heels. He hit the floor, spilling a table with china trinkets that shattered loudly enough to bring Jewel through the door at a gallop, shrieking and wringing her apron as if it were the neck of last year's Christmas goose.

Wobbling weakly on her knees, Bonnie stared at the gape-mouthed servant and said, "He tripped."

"Milooord!" the servant screamed before spinning out the door.

Bonnie looked again at the doctor. He was out cold. She wasn't feeling too well herself, she decided. Satisfied that she was still safe from Birdie Smythe, she crawled back under the covers, rested her head against the satin-slippered pillow, and fell asleep almost immediately.

She thought, but she couldn't be certain, that she slept another three or four days before rallying her strength to sit up. In the very back of her mind she recalled stumbling toward a manor house, falling through some towering double door, and spilling hard onto a black and white marble floor. She'd been wet. She'd been cold. She'd been terribly ill. But she felt better now. And stronger. For the first time in days hunger rumbled in her stomach.

Very tentatively she rolled from the bed and leaned against it until the world stopped tipping. Her knees were weak. She took one step, then two, still gripping the bed until she was certain she was strong enough to walk. So far so good. If she could just make her way to that door, she thought for certain she would find someone to help her. There had been enough people hovering around her throughout the last days (weeks?), they should at least have the decency to be here when she needed them.

She was halfway across the room when she caught a glimpse of herself in the cheval glass. Her first thought of the tattered urchin she saw there was, "Now ain't that a pitiful wretch." When she realized it was herself, a flash of shame swept over her that burned her body like fire. The last time she'd looked in a mirror had been the afternoon of her father's death, four . . . no, five years ago.

Her father . . .

The old nightmare resurfaced and she realized that during her fever the memories of her father's murder had been prevalent in her mind. She vaguely remembered calling out in her delirium, crying for her da, and with that recognition, she staggered. Bloody hell, what had she revealed to these people? For five horrible years she had lived with the secret of her father's death. Having witnessed his murder, she'd run from the killer, hiding for days on the cold, rain-drenched moors, convincing herself that if she turned up at the authorities with her story, the monster would find a way to finish her too. For that reason, throughout her grueling years at Caldbergh, she'd never disclosed her last name to anyone.

She glanced again at her image in the mirror, then closing her eyes, she turned away, feeling anger and pain and humiliation rise in her throat bitter as bile. Birdie Smythe had done this, he and his cohorts. They'd done their best to turn them all into animals, helpless mindless animals so the alternatives they eventually offered would seem too good to resist. Oh yes, she understood it all now; why certain girls were never mistreated as badly as the others, never manhandled by their filthy attendants, and were constantly separated from the boys.

The smell of food brought her back to the present. Standing in the doorway gripping the frame with all her strength, she closed her eyes, savoring the mouth-watering aroma of roasted beef. God, how long had it been since she had last sunk her teeth into food that wasn't half bad or half cooked or overcooked or . . .

Her stomach knotted, took hold of her breath so suddenly that she bent double with the pain. Nausea swept over her in a stranglehold, and had there been anything at all in her system to vomit, she would have lost it right there on the floor. Instead, the dry heaves twisted up her insides until she thought for certain her guts were being torn apart.

When finally the spasms had passed, Bonnie took a deep breath, straightened, and ventured forth again, noting for the first time the grandeur of her surroundings. Bloody hell, she thought. Where am I? Perhaps I've died. Perhaps this is what heaven really looks like.

There were gleaming gold adornments sitting about here and there. The ceiling high above her head was a mixture of snow-white swirling curling moldings that might have passed as clouds. Then, on closer inspection—her eyes widened— along the ceiling there were a half dozen naked and tubby cherubs, blowing trumpets and tiptoeing across a long line of puffy clouds.

A burst of laughter rolled up the stairwell not far down the hallway. Bonnie listened to the masculine sound. Somehow she'd never imagined God sounding so human. That wasn't God, she finally decided. While the laughter was pleasant to hear, she knew that God would *boom* more, or growl—like someone's gruff but kind grandfather.

She continued to walk, keeping close to the wall for support. When she finally reached the stairway, she swayed against the balustrade, gripping the smooth and polished mahogany with both hands while focusing on the group of men below.

"And there was the time Damien and I sneaked into Professor Corocan's lounge and *borrowed* his lecture. We rewrote it completely, inserting some very specific and personal information we knew about Corocan's—shall we say—relationship? with a certain wife of a colleague. The bloody frogfaced bastard nearly choked on his tongue the next day when reading it aloud!"

The laughter again. Bonnie flinched at its intensity, then focused more sharply on the golden-haired storyteller. He continued to speak, slurring an occasional word now and again, sending his companions into gales and fits of uncontrollable laughter. They all held drinks in their hands. With each burst of merriment they sloshed the amber liquor over the rims of their glasses, spilling it on the floor or on the toes of their shoes.

They have all the manners of a workhouse waif, she thought.

She found her attention shifting from one face to the next, searching out the one called Damien, wondering if she would know him if she saw him, suspecting she might. His face had come and gone in her dreams often enough, though at times she had wondered if he wasn't a product of her fever dreams after all. She had imagined him holding her. Other times she had visualized him standing before the hearth, his back to her, or at the window or beside her bed, his hands in his pocket, his eyes on hers, kind and concerned. And there was his voice, deep and rich and so melodious . . . like her father's . . .

Sighing, Bonnie focused again on the group of men below, studied the one with gold hair once more, then moved on. She paid the balding man a mere second's consideration, then narrowed her eyes at the reed-slender gentleman whose apparent inability to move his upper lip when he spoke became instantly irritating. There were two other men, but she discounted them as well. This Damien fellow simply wasn't among them, Bonnie concluded.

"Gentlemen," came a droll, if not bored voice from somewhere beneath her. "Dinner is served."

"After you," said the golden-haired man to his companions.

"Oh, by all means," his friend responded, "after *you*, good sir!"

Bonnie rolled her eyes. She was starving and they were arguing over who would be first to the bloody table. If they waited another five seconds she would beat them all to the food and not think twice about it.

Just then they burst into another fit of laughter and moved in a group out of the vestibule. Someone said, "Shouldn't someone fetch Damien?"

"Bugger Damien," came the rejoinder.

Another gale of laughter.

A door opened somewhere to the left. As a shadow moved

across the floor, Bonnie stepped around the balustrade for a better look, then stopped short as the tall, dark-haired man walked gracefully into the foyer. She couldn't see his features clearly at first, but when he stopped abruptly at the sight of her, she was gripped by a strange, almost painful awareness as she stared down into his hard face.

She decided it was an intensely masculine face, with a straight, strong nose that seemed to flare a little at the nostrils. A thrill of fright, and something else, raced through her veins as she noted how tall, how broad shouldered he seemed, even from this distance. There was a careless elegance in the way he was dressed—black velvet jacket that fit those shoulders like a glove and a spotlessly white cravat tied and tucked beneath his chin in the most intricate manner. There was an aura of recklessness, of tethered male passion about him that the other men had not possessed in the least. And those eyes—dear God, those eyes. Green as bottle glass, they were, and just as cold. They bore through her as forcefully as a frigid northern wind, taking her breath away.

Frozen, like some small, frightened, and weakened animal, she grasped the stair rail with her right hand, unable to tear her gaze away from his while he appeared to assess her. And in one agonizing flash the image of herself in that mirror blinded her mind's eye: a reflection of a wasted, dirty waif, hollow in cheek with matted, dull black hair tumbling beyond her hips. She felt again that bitter, burning disgust crawl up her throat, but she swallowed it back and slowly released her pent-up breath in a sigh, feeling her shame replaced by an unreasonable anger.

How dare he look down—or up—his nose at her.

"Damien!" came the chorus. "Sup's on, old man!"

Damien responded simply, "Jewel!"

Like a leprechaun the servant appeared from the shadows, wringing her wet hands in her apron. Behind her came a tall, stiff manservant whose bearing dimly reminded Bonnie of a corpse. They both stopped behind Damien and looked up at Bonnie at the top of the stairs.

"Gum!" Jewel said. "She's up."

"Shall I hide the silver now?" queried the manservant.

"That won't be necessary . . . yet," came the flat reply. "But get her abed immediately."

"Yes, milord, immediately," was their response.

Yet there was no movement, at least not right away, Bonnie noted. She thought with smug satisfaction: They're afraid of me. The idea pained her a little, just a short, sharp jab as if she'd pricked her finger on a rose thorn, except the pain was in the vicinity of her heart. She raised her chin and righted her shoulders, or tried to. She wasn't certain she'd pulled it off. Her knees had grown so suddenly and horribly weak it was all she could do to continue to stand. She managed to meet those green eyes head on, with as much pride and contempt as she could muster.

Bloody aristocrat, she thought, damn blue blood, friggin' high stockin'—

Suddenly Jewel was barreling at her up the stairs, the manservant not far behind. Damien, as if reading her thoughts, raised one dark brow and with faint humor touching the firm line of his lips, he quit the vestibule.

She looked then at Jewel.

"Ye'll be a nice lass," the woman said. "Y' won't be doin' nothin' naughty like, now will y'? His lordship says yer to get back into t'owd bed and—"

"I'm hungry," Bonnie stated.

"Yer meal'll be comin' soon as it's been placed for his lordship's—"

"I'm hungry now."

"First we'll get y' back in the bed. His lordship—"

"Bugger his lordship. I wager he's never been hungry."

Jewel's face flushed the color of a ripe plum. "Now, that ain't no way for a young lady t' be speakin'."

"I ain't a young lady."

"His lordship has been most accommodatin'—"

The aromas wafting to Bonnie from the dining room made her mouth water again. She grabbed hold of the stair rail and ran her tongue over her suddenly dry lips while she fought the vertigo that made the room spin around her. There were brief flashes of memory, pictures of Birdie Smythe sitting down to a table laden with fresh roasted meats and pastries and vegetables while she and a dozen others sat down to a bowl of gruel and moldy bread, the smell of Smythe's fare buzzing in their nostrils like angry bees.

"Bloody bastard," she said aloud, then hearing Jewel's gasp of surprise, she blinked one last time at the terrified servant and turned back toward her room.

Three

Bonnie stared at the bowl of broth a full ten seconds before she hurled it across the room. It wasn't out of anger that she flung it. More like frustration and desperation. She knew full well that the high and mighty Earl, along with his cronies, was feasting on roasted beef, and it was, no doubt, the high and mighty Earl who had ordered that insipid mutton broth to be foisted upon her. No doubt it was something he normally fed to his bloody pigs. God, how she loathed the aristocracy!

Turning her furious eyes on Jewel, who by now had dashed toward the door, skirts in hand and cap flopping off her head like a limp white flag, Bonnie railed, "Food! I'm starvin' to death and yer givin' me sheep's piss!"

"But his lordship—"

"His lordship can take a flyin' leap off the bloody Buttertubs as far as I'm concerned. Either I get to chew my friggin' dinner or his lordship . . ." Not bothering to finish, Bonnie lay back on the bed. "Point taken," she mumbled, smiling a little at her own cheekiness as Jewel fled the room. It was a foregone conclusion that if one was to successfully communicate with the aristocracy, one did so loudly enough so as not to be ignored.

Another ten minutes passed before Jewel returned, tray in hand. Bonnie stared at the bowl of broth in disbelief. But as she reached to sling it the way of the first bowl, Jewel said, "I wouldn't if I was you." Her button-black eyes widened as Bonnie looked up. Stepping a little farther from the bed, Jewel cleared her throat. "His lordship says, um, beggin' yer pardon, 'Tell the young lady t' enjoy her broth, sheep's piss or not. If she flings it again she'll either starve or I will personally see to it that she's spoon-fed every drop of—um—sheep's piss in Yorkshire.' "

"He did, did he?" she asked softly.

"Oh, aye."

"Are y' thinkin' he meant it?"

Jewel's head bobbed up and down. "Be a nice lass and sup it. It couldn't be no worse'n wot yer fed at Caldbergh, if ye don't mind me sayin'."

"But I ain't at Caldbergh," Bonnie replied. "And them bloody bastards downstairs are eatin' roasted beef and puddin's, I vow."

High color dotting her cheeks, Jewel wrung her hands and beseeched Bonnie, "Beggin' yer pardon, but his lordship ain't exactly in a fine frame o' mind these days. So be a good lass and drink yer meal, if y' please. I'll do me best t' see yer sent somethin' more substantial come mornin'. It's joost that his lordship feels yer better off with eatin' somethin' less—um—"

"Substantial?"

"Aye." Jewel nodded again. "That'd 'bout sum it up, I s'pose."

Bonnie stared down at the broth again. It wasn't altogether unappetizing, she decided. It might possibly tide her over until she could find a way to filch something more "substantial." Giving the spoon on the tray only a moment's consideration, Bonnie picked up the bowl and tilted it to her lips, wiping her mouth with the sleeve of her gown when she was done. She then pinned the gawking servant with her eyes and said, "You can tell his bloody lordship that I'm much obliged."

Without replying, Jewel took the tray and left the room.

Bonnie lay back on the bed. The broth had been good, but hardly satisfying. If anything, it had only whetted her appetite for something more.

She stared at the ceiling, thinking sleep would come. Occasionally the distant laughter from the dining room would reach her, as did the food smells. Besides the roasted beef and Yorkshire puddings there were roasted potatoes and green peas (she could smell them), and although while once upon a time she wouldn't have eaten a pea for all the shillings in

England, *now* she would gladly pay that much—or more—for a bowl of the mushy green slop.

Finally she dozed. She awoke an hour later in a cold sweat, feeling as if she were going to die in the next five minutes if she didn't get more food to eat. She thought of calling for Jewel, then reconsidered. Since the woman seemed terrified of his high and mighty lordship, Bonnie suspected she could hardly coerce the servant into pilfering her more food.

Well, she thought, it wouldn't be the first time she'd been forced into stealing for her survival.

As before, she left the bed, assured herself she was strong enough to walk, then made her way from the room and down the corridor to the stairway. Once there she hesitated. It was a very long stairway and very steep, making Bonnie wonder if she was really all that hungry after all. What if she were caught, as surely she would be? What if she were suddenly to look up and find a pair of glittering green eyes staring back at her? The image of her host, casually poised at the bottom of these stairs, his face full of light and dark and something else—threat? anger? confusion? shock!—and tilted up toward hers, made her slightly dizzy, so she was forced to grip the handrail even tighter.

That one would be trouble, she thought. He would be cold-hearted as a bloody trout—any man who would force mutton broth on a starving orphan would have to be coldhearted—and would probably see her in prison for filching one crumb of his stinkin' puddin's. Oh, she knew his type. The aristocracy all thought themselves God's gift to mankind, using the common man as fodder for their self-esteem. Swines.

She took an unsteady step, then another and another, expecting to be discovered any moment by Jewel or any one of another dozen or so servants who must inhabit the great house. But as luck would have it, no one entered the vestibule. Bonnie reached the bottom step, weak-kneed, trembling not only with hunger but also with the realization that just beyond those doors was all the food she could eat in a lifetime. The thought made her salivate so strongly she was forced to press her hand over her mouth for fear of humiliating herself even further.

From some different part of the house she heard the men's voices, rising and falling in pitch. Apparently having finished their meal, they had moved off to smoke or do whatever it was that blue bloods did after gorging themselves on beef and puddin's. Perhaps ravishing the comeliest maids. She had read in a book once that lords of the realm had been notorious for that sort of thing . . . back when folk clattered about in suits of armor and such. The lords ripped roasted meat off the bone with their hands, ate with their fingers, gulped wine by the goblets, then buggered the first serving wench they could get their greasy paws on.

Bonnie shuddered.

Still, with hunger driving her onward, she tiptoed to the nearest doorway, gown hem trailing on the floor by several inches, hair brushing the backs of her thighs. Peeking around the door frame, she found another long corridor, gave it a momentary inspection up and down, then continued, following her nose as the aromas became so strong her jaws began to ache.

At last! Bonnie stood in the dining hall's immense double doorway, stared toward the table that would have seated twenty easily, then at the sideboard with its gleaming silver chafing dishes still smoldering with food. She gaped a full half minute before realizing that she had begun to cry. Every punishment for thieving that she had ever heard flashed through her mind's eye, and she did—she honestly did—consider turning her back on the luscious-smelling temptations . . . for all of two seconds. She then lunged at the bowl of peas with the ferocity of a hound on a hare.

She had no more than cupped a palm full of the green peas when a full-bodied voice behind her said, "Hullo, what's this?"

Bonnie jumped, spun, and with a dexterity that surprised even herself, grabbed a heavy silver knife from the table. Glowering at the grinning, golden-haired intruder, she declared, "One bloody step toward me, y' smarmy bastard, and I'll cut y' from here t' Sunday and back."

"Indeed," he responded, "with a butter knife?"

She glanced at the round-bladed utensil.

"I highly suggest the meat carver," he continued, his blue eyes twinkling. "That would, beyond any shadow of doubt, deter me from taking even the slightest step further into this room. Shall I wait until you fetch it?"

Bonnie inched toward the vicious-looking weapon lying to one side of the largest chafing dish. As her gaze fell on the succulent beef, however, her stomach took such a turn she nearly collapsed.

The stranger cleared his throat. When Bonnie looked around she found him leaning one slender but erect shoulder against the doorjamb. His classically handsome face smiled at her very pleasantly.

"I dare say we've never met," he said. "My name is Philippe Fitzpatrick. And you must be . . . don't tell me, let me guess." He tapped his lower lip in contemplation. "Ah, by Jove, I've got it! You're the chit . . . or was it baggage? . . . no, I'm certain it was something more colloquial. Aha! Urchin! Urchin it is. How do you do, Miss Urchin?"

Bonnie's eyes narrowed. Her lower lip began to tremble.

Philippe stopped smiling. "By gad, I suppose that wasn't a very nice thing to say, come to think on it. I was only jabbing at old Dame. He's the one who . . . what *is* your name?" he asked.

She didn't respond, just turned her back to Philippe Fitzpatrick and stared down at the roasted beef while tears formed in her eyes. She wiped her nose with the back of her hand, not daring to sniffle.

"What are you doing here?" came the voice, kinder now and without its flippancy.

"Wot the bloody hell does it look like I'm doin'?"

"About to faint, I should think. Could do with some assistance, I suppose? Of course you could. Where should we begin? The Yorkshires are delicate and light. How about there?"

Bonnie cocked her head and peered warily at the man through her curtain of hair.

Having retrieved a china plate from the sideboard, he used the tongs to grip a slice of crisp brown pudding, which he placed in the center of the plate. He then lathered on gravy, surrounded it with meat, potatoes, and peas, and placed it in Bonnie's hands.

"May I offer a suggestion?" he asked.

She nodded, still suspicious.

"Take the back stairs. There is much less likelihood that

you'll be discovered there." Smiling in an offhanded manner, he clasped her shoulders and directed her from the room, down a hallway to her left, then said, "Have a good go at it, lass."

Bonnie walked on, paused, and looked back. Philippe Fitzpatrick was smiling again, a sly smile, as if he had suddenly discovered something that could change the entire course of history. Finally, she turned down the hall, found the stairs, and began the long climb up. She made it only halfway, however, before she roosted, balanced her plate on her knees, and began to eat.

"Do you know what I recall best about this room? Hmm? Damien, are you listening to me?"

Damien looked over the top of his cards at Frederick Millhouse. "It's your ante," he said.

"It was that summer we both turned nineteen. Do you recall it?"

Damien stared down at his royal flush, reached for his cigar, and sat back in his chair. "Your ante," he repeated.

"Your mama put on that marvelous ball-assembly in celebration of your birthday."

"Actually it was a ridotto," Claurence Newton called out from his chair beside the fire. "I recall because I came as a highwayman. Was twice stopped on my way here, by Jove. I came to fear for my life, I dare say. Shan't do that again."

Damien looked around as Philippe entered the room saying, "I recall that eve very well. I'm certain Dame does too, unless he's completely lost his mind."

Damien raised one brow as his friend ambled across the carpeted floor and fell onto the leather settee. Philippe lay his head back and stared, grinning, at the ceiling. "We sneaked that wench into the assembly, which wasn't hard, I suppose, since we were all in masquerade."

Claurence added, "As I recall she won first prize for best getup."

"It weren't even getup," Freddy said, then giggled like a boy in knickers. "If they'd known she was a real strumpet, I wager we'd've had a riot on our hands."

Philippe rolled his head, winked one blue eye at Damien, and said, "It was an evening to remember, eh, Dame?"

Grinning, Damien inclined his head toward his cards and tapped them gently on the table as those memories came swirling back in a rush. His gaze drifted back to Philippe as his friend laughed and continued.

"We all stood guard outside the door, just to make certain no one intruded."

Freddy snickered again, his face turning beet red to match the color of his hair.

"I wager it's the last woman Freddy's had," Claurence replied.

"Careful!" Philippe laughed. "Old Fred's liable to let go with something rude again, like he did in Corocan's last lecture of the year."

"One for auld lang syne, you might say." It was Claurence again.

Still smiling and eyeing Damien, Philippe said, "It was a true friend who would share such a present with the lads."

"It was your money," Damien replied.

"Aye, but it was your wench. Bloody good one at that, as I recall. Did you enjoy her, Dame? I can't say as I recall your testifying one way or the other."

Claurence replied, "Not having anyone to compare her with at the time, it would have been difficult to judge, I should think."

"Aye, but I think Damien is man enough now to know a thoroughbred when he sees one. Eh, Dame?"

"Did I hear my name mentioned?"

All heads turned toward Marianne.

Smiling, her hands on her hips, she stared back into their smirking faces and said, "Thirty-two years old, each of you, and you're still tittering like a bunch of hot-blooded young pups after a bitch. *When* will you ever grow up?"

Leaving the settee, Philippe wrapped one long arm around her waist and said, "Never, as long as there are women as beautiful as you around to tempt us."

Marianne shrieked in pleasure as Philippe buried his lips

against her throat. When his hand caught her breast and squeezed, she cried, "Are you jealous yet, Damien?"

"He's thinking about it," Freddy responded.

"Let me know the moment he turns green," she cried, then wrapped her arms around Philippe's neck and met his kiss with enough feeling that Damien supposed he should feel some jealousy. After all, before she'd left to visit some "sick friend" in York three days ago, he'd spent the better part of the week making love to her. He tried, he really tried, to conjure up some slight twinge of the green-eyed monster in himself, but it never came. He couldn't even pretend. The only emotion to sweep him in that moment was chagrin. Chagrin that he, over the last five years, had turned into a man like his father, or a man who closely resembled him, while "the lads" were as devil-may-care as they had always been.

Damien dropped the cards on the table, game forgotten. The wine and food had given him a headache. He needed some air. Marianne's laughter and Freddy's sniggering had begun to grate on his nerves. Grow up, he thought of saying. Instead, he excused himself and strode from the room.

Once outside, he leaned against the wall and closed his eyes. He had turned into his father all right; he was a stiff-lipped replica of Joseph Warwick, Baron of Middleham. Damn Randolf to hell for dying and doing this to him. Braithwaite's obligations lurked like vultures in every shadowed corner of the ancient house, behind every sculpture, every painting, every antiquated relic within these fifty-seven rooms. He was Jerome Abernathy, Earl of Burnsall, all over again. He wanted to dig his own mock grave on the green and bury himself in it. He didn't want the restrictions that came with his father's title, or the obligations that came with his ancestry. He yearned to go home to Vicksburg and feel the cool, damp earth between his fingers. He ached to turn his face up to the sun and let it warm him. He desired the freedom to be his *own* man, dammit, and not the man his English peers expected him to be, neither earl nor a half-sotted n'er-do-well with the maturity of an eighteen-year-old. So where, exactly, did that leave him? Empty and lonely and homesick. Christ.

"Beg pardon, milord," came Jewel's timid voice from the shadows.

Without opening his eyes, Damien said, "Yes, what is it?"

"It's the lass, sir. Y' see, I went to her room to check—"

"Lass?"

"The young lady from Caldbergh, milord."

"Ah." He opened his eyes, blinked away the ghost of Damien past, and turned on the servant. "What about her?"

"She weren't in her bed, milord, and—"

"Not in her bed?"

"No, milord."

He waited. "Well . . . ? Where *is* she, Jewel?"

"On't back stairs, milord. I think you should come."

He followed Jewel through the corridor, past the dining hall, continuing until they rounded the corner and came to the stairs. A pair of slender white legs greeted him first. His eyes wandered from the tips of her toes, up over her calves, beyond her knees to her thighs, where her gown lay bunched in a ball between her legs. From her hips up she lay in shadow. He squinted to make out if she was dead or fainted or fast asleep. Beside her on the stair was a plate of congealed gravy and beef scraps.

"Shall I call you a man, milord?" Jewel asked.

"You're looking at one," he replied.

"Yes, milord. I was meanin'—"

"I know what you meant, Jewel." When the servant continued to hover, he looked at her directly and said, "That will be all, Jewel. I will see the young woman back to her room myself."

"Aye, milord." Bobbing once, Jewel bounced down the stairs, then was gone. Damien remained, staring down at the girl a long while before going to one knee and heaving her up into his arms.

Her head nestled against his shoulder, snuggled, cheek pressed against his thin lawn shirt, smearing it with gravy. Damien did his best to frown, though a smile toyed with the corners of his mouth. "Nuisance," he said softly. "You've gotten your belly full, I see, and will no doubt pay for it tomorrow. It'll serve you right, Bonnie."

He carried her back to her room and placed her in bed, making certain the covers were tucked neatly beneath her chin. He wondered how old she was. Fourteen? Fifteen at the most, he reasoned. He brushed a tendril of black hair from her cheek, lingered, brushing his knuckle over the high contour of her cheekbone. Until he caught himself, jerking his hand back as if he'd been burned. He stood, unable to do anything then but stare down into her young face, entranced as he was by the sudden shocking and strange feeling that passed through him. His earlier irritation toward the lads diminished, replaced with . . . what? Chagrin over his dissatisfaction of being forced back to England? Of finding himself heir to a king's fortune when he'd rather be tilling Mississippi dirt? Before him slept a girl who owned nothing, yet she had stood atop the stairs and faced him with all the fierce pride of a young warrior.

His hand drifted again to her cheek. In sleep her face was gentle; her mouth carried a hint of a smile. The certainty of her innocence and loneliness, of her pariah existence, filled him with an unsettling, hedonistic craving to awaken her and proceed to reward her with every material possession of which she had been denied during her lifetime. He would feed her the richest foods so all traces of hunger were eliminated from her gaunt features. He would clothe her in the finest materials the couturieres of Paris and London could supply.

Why?

Because of some absurd notion that he did not deserve this fortune which his father and brother had bequeathed him? What, after all, had he—or they—done to merit it? Was this idea of generosity due simply to guilt or restlessness or . . .

He touched Bonnie's mouth with the tip of one finger. A long dormant feeling roused inside him, like a dragon—long suspected of being dead—suddenly, unexpectedly awakened. Abruptly, he turned toward the fire and busily prodded the ashes, shoveling a bit more coal into the grate, then chastising himself because it was already so warm in the room he'd begun to sweat. He paced. He stopped. He covered his face with his hands and thought, great God, what is happening to me? For an instant the image of his Vicksburg plantation had evanesced into a vision of Braithwaite and merry children and . . .

He caught himself staring down at Bonnie while the sweat collected along his brow and ran down his temple to spill on the front of his shirt, near the gravy stain. He told himself that since she was so much better, tomorrow he would contact Birdie Smythe and let him know that his escapee was on the premises. Of course he would point out that she should remain at Braithwaite until she was well enough to survive Caldbergh again.

But she was definitely going back.

He had enough responsibilities weighing on his mind without a Caldbergh upstart adding to them.

"Damien?"

He looked around to find Marianne watching him from the doorway.

She smiled. "So here you are. Is Bonnie all right?"

"Right as rain," he drawled. "See for yourself. Having indulged herself in half of Braithwaite's larder, she will sleep until this time tomorrow, I highly suspect."

"How very encouraging."

He grunted to himself before turning back to the fire. He heard Marianne rustle up behind him. Her hand gently touched his back.

"She's a very precocious young lady."

"I would hardly call her that."

"Precocious?"

"A lady."

"Oh, but she could be, I think. With a little guidance, of course."

He stared harder into the fire.

"You don't really intend to send her back, do you?"

"Certainly. Have you forgotten, Mari, my tenure here is only temporary."

Sliding her arms around his waist, she whispered, "I had hoped I had convinced you to stay."

"No chance."

"Damien?" She hugged him close, pressing her face against his back, running her hands slowly across his chest. "Did you miss me these last few days that I was gone?"

"I've been busy . . . and the lads . . ."

"Is it so difficult for you?"

He frowned, knowing her meaning but refusing to acknowledge it.

"Louisa did this to you. You won't ever admit to a woman that she means something to you, will you, Dame?"

"I don't wish to talk about it."

"You should marry."

"I said—"

"Have children."

"I—don't—want—children," he stated, turning slowly to face her. "And what need do I have for a wife when I have one right here?"

Marianne stepped backward, her face paling until all that was left of color was the two bright spots of rouge on her cheeks.

He continued. "Grant you, you are someone *else's* wife, a fine example of fidelity if I ever saw one. Not only can't you be faithful to that fop of a husband of yours, but you can't even be faithful to me. Do you think I don't know who you were seeing while you were in York these last three days?"

She shook her head.

Damien laughed sharply. "You were screwing Gene Spears, and we both know it. I have the suspicion that if I were to hike your skirts right now I'd find him smeared all over those beautiful white thighs."

She rocked slightly in her surprise, too stunned to do anything but shake her head. "This—this is so unlike you," she finally managed. Then trying to smile, she said, "Perhaps you are—are jealous, just a little?"

"You're not denying it," he said softly.

"It really isn't any of your business." She backed away. "What in God's name has come over you?" she whispered, then lowered her eyes. Relaxing somewhat, she began to laugh. "Oh. I should have known. Why didn't you just say what the problem was, darling?"

And admit that his erection had nothing to do with her? Admit that the pressure in his loins had been there since the moment he'd seen a child's white legs revealed by candlelight, only to have it grow stronger when he'd touched her face with his fingers?

Marianne stepped up against him, ran her hands over his shoulders and around his neck. "Why didn't you say so?" she asked again. But as she forced his mouth down to hers, he found his eyes drawn back to the face on the bed. Groaning, he closed his eyes, buried his hands in Marianne's hair, and kissed her.

Four

His high and mighty lordship had been right, and she knew it. Every time she heaved over the chamber pot that night Bonnie visualized Damien's face smirking back at her and saying: "I told you so, chit, baggage, urchin. I told you your shriveled stomach was not going to tolerate more than sheep's piss for a while. Ha bloody ha ha ha!"

He hadn't really said that, of course. He and that red-haired harlot had practically suffocated each other with their mouths before they had finally stumbled out the door in each other's arms.

Hanging upside down from the bed, she heaved again and thought, This is it. I'm dyin' for certain this time. *Here lies Bonnie Eden, orphan at ease, found dead in her bed with chucked up mushy peas. May she rest in friggin' peace.*

Bonnie fell back against the bedclothes, wiped her nose and mouth with her gown sleeve, and waited for the spasm to pass. When she was certain there was nothing left to come up, she climbed from the bed, took the fine china pot decorated with pink rose garlands, and walked to the window.

Lifting the chamber pot to eye level, she admired the delicate curvature of the china container and thought the roses were nice, in a prissy sort of way. Her mother might have liked it; Bonnie remembered she'd had a weakness for roses. There had been trellised roses running 'round their fence back home. But her mother had never owned anything as fancy as this. If she had she would not have wasted it on something like a slop jar. More than likely she would have used it as a serve-up for stew, then left it out on the sideboard for decoration, hoping to add a little color to the otherwise drab old

45

place. The only *chamber* pot they'd owned was a tin bucket big enough to fall in if one wasn't careful. She had asked her ma once why they thought they had to own a chamber bucket big enough to accommodate the Queen's army, and her mother had replied, "Cause yer da drinks too much at the pub."

Bonnie had always wondered what that had to do with anything.

Bonnie shoved open the window and turned her face into the cold, wet wind, breathing deeply, feeling the air slice into her damaged lungs like a razor blade. Then she tossed the jar out the window and listened as it shattered on the veranda below. Then she returned to bed.

The next morning Bonnie awoke to find Jewel hovering at the end of the bed, her eyes as round and shiny as shoe buttons. Her face looked the color of bread dough. Feeling her stomach rumble, Bonnie grinned and thought, Bring on the sheep's piss, lovie. Bring on a whole friggin' herd's worth. I'm bloody starvin'.

But Jewel said only, "Y've done it now, y' know. His lordship is livid with anger and—"

"Done wot?" Bonnie asked. She was still half asleep and too groggy to fully comprehend what the jittering servant was talking about.

"Y've destroyed a family heirloom. An antique."

Bonnie rubbed her eyes and took a visual turn around the room before scratching her belly. "Wot?" she stated again.

"The chamber pot."

"The . . ."

"Chamber pot. It's been in t' family for past hundred years."

Bonnie kicked back the coverlet. "Well, it's about time he got rid of it, I should think."

"He's threatenin' to turn you over to the workhouse, lass. I think you should know."

That grabbed Bonnie's attention.

"If it weren't for Lady Marianne, he would've done so already. Lady Marianne is—"

"I bloody know wot she is," Bonnie interrupted. She would have had to have been brought up in a cave or a convent not to. "How was I to know the pot was a bloody an—"

". . . tique," Jewel finished. "Y' might've asked."

"I weren't in the mood t' ask. I'd just finished purgin' m' gut, ya know."

"His lordship told y'—"

"Giver over," Bonnie snapped. "I've had it t' me bum with hearin' wot his lordship thinks."

Color had, by now, crept into Jewel's face, her cheeks glowing pink not unlike the roses on the slop jar Bonnie had tossed out the window the night before. Her hands were twisting nervously in her apron as she said, "Yer attitude toward his lordship leaves a lot to be desired, me thinks— you don't even curtsy when he walks in the room—after all, if it weren't for his lordship you might be dead by now."

Bonnie could find no retort to that. The servant was right.

Jewel pointed to the bucket in the corner. "Yer to use that from now on until ye can be trusted with somethin' nicer."

Bonnie rolled her eyes and slid from the bed. Looking at Jewel directly she said, "I don't need any help usin' it, thank you." When the servant turned toward the door, Bonnie added, "And y' can tell his high and mighty that it'll be a bloody cold day in hell before I go t' one knee for him. And y' can tell 'im that from now on he should deliver his own sermons, unless he thinks he's too damn good t' catch himself in my lowly presence. In that case he can take his heirloom slop jars and eat his dinner from 'em, if you know wot I mean. I ain't talkin' beef and puddin's either, ya know."

Jewel slammed the door behind her.

Bonnie stared at the door, the smile on her face fading as the servant's footfalls diminished down the hallway. She thought of going after her and asking her, in a nicer voice, not to tell his high and mighty any such thing. She was in no great hurry to return to Caldbergh Workhouse. In truth, she had no intention of returning there at all, but what his high and mighty didn't know wasn't going to hurt him none.

She was surprised to find that she did feel somewhat guilty over his lordship's chamber pot. Guilt was something that belonged to the sheltered Goody two-shoes of a child she had been when first arriving at Caldbergh. She'd learned soon enough that conscience had no place in a world where survival belonged to the fittest, fastest, and cruelest. She had to give as good as she got, or she starved or froze.

Bonnie still recalled the morning, two days after her internment at the house, when she awakened to discover someone had stolen her shoes off her feet during the night. She had spent the next two frigid months without shoes. She had been trying to sleep one afternoon, huddled on her pallet on the floor, when Birdie Smythe had strolled in with his birch switch and announced to the room full of shaking, half-starved girls that a pair of shoes was available for the taker. Bonnie had been the first to her feet, shouting and waving her arms like a lunatic, wondering why she was the only one to be doing so when there were a half dozen girls who had outgrown their shoes or whose shoes had fallen apart weeks ago, leaving them barefoot. Twenty-two faces had turned on her, emotionless full moons with dark, hungry craters for eyes. But no one had said a word. Not one word because they knew already what she found out soon enough.

The shoes belonged to Helen Brown.

And Helen Brown was dead.

It might not have been so bad if Smythe had simply dropped the shoes into Bonnie's eager hands, allowed her a pat on the head and a, "Enjoy them with good health, you little tramp." But that wasn't Birdie's way. She had been forced to march up to Helen's corpse and remove the shoes from her feet. It had taken her the better part of a half hour to work up the courage to do so and, as Bonnie recalled, that had been her last struggle with conscience. When putting the shoes on her own feet she had been horrified to find they were still warm. She had made a mad dash into the yard and vomited, not beef and puddin's but bile and disgust. But she had kept the shoes, even fought over them a time or two—she figured she owed Helen Brown that much. Still, no one at the workhouse much messed with her after that. They were afraid to, and rightly so, Bonnie surmised.

Bonnie was definitely feeling stronger now. Her fever having completely broken, her skin felt cool, though the ache in her lungs was still apparent each time she took a breath. She was bored, which was certain proof that she was getting better. Perhaps it was time to take a look around, maybe check out the possibilities for future money-making ventures. In other words, pinpoint whatever she wanted to heist before bidding his high and mighty a fond fare thee well.

She looked about for her clothes. They were gone.

She left the room and strolled a bit wobble legged down the corridor to the head of the stairs. There was certainly a lot of activity, servants dashing this way and that, some polishing silver, others on their hands and knees scrubbing the marble floor. Just watching them made her tired, so she turned back down the hall, deciding her exploration here could be just as productive.

She had walked a good way down the corridor when she heard the laughter. His and hers. She froze. The image of them together—as they had been the night before—came like a highland wind, jarring and disconcerting in its magnitude. The night before, she'd watched Damien alone for a while, watched how he paced about her room like a caged cat. She had only wanted another glimpse of his features. Those pagan features. There was something of the devil about him that frightened and amazed her. He simply did not fit her image of what an aristocrat should look like, neither pale nor rigid, though there was that implied here-I-am-and-ain't-I-grand? glint in his eyes when he looked at her.

Bonnie frowned when she recalled his standing by her bed, his fingers gently pushing her hair from her face when he thought she was asleep. Then soon after the woman called Marianne had come in, spoiling it all, and Bonnie had been forced to watch her stroke him until he kissed her. But even as his mouth moved on hers, Damien had looked over to Bonnie. She had continued to sleep—pretended to sleep— though her breathing had somehow run away from her. That was when the nausea had hit her, and for the next five minutes she had lain perfectly still, praying that they would leave before she humiliated herself.

"The guests should begin arriving this afternoon," the woman Marianne was saying now. "It'll seem like old times, won't it? All of us together again; it'll be just wonderful."

No response. Then finally, "What's this?"

"I wanted to give you your birthday present early."

"I thought the party was my present." There came a rasping of paper, followed by silence.

"Do you like it?" the woman soon asked.

"Yes." The word smiled. Bonnie smiled too, hearing it. "It's very nice, Mari."

"I love you, you know."

"I know."

Hearing those words "I love you," Bonnie suddenly turned on her heel and returned to her room. She wondered if her fever was returning because her face burned and her heart raced so sickeningly fast she thought she might faint before falling onto the bed.

I love you.

She heard it over and over in her mind until a confusing and unreasonable anger replaced her earlier sickness . . . anger at his lordship, anger at his lover, and anger at herself for caring about what the two of them shared. Who was she, after all, to even imagine that his concern over her well-being had meant anything special? No doubt she had imagined it all anyway. His standing at her bedside, his holding her in his arms as she battled her delirium, had no doubt been only that—delirium. Another of her fanciful fantasies that had enabled her to survive five torturous years at Caldbergh and remain sane. Besides, his high and mighty had made himself perfectly clear the evening she had stood atop the staircase while from below, he stared coldly at her with his frigid green eyes, assessing her appearance and passing judgment.

Marianne's laughter rang out again from the hallway, and wiping her tears with the back of her hand, Bonnie rolled from the bed and hurried to the outer door, where she peeked down the corridor. Marianne, dressed in emerald-green satin, stood facing Damien, who was dressed in formal black attire. She was pinning a white rosebud to the lapel of his coat.

Bonnie backed away, the image of Marianne's finery engrained on her mind's eye. She walked to the cheval glass and stared at her reflection. Then she gazed at the tortoise-shell comb on the dresser and picked it up. What was the use? she asked herself. She could look like the frigging Queen of England, but the fact was, she was a waif. A wretch. An urchin from Caldbergh. And his high and mighty wasn't about to let her forget it for a moment.

A knock on the door interrupted Bonnie's thoughts. She turned to find Philippe Fitzpatrick grinning at her from the doorway.

"Hullo," he said.

She ran and jumped in the bed, pulling the counterpane to her chin.

"Remember me?" he asked.

"Aye," she replied. "Y're the one that 'bout killed me with all that bloody beef and puddin's."

"You don't say. Well, I do apologize. May I come in?"

"Why?"

"To say hullo, of course."

"Y've already said hullo."

"Oh. Well, would you like me to leave?"

Bonnie chewed her lower lip before saying, "Well . . ."

The door creaked open a little more and Philippe, smiling, slipped into the room. In his hand he held a tray of food. "Bumped into Jewel on her way up with your tea. I decided to save her the trip as I was considering coming up anyway."

"Just t' see me?"

"Certainly."

Bonnie stared at him suspiciously. "Give over," she finally said. "Why would y' wanna do that?"

"Because I like you."

Bonnie frowned.

Impeccably attired in a dove-gray jacket and striped trousers, with a white lawn shirt beneath and a white silk cravat at his throat, Philippe approached Bonnie cautiously before saying, "Promise you won't lunge at me with another butter knife?"

Grinning, Bonnie narrowed her eyes and said, "I promise."

"You won't hurl a china chamber pot at my head?"

"No."

"Smashing!" he exclaimed. "Does this mean we're friends?"

Bonnie eyed the food in Philippe's hands before looking back at him. "I can't imagine wot we could possibly have in common."

"Damien, of course."

"Oh," she replied. "Well then . . . sit down."

Damien looked out over the gathering of friends and smothered back his yawn. He had smiled his way through the last hours, and he had had about enough. He didn't like being reminded of his birthdays anymore, and seeing this group of rousers only reminded him that he was thirty-three going on sixty-three. This was their life, surviving on milk punch and champagne and caviar, living from one season to the next. Meanwhile, back in Vicksburg, everything he valued was about to be blasted to kingdom come.

Pushing open the French doors, he stepped from the overcrowded ballroom into the night. Around noon the rain had ceased, as had the wind. As he looked toward the dark sky he saw the shadows of clouds skirt across the quarter moon and spattering of stars, then heard the distant baying of his hounds, which reminded him that tomorrow at dawn he would be expected to lead guests on a bloodcurdling romp over the moor, chasing fox. He wasn't looking forward to it.

"He's not so bad, lass. A bit jaded, I suppose, after living among barbarians these last many years. But he's a likable sort if you'd give him the chance."

Fitzpatrick? Frowning, Damien looked about the shadows, wondering what young lady his old friend had managed to woo into the dark.

"He's a bloody ogre," came the response.

Philippe Fitzpatrick chuckled. "Perhaps intense would be a more appropriate description of Warwick. He is intense, I agree, Bonnie; perhaps a stick-in-the-mud, but he wasn't always so. There was a time when he laughed—"

"Give over," she interrupted. "He don't know how."

"But he does! By the Queen's innocence, Damien used to be a congenial fellow."

"He was gonna send me back t' Caldbergh for breakin' his bloody slop jar."

"Bluster. Damien is full of it."

"He's bloody well full of somethin', I vow."

Stepping further into the dark, Damien looked harder through the shadows, then up to the second floor wrought-iron balcony. Two pairs of legs jutted from between the ornately scrolled rails and dangled over the ledge, the longer draped in striped trousers, the other naked from the knees down. He watched the tiny white feet swing back and forth above his head.

"Wot's this?" came Bonnie's voice.

"Goose pâté on toast point," Philippe told her.

"Pat-tay?"

"Goose liver paste."

Damien watched as the pâté on toast point splattered on the veranda at his feet, missing his toe by inches.

"Disgoostin'," Bonnie said, giggling.

"Sir," came Stanley's voice from the door. "Your uncle has arrived . . . sir?"

Damien turned his eyes to his butler, frowning. "Beg pardon?" he asked. His mind was still grappling with the fact that his friend was lagging about the dark with the urchin from Caldbergh.

"Sir Richard Sitwell has arrived," Stanley repeated.

Reentering the room, Damien closed the doors behind him. He followed Stanley into the vestibule, stopped, and watched the newcomer pace. He noted that his uncle had added a few inches to his girth and his face had taken on the ruddiness of a man who still enjoyed his port to extremes, which made Damien frown. Bluff and bluster, was the old codger, with a temper that had been known to put him on the wrong side of Britain's social circles on occasion, not to mention on the wrong side of Damien's father. But where Damien had always been concerned, Richard's heart was as big as all Britain and as soft as goose down. Finally Richard looked up, and Damien smiled.

Throwing open their arms, they met and embraced for a full minute, Richard hugging Damien so tightly he could hardly breathe. Finally backing away, they studied each other speculatively. "By God," Richard said with a catch in his voice and a tear in his eye. "Damien, for a moment I hardly knew you."

"Have I changed that much, Uncle?"

"Aye, lad, you have. You have!" Catching Damien's face with his hands, Richard sighed. "You went to America a lad and came back a man."

"Thank you. I think."

"Am I too late for the celebration?"

"Hardly. I'll be lucky to see the last of this bunch by week's end."

"Just like the good ole days, eh, lad?"

Right, Damien thought, just like 'em.

Taking his uncle's arm, Damien moved away from the music, down the longest gallery toward the back of the house. Damien called out to Stanley that he would appreciate privacy, a decanter of brandy, and another of port. Upon reaching the parlor, Damien shut the door, closed his eyes, and thanked God that there was still a corner of Braithwaite that wasn't filled to overflowing with high-spirited revelers.

After throwing his coat over the back of a chair, Richard spread his hands before the fire and said, "Damn cold spring, Damien. The worst in years. How was it in the colonies when you left?"

"Warm."

A soft rap at the door intruded. Stanley entered, a decanter of brandy, one of port, and two snifters on a silver tray balanced on one hand. The servant poured each man a drink before exiting the room, closing the door softly behind him.

Richard Sitwell said, "There goes a good man. I wager you don't find loyalty like that back in Mississippi."

"No," Damien replied softly, "you don't."

They stared into their drinks, listening to the distant music. Finally Richard dropped into a Queen Anne chair, sipped his port, then looked at Damien directly.

"To say I was stunned upon receiving your letter is an understatement."

"No doubt."

"Before leaving London I spoke at length with Palmerston. He will do what he can to convince Parliament to see you, but he is only one voice among many. England, as you know, does not well receive the news about the war, Damien. She wants no part of it."

"I highly suspect she will think twice when her cotton supplies dry up." Walking to the fire, Damien stared into the flames before turning the glass up to his mouth, then he added, "You know that England demands five-sixths of the South's raw cotton crop. Without it, some four hundred thousand English mill workers will find themselves unemployed."

Richard shook his head. "In theory that seems a fine war plan, Damien. But while you've been in America, circumstances have changed. The London *Economist* has been reporting for two years about the overproduction of cotton fiber and textiles in England. Last year half the mills in Britain were shut down by the glut, including a number of our own. Many French mills are also idle. Just last month the *Economist* calculated that the country has something like a three-year surplus of raw cotton to contend with. In fact, Lancashire mill owners are even now unloading their warehouses and shipping the cotton back to New England.''

Damien closed his eyes. ''Which doesn't help the South in her attempts to cut off cotton from the North.'' More angrily, he added, ''And it sure as hell is not going to help me when it comes time to sell my crops.''

''No,'' Richard said. ''It won't.'' Sitwell continued to silently watch Damien for several minutes. Finally he said, ''Why did you hotfoot it out of London so quickly? You might have met with more success had you spoken to Palmerston yourself.''

''I had obligations, Uncle. Braithwaite—''

''Humbug! Braithwaite has been idle since your brother's death. Did you expect her to crumble to the ground in the fortnight it would have taken you to face Parliament?'' When Damien didn't respond, Richard pursed his lips and said, ''I see. I wouldn't have thought it of you, Dame. Cowardice has not, until now, run in the Warwick veins.''

Damien shot his uncle a hot glance.

''Forgive me if I have opened old wounds. I didn't realize they still bothered you.''

''They don't.''

''No?''

''No.''

''Then the fact that Louisa was in town at the time you arrived in London had nothing whatsoever to do with your rushing off to Braithwaite before stopping even to see me?''

''Absolutely nothing.'' Damien poured himself a second brandy before facing his quizzical uncle again. ''I may have left England with my pride sorely battered, Uncle, but I assure you, my success in Vicksburg has helped remedy that. I really do not give a damn what my peers think of me.''

Richard studied him severely before saying, ''Then you are over Louisa completely?''

Damien took a drink. ''Completely.''

''No lingering trace of love?''

He turned away.

"Forget the wench and what she did. Put it behind you and settle down, Damien. Get married and—"

"For God's sake, why is everyone so eager to get me married? You would think I was the only man who ever existed who had not strapped himself down with wife and brats by his thirty-third birthday."

"I know that marriage was important to you once."

"Once. I'm married to my Vicksburg plantation, Bent Tree, now. She occupies my days and nights. There's no time for courtship and all the crap that goes with it."

Richard's eyebrows shot up.

Another knock on the door brought their heads around. Stanley reentered the room, tight-lipped and frowning. Dropping his air of formality, he centered Damien with a look and said, "Miles Kemball has arrived."

A shadow fell over Stanley's shoulders. Miles Kemball Warwick shoved the door open further and stepped into the room. Smiling, he said, "Hullo, Dame. Happy birthday."

Damien stared into his half brother's face, feeling anger rise like sudden fire inside him. The meeting had been inevitable—Miles did make his home at Braithwaite, after all, when he wasn't gallivanting over Europe with his bed-hopping Parisian mother. Miles Kemball Warwick was the true black sheep of the Warwick family, the skeleton in the closet; Joseph Randolf Asquith Warwick, Earl Warwick's bastard son by an opera singer from Paris. He was the evidence that men of the realm had moments of weakness, were base enough to be human. They just prayed to the Almighty that they never got caught at it. Joseph Randolf Asquith Warwick, Baron Middleham, Earl Warwick had been caught.

Damien turned slowly toward the mantel and placed his snifter on it.

"Don't everyone jump with glee," Miles continued. "You all look as if you've just seen a ghost."

"We should be so fortunate," Damien said quietly, still facing the fire. He didn't trust himself to confront Miles yet. Not yet.

"Now, is that any way to greet your brother?" Miles asked. Then, noting Sitwell in the shadows, he said, "Well, it seems this is quite the·family reunion, isn't it? I suppose I'm fortunate to have happened upon this rather auspicious occasion, or was my invitation perhaps lost in the mail?''

Damien slanted a look toward his uncle, wondering if Richard had known all along of Miles's arrival in England from Paris. Richard returned his expression with a touch of chagrin that told Damien he had.

''As usual, Dame, you've thrown a bash that Yorkshire will be remembering for months to come. How do you do it?'' Miles looked from Damien to Richard. ''No one is speaking. Have I stumbled upon a game of charades or have you all lost your tongues?''

Richard left his chair. ''You have lost your mind, Miles. Why ever did you think you would be welcome here?''

''This is my home as much as it is Damien's.''

Stanley huffed as he turned toward the door and left the room.

A smile curled Miles's thin mouth as he looked back at Damien. ''London is stewing with the news that you're back, Dame. Conjecture is you avoided town for a reason. Wonder what that could be? Shall we all guess?''

Damien turned back to the fire. ''Get rid of him, Uncle,'' he said through his teeth, then with more emphasis, ''now.''

Acknowledging the tone for what it was, Richard approached Miles and clasped his arm. ''I'll see you out.''

''Nonsense.''

''Damien does not want you here.''

''Do I care?''

''Pray, do not make trouble, lad.''

''My name is trouble, Uncle. Seems I recall you mentioning that off and on as I grew up.''

''And deservedly so.''

''Take your hand off me.''

''Once you are outside Braithwaite's door.''

''I'm warning you.''

''Will you call me out?''

''Damn tempting thought.'' Miles glanced at Damien, who had turned from the fire. ''Seems the last time we saw each other, Damien, it was down the barrel of a gun. I wonder why you didn't fire. That touch of yellow down your spine, perhaps?''

"A waste of a bullet," Damien replied. "Not worth the farthing it would take to pack a new one."

"As the Earl you needn't worry over such trivialities any longer. Perhaps you would like another go? Perhaps my trigger won't jam this time."

"I trust it didn't jam when you pointed your barrel at Randolf."

The sharp crack of green kindling burning and the sudden rise of music from the distant ballroom heightened the silence that fell between Damien and his half brother. Very slowly Damien crossed the room, his eyes never leaving Miles's. When they stood toe to toe, he said, "Did you kill him?"

For an instant Miles looked stunned. "Don't be an idiot. I was with Mama in Paris at the time. Ask her if you wish."

"She'd lie. Just as she lied when she said you were sired by my father."

"Since I suspect that you think I killed Randolf, nothing I might say contrary to the fact will alter your opinion. But I might add, should you go about bandying such malice about the dales, I might be forced to face you down again. My reputation is at stake."

"Do you mean your reputation as an illegitimate son of a whoring opera singer or that of a simple reprobate?"

Richard did his best to step between the men. He succeeded only in treading on Damien's toe. Facing his green-eyed nephew, he said, "Beg your pardon."

Damien gently, but firmly, shoved Richard aside. His eyes still fixed on Miles's seething features, he barely heard the door open and Richard's footsteps pounding hurriedly down the hallway. "Well?" he taunted. "Which is it?"

Miles's gray eyes narrowed. "Careful what you say, Brother. You may come to regret it before long."

"I doubt it."

"Why, Dame, I fear you've grown into a bully."

"You bet."

"Fisticuffs with your guests is hardly appropriate behavior for an earl. Is that how you spent your time in the colonies? Oh yes, they are rather barbaric over there, aren't they? But then you always did have a touch of the savage in you, until it came down to face-to-face—or fist-to-fist—contact. *Our* father used to lament on it regularly, as I recall. Said you were too softhearted—or was the term 'yellow' used instead?''

Damien did his best to swallow back the anger that made him visibly shake. He had always prided himself on not buckling under Miles's blatant attempts to goad him into rage. But he was no longer the man—or boy—he used to be.

Wetting his lips, he said, ''What say we step outside and discuss this matter further?''

The smirk on Miles's mouth faltered slightly. A flash of something closely resembling disconcertion flitted through his gray eyes. ''Come now, Damien. We are gentlemen—''

''*I* am a gentleman. *You* are a snake. Now, will you step outside on your own or must I escort you? If I am forced to escort you I shall do so by way of the ballroom and my guests. What will it be?''

Miles sneered. ''You're an ass. But then, you always were. A pompous ass, and I will take pleasure in smearing your face in Braithwaite's dirt.''

Damien moved back and lifted his arm in invitation toward the French doors. His eyes narrowed icily as he said, ''We'll see who's yellow now. After you.''

Bonnie stared at the door a long minute, wondering what news could be so important that Philippe Fitzpatrick would whoop and jump as if he'd just dropped a hot coal in his lap. She looked down at the toast point, minus its goose liver, and stuck it in her mouth. Chewing, she walked out the door.

Standing at the top of the stairs in the shadows, she gazed down the long flight of steps at the guests who were all hurrying from the ballroom, crossing the vestibule, and rushing out through another door. Bonnie turned and walked down the corridor in the same general direction, wondering at the murmur of excited voices below her. At the far end of the hallway she came to a room. The door was open, and without a thought or a moment's consideration that the chamber might be occupied by one of his high and mighty's guests, she strode toward the open French doors, walked out on the balcony, and gazed down into the garden.

A circle of onlookers was gathered around a pair of men who looked ready to go at each other with their fists. On second inspection she noted that, from the looks of their

muddied shirts, they had already taken a swing or two. Then
her hand, with its triangle of toast, halted halfway to her
mouth as she noted that the man with his teeth bared like a
rabid fox was her host.

"Bloody hell," she said aloud. "Would y' look at that."

The crowd roared as Miles swung again. His fist glanced
off Damien's chin, and as Damien stumbled backward Miles
tripped and fell to his knees. Damien retaliated with a swift
kick toward Miles's belly, but Miles grabbed his foot, twisted,
and sent Damien spinning toward the ground.

"By gad," came Fitzpatrick's familiar voice above the excited throng. "Millhouse, I withdraw my wager. One hundred pounds on Kemball!"

"Fifty more!" came another.

As Bonnie leaned over the banister to see better, a stout
man came barreling through the onlookers and announced
with flustered authority to Philippe, "This is outrageous! You
were to have stopped this insanity, and instead you are wagering on its outcome!"

The crowd roared again. Damien, blinking mud from his
eyes and having regained his feet, swung his fist at Miles's
jaw with all the power he could muster. He missed. In turn
Miles brought his knee up squarely into Damien's stomach.

"Twenty on Kemball!" rang out another voice.

The men met in center circle like two rams butting over
breeding rights. Bonnie winced as she heard them come together. She closed her eyes, albeit briefly, while the brutal
slap of flesh against flesh reverberated in the air. Much to
her surprise she found herself cheering Damien on. Caught
up in the excitement, she ran up and down the balcony,
swinging her small fist with each of his thrusts, whooping
when he connected, groaning when he didn't. It was David
and Goliath all over again. His high and mighty was a cru-
sader for all the starving urchins throughout the land. Van-
quisher of hunger. Rectifier of all unmentionable sins heaped
upon the starving orphans of the world!

"Yes!" she cried aloud. With one final swing that took her
halfway over the wrought-iron balustrade, she stared down at
the fifty or so stunned, upraised faces who were regarding
her.

Oops, she thought.

It was Philippe who jumped over a prone Damien, who, with his chest heaving, glared up at Bonnie with as much anger as he had sneered mere seconds before at his adversary. Waving his hands over his head, Philippe called out, "Don't move, Bonnie! I'll be there directly! Hold on, lass, I'm coming!"

Bonnie tried to smile, but the iron grill cutting into her stomach wouldn't let her. She wondered why Philippe was so adamant about her remaining where she was, with her feet sticking up in the air behind her and her hair cascading like a black waterfall toward the ground. It really was uncomfortable. And embarrassing. Judging by the look on lord high and mighty's face, she was apt to find herself plunked on Birdie Smythe's doorstep by morning.

Then there were hands grasping her waist and hauling her back. Philippe righted her on her feet before turning her around.

"Are you all right?" he asked.

Bonnie noted his chest was rising and falling from exertion, and it suddenly occurred to her: He had been under the mistaken assumption that she was in dire need of saving. Smiling brightly and feeling truly delicate for the first time in years, she nodded and said, "Y' saved m' worthless life, it seems. I'll be forever grateful, sir." She batted her lashes; she'd heard once that femme fatales did that sort of thing when they were rescued.

Cocking one blond brow, he looked hard through the shadows before saying, "Think nothing of it, lass. . . . Do you have something in your eye?"

Bonnie frowned and turned away. Glancing back over the railing and finding the crowd dispersed and the fighters gone, she said, "Wot's all the fuss over?"

"Just Damien welcoming his brother home."

"Well," she said, turning to face him again, "seems Damien's got a peculiar hospitality."

"So it does." He beamed her a smile and offered his arm. "What say we change you out of that gown and into some clothes? You, my dear young lady, are about to attend your first gala ball."

Bonnie stopped and pulled back. "No, I ain't."

"Yes, you are."

"No, I—"

"Think of it: all the bloody food you can eat."

"But *he'll* be there. Won't he?"

"Aye. They'll all be wishing him a happy birthday, I wager. Can't you imagine him looking up and seeing your smiling face there too?"

"It'd serve him right for bein' such an ogre t' me just cause I broke his chamber pot."

"My thoughts exactly."

Five

Miles Kemball pressed a cloth to his bloody lip before facing his uncle. "If you have come here to ask me to leave Braithwaite, save your breath. As you know, my father stipulated in his will that I be allowed full privileges concerning my right to live here."

"He also left you enough yearly allowance so that you might choose to reside elsewhere."

Miles glanced in the mirror, noted the swelling around his eye. He tossed the cloth to the floor. "I grew weary of Paris."

"I doubt that. You somehow heard that Damien was home and, as always, you decided to make trouble. By gosh." Richard huffed. "You are a dislikable sort, Miles."

"Like father like son." Miles grinned and tucked his clean cravat more snugly into his shirt. "I must admit, the changes in Damien surprise me. I suspect my stay at Braithwaite may prove to be more stimulating than I had anticipated."

"Meaning you intend to cause trouble."

"I'm not home five minutes and Damien is insulting my birthright, accusing me of murdering Randolf, doing his best to pound my face into mush, and you are insinuating that *I* am the troublemaker here."

"The two of you cannot abide in the same house, much less the same city, without there being trouble. You know that, yet here you are."

Miles slid his suit coat on over his brocade vest and studied his reflection in the mirror. "Perhaps I've decided to turn over a new leaf. Start fresh. Perhaps I've come home to make peace with Damien."

"I find that highly unlikely."

Miles laughed sharply. "Talk about the pot calling the kettle black." He faced Richard. "You can't stop swimming in port long enough to come up for air, old man. You've made a botch of the Warwick estate and, as I understand it, you've been forbidden membership in half the clubs in London because of your gambling, drinking, and temper." He watched Richard's countenance turn red, and he chuckled. "I wonder what Damien's reaction will be once he sorts out the reason for Warwick's business failures. Granted, I boggled a few when I was in charge, but I sure as hell didn't bring the entire damn fortune threatening to crumble the way you have."

Miles walked to the chair where Richard sat staring at him with rummy eyes and slack jaw. The old man's hands were clasped in his lap, trembling. Leaning forward, Miles gripped the chair arms, and with his face inches from Richard's, said, "This all should have been mine, you know. I was Joseph's first born, legit or not. Damien seems to forget that, and I am here to remind him that I will not be ignored. And another thing. Should you decide to encourage this asinine idea of Damien's that I was somehow responsible for Randolf's death, I will remind him that *you* were in residence at Braithwaite then, and *you* were overheard arguing heatedly with Randolf just hours before his death."

Richard's cheeks drained of color. He opened and closed his mouth without speaking.

Miles smiled. "According to my sources, Randolf threatened to release you from your duties—"

"That is a lie!"

Richard attempted to stand. Miles shoved him down into the chair and said, "We all know that the only reason my father tolerated your ineptitude and drinking was because he was married to your sister. We also know that it was his influence that kept you from being totally shunned by your so-called peers. A lie? I don't think so, Sitwell. I can recall many a night I overheard Joseph criticizing some business transaction you'd bungled. I heard him, time after time, give you one more chance to sober up and iron out the mess you'd made at the mills. Face it, old man, you're a lush. A wretch. Without the Warwick ties, you would be practicing law from some tenement in the East End representing drunken scum just like you."

Richard turned his head and closed his eyes. His voice shaking, he said, "You cold-blooded bastard, have you no soul, no compassion whatsoever?"

Miles closed his fingers over Richard's fleshy chin and angled the man's face toward his. "Ever wonder why an aristocrat's blood is blue? Now you know. It's because it's Goddamn freezing, Richard. As I said earlier, like father like son. I learned early to give as good as I got. I learned to strike the first blow—'hit 'em low when they least expect it,' as Joseph used to say. To do anything less is a weakness. And we both know how my dear papa loathed weakness, *don't* we, Richard?"

Miles moved to the door before stopping. Straightening his jacket, he glanced back at Richard and smiled. "You look as if you could do with a drink. Be my guest." He motioned toward the decanter on a table near the wall. "Now, if you'll excuse me, I think I'll join the celebration. It would be remiss of me not to be on hand when the guests wish the Earl a happy birthday . . . wouldn't it?"

Laughing, Miles quit the room. His step slowed, however, as the shadows of the corridor swallowed him in darkness. He listened to the music and heard the merriment of the guests. He looked up and down the corridor, noting the many objets d'art lining the walls. It should have been his. All of it. He'd licked Joseph Warwick's boots so many times he felt sick thinking of it, and all the old man saw fit to leave him when he died was a pittance of an allowance. The meager annual income hadn't been so hard to stomach since he knew he could get what he needed from Randolf. Just like Joseph, Randolf could be easily manipulated into forking over a few hundred quid every now and again. After all, he and Randolf hadn't got along too badly while they were growing up. Birds of a feather, and all that.

But now Damien had it all. Damien, who had always seen through Miles's every motive. Damien, who, despite—or perhaps because of—Joseph's influence, had thumbed his nose at propriety and custom. He'd rebelled against everything the Warwick reputation stood for, yet he had inherited six estates throughout England, one in Wales, a half dozen textile mills, and four of the highest producing lead mines in Yorkshire.

Leave it to Damien to fall into a cesspool and crawl out smelling like a rose. But then, that had always been the way of it. Despite Damien's obvious refusal to buckle under Joseph's attempts to turn him into a "chip off the old block," as he had Randolf and himself, Miles had always suspected that Damien had secretly been Joseph's favorite. He'd noticed the warming in the old man's eyes when Damien entered a room. He'd witnessed, unbelievably, a tear in Joseph's cold green eyes as he stropped Damien's bare backside for protecting the identity of some poacher.

Miles could still remember the look on Damien's features as the leather cut into his flesh time after time. Damien had wanted to throw his hands back to protect himself from the blows, but he hadn't. He'd only stood there with his hands clenched at his sides and tears running down his face. When Joseph had demanded the name of the poacher one last time, Damien's only response had been, "He needs the goddamned meat more than you." The next day Miles had followed Damien into the woods and had discovered the poacher was a tenant farmer from a nearby estate. Yet when he'd hurried home to his father with word of the man's identity, Joseph had only looked down his nose at him in disgust.

The applause from below brought Miles back to the present. So Damien had it all now, not only his father's respect, but the money as well. Yet, according to gossip, he didn't want it. Well, there had to be something Damien *did* want just as much as he, himself, wanted Braithwaite. He'd find out what that something was. He had before, after all, and the outcome had been glorious.

Bonnie refused the loan of one of the maid's dresses and informed them all that she was going no place without her breeches. Eventually they were grudgingly delivered, freshly laundered and patched. She allowed her hair to be brushed out, braided, and looped around her head. Chancing a glance into a mirror, she decided she looked fairly presentable, considering.

Fitzpatrick seemed pleased. In fact, Bonnie thought he looked absolutely ecstatic. His eyes lit up, his face broke into that smile that said *I know a secret and you don't and I'm not going to tell*, and then he began to chuckle.

"I ain't sure I want t' do this," she told him pointedly.

"Food," he responded. "Keep thinking food. Beef, lamb, pork—"

"No mushy peas," she interrupted.

"No mushy peas. Potatoes. Carrots. Puddings. Petit fours."

"Petty wot?"

"Bite-sized cakes with marzipan icing. By gad, they'll melt in your mouth." He took her arm and led her down the stairs. "Remember. Don't let him intimidate you."

"Y' sure he won't send me back t' Caldbergh for this?"

"I give you my word. I will take all the credit when this is over."

They had no more than reached the bottom landing when they were surrounded by the gentlemen Bonnie had noted standing around Philippe the day before. They all looked down their noses at her, eyebrows raised, teeth showing in smiles.

"Hullo," they all said.

Bonnie glared.

"She's a mite thin," the tubby one with red hair stated.

"Yer not," Bonnie responded, looking pointedly at his girth.

"Doesn't say much," the taller one commented.

"Least I manage t' move m' bloody lips when I talk," she retorted.

"Touché," Philippe declared.

"Two wot?"

"Never mind." He smiled. "Come along."

In the lavender drawing room, Damien sat in his wing-back chair before a fire, holding a piece of raw meat to his eye and brooding.

"Please," Marianne beseeched him. "Cook refuses to bring out the cake until you make an appearance."

Richard, looking shaken, sipped his port, then said, "I warn you, Nephew, that Miles intends to make trouble. You should never have let him goad you into losing your temper. I'm surprised at you, Damien. You were always so good at ignoring the scoundrel. I dare say, it's a good thing you did not approach Parliament while you are thrashing about in

your present state of mind. We might have found the Warwick good name besmirched.''

"My heart bleeds, Uncle. It truly does." Damien threw
the meat into the fire, where it hissed and fried upon the
embers. "You might have told me the son of a bitch was in
the country.''

"I was hardly given the opportunity. I did not realize he
was on my heels.'' Richard rewarded Marianne with a tight
smile as she fetched him another port. Then he said, "Besides, you seemed so concerned about this war business and
your home in Vicksburg—''

"Oh, please," Marianne interrupted. "Must we discuss
that dreadful war tonight? This is Damien's birthday, after
all.''

"Ah, yes." Richard nodded. "I shall dash off a dispatch
to the Confederacy and ask them nicely to cease their talks
of war in honor of the event." At Marianne's stern look, he
cleared his throat. "Very well, we'll change the subject. I
hesitate to bring this up now, Damien, but have you forgotten
to tell me something?''

Damien cocked one black brow and looked up at his uncle.
One eye, enlarged by Richard's monocle, stared at him in
return. "To what are you referring?" Damien asked.

"The child.''

"The child?''

"The one who was about to throw herself off the second
floor balcony.''

"Ah.''

"That is Bonnie," Marianne replied.

"Ah, well." Richard sampled his port. "That explains
it.''

Detecting sarcasm in his uncle's voice, Damien explained,
"She's an urchin from Caldbergh.''

"Caldbergh! Great Caesar's ghost, what is she doing
here?''

"Making a spectacle of herself it would seem.''

Mari caught Damien's hand and pulled him from the chair.
"You must get back to your guests. I'll explain Bonnie to
your uncle and we'll join you soon.''

Damien left the room and stood in the corridor, his eye

throbbing like a toothache and his side aching each time he breathed. He remembered his last birthday.

Charlotte Ruth Montgomery had thrown him a surprise party on the banks of the Mississippi. He'd been surprised, all right. He'd known for some time that Charlotte Ruth was enamored of him. And if he was honest with himself he must have been more than a little interested in her, or he might never have followed her down that winding river path to the "secret place" he'd heard so much about.

At eighteen, Charlotte Ruth was a beauty who would turn a man's head in a minute, and she knew it. She could taunt a man into a rutting fever with a flash of her sparkling blue eyes. She had lured him down to the secret place with hints that maybe, just maybe, she might allow him to kiss her. After three months of dining and dancing and wooing her in the company of her mother, father, grandmother, two brothers, and three sisters, not to mention a negro mammy who would have taken his head off with one swipe of her meaty palm if he'd shown Miss Charlotte the slightest disrespect, he was more than ready for a little privacy with the beautiful Charlotte Ruth. Imagine his chagrin when he'd taken her in his arms, only to have a hundred people leap at him from the trees and scream, "Surprise!" That night, when he had been left alone with Charlotte Ruth's father and two brothers, things had become somewhat tense. They were expecting him to ask for Charlotte's hand. He didn't ask and Charlotte Ruth came down with a headache that lasted just short of two months, until he began seeing Melinda Bodeen from Natchez parish.

Christ, it was no wonder he hated birthdays.

For the life of him Damien could not yet force himself to join the party. He wandered down the gallery, idly studying the portraits on the walls. Some were of his father's ancestors. Others were of his mother's. He came to a little-used drawing room, noting that it was brightly lit and judging from the empty glasses set about the furniture, had recently been occupied by a few of his guests. He was about to turn away when the sound of kittens mewing caught his attention. He looked toward the distant French doors. He crossed the room.

Torchlight lit the veranda with a soft yellow glow. He

glanced toward the darker rose garden beyond and, finding nothing, was about to turn back when he heard a whisper.

"Here, kitty. Kitty, kitty."

Damien crossed the veranda and searched among the roses growing along the path leading to the garden. He discovered Bonnie sitting cross-legged between two bushes. In her lap was a basket with three kittens.

She looked up and saw him. Her eyes wide, she grabbed for a taffy-colored puss and did her best to shove it back in the basket.

"What have we here?" Damien asked.

"Kittens," she said.

"Whose?"

She shrugged and her eyes challenged him again.

He walked to the edge of the roses and stared down at Bonnie while she stared up. Neither of them smiled.

"What are their names?" he asked.

She appeared thoughtful, then replied, "Winkin, Blinkin, and Nod. From the nursery tale—"

"I am familiar with the nursery rhyme."

Bonnie hugged the kittens close. "Do y' like cats?" she asked softly, surprising him with the feminine quality of her voice. She sounded nothing whatever like the urchin from Caldbergh.

He stooped before her and scratched between the ears of a white kitten with a black circle around its eye. "Never trusted them much," he replied. "They're a lot like women. You never know when they're going to turn on you with their claws bared."

"Oh," she said. "Y' mustn't like women much."

"That would depend on the woman."

"I suppose y' like the red-haired one a lot."

Damien laughed. "Yes, I suppose I do."

Bonnie scooped up a kitten and buried her face in its downy fur. Then she tipped her head and grinned at Damien.

"Y' ain't much of a fighter," she told him.

Damien touched his eye and winced. "I got my share in."

"My da told me once that there are only two things a man is liable t' fight over. A horse or a woman . . . Y' don't look like a man who would fight over a horse."

"Your father must have been a very astute man."

"He was," she stated decidedly. "The smartest man in the world, I suspect. And the handsomest. Well . . ." She glanced at Damien, then looked away. "Perhaps the second handsomest," she amended quietly.

Damien watched Bonnie a moment longer, noting, not for the first time since joining her, that she looked very different with her hair brushed and braided and swept back from her face. He found himself wishing it wasn't so dark, that the light from the house reached a little further into the garden so he could better see her features.

Taking a deep breath, Bonnie glanced about their surroundings and said, "Nice roses."

"Thank you."

Looking a little dreamy, she caught a bud in her hand and broke it off. She twirled it between her fingers before saying, "Ain't it amazin' how somethin' so plain can blossom open t' be somethin' so delicate and beautiful?" Her gaze came back to his. She smiled brightly and handed him the flower. "Happy birthday," she told him.

Damien accepted the rose, his fingers brushing hers. He stood and looked down through the shadows at her. "The cats are yours if you want them."

She didn't respond, just gathered the squirming, mewling kittens close and laughed as they batted her hand with their paws. The idea occurred to Damien that he'd just as soon spend the remainder of the evening here, sitting in the rose garden and listening to Bonnie laugh. The light cheerful sound reminded him of music, of childhood, of innocence. It filled the darkness around them and inside him with a brief glimpse of sunshine, and something else. He couldn't quite place the sensation, but it felt warm and arousing. Soothing, yet disturbing. As she turned her startlingly wide blue eyes up to him again, he felt a deeper stirring of emotions that were as unexpected as they were unwelcome.

He smiled then, and she smiled back. "Think you can leave your furry friends long enough to eat a piece of birthday cake?" He extended one hand to her. She regarded it, hesitant, before cautiously taking it in her own. He helped her to stand, and for a moment as she stood there before him, the top of her head barely reaching his chin, the ache to take her in his arms and hold her washed through him like a slow fire.

* * *

It was the biggest cake Bonnie had ever imagined, even in her dreams. Three cooks rolled it into the ballroom on a table with wheels. On the top tier, painted with gold-colored icing, was the likeness of a bear rearing up on its back legs. Within one paw it held a ragged staff. Around the emblem were burning candles, and written across the bottom tier was, "KINGMAKER."

A sigh of awe rippled through the crowd at the sight. As Bonnie, hiding in the back of the room, looked as best she could over the crowd's shoulders, she saw Damien's face melt into an expression of pleasure. He gazed down into Marianne's eyes, and before the entire audience, kissed her firmly on her smiling mouth.

Bonnie took that opportunity to slip from the room. She had not cared for the idea of joining in this celebration, although she had been more than a little surprised to be treated as cordially as she had been by the guests. Following Philippe's advice earlier, she had kept her mouth closed during introductions, though she had burned inwardly each time he had explained that, out of the goodness of his heart, Damien had saved her from a wretched fate at Caldbergh. Bonnie surmised that she would rather be regarded with curiosity than with pity. And she'd rather rot, hungry in her room, than be subjected to watching Damien kiss his mistress before a roomful of people.

She was about to retreat up the stairs when a voice behind her said, "Who the devil are you?"

Bonnie looked back over her shoulder in surprise. A man with curling red-brown hair stepped from the shadows and approached her. A flash of fear swept through her so suddenly that Bonnie almost lost her footing, as well as her breath. She stumbled and would have fallen had he not grabbed her.

"Who the blazes are you?" he repeated.

Bonnie glanced at the fingers gripping her wrist and did her best to pull away. Finding her voice, she said as calmly as possible, "Yer hurtin' my arm."

"I'm liable to hurt more than that if you don't answer me."

"I live here."

"Try again."

"I'm tellin' ya—"

"Miles!"

The man gripping Bonnie turned away, dropping her arm. A portly stranger approached them, his heavy gray brows drawn over his eyes. Stopping at the foot of the stairs, he studied Bonnie with a speculative expression, then said, "Please forgive my nephew, young woman. Miles has a tendency to forget himself on occasion." Addressing the man called Miles, the older gentleman frowned. "Marianne tells me Bonnie is a temporary guest at Braithwaite, so do try to curtail your less-than-savory manners for another time." To Bonnie, he added, "I am Damien's uncle, Richard Sitwell. This is Damien's half brother, Miles Kemball."

"Warwick," Miles supplied.

"I trust that he hasn't hurt you?" Richard asked.

Bonnie rubbed her arm where Miles's fingers had gripped her. She did not respond. She was too busy struggling to control all the old fears that had resurfaced the moment the man's voice had come at her from the shadows. The need to run and hide was suffocating and made her already weakened limbs quiver with distress.

Forcing herself to stand, to turn, to climb the stairs without looking back at the men was an effort. But she managed it. Shoulders squared and head up, she walked as calmly as possible to her room and shut the door behind her.

Bonnie closed her eyes and waited for the shaking to cease. It didn't. It was still there when she opened her eyes and glanced around the room. Each looming fixture cast dark patches over the floor. She searched each one before she left the door and walked about, assuring herself that everything was fine. She was alone and safe and . . .

Bonnie stopped and hugged herself tightly, holding in the terror, refusing to acknowledge its grip on her senses. But she was losing control. Hysteria was boiling at the base of her throat. Soon there would be the blackness, and all the nightmares would return, and the memories . . .

"No, no," she groaned.

She pressed her palms against her temples as if she could make the images go away, force them back into the shuttered recesses of her mind where they belonged. But it didn't help. The roaring was there, and the blackness too, pulsing in and out like some breathing thing, the same thing that had chased her through the rain and darkness with blood on his hands.

Groaning, Bonnie fell against the wall and slid to the floor, drew her knees up to her chest and covered her head with her arms. "Please, God, make 'em go away," she whimpered. "Please . . ."

Damien stared at the ceiling. The idea that at dawn he would be galloping over the moor chasing fox made his head ache worse. Beside him, Marianne was fast asleep, her soft breaths stirring the red strands of hair which had fallen over her face. She was delectable and enchanting. Looking at her made him smile, made him forget for a moment that just down the hall Miles Kemball slept.

Damien rolled from the bed, wincing and touching his eye, then his ribs. Quietly he walked to the chairs and table before the hearth, intending to merely sit and think for a while, perhaps sort out the troubling concerns that had been plaguing him of late. Seeing the pale yellow rose on the table, he picked it up. Due to the heat from the fire, the tight bud Bonnie had given him had opened, unfolded its delicate petals in full bloom. Raising it to his nose, he smelled it, recalling the girl's face—how it had shone as she handed the flower to him. He shook his head free of the memory, slipped on his clothes, and left the room.

He was feeling trapped again, and it had nothing to do with his bruised body or his battered pride. It wasn't the first time he'd been bested by fists. More than likely it wouldn't be the last. But he'd be damned and dead in his grave before he would let Miles get the better of him again. If he was forced, by his father's decree, to allow Miles to live here, he must do his best to ignore the ne'er-do-well. It wouldn't be easy, considering what lay between them, but for the sake of his own sanity, he would try. There were more pressing problems to deal with. He must be mentally prepared to face Parliament. Physically he should be at his peak if he was forced to take up arms to protect Bent Tree.

Damien stopped at the top of the stairs and gazed down into the darkness. How many Warwicks had stood in this very place, considering their futures, their pasts? So many plans to make. So many decisions. He could remember his grandfather standing here, pondering some grand vision as he stared out into the blackness of the immense house. "Ah, Braithwaite, you are a grand old girl," the old man had whispered, oblivious of the small boy who crouched in the shadows, watching. Damien could remember, too, the many times he'd sat on his grandfather's lap while his ancestry was explained in colorful detail.

Middleham Castle, Windsor of the north, had been begun by Robert FitzRandolph in 1170, and was connected with the powerful Neville family, one member of which was the great Earl of Warwick of the War of the Roses. In those days these grounds had witnessed scenes of princely magnificence, lordly occasions of state, wild revelries, and gorgeous retinues. The feudal baron, Warwick the Kingmaker, had lived in regal state in Middleham's grand fortress. It was said that six oxen were eaten at his breakfast feasts. King Richard had married Warwick's daughter, the Lady Anne Neville, and had lived for a time at the castle. Edward, Prince of Wales, had been born in the round tower. But after Richard's fall at Bosworth the reign of the Plantagenets ended, and so did the grand days of Middleham. King Richard's successor, Henry Tudor, had allowed the great castle to fall into ruin, and in 1546 his son Henry VIII had ordered the castle to be blown to bits. Eventually, just a short distance from the ruins, had risen Braithwaite. Mammoth. Dignified. A cornerstone of the Warwick pride and empire that still dominated the Pennine hills and valleys in West Yorkshire. Damien could still recall his grandfather sighing and saying in a dreamy voice, "Ah, my young Damien, if only the War of the Roses had ended differently. If only . . ."

Damien closed his eyes. What would his grandfather say to him now if he were here? His old heart would have been shattered, just like Middleham's walls, had he known that someday his grandson would turn his back on an ancestry and titles so old and prestigious. That he would immigrate to America and take up a rebel's cause and beseech the Queen on behalf of a foreign soil.

That thought stopped him. Not for the first time the idea, *What the hell am I doing in Mississippi?* rose unbidden and unwelcome to his mind. He found himself questioning his loyalty to Bent Tree as thoroughly as he had questioned it for

Braithwaite. More and more the realization that he was a man caught between two countries presented itself, and he was frequently at a loss as to what to do about it. What did either of them have to offer? Braithwaite, of course, was his heritage and worth a fortune far exceeding that of most of his peers. Bent Tree was challenging and demanding. It was proof positive of his worth. In Vicksburg he wasn't simply the son of an earl, but his own man.

He felt a little like a bigamist. He'd deserted one distinguished but boring lady for the forbidden thrill of a vulgar mistress. He was married to both, and no longer totally in love with either. Something was definitely missing in each relationship, and he couldn't put his finger on what it was. Perhaps it was better that way for the time being. He was finding that the choice he had to make between Braithwaite and Bent Tree was difficult enough—even more so than he'd imagined. He needed no other outside forces complicating the issue.

Deciding to return to bed, Damien started back to his room when the sound of weeping stopped him. He listened hard and heard it again. He walked directly to Bonnie's door. Standing in the darkness he tried to convince himself that he had no business coming here. The girl haunted and disturbed him. Yet . . .

Over the days, she had become like a bright, burning light in an otherwise lusterless cosmos. While in her company his lethargy left him. He yearned more often than not to bask in her presence and allow her warmth to thaw the nagging chill inside him. He had, in an odd sense, come to rely on her.

He eased open the door.

A single shaft of moonlight spilled through the window, over the floor, and across the empty bed. Damien searched the room, his gaze lingering on each shadow. Then he found her, huddled against the wall near the wardrobe, her knees drawn up to her chest, her small face buried in her hands. Her shoulders shook violently, spasmodically with the force of her tears.

He cautiously approached Bonnie, then bent on one knee beside her. She must have sensed his presence, for suddenly her face, tiny within her cloud of black hair, turned up to him. It looked pale with moonlight. There were silver tear streaks running down her cheeks.

"For the love of God," he whispered, "what is wrong with you, lass?"

Suddenly Bonnie was against him, her arms around his neck, her face buried in his chest, her small body heaving with her emotions. His arms at his sides, he stared out the window at the sheets of moon-kissed mist blanketing the moor. His first instinct was to wrap his arms around the girl's frail form and comfort her. Once in his life, he would have. Now he only fixed his eyes on the eavesdropping moon and forced his hands to remain at his sides, rebelling with all his strength against the instinct to hold her.

Damien swallowed. Her breath was warm, her tears hot against his chest. Her small hands dug into the flesh of his nape, burning.

She wept harder. She clung to him more tightly, so tightly her every curve was melded to him, so forcefully her heart thumped against his like a frightened rabbit's. "Don't let him hurt me," she pleaded.

With a will of its own, his hand came up and hovered against the back of Bonnie's head before burying itself in her hair. He hugged her close, closing his eyes as a flood of warmth rushed through him. "It's all right, Bonnie. No one's going to hurt you here. You're all right, lass."

The words soothed her. Damien eased down onto the floor and leaned against the wardrobe, cradling Bonnie in his lap and against his chest. Her hair spilled softly over his arms and hands and legs. Still she clung like a terrified child to his neck. He could feel her eyelashes bat softly against his throat like a butterfly's wing.

"Are you awake now?" he asked.

Her head moved up and down.

"Bad dreams?"

She sniffed and nodded.

"Too much birthday cake, I wager. Did you enjoy it?"

Bonnie shrugged.

"A bit rich," he said. "The icing could have used some trimming down, I think, though I would never tell Cook that. He's a bit funny about that sort of thing."

As she shifted a little in his lap, Damien's body responded

with a startling jolt that was almost painful. It was appalling really. Disgusting. He suddenly found himself doing his best to picture Marianne in his mind: her beautiful glossy red hair, her wickedly teasing eyes, her silk underwear that could turn a man into a rutting animal . . . which is what he felt like at that very minute, and Marianne had absolutely nothing to do with it.

Finally Bonnie lifted her head. Nose to nose she stared into Damien's eyes, her own like two dark, glistening saucers surrounded by the longest eyelashes he had ever seen on a female. Then the tip of her small pink tongue darted out and licked a trembling tear from her upper lip. Another tear slipped down from the outer corner of her eye, and before he could stop himself he raised one hand, caught the glistening drop with the pad of his thumb, and wiped it away.

"Would you care to tell me what it is you're frightened of?" he asked softly.

She appeared to consider the idea, then shook her head.

"You cry out for your father. Is he dead?"

"Aye." Bonnie sniffed and wiggled again on his lap.

"And your mother is dead too."

"Died of consumption."

"How long have you been at Caldbergh?"

Frowning, Bonnie said, "You ask too many bloody questions, y' know."

"I'm curious is all. You've been here for a while now, and I don't even know your last name or where you're from."

"Why should you care?"

The directness of the query set him back. She was right. Why should he care? What difference would it make in his life if he familiarized himself with her circumstances? He'd reminded himself a hundred times during the last three weeks that he had too much to cope with now; why add to the burden? Yet, here he was, holding on to some grubby little urchin from a workhouse, feeling as if her smile, indeed, her very presence, could somehow save him from completely falling apart as he awaited news from Parliament and Vicksburg.

"Well?" she prompted.

Damien shrugged. "I suppose if we intend to reside in the same house we might as well know one another."

"I know who *you* are," Bonnie said. "I know a lot about you."

"Oh?"

"I hear the servants talkin'."

"Ah. An eavesdropper. I'll be certain to speak in whispers from now on when discussing matters of importance."

She giggled. "I know y' just turned thirty-three. Y' enjoy reading someone named Shakespeare—"

"How do you know that?"

"Cause I seen the book Lady Marianne gave y' for a present."

Surprised, Damien asked, "Can you read?"

"Course I can read." She rolled her eyes. "D' y' think I'm completely daft?"

"Then you went to school."

"Sometime. When m' mum and da didn't need help with the chores. M' mum taught me when I was at home."

"I'll bet you lived on a farm."

"Sorta. We had a few cows and chickens, and a sow named Sue. M' da named her that cause she reminded him of a lass he almost married."

They laughed.

Damien nudged a tendril of dark hair behind Bonnie's ear. "Your da sounds like a man with a sense of humor."

"Aye. He had lots o' dreams too."

"Such as?"

"He wanted t' raise sheep."

"Sheep! Good God."

"And just wot's wrong with sheep?" Bonnie demanded.

"They smell, for one thing."

"I like sheep. I always imagined m'self marryin' a sheep farmer one day."

"That's a first. Most young women dream of marrying a prince or some such nonsense."

"Give over." Bonnie laughed. "Wot would a bloody prince want with me?"

"Stranger things have happened, little girl. Haven't you read the story of Cinderella? No? A handsome prince meets a poor but beautiful girl in his kingdom. They fall in love and are married."

Silence seemed to swallow them then. Bonnie looked away. Damien dropped his hands to his sides.

A full minute ticked by before Bonnie made herself crawl from Damien's lap. She walked to the window. "Rubbish," she finally said. "It's one thing t' read fairy tales about such things, but another t' really believe it could happen. Besides, I think bein' married t' some nabob would be borin'. No offense intended," she added, glancing Damien's way. His face appeared pale in the moonlight, his eyes dark. His hair had tumbled over his brow, thick and black. She took a breath.

"Why?" he asked quietly.

"Y' got nothin' in common for one thing. Say—" She hesitated. "Say if . . . if you and me was t' get married . . ." She gazed out the window and laughed, or tried to. She listened for some similar response from Damien, but there was only silence. "Y' don't even like sheep. I'd be wantin' t' talk lambin' and y'd be discussin' wot lord such and such done down in Parliament. I'd be wantin' t' picnic out on the moor and y'd be yearnin' t' have tea in some stuffy ol' parlor in some stuffy ol' manor house with some stuffy ol'—"

"I don't like tea."

Bonnie closed her mouth.

"I do like picnics."

"With goose pâté and petit fours, I reckon."

"A loaf of bread, a round of cheese, a nice bottle of wine, or a pint of ale."

"Give over." She gripped the windowsill. " 'At's a plowman's lunch. Wot would a nabob like you be doin' eatin' food like that?"

She could feel him staring at her. A heartbeat passed before he responded. "You don't like me, do you?"

"I don't like wot y' are." She faced him again, and found him frowning.

"Which is?" he asked.

"Y' got no idea wot the real world is like. Y' don't know wot it's like to work all yer life so there's calluses upon calluses on the palms of yer hands. And after all that work y' still got naught t' show for it. When was the last time y' ever had t' worry over losin' yer home cause of debts? A home you'd struggled t' build with yer own two hands and the sweat from yer brow. How would y' feel watchin' some stranger come along and take it from y' cause y' can't pay yer bloody taxes cause y've been too ill t' work or cause y' was injured doin' yer job and can't work.''

"I think you judge me too harshly, Bonnie. Why don't you get to know me before—"

She turned on him angrily. "I don't want t' get t' know ya. In fact, I was just thinkin' that I aught t' get out of here. I'm feelin' better now and there's really no reason why I shouldn't leave.''

Bonnie stepped back as Damien rose to his feet. Even with distance between them he seemed formidable, frightening. She stared up at his face and felt more helpless than she ever had at Birdie's hands. There was something going on inside her that left her feeling out of control, and that was a dangerous state in which to be, at least in her world. Still, it was hard not to recall how those arms had felt around her. God, how long had it been since she had actually experienced any form of tenderness? In truth, how many hours had she lain in this bed imagining Warwick's arms holding her?

That realization stunned her. The very idea that she had stood in this man's presence these last minutes and ached with the silly fantasy that this bloody nabob would actually see her as something more than an urchin from Caldbergh made her feel ill with humiliation.

"Friggin' nabob, why don't y' just get the hell out of m' room?''

He didn't move.

"Are y' daft? I said t' get out of m' room. Y' might own half of bleedin' Yorkshire, but y' don't own me. I don't *want* t' get t' know you. Understand? Warwick? I don't bloody like y' or wot y' are. The sooner I see the back of y' and this friggin' mausoleum the better.''

Damien's look became cold, his eyes hard, and his mouth tight. His stance, once casual, now appeared rigid as he clenched and unclenched his fists at his sides. "Since you chose to regard me in that manner, I will remind you that this is *my* room. My house. And yes, my bloody village for all that. The air you breathe as long as you reside here is mine. So is the food you eat and the water you drink.''

Raising her chin, Bonnie stared back at Warwick defiantly. It wasn't easy. She suddenly felt a little like a hare cornered by a hound. At any moment she expected him to leap at her with his teeth bared and tear her into little pieces.

Yet, he didn't. He only rewarded her with a disapproving snort and a sudden flash of his white teeth as he laughed. She was again uneasily conscious of the feeling of leashed power that emanated from him, and for a moment she questioned the wisdom of aggravating him so. Still, it couldn't be helped. She couldn't allow herself to believe that what had passed between her and Warwick moments before had been anything special.

Uncomfortably aware of her increased heartbeat, she angrily thrust up her chin, and doing her best to keep her voice as dispassionate as possible, asked, "Since this house is *yours*, as well as this village and the air we are breathin', just wot does that make me?"

"Baggage."

The word stung. Bonnie stiffened and, unable to help herself, spat, "Bastard!"

A hint of a smile lurked on Damien's mouth as he continued to regard her without emotion. "While your mama was teaching you to read, didn't she also teach you that young ladies do not swear?"

"Wot I say and how I say it is none of yer bloody business."

The smile left Damien's mouth, and his shadowed features fell into their more familiar hard lines. "Wrong, urchin. Since you were kind enough to remind me of my privileged position in life, I will now remind you that, as master of Braithwaite, I make the rules. Being the uninvited baggage that you are, you follow them or leave."

"Well, I'm planning t' do just that!" Bonnie cried. "I'd rather tolerate Birdie Smythe ever'day for the rest of me miserable life than t' have t' bear yer stupid hierarchy one more bleedin' minute!"

"So," he said dryly, "what's keeping you?"

"I'll leave then!"

He raised one eyebrow.

Without considering the ramifications of her actions, she stormed to the bedroom door, flung it open, and left. She had marched all the way to the stairs before she realized what exactly she *was* doing. It was well after midnight. Where would she go? No way was she *really* going to return to Caldbergh and submit herself to Smythe's fiendish plans.

Hesitating, she glanced back down the hallway. Warwick was nowhere in sight. What had she expected? That he would run after her and beg her to stay? What was she to him, after all? An urchin. Chit. Baggage. Brat. A waif with little more than the clothes on her back, a saucy tongue, and a voracious appetite. An orphan who had stumbled into Braithwaite in error and sickness and desperation. She was nothing to him but trouble, and if there was anything the aristocracy avoided, other than outright scandal, it was trouble.

Still, she wouldn't back down. There was her pride she must deal with, bruised as it was already. She reminded herself that for the last five years she had survived Birdie and Caldbergh and the indifference of the ignorant populace. If she must, she would survive Warwick's turning her out as well.

Head up and shoulders squared, Bonnie descended the stairs. She had just reached the front door when Warwick's deep voice called through the darkness.

"Bonnie!"

She froze, then turned slowly back to the stairs. He stood poised at the top of the staircase, a silent shadow. Finally he moved partially down the steps into a halo of soft moonlight that spilled through a window near the door.

"It's late," came the words, sounding strangely urgent. She stared harder through the shadows. His eyes seemed disturbed, cold and icy one instant, haunted and slightly wild the next.

"It's late," he repeated more forcefully, and this time a grim smile flickered in his eyes and across the pressed line of his mouth. It was as if he was laughing at himself, as much as at Bonnie. "I suggest you wait until morning before taking leave of Braithwaite," he continued. "After all, it may well be the last decent bed you sleep in for a very long time."

Taking one step closer to the stairs, she asked, "Are y' askin' me t' stay, Warwick?" She held her breath.

The reply was a moment in coming. "I am not," he responded shortly. "I am *allowing* you to stay. At least until morning. Then we'll . . . discuss it."

She stood in the damp chill, trembling. It might have been due to relief, but somehow she sensed it was more than that. Watching him closely, Bonnie approached the stairs and began the climb, slowing as she neared him.

Raising her sight to his, she found his eyes hard and speculative, staring back into hers with a fierceness that took her breath away. It was a duel between them—she fighting to remain cool and indifferent, and he deliberately taunting her with his aloofness. Forcing herself to breathe, Bonnie said, "I'll be gone first thing in the mornin'. Y'll not be troubled by me another day. That should please you."

He started to respond, but didn't. Instead, he crammed his hands into his pockets and looked away.

Heart racing in her chest, she started up the stairs, calling back in her most mocking voice, "Good night, *my lord*."

It was a moment before the soft words came from the darkness below.

"Good night, Bonnie."

Six

Damien took Marianne up against a rowan tree. With the skirt of her habit hiked to her waist, he drove himself into her while somewhere in the distance the dogs were baying like the hounds of hell.

"Damien!" she cried, "what in God's name has come over you?"

Damien closed his eyes and did his best to block the image of blue eyes and raven-black hair from his mind. But it wouldn't leave him. Even as Marianne wrapped her legs around his hips, even as he moved his body in and out of hers, he imagined it was Bonnie he was holding. It was disgusting, perverted. He would probably go to hell for thinking it. She was a child, for God's sake. An innocent. Unaffected by all the pomp around her. And the most beautiful young woman he'd met in a very, very long time.

Marianne gasped as his fingers dug into the tender undersides of her thighs. He drove her harder against the tree, panting, sweating inside the confining shirt and form-fitting hunt coat. He heard her whimper, and the realization of what he was doing hit him full force. Very slowly he set Marianne on her feet and slid his body out of hers. He turned away and rearranged his trousers. Marianne did her best to smooth down her crushed velvet skirt as she eyed him guardedly.

"Well?" she said. "I think you owe me an explanation. Is your recent behavior due to something I've done?"

He shook his head and yanked the cravat from around his neck. He wiped his face with it.

"You woke me in the middle of the night like some rutting stag and now this."

"You don't like it?" he snapped.

"No. I don't. You're not making love to me, Damien. You're taking out your anger on me. I understand you're upset—"

He whirled on her so suddenly that she stumbled back in surprise. "You understand nothing, lady. I'm sitting around this—friggin' mausoleum—waiting for some high official to make up his mind whether or not he's going to give me the time of day, while any moment I expect a dispatch from Vicksburg informing me that everything that means anything to me is about to be obliterated."

"Damien, there is always Braithwaite—"

"I don't give a damn about Braithwaite! Jesus, Marianne, don't you understand? Bent Tree is six years of my life. It is *my* accomplishment. Not my father's or grandfather's; it's mine. By the sweat of my brow I turned a plot of worthless land into something rich and productive." He held out his hands, palms up. "I didn't get these calluses from hunting fox or playing snooker or passing time at White's. I worked for them, Mari. I worked so damned hard there were times I couldn't even make it back to the house to sleep. I'd collapse under some bush or tree or wherever the hell I happened to fall and that's where I spent the night."

Dropping his hands, he shook his head. "You don't understand, do you?"

Marianne looked away and, without responding, walked to her mount. The sleek mare whinnied and thrust her velvety muzzle into her hand as she gathered up the reins. Turning back to Damien, Mari asked, "Shall we catch up to the others? I'm certain by now they have grown aware of our rather conspicuous absence."

"Go on without me."

Wary of his mood, she mounted her horse, and without another word, rode off. Damien watched her go, her name on the tip of his tongue as he considered calling her back and apologizing. He was appalled by his behavior. For the love of God, he had tackled and tamed a wilderness in Mississippi, but suddenly he couldn't control his mind *or* his body.

His entire life was unraveling, and there didn't seem to be a damned thing he could do to stop it. He hadn't even been totally truthful with Marianne. The problem of Vicksburg and Parliament was suddenly getting muddled up with thoughts of some homeless waif who thought life with a prince would be boring.

He didn't call Marianne back. Instead, he reached for his gelding's reins and swung his leg over the horse's back, settling into the saddle with an ease that came from spending much of the last five years on a horse as he oversaw the building of Bent Tree and the planting and harvesting of his crops.

He headed back to Braithwaite, pushing the animal to its limits, doing his best to drive away the conflicting emotions inside him. By the time he arrived at the house the horse was lathered and its sides were heaving with exhaustion.

Tables and chairs had already been arranged on the meticulously manicured lawns. Servants hurried here and there as they prepared for the returning hunters. China was being set out. Great urns of coffee and steeping tea were being arranged on long tables beneath brightly colored canopies with flapping pennants. Decanters of liquors were readily available as well.

As Damien dismounted, leaving his horse with a groom, Jewel hurried to him with a cup of coffee steaming into the brisk morning air. "Yer coffee, m'lord. Will the others be 'round directly?" she asked.

"Soon." He took the cup and saucer; his hands were shaking.

"Would there be aught wrong, m'lord?" Jewel asked, her shining eyes concerned.

"No. Nothing." He sipped the brew, finding she had laced it perfectly with brandy. He looked down at the conscientious servant and offered her a quick smile of approval. She beamed in return. "Is Miles about?" he asked.

"I ain't seen him this mornin'," she said with a sniff of disapproval.

He drank again, allowing the coffee to soothe him as he gazed out over the rolling Pennine fells. A lazy sun stirred the mists into long, swirling fingers of gray. The thought occurred to him that he'd actually missed the English mornings the last years.

Unconsciously, his sight shifted back to the house, to Bonnie's bedroom window. Finishing the coffee, he handed the cup and saucer back to Jewel and said, "What about the urchin . . ."

"Bonnie," she reminded him.

"Right. Bonnie. Has she gone yet?"

"Gone, m'lord? Was she supposed to?"

"Is she still here?"

"I couldn't say, m'lord."

"What about my uncle? Is he about?"

"No, m'lord. He's kippin' in this mornin'. We're to awaken him at nine, m'lord, not a minute before, not a minute after."

Damien frowned. It seemed the older Sitwell got, the more eccentric he became. "Let me know when he's up," he told Jewel. "I'll be in the library if you need me."

Jewel bobbed a curtsy, then hurried off as Damien strode toward the house, flicking his riding crop against the heel of his knee-high black leather boots. Upon arriving at the library door, however, he stopped short. Miles, dressed in his riding coat, breeches, and boots, was lounging in the chair behind the desk. He grinned at Damien.

"Well, if it's not the earl himself. What's wrong, ol' man, have you grown weary of tallyho and all that rot?" Miles clicked his tongue. "Our father wouldn't have approved, you know."

"What the hell are you doing here?"

"I had every intention of joining the hunt. I truly did. But I was a bit late out of bed—someone forgot to wake me—and as I was considering riding out to join the revelers, I was met at the door by a courier." Smiling, he held a letter up between two fingers. "This came for you just minutes ago."

Damien moved to the desk and snatched the envelope from Miles's hand. He recognized his overseer's writing immediately.

"Bad news," Miles announced, leaning back in the leather chair.

The seal on the envelope had been broken. Miles had obviously read it. However, the fury Damien might have felt at

Miles was dampened somewhat by the dread of reading the letter. He slowly slid it from the envelope and opened it.

"Seems the troops are getting restless, Dame. A dozen black men laying down their picks and shovels and marching off to join the Union army doesn't bode well for future cotton pickin', does it? As your overseer says, 'A dozen today, maybe two dozen tomorrow.' So who the devil is going to be there to protect hearth and home when Lincoln's armies march into Vicksburg?"

Damien crumpled the letter in his fist.

Miles left the chair, walked around the desk, and stood eye to eye with Damien. "How does it feel to have something you love yanked right out of your life, my lord? I mean taken away and there isn't a damn thing you can do but stand by and watch it happen. A bit like being punched in the gut, ain't it? Makes you want to hurt something or somebody. It makes you want to vomit, don't it, Dame?"

"Go to hell."

Miles threw back his head and laughed. Then he said, "By the look on your face I think you've beat me to it." He glanced about the library. "Enjoy your Gehenna, my lord. You deserve it."

Miles left him. Damien listened to his footsteps echoing up the gallery, then he flung the crushed letter to the floor and followed. By the time he reached the vestibule Miles was nowhere in sight. Standing at the foot of the stairs, he slapped the riding crop against his boots and thought to himself that if he went after Miles now he would later regret it. Miles was right. The helplessness and frustration he felt in that moment made him feel out of control. Sick. Furious. He'd done his best to prepare himself for the inevitable. Everyone had warned him, even when there were only whispers of war, that Damien's idea of working free blacks at Bent Tree would backfire. He had anticipated that backlash. He understood the men's feelings. He couldn't expect them to side with a people who were enslaving their own kind.

What he hadn't anticipated was his own reaction to being forced into the position he was in now. Jesus, what was he supposed to do? He couldn't even call himself an Englishman any longer. He found his peers' ideals shallow and their pastimes frivolous. Yet here he was waiting to beseech Parliament on behalf of a people whose ideas on slavery he didn't totally believe in either. And Braithwaite. What the devil was he to do about it? How was he to just walk away and pretend it never existed? How could he turn his back on a heritage his ancestors had fought and died to provide him?

He closed his eyes. When he opened them again he was gazing up the stairs, the memory of his confrontation with Bonnie the night before prevalent in his mind. Now there was the girl to contend with. What was the matter with him? What the *hell* was happening to him? Regardless of all his problems, Bonnie seemed to be constantly on his mind, popping up at the most inopportune moments. He couldn't even make love to Mari any longer without experiencing the insane notion that it was Bonnie he was holding.

He shook his head and laughed dryly to himself. He must be bored. That had to be it. That or he had totally lost his morals or his mind. He couldn't even put his finger on the reason for his lusty obsession. Yes, Bonnie was pretty, in a simple sort of way. Perhaps that was it. The urchin from Caldbergh posed no threat to his plans. She made no demands on his time. She was uncomplicated, unaffected. She could find joy in a basket of kittens and a rosebud while Marianne and all those women like her measured their happiness in wealth and title. Bonnie dreamed of marrying a sheep farmer.

A sheep farmer.

He wondered if she would settle for a ruined cotton planter.

The idea hit him like a lightning bolt. Damn, he *was* going crazy. The stress was getting to him. Marry that little guttersnipe? Ha! . . . Besides, she didn't even like him. She'd told him so last night. After he'd saved her life, she couldn't wait to be rid of him. The sooner she was gone the better, he told himself in no uncertain terms. Out of sight, out of mind, as the old saying went.

He took the stairs two at a time, walked determinedly into the sitting area outside her room, and stopped at the door. It was partially open, enough for him to see that the bed, though rumpled, was empty. He drew a long breath as it occurred to him that she might already be gone. He was about to shove open the door when her singing voice came to him like a melodious lullaby.

You call it dishonor
To bow to this flame,
If you've eyes look upon her
And blush while you blame,
Hath the pearl less whiteness
Because of its birth?
Has the violet less brightness
For growing near earth?

His eye caught the vision in the cheval glass. Naked, Bonnie stood with her back to the mirror as she busily scrubbed her arms the best she could with water from a blue and white porcelain washbowl. Her fall of black hair covered her back completely, trailing over her buttocks to her thighs. There the wispy ends curled generously, offering him frequent glimpses of her snow-white flesh and the alluring separation between her buttocks. Damien viewed her with half-admiring half-hostile eyes, feeling the stirring in his body again, the restlessness, the ache. For an instant he imagined himself storming into the room, throwing her onto the twisted sheets, and covering her body with his. He imagined her response. She would fight and claw like a she-cat, no doubt.

His eyes narrowed, he allowed a thin smile to curl his mouth. Then, quickly, he came to his senses. He was erect. He was sweating. If he didn't escape now . . .

He reached with his crop and shoved the door open. Suddenly there was a flurry of activity. By the time he centered his sights on the girl she was gripping her nightgown against her breasts like a shield. Her eyes wide, she stared into his face, her small body trembling with what must be rage at his brazen, unannounced entry.

Stopping at the foot of the bed, Damien raked Bonnie with his eyes. "So," he snarled softly, "I see you haven't gone."

"How—how dare you," she sputtered. "Of all the—"

"My house. Remember? My room . . ."

Bonnie angled her chin at him defiantly. "And y' can bloody well have it! If y've come all the way up here just t' tell me t' get out—"

"On the contrary, brat . . ." He glanced toward the bed and flipped the end of his crop back and forth over the toe of one boot before refocusing his gaze on her. Two spots of hot color blazed on her cheeks. Her soft lips were as red as cherries and parted in anticipation as she awaited his next move.

Raising the tip of the crop, he drew it gently down the side of her face, her neck, trailed it over one bare shoulder to stop just above her fist where she gripped the gown to her breast. "You may stay . . . as long as you behave in a manner befitting Braithwaite and those who reside here. You will, however, remain in your quarters until these guests have all returned to their own homes. That should be only—oh . . ." He stared into space. "This time tomorrow. Then you may come out, and we will address the little problem of what to do with you next, who you are, and what you were doing running away from our friend Smythe in the first place."

Before Bonnie could form a reply, Damien pivoted on his heel and strode to the door. He paused and looked back. Bonnie's complexion was now completely ashen, her eyes two huge violet jewels in her face. His gaze lingered on her angrily heaving bosom and the wrathful slant of her full mouth before he added, mockingly, "Don't thank me . . . yet. I'll let you know this time tomorrow just what sort of compensation my philanthropy will cost you. Have a pleasant day, baggage."

Damien left the room. He had just arrived at the stairs when his uncle joined him.

Richard, his face appearing pinched with fatigue, regarded Damien with concern. "You look like hell," he said.

Raising one eyebrow, Damien replied, "You don't look much better. What's your excuse?"

"I don't sleep well. It must be my age."

"Or the bottle of port you put away before falling into bed."

"By gad, that's not very nice," Richard declared.

"I'm not in the mood to be nice."

Richard slowed his descent of the stairs. "Perhaps I should retire to my room until later."

"Perish the thought."

Damien entered the library and waited until his uncle was seated behind the massive walnut desk before offering him a cigar. Richard shook his head and waved it away. "I've sworn off," he said. "But I wouldn't mind a port."

"A little early for that, isn't it?"

"Good God, you sound like your father. Does this mean I must now be forced to answer to my favorite nephew each time I have an itch for a drink?"

He wasn't in the frame of mind to deliberate the matter, so he poured Richard a port and handed it to him.

Richard took a generous swallow before relaxing in his chair. Damien didn't miss the nervous glance his uncle made toward the ledger on the desk. He supposed he should confront Richard about the mess he'd made of Braithwaite's books; although he'd prepared himself for the dreaded confrontation, he hadn't been able to bring himself to do it. Perhaps because he had not anticipated the changes in his mother's brother. Richard had aged dramatically in the last years. He looked like a man of seventy-three instead of fifty-three. Obviously, the man's health wasn't good. Stress, along with drinking, had taken their toll.

Aside from that, how was he supposed to dismiss his own uncle from a position he had dedicated his entire life to? How, when, while Damien was growing up, that very man had loved and nurtured him more than his own father had?

Richard pursed his mouth and ran his fingers idly over the ledger. "It's in a real mess, isn't it?"

Damien nodded.

"Well, I told your father that he should never have put Miles in charge of those mines. That's when the trouble started, you know. Joseph was a fool for pulling you out. But you know how your father was about Miles. Always conscious of obligations, et cetera. I suppose he felt as if he owed the lad something, considering, but you would have thought allowing Miles to live here at Braithwaite as he was growing up would have been enough."

Glancing away, Damien said, "I really don't care to go into that this morning."

"Ah, well. Don't blame you, my boy. I was just curious over how deeply you've delved into the books so far."

Noting the slight tremor in Richard's hands, Damien feigned a disinterested shrug. "I've had other things on my mind."

"You do realize that financially the Warwick estate is on the verge of being crippled."

"With a great deal of effort, I think she can be saved."

"Gunnerside Mine is closed down. I really did do my best to rectify the mess Miles made of it, but his incompetence during his tenure as supervisor hurt us. Now everyone is fleeing to Durham to work in the damnable collieries. You might consider selling your assets now, Damien, before it's too late."

Damien studied his uncle's agitated features.

"Should you decide to reinvest, I have a suggestion. I have looked into purchasing some iron properties outside Cleveland. They will take a great deal to modernize, but it might be worth the effort in the long run—"

"I don't think so."

"But I recently spoke with Henry Bessemer while he was in London. We discussed the purchase of one of his converters for the mills and—"

"The mills are a dying issue, Uncle. In my opinion we would be better off shutting them down completely and paying what few workers remain a fair settlement."

Richard laughed uneasily. "Sounds as if you have delved into the books deeper than you're letting on, Damien."

"Enough to know that we can't afford to buy Bessemer converters."

Deciding to change the unpleasant subject, Richard said, "So tell me. Has Marianne decided to finally divorce Sir Harry Lyttleton and his bevy of young men and return to Vicksburg with you?"

Damien leaned negligently against the mantel, his arms crossed loosely over his chest. "You must be lapsing into senility, Uncle, if you think for a moment Marianne would give up the freedom marriage to Lyttleton affords her or that I would marry her if she were available."

"My pardon. I misinterpreted that glint in your eye as fondness. Instead it is simply lust. However could I make such a mistake?"

"Age and too much port."

Sitwell snorted. "I thought perhaps you would marry that girl—let me see, what was her name? You mentioned her in that letter you wrote me last year . . ."

"Charlotte. And, no, I do not intend to marry her either."

"When *do* you intend to settle down?"

"I don't intend. Ever."

"Bah! Of course you will. Find yourself some sweet innocent, Damien, and get married."

A lazy smile on his mouth, Damien approached the desk. "This coming from a man who has, in all his fifty-three years, never been married."

"Yes, well I regret it now when I see my friends entertained by their grandchildren. You are my last chance, Damien. I would dearly love it if you gifted me with a passel of great-nieces and nephews before I am too old to enjoy them. You always loved children."

"Did I? I cannot recall."

"Of course you did. And do. Look what you have done for the Caldbergh child upstairs. Don't deny you have a soft spot for the young ones."

Damien's face suddenly went dark, causing Richard some curiosity. "Is something wrong?" he asked. "Every time I mention the lass you cloud up like a moor fog at dark. Marianne tells me she's a delight."

"A delight!" Damien barked a laugh. "She's a bloody pain in the ass, and for twopence I'd haul her undernourished backside back to Caldbergh."

"So why don't you?"

"I will," he hedged, "just as soon as the opportunity offers itself."

"What's wrong with now? I'll ride with you, if you'd like. I wouldn't mind a few hours out. I was beginning to feel a bit hemmed in." Richard finished his drink and placed the empty glass on the desk. He left his chair.

Damien, however, stood his ground, legs planted firmly apart, face revealing that shut-in expression he knew his uncle had seen so often as he was growing up.

"Is something wrong?" Richard asked. "Is a ride to Caldbergh not convenient now?"

"No," Damien said dryly. "It isn't."

"Then perhaps later."

"Perhaps. I'll let you know."

"I met the girl briefly last night. I imagine she would make for rousing conversation. If she is going to be here a while, I might have a go at it."

Damien's lip curled with amusement. Picking up a crystal

paperweight from the table, he turned it one way then another, watching as it refracted the light through the window into bands of colors. "I cannot imagine why anyone would wish to spend one moment of their valuable time in the urchin's company. She's quite disarming."

"How do you mean, Damien?"

"Foul."

"Ah."

"Ill-tempered."

"Rather like you."

"Belligerent. Stubborn—"

"She's very pretty."

"Pretty! Ha!"

"Like a rough diamond just waiting to be cut and polished, so Marianne says."

"Then Mari is senile as well. There is nothing remotely pretty about that spitting little cat upstairs. I'd rather wrestle a Bengal tiger."

"Oh ho!" Richard declared. "She sounds fascinating! Just the sort of woman to keep a man on his toes, I should think."

Damien placed the paperweight back on the desk and grinned.

Bonnie paced the room, furious at herself for standing before his high and mighty and taking his abuse without speaking a word in her own defense. Gravely she walked to the window and looked out on Braithwaite's grounds.

The hunters had returned several hours ago and enjoyed their breakfast alfresco. Bonnie had watched Philippe strut about the gathering waving his foxtail under his friends' noses; they had laughed; his friends, Claurence and Freddy, had jested with him, then everyone had returned to the house to make ready for the grand ball to take place at Braithwaite tonight.

Throughout the day, from her doorway, Bonnie watched the servants rush from one room to another, carrying laundry or water or drinks or food. The guests' own servants rushed about as well, dictating to Braithwaite's staff just what it was their mistresses or masters wanted or needed for his or her toilette. Unable to tolerate any more of the madness, Bonnie took the first opportunity she could find to sneak down the back stairwell and exit the rear of the house. She didn't stop running until she reached the stables.

Here, too, she was met with bustling activity as the grooms and drivers busied themselves with polishing and waxing the coaches and exercising and currying the horses. Young boys ran up and down the long, brick-floored building carrying pails of steaming mash, buckets of water, armloads of blankets, and curry combs. Several, on their hands and knees, scrubbed the floor with stiff-bristled brushes until the red brick glistened.

Bonnie backed away and looked out across the grounds at Braithwaite's townscape of tiny buildings with pitched slate roofs and towering chimneys, each belching gray smoke into the sky. There were gateways and covered walks. In the distance was a great grassy yard with lines and lines of laundry flapping in the gentle breeze. Startling herself, she realized that she had begun looking on it all with a sense of pride. That would never do. She had learned early that there was nothing permanent in life. People lived and died. Material possessions lasted until they broke or wore out, then they were discarded with precious little thought. Braithwaite was only a stopover. She must remember that. There was no way she was going to subject herself to Warwick's dictates just for the sake of some short-term security.

"So we meet again," came a voice behind her.

Bonnie looked over her shoulder and recognized the man she had met at the foot of the stairs the night before.

"I'd like to apologize for my behavior last night," Miles said. "I must have seemed like a beast coming at you in the dark like that. It's no wonder you were frightened." He offered his hand. "I'd like to start over. What do you say?"

Bonnie glanced suspiciously at his hand. With some effort she placed her own in his. He held it gently.

"I understand you've been very ill. I trust you are fit enough to be out?"

She nodded.

"Wonderful. I was just about to take a walk. Would you join me?"

Bonnie remained where she was, as Miles continued to smile and charm her with his pleasant attentiveness. He was a fine figure, really, despite his air of dissipation and the

deep, sardonic grooves on either side of his mouth. Standing
just over six feet, and, from what she could recall from the
previous evening's activities, just slightly shorter than Damien, he was as well muscled and lean as his brother. His
complexion, however, was not as dark as Warwick's, Damien's being as bronzed as a Gypsy's. Miles's eyes were not
green, but hazel. His mouth was thin where Damien's was
sensuously full. But at least *his* mouth smiled instead of
sneering, which allowed Bonnie to relax somewhat in his
presence.

She decided to join him. They walked down a brick pathway until they came to an area wherein a groom was brushing
down the most beautiful horse Bonnie had ever seen. She
stopped and stared in awe as the animal tossed his delicate
black head and stamped his feet.

"Lovely, isn't he?" Miles said. "That is Gdansk, full Ara-
bian. At one time breeding horses was my father's passion.
After he died, however, Randolf sold them off—except
Gdansk, of course."

"Does he go well?" Bonnie asked.

"Occasionally. He's a funny old bugger and highly particular about who he allows to approach him. We keep him for
stud mostly. Many of his offspring have gone on to compete
and win some of England's most impressive races."

They continued down the winding path, passing cultivated
beds of flowers whose long stems were heavy with unopened
buds. There was a marble bench situated before rose bushes.
Miles ushered Bonnie to it and sat down beside her, crossing
his legs and smiling again.

"Would you mind if I smoke?" he asked.

Surprised that he would ask, Bonnie shook her head.

After lighting the fragrant cheroot, Miles said, "You don't
say much, contrary to what I've been told. Are you frightened of me?"

"Should I be?"

"Wary, perhaps, but not frightened. I don't normally rush
about the countryside devouring little girls." Then, with a
wicked, teasing glint in his hazel eyes, he winked and added,
"Of course I haven't run across many as pretty as you." She
must have looked stunned, for he laughed. "You *are* be-
witching, Bonnie, even if you do try to disguise it with those

dreadful breeches. I wager if you put on a dress you would have every lad in Yorkshire beating a path to your door.''

"I ain't int'rested," she told him pointedly.

"No? Too young yet, eh?''

"I ain't *that* young," Bonnie said. "I'm older than I look.''

"Oh?'' His curiosity clearly piqued, Miles focused on her face. A cool smile on his lips, he asked, "Just how old are you?''

Bonnie opened and closed her mouth, biting off her response. Under Miles's intense scrutiny she couldn't subdue the faint wave of color in her cheeks as she concluded that the more left unsaid about herself the better. With an uncertain smile, she met his look and said, "Old enough t' know when t' keep m' mouth shut.''

Miles laughed and Bonnie once again relaxed. She decided he was a pleasant sort, though she did not dismiss the crafty glint in his eye for anything other than what it was. She knew a rogue when she saw one.

In that moment Stanley appeared walking briskly down the path. Both of his bushy gray eyebrows rose when he found Bonnie sitting a hand's distance from Miles.

"Good lord," he exclaimed. "There you are! Do you realize the earl has had the entire staff running about like ants trying to find you?''

"The earl can take a flyin' leap—''

"My dear young woman, I am well aware of your and his lordship's shared animosity. However, as long as the earl is so generously offering you his charity—''

"Charity!'' Coming off the bench in one leap, Bonnie faced the dumbstruck butler. "If y' call being browbeaten, chastised, taunted with a whip, and ordered t' suffocate behind closed doors for days at a time charity, then I shudder t' imagine what his definition of *cruelty* might be. No doubt chained t' a rack in the bottom of some cold black dungeon!''

Drawing himself erect, Stanley raised one eyebrow and said, "I should think not.''

Leaving the bench and placing himself between Stanley and Bonnie, Miles said, "I apologize, Stanley. This is my fault. I invited the young lady for a walk and lost track of the time. I'll explain to Damien if you'd like. In the meantime . . .'' He smiled at Bonnie. "You'd better get back to your room. Too much of this fresh air too soon might be detrimental to your recovery. We wouldn't want a relapse, would we?"

When she didn't respond, Miles placed a gentle hand on her shoulder. "Off with you now. Perhaps we'll have tea together later. Would you like that?"

After a moment's hesitation, Bonnie nodded.

"Capital! May I call on you say around five?"

Staring up into his twinkling eyes, Bonnie did her best to ascertain the truth behind this undoubtedly false consideration. Yet she found nothing there to belie the friendly words. For an instant she was swept with the silly urge to cry, then as quickly she mentally dashed the feeling away. She had not survived the last five years by being tough only to weaken now.

Miles watched Bonnie follow Stanley up the walk, then he sat down on the bench. He smoked his cigar. So, his eyes hadn't deceived him the night before. The young woman from Caldbergh was a fetching little thing, despite her beggar's attire. He hadn't lied when he'd told her every lad in Yorkshire would be around if she put on a dress. Knowing his brother, he suspected that was the very reason Damien hadn't packed her up and moved her back to Caldbergh since her recovery. She'd be the kind to turn his head, of course. He'd always been drawn to the unpolished types. It was that touch of rebelliousness in him, Miles supposed.

Miles had just tossed the stub of his cheroot to the ground when Damien approached. He'd barely left the bench when Damien drove both flattened hands into his chest hard enough to knock him down again.

"You stay away from Bonnie," Damien warned him. "If you so much as look her way, you'll live to regret it."

Too stunned to respond, Miles only gazed into Damien's dark face and waited for him to continue. But he didn't. He only spun on his heels and stormed up the walk without looking back.

Miles laughed.

For the next several hours Bonnie sat by the window and gazed over the green Pennine fells. Occasionally she thought she caught a glimpse of the river Cover, coiling its way over the countryside with flashes of silver as the setting sun was reflected from its smooth surface. She watched patches of scarlet bracken blaze like flame as the sun turned gold then orange and finally copper before disappearing beyond Great Whernside.

She thought of Damien holding her the night before.

She recalled how good it had felt. For the remainder of the night her dreams had been wonderful images of tenderness and peacefulness. No nightmares. No night sweats. No crying out in the dark with fear and loneliness. His concern for her had been real. Yet why would a nabob like Warwick care whether she lived or died? Most people—even those of her own class—would have tossed her out on her ear after her display of bad temper. It had been a man of her own class who'd turned her into Caldbergh for filching a piece of meat, after all.

Careful, lass, she thought. Don't be thinkin' for a minute that Warwick is any different from anyone else. Just because he gave y' a basket of kittens and wiped a tear from yer cheek don't mean he wouldn't toss y' out on yer ear if y' crossed him too badly. He was about t' do just that the night before, remember. He would've done too, if it hadn't been after midnight. And although he marched int' this room this mornin' like he was the bloody King of England and announced you could remain in his kingdom a while longer, don't dismiss the fact that he ordered y' t' stay in yer room away from his guests—like y' had the friggin' plague, or somethin'.

When five o'clock finally arrived, Jewel delivered Bonnie's tea, alone. Bonnie stared at the plate of confections, then toward the door before saying, "But Miles—"

"Ain't comin'."

"Why not?"

" 'Cause his lordship says so, that's why. His lordship told Miles in no uncertain terms that he was to stay away from you. And it's just as well," Jewel added, hands plunked on her ample hips. "Miles Kemball is big trouble, if y' ask me— if y' ask most of England fer that matter. And one more thing, lass—his lordship don't take kindly to yer disobeyin' his direct orders, so when he gets steamed at you, it's the rest of us what got to pay the price."

Speechless, Bonnie stared until long after the servant had

quit the room. Then furiously she paced the floor, her fists clenched at her sides. How dare he treat her as if she were some animal to be locked in a cage! To be acknowledged at *his* whim, to be denied the companionship of another human being!

Spinning, she grabbed the china teapot and hurled it out the window. The plate of confections followed. ''We'll see about that,'' she whispered under her breath. ''We'll just see about that.''

Seven

Damien entered the long reception room where the music and dancing had already commenced. Unlike the ball of the night before, which had been much less formal, this time the guests were arrayed in full splendor. The room itself sparkled with glowing chandeliers, banks of greenery, and massed bouquets of flowers, many of which had been grown in Braithwaite's own conservatory, placed on tables covered with royal blue linen cloths, the Warwick color.

Damien couldn't help but smile. Marianne, as usual, had an eye for detail. There was not one hostess from Yorkshire to London who would not call on the Lady Lyttleton when making arrangements for such a gala event. All of England loved her, in one way or another. No one would bat an eye if she suddenly decided to divorce her husband. For a moment he considered the possibility, imagining that, though she denied it, she would gladly begin the proceedings tomorrow if he asked her to marry him tonight. She might even be faithful to him, for a while. It would be a convenient arrangement, no doubt.

He saw her then, surrounded by her usual admirers, among them Philippe and Claurence and Freddy. She wore a gown of royal-blue silk, only a shade lighter than the linens on the tables, with a scattering of tiny diamonds pinned in her hair. As always her décolletage was daring enough to make the most honorable married men in the room take a second appreciative look.

The musicians, behind a screen of palms and ferns, had begun to play a spirited Chopin piece. If Damien remembered correctly, a polonaise would be next, then another waltz and then a polka. Another waltz would follow, and that would be his dance with Marianne. As it was, she was now being swept onto the floor by a snickering Freddy.

Damien was about to join Philippe and Claurence when a hand on his arm stopped him. He turned to find Miles at his side, smiling pleasantly.

"Damien, I'd like a word with you, if you don't mind," he said.

Damien looked at the hand on his sleeve, then back at Miles. "I do mind," he replied as evenly as possible. "And take your hand off me this instant."

"Dame . . ." Moving closer, Miles said, "Please. We aren't children any longer. I've been giving the idea a great deal of thought throughout the day, and I honestly feel it's time we buried all the old animosities and started over."

For a long minute Damien studied his half brother in silence. Then, unemotionally, he removed Miles's hand from his coat. "Go to hell," he said softly. "And don't ever come back."

"You're being unreasonable."

"Am I? I don't think so. The only thing unreasonable about me is the fact that I allow you to remain at Braithwaite in the first place."

"This is my home as much as it is yours."

"Bullshit."

An uneasy smile flickered over Miles's mouth. "The least you could do is hear me out," he stated.

"There is nothing you could spit out that I would be remotely interested in hearing."

Until that moment Damien had not noticed the silence. The orchestra had ceased playing, and as he slowly looked toward the dance floor he found a stunned audience watching his display of temper with expressions just short of horror.

Suddenly Richard was beside him, speaking quietly. "Perhaps you would care to share a port with me in the library, Damien. We can talk. Perhaps cool down before someone does or says something he may regret later."

Taking a deep breath, Damien looked at his uncle.

Richard regarded him levelly. "It would seem," he said calmly, "that you have a captive audience."

"So it would," Damien responded. He let out his breath

in a rush before turning his back on the spectators. As he moved to quit the room, however, Miles's voice rang out through the silence like bells.

"I am deeply sorry you feel that way, Damien. I had so hoped we could put our differences behind us and start afresh."

Damien did not stop walking until he reached the gallery. Leaning against the wall, he closed his eyes and did his best to steady his breathing, then he followed Richard to the library. He entered slowly, his expression serious and a little drawn. Richard had already seated himself behind the desk and had placed a decanter of port and two glasses before him.

"Have a drink," Richard ordered. "You look like you could use one."

"I don't like port."

"Drink it anyway."

He did, tossing it back in one swallow. He shuddered.

"You played right into his hands, you know," Richard said.

"I know."

"You looked like a right jackass out there."

Damien raised one eyebrow and reached for the bottle of port. "Thank you for your support."

"He might be serious."

"And pigs will fly. You know Miles does nothing without some ulterior motive."

"Realizing that, you should do your best to avoid antagonizing him."

Damien poured himself another drink.

Richard sat back in his chair. His face looked ashen against the dark brown leather. "Take it from a man who knows, Nephew. All this anger toward Miles will consume you someday."

"My dislike for Miles is the least of my problems."

"I understand that. But if you continue to allow it to grow, it will eventually hurt—if not destroy—you. Put it all behind you or you are liable to wind up a wretch like me. I cannot look forward to my old age on account of my misspent youth."

"Regrets, Uncle?"

Richard stared at his glass. In a quieter voice, he said,

"Regrets? Good God, yes. So many I could not begin to name them, my boy."

"You could always start fresh."

He shook his head. "The damage I have done could never be merely swept aside and forgotten. Some of it is simply too ghastly. It is too late for me, Damien, but it's not too late for you. I fear you are cursed with my disposition, and I will warn you, get a good grip on it now or you may face the rest of your life in despair and remorse. Put this burning hate and need for revenge against Miles aside and dwell on the positive."

"There seems to be little that is positive in my life right now."

"You're young, wealthy, titled, and handsome."

"And about to lose everything I own in Vicksburg."

"Start over."

Damien laughed, then drank his port. "Just like that," he said.

"You did it once. Look around you and see what resources you have at your disposal."

In that moment the door flew open behind him. Damien spun to find Freddy gawking at him with a fish-faced expression, eyes bulging and mouth opening and closing without a word.

"It—it's the urchin," he finally managed. "You'd better come."

Damien slammed the decanter back on the desk and followed Freddy out the door, back down the gallery to the ballroom. He stopped abruptly at the sight of Bonnie standing spread-legged in her breeches, arms akimbo, in the center of the dance floor.

"What the devil is going on here?" he demanded.

"I'll tell y' wot's goin' on, yer high and mighty lordship. I refuse t' be locked up in that bloody torture chamber a minute longer."

A gasp of startlement reverberated through the room.

Damien narrowed his eyes. Raising one hand, he crooked a finger at her and said, "Come along and we'll discuss it."

She shook her head.

"Urchin—"

"M' name's Bonnie."

"This is neither the time nor the place to discuss this matter. If you would like to join me in the library . . . ?"

With a toss of her black hair and tilt of her ornery chin, she said, "No."

Hands clenched at his sides, Damien approached the girl. The closer he came the wider went her eyes. Yet she did not back down, although by the time he stopped before Bonnie her face had turned as white as the marble floor beneath their feet and her body had begun to tremble.

For some inexplicable reason in that moment words failed him. All the anger and chastisement he had briefly thought to hail on her small shoulders settled calmly inside him. The curious buzzing of voices surrounding him faded to nothing. Suddenly there was only Bonnie, with her wide-set, snapping blue eyes, and her gently tipped-up nose boasting a smudge of dust on the end. The hair surrounding her face was unencumbered by ribbons and combs and diamond or pearl pins, but curled riotously and freely over her shoulders and beyond her hips. But it was the mutinous set of her luscious mouth that made him almost smile, made him almost laugh. Fortunately he caught himself on the very verge before it was too late.

Forcing his thoughts back to the problem at hand, he said more quietly, without a dictatorial tone in his voice, "If you will kindly step outside, we will leave these good people to their entertainment and discuss this matter privately."

"And if I don't?"

"Then I will forcibly remove you."

"Y' think so?"

"No, urchin." He smiled coldly. "I *know* so."

She stared, or rather glared, up into his face a full half minute before her good judgment seemed to get the better of her. Without even a glance at her audience she marched from the room, head high and fists swinging. Damien watched her go before allowing his eyes to scan the crowd with an air of nonchalance. Some forty people stared back at him—all friends, all smiling, all looking as if they had just witnessed the coronation of a new queen. But none looked quite so amused as Marianne and Philippe. Though Marianne's face was mostly hidden behind her fan, he knew by the upward tilt of her eyes that she was laughing. And Philippe's shoulders were positively shaking with mirth.

Rewarding them all with a mocking bow, he said, "Please, do carry on with your dancing." Then he offered them his back and strode from the room.

Bonnie stood in the center of the gallery as she had in the ballroom, hands on hips and chin thrust out in defiance. Damien did not hesitate but grabbed her and began propelling her down the hallway toward the stairs.

"Bloody hell!" she cried. "Yer hurtin' m' bleedin' arm!"

"I am likely to hurt more than that if you pull this sort of stunt again, baggage."

"Take yer hands off me! Y've got no right—"

"Oh, yes, I do. I most certainly do."

"No!" Digging her heels into the Turkish carpet, Bonnie did her best to extricate herself from Warwick's punishing grip. The hold only tightened, and this time when she threw her head back and met his blazing eyes, she saw that his face was no longer amused, but was dark and dangerous as a summer storm. She didn't care. Her anger had been fueled the last few hours by the memory of his earlier ultimatum and the fact that he'd sequestered her in her room like some ill-tempered, disobedient child. "Take yer hands off me before I scream," she shouted.

"Nonsense. You wanted my undivided attention and now you've got it. Come along like a good little girl. I have no desire to air our dirty laundry to a house full of guests."

"Good little girl!" She almost choked.

"I do realize that is sorely stretching the boundaries of the imagination."

Something in his tone told Bonnie that to press the matter at this point would be unwise. So she obeyed him for the time being, much to her own displeasure, and took the next few minutes to collect her thoughts.

Something was going on here that was highly unnerving. All the fury she had worked up while confined like a leper in her room all afternoon had turned into an unaccountable anticipation and thrill the moment Warwick entered that ballroom. Her inability to speak those few moments had not been out of fear or even anger, but out of . . . what? Dare she admit even to herself that her longing to simply reach out and place her hand on him had totally shattered her resolve?

Having scaled the stairs with ease, Warwick escorted Bonnie to the end of the hall, kicked the bedroom door open, and shoved her inside. She rubbed her arm as he proceeded to pace across the room. She could not take her eyes from him, though she tried. Oh, how she tried! But he was, by far, the handsomest man she had ever seen. Even more handsome than her father, and she had always believed him to be the handsomest scoundrel in all of England. Why had she suddenly realized it now? Now, when she had made up her mind to leave Braithwaite just as soon as the guests were abed?

Bonnie was so lost in her musings that she did not realize at first that Warwick had stopped pacing and was now standing stock-still, regarding her. His look was no longer as murderous as she might have suspected. Far from it.

"Say what you have to say and be quick about it," he prompted. "I have guests, in case you haven't noticed."

The idea of telling Damien good-bye settled in her stomach like a stone. She couldn't do it. The very idea of it made her feel as if she were coming down again with the grippe.

"Well? . . . Well!"

"Do you have t' yell at me all the bleedin' time?"

"I wasn't yelling."

"Aye, y' were yellin'. Yer always yellin'. At me. At yer brother. The help. Poor Jewel turns into a jitterin' bag of bones ever'time she sees y'. Yer sneerin' at Philippe or jeerin' at that red-haired woman—"

"Marianne. And I don't jeer."

"Y' bloody well do, and I don't mind tellin' y' I'm sick t' death of hearin' it. Wot have y' got t' be so ornery about anyways? Y've got a lovely home an' family an' friends who love y'. A man yer age ought t' be married with wee babes on yer knee and here y' are stompin' around the countryside darin' everyone y' meet t' try an' knock that bleedin' chip off yer shoulder. Wot's got y' so riled, anyhow? If y' were a woman, I'd swear y' were in a perpetual state of the monthlies."

One black eyebrow shot up, and anticipating Warwick's verbal backlash, Bonnie braced herself for the eruption. It was just as well. She'd rather leave Braithwaite with Damien's curses still ringing in her ears. It'd only serve to remind her that, had she decided to stay—which she had never *really* considered—her life would have been as miserable here as it had been at Caldbergh.

Yet, he did not yell. The tension left his shoulders and his stance relaxed.

Bonnie's heart lurched in her breast as she looked into his eyes. She suddenly realized that the sight of him always did that to her, and she resented it—resented, too, his unabashed masculinity as he stood there, arms crossed loosely over his chest, eyes gleaming mockingly between thick black lashes. Oh yes, Warwick unsettled her, making her, for the first time since she'd been interned at Caldbergh at the age of twelve, totally aware of the femininity she had tried so hard to hide from Smythe, though at times she had ached so badly to be the girl she once was that she thought she might die.

"Well?" she asked suspiciously. "What are y' waitin' for? Go ahead and chew my butt off cause I embarrassed y' in front of yer hoity-toity friends. Get it over with and quit starin' at me like that."

Damien's lips curved in a smile as he shrugged off Bonnie's efforts to antagonize him. "And be accused of being an ogre again? Not on your life, sweetheart."

At first Bonnie was taken aback by this sudden complacency. There was a strange glitter in his green eyes, and she didn't like it. The assessing quality of his gaze exaggerated her growing uneasiness, and she backed away. She suddenly felt as if she had been stripped of her clothes and the gauze beneath her shirt that kept her breasts flattened to the size of a young girl's.

"As a matter of fact," Warwick continued, "I had every intention of repeating my earlier offer for you to remain at Braithwaite, reemphasizing, of course, that should you do so, you are to behave yourself, as much as you are capable of doing, that is. Should you cooperate, I'm certain you will find that I am not nearly as unlikable as I seem. I do realize certain allowances must be made for your upbringing and background, but those are shortcomings that can be remedied to some degree."

Bloody hell! He made her sound as if she were some appalling disease to be cured with calomel and James's Powders!

Bonnie's eyes widened as Warwick approached her. All at once she was assailed by conflicting emotions. Uppermost was the acute awareness of him as a man. There was his wide mouth, no longer tight with anger or irritation but turned up gently at the corners. His nose was straight and aristocratic, his eyes heavy lidded as he peered down at her. She was unbearably conscious of the fact that his mouth was so very near her own. For the first time in her young life she was tempted to rise to her toes and press her lips to a man's. She wondered remotely what his reaction would be.

Sliding his hands into his pockets, Warwick looked around the room. He stunned her by suddenly admitting, "I don't like this house. It's cold and drafty and dark. When I was a young child it frightened me. Then, there were furnishings with gargoyles carved into their facings. I imagined they were devils waiting to pounce on me in the dark. When I finally explained to my mother why I was frightened of going to bed at night, she ordered the damned furniture to be removed from my room. My father had it put back. He said any Warwick worth his heritage would confront the devil face-to-face and refuse to retreat." He shook his head. "I was only six or seven. I couldn't understand why a boy as young as I was should be expected to face down the devil." He looked at Bonnie. "Do you, lass?"

When she didn't respond, he said, "Of course he never treated me like I was a child. My brothers and I were always noble young men and forever conscious of our position in life. It wasn't much fun. I'd see our tenants' children playing and I'd resent the hell out of it. Occasionally I'd sneak away from the house and join them. He found me once and whipped me with a crop in front of my friends. He told me I'd never amount to anything, that it was just as well that I was second born because if the Warwick title ever fell into my hands I would bring disgrace to the name. I responded that I didn't give a damn; he didn't speak to me, or look at me again for six months. Not one word. Not even a glance. I might as well have been dead.

"Six years ago I left England for America. I told myself it was because I was running away from an unfortunate set of circumstances in my life at that time, but now, thinking back, I wonder. I'd never been one to care *what* my peers thought about me, so the excuse of going away long enough for the gossip to die down really doesn't hold up. I had something to prove to the old man and to myself. But he up and died on me before I could. Now there is a war in America. That war could destroy everything I fought to accomplish. Bent Tree is proof of my worth, Bonnie. No one seems to understand that.'' He took a deep breath and released it slowly. Then, as if realizing for the first time that he had just confessed something very personal to her, he squared his broad shoulders and abruptly brought the subject back to her.

''Have you anything left to say before I rejoin my guests?'' he asked.

Her heart racing, Bonnie shook her head.

''Not even an apology for that tantrum?''

She shook her head again, more adamantly this time.

Damien gently nudged an errant curl off her face and tucked it behind her ear. He allowed his finger to trace the high contour of her cheek, down to the corner of her soft mouth. Her entire body tensed, and noticing, he backed away, dropping his hand once again to his side. His eyes turned a little harder, a littler colder; his mouth flattened in mild irritation.

Damien did not speak again but turned to the door, started to close it, then throwing one last glance back at the girl, left the door open and quit the room. He walked to the top of the stairs before stopping. He gripped the balustrade with both hands and listened to the music pulse in three-quarter time below him.

What the blazes was he doing explaining himself to some waif from Caldbergh?

Why should it matter to him *what* she thought?

But it did matter. God help him, it did.

Eight

At just after midnight, Bonnie made her decision.

She would leave Braithwaite. She had no choice. She would accept no charity from any man, least of all one like Warwick. It was his kind, after all, who had ruined her life so irrevocably. It was his kind who chose to ignore the plight of the poor and homeless, to look down their noses at the rest of the world, and to scoff at what they would, could, never understand. How could she have forgotten that these last few days?

Actually, she knew how. And that's why she had decided to leave now, not to wait another moment. If she hesitated she might never leave . . . and then what? A life doomed to a worse hell than that of Caldbergh assuredly. For it was becoming harder and harder to stand by like a mute shadow and watch Warwick with this strange new longing growing in her breast. Someday he would marry—if not the woman called Marianne, then someone, surely. And there she would be, like a child watching wistfully from a distance, her nose pressed against that cold window of longing and class separation.

If she hung around, she might start to believe that he wasn't so bad after all. She might begin to think he wasn't so different from her, that life hadn't exactly been a bowl of cherries for him either, despite his apparent wealth. She might even imagine that he was unhappy and lonely and *that* was the cause of his enormous anger, not only toward her, but also toward everyone else around him. She might even decide she liked him . . . or worse. She might begin to imagine that she was falling in love with the bleedin' nabob. Best to nip it in the bud before the attachment grew any stronger.

She waited until the music had ended and conversations ceased. She lay in bed pretending sleep as the door of her room opened. Someone stood there for long minutes watching her. She could not be certain it was Warwick, but she sensed that it was. Her heart raced. Every nerve began to tingle with anticipation. It was all she could do not to lift her head and allow her eyes to feast one last time on the face that would forever haunt her dreams and memories. But she continued to lie perfectly still, even as the pleasant aroma of brandy touched her nostrils. Even as the whisper of his satin-lined coat brushing against his shirt hinted of his habitual restlessness. Then the door closed quietly again, and she was alone.

Somewhere deep in the bowels of the house a clock struck two as Bonnie made her way as soundlessly as possible down the stairs. Her pillowcase, already full of pewter candlesticks, rattled only slightly. She had taken nothing of great value. Simple trinkets, but fine enough to fetch a few quid when she reached York. She would make a quick stop by the larder and lift enough food to last her the journey. A week's worth would be more than ample, she reasoned, and would hardly be missed by the staff.

Having first made several wrong turns, Bonnie finally located the larder just to the right of the gun room and to the left and just down the hallway from the kitchen, the scullery, and bake room. She poked about as best she could through the many cabinets and shelves lining the walls. She chose two small rounds of Cheddar cheese, a loaf of bread, a tin of tea, and bits of beef, ham, and pork that had been leftover from dinner that night. She then lobbed in a chunk of Warwick's birthday cake for good measure. Deciding that was as much as she could comfortably carry, she turned back to the door and plowed straight into Stanley's chest.

"Blast it!" she cried, more from surprise than fear. Feet scurried beyond them as several servants entered the room, holding their lanterns high in the darkness.

"I knew it!" someone declared. "I tol' y' it weren't no rat."

"Oh, but it is," Stanley replied in his usual droll voice.

"A very big rat, I declare. Would one of you kindly fetch his lordship?"

The women's pale faces and wide eyes looked around at each other.

"If you please," Stanley stressed.

Bonnie frowned as one of the young women broke away from the group and disappeared into the darkness. Feeling panic rise inside her, Bonnie carefully placed the pillowcase on the floor and nudged it away with her foot. She looked at Braithwaite's butler again.

"There. Y' can have it back. I'll just leave and y' won't have t' bother his lordship; I'm certain he must be tired after dancin' all night."

"How very accommodating of you, I'm sure."

"Look." She stepped slightly closer and lowered her voice. "Y've all wanted me out. Y' didn't want me here in the first place. So here's yer chance. Just let me go, Stanley, and I'll never darken yer doorway again. I swear!"

Stanley pursed his lips in apparent consideration.

Bonnie eyed the room beyond him. Before Stanley could react, she darted past him, scattering the tittering servants as she raced for the door.

She had no more than set foot in the hallway when she was stopped dead by an arm around her waist, hauling her off her feet so they pummeled air and her arms flailed helplessly. It took a moment before she realized it was Warwick who gripped her. He held her so tightly about her midsection that she could hardly get breath enough to scream, "Let me go! You can keep yer bloody pewter and food. I don't want it! I don't need it! I don't need you, so let me *go!*"

She twisted around so she was able to beat at his bare chest. He only gripped her more tightly to him, using his arms to force hers down to her sides.

"You conniving, treasonous little bitch," he hissed in her ear. "After I spilled my guts to you this evening. After everything I've tried to do for you, you'd sneak off in the night like a thief. I might have known I couldn't trust you. Stanley!" he shouted.

"Yes, sir."

"What's the damage?"

"Slight, sir. A few pewter candle holders and some food is all."

Bonnie continued to squirm. Finally Warwick placed her back on her feet. Still gripping her arms, he shook her so hard that her teeth rattled, and said, "Why, damn you? Why, you little thief, when I've done everything in my power to make you feel at home?"

"It ain't *my* bloody home!" she cried.

"Indeed. How remiss of me to forget, *urchin*. Perhaps you would be happier back at Caldbergh?"

Bonnie froze. Fear choked her voiceless as she stared into Damien's face. His features, tight with barely suppressed rage and lit only by a nearby flickering lantern, looked more than a little menacing.

"What's wrong, baggage, cat suddenly got your tongue? What happened to your usual witty repartee? Come now, don't be shy. Perhaps you'd like to explain why you decided to bite the hand that feeds you. Go on. We're all waiting."

Warwick released her. Hands planted on his hips, he waited.

Unable to meet his eyes, Bonnie stared at the patch of soft, curling black hair on his chest and stubbornly refused to answer. How could she explain that the animosity she'd once felt for him had turned into something unsettlingly close to fondness? That if she didn't escape now, there would be no turning back, at least where her heart was concerned.

"Very well," he said. "You leave me no choice. At dawn you will be returned to Caldbergh."

The eavesdropping servants gasped.

Bonnie closed her eyes, uncertain if she had actually swayed in dread, suspecting she had. She held onto her sanity the best she could while finally forcing her eyes up to Warwick's. She longed to wet her lips, but there wasn't enough spit left in her entire body to do it.

"Nothing to say in defense of your actions?" he taunted.
"No. I shouldn't think so. Very well. Stanley!"
"Yes, sir."
"Have you the key to the coal room handy?"
"Cook should have it, sir."
"Get it. Then join the girl and myself there."

There was silence before Stanley replied, "I don't understand, my lord."

"Since the chit has chosen to act the criminal, she will be treated as such. Bonnie is to remain in the coal room until morning, under lock and key, as befits her behavior. I want her away from Braithwaite before the guests are afoot."

"Yes, sir. I will see her to Caldbergh myself."

Bonnie was ushered down the corridor to the coal room. She stared into the pitch-black quarters for a long, silent moment before managing to say, "Can I at least have a light, please?"

Someone came forward and handed her a lantern. She gripped it with both hands before stepping over the threshold. She heard Stanley's voice say sympathetically, "Hang tight, lass, it's only three hours until sunup."

Bonnie turned, catching a glimpse of Warwick as he stood in the shadows outside the room. For a moment she almost believed—no, that couldn't be distress twisting those handsome features. Then the door clanged shut between them.

Damien paced the apartment, doing his best to rationalize his behavior, not only to Marianne but also to himself.

"We have given her everything, Mari."

"Not everything," she said from the bed.

"Comfort, food—"

"Compassion?"

Damien walked to the window.

"Well?" she prompted. "Have you, even once, shown Bonnie that you understand her plight?" Marianne left the bed and walked to the fire. "Can you imagine what her life must have been like at Caldbergh? My God, Damien, I hear those children spend hours grinding stone to dust."

Marianne turned to face him, her face white. "They were hunting Bonnie with dogs," she said hoarsely. "She was nearly dead. Can you in good conscience send her back there?"

"She was attempting to rob us blind, Mari."

"What are a few candlesticks to you, my lord?"

"It is the principle—"

"You and your high and mighty principles! The child is crying out for love and attention, and yet you lock her in her room like an animal, thinking if you simply feed her occasionally she might be satisfied.'' Marianne approached him, her hair like a mantle of fire over her white shoulders. ''What is it with you? The Damien I once knew had a heart as big as all Yorkshire. Like his kind, gentle mother, he might have wept a few tears for an urchin named Bonnie.'' Her eyes searched his features, and she shook her head. ''I didn't want to admit it to myself, but that man no longer exits, does he, my lord?''

''That's enough.''

Marianne laughed sharply. ''Are you going to throw me out as well? Have you finished with me so soon, my lord? No response? Then let me inform you that if you send that child back to Caldbergh at dawn, I am leaving for London just as soon as the guests have departed.''

Damien regarded Marianne in silence while he considered her ultimatum. Then he said dryly, ''I'm certain your *husband* will be glad to see you. That is, if he's returned from buggering his young men in Paris.''

''Right now even Harry would look more welcome to my eyes than you, my lord. Harry may have his foibles, peculiar as they may be, but at least he has a soul.''

Turning on his heels, Damien left the room. He did not stop until he reached the vestibule, then it was to look blindly through the dark and wonder why he had retreated, why he hadn't stood toe-to-toe with Marianne and spelled out his reasons for sending Bonnie back to Caldbergh. After all, he had thought them out in his mind so many times during the last weeks that he knew them by heart.

He didn't want or need the responsibility.

She was trouble, and he had enough of that in his life right now without taking on any more, thank you very much.

Besides, he would be leaving England soon, and he didn't need any attachments holding him back.

He shoved his hands in his pockets.

Bonnie had tried to rob him. After everything he had done for her. He'd stood before her like a fool, confessing his personal and private thoughts, believing she'd understand his motivations as none of his peers seemed to be able to. He'd confided in her, for God's sake. She'd rewarded him by stealing his pewter, by sneaking out into the night without a fare thee well. And when caught, she hadn't even apologized.

He walked through the house, down the gallery, down the long corridor to the kitchens and larders, and finally to the coal room. A faint light shone beneath the door and reflected dimly on the key that lay on a table near the wall. He picked the key up and shoved it in the lock, gave it a twist, and the door swung open.

Bonnie lay curled up in the corner of the farthest wall, her hair as black as the coal and soot surrounding her, her eyes as dark as they turned up to his.

"Why?" he asked simply.

She didn't respond, just looked at him fixedly with her glazed eyes and her face as white as a sheet.

"If you apologize, perhaps I'll reconsider."

Bonnie turned her head to the wall. Then she rose slowly to her feet. In that instant she didn't look like a child, not the trembling, frightened girl he had occasionally found weeping from bad dreams. She seemed immeasurably older and harder. There was a maturity around her eyes and mouth that made him question, for a moment, whether she really was as young as she oftentimes appeared.

Bonnie stepped carefully around and over the heaps of coal strewn about the tiny quarters, walked directly up to Damien, and stopped. As he gazed down into her tempestuous eyes, ablaze with anger, he felt his wounded pride and resulting fury give way to something else, a reluctant admiration for the fight and courage he himself had apparently lost sometime during the last few years. He briefly wondered if that was why the girl antagonized him so, then with a flash of honesty he admitted that it was only *one* of the reasons.

Raising one hand, he placed it gently against Bonnie's face. He smiled. "Do you apologize?" he asked. "Do you swear you will never do anything like this again, Bonnie?"

A heartbeat passed before she said, "Go t' hell . . . m' lord." Then she spat in his face.

Damien stood in the open doorway, watching as Bonnie climbed aboard the coach with Stanley. Marianne stood at the curb, her morning dress fluttering in the brisk dawn breeze. Her face was drawn as she turned back to the house.

As she reached the doorway where he stood, she paused long enough to say, "You are the most heartless bastard I have ever had the misfortune of knowing."

He grabbed her arm as she tried to edge past him. "Am I to condone the fact that she was attempting to rob us blind? For God's sake, Mari, we showed her every kindness, and this is how she repays us. Besides, she'll be better off at Caldbergh. They are equipped for handling difficult children."

"Children? God!" She laughed. "Not only are you heartless, you're blind. Haven't you ever questioned why Bonnie was running away from Caldbergh?"

"What would you have me do? Turn her over to the authorities, who would no doubt bring her right back to Caldbergh, or worse, lock her in prison? Or perhaps you would have me turn her out to beg. How long do you think she would last out there, Mari?"

"You might have allowed her to remain here, Damien."

He looked back down the road where the coach was disappearing around a bend. Recalling his and Bonnie's earlier meeting, he said dryly, "I offered her the opportunity. Obviously she chose to decline. Besides . . ." He leaned against the door frame and crossed his arms over his chest. "As you may or may not recall, I will be taking leave of Braithwaite soon. What would happen to Bonnie then? Do I allow her to stay here and be raised by servants?"

"There are schools."

"Good God." Damien laughed. "The next thing I know you'll have me adopting her, or some such nonsense. Besides, there isn't a school in England that would take her as she is."

Marianne's spurt of irritation with him apparently having subsided, she regarded him with interest. "It seems you *have* given this matter some thought, after all."

"Of course."

"So tell me. How do you really feel about the decision you just made?"

"Bonnie made it. She chose to leave Braithwaite herself," he reminded her.

"Perhaps." Marianne looked back out the door. "Why

did you send her away, my lord? It wouldn't be because you've actually grown fond of her, would it?''

"That's illogical. Were I fond of her, why would I want to get rid of her?''

"To make life easier, of course. I told you once that you'll be reluctant to admit your feelings for another woman. By sending Bonnie away, you won't be forced to face up to the realization that she means something to you.''

He made no response. The statement was too ludicrous to even acknowledge.

"I have a feeling we haven't seen the last of that young woman, my lord. Would it please you if she again turned up on Braithwaite's doorstep? If she decided to change her ways and . . . adjust?''

Damien ran one hand through his heavy black hair as he considered his reply. Finally he answered truthfully, "I don't know.''

Marianne considered him a moment longer before smiling. Then without another word she returned to their room, leaving Damien alone to contemplate his actions. He told himself over and over again that the decision to send Bonnie back to Caldbergh was the right one; he was thinking of her welfare, and it had nothing to do with the effect the girl had had on his better judgment since she arrived. Had nothing to do with the fact that he could not concentrate on all his problems because the memory of her haunted eyes kept creeping into his thoughts day and night. Even as he stood staring down the now-empty road, other memories of Bonnie came back— the sight of her small figure fighting so valiantly for life; the blazing fury in those bluer-than-blue eyes each time she came up against any threatening obstacle; the way her rosebud shaped lips could curl in pleasure then twist in anger in the blink of an eye.

With reluctance he admitted that at some point during these last few weeks he had come to feel responsible for Bonnie. Only responsible? It was more than that and he knew it— though it irked him like hell to admit it. He'd been drawn to the girl since the night she'd arrived at Braithwaite. And with that awareness his thoughts drifted in a direction he had been very careful the last five years to avoid.

Damien stepped out of the house, down Braithwaite's front

steps. The wind wrapped around him, stinging his cheeks and ruffling his hair. He took little notice. The effort to dam the flow of memories took all his strength, yet he knew the battle was lost even before it started. He was weary of fighting it, so weary. Through the years he'd managed to keep it buried like a sleeping beast in the deepest recesses of his mind. Occasionally it would rouse and threaten to overwhelm him, but somehow he would manage to soothe it back into submission. But since returning to England—more so since the girl had stumbled into his life—those memories would no longer be denied. With despair he remembered the woman he had loved—Louisa Thackeray.

Closing his eyes, his fists clenched so tightly that his knuckles shone white beneath his tanned skin, he let the betrayal and fury avalanche through his mind once again. His hands shaking, he thrust them through his hair and tried futilely to overcome the past and what it had cost him. It was over. Finished, he told himself. He couldn't allow all the old fury to continue gnawing away at his insides or it would destroy him completely. Already it had turned him into a shadow of his former self. He had closed himself off to everything except ambition. Somehow the challenge of conquering that wild Mississippi land had been vast enough to bury all else the last years: friendship, pain, memory . . . love. How ironic that it had taken a homeless waif, helpless and innocent—the very qualities he had so loved in Louisa— to unleash all those dormant feelings inside him.

Ah, you fool, he thought disgustedly, you fool.

Bonnie knew by the landscape that any moment the coach would top the ridge and there would be Caldbergh and Birdie Symthe. She had little time to waste if she was going to convince Stanley to release her before they arrived.

"Stanley," she said a little frantically, "if y'll just drop me here, I'll see m' own self back t' Caldbergh."

He raised one eyebrow in obvious disbelief.

"They'll beat me," she said. "They will. With a strop. Then they'll lock me in a dark hole for days."

"Nonsense." Stanley looked away.

Time for total honesty, she thought.

"They sell girls int' prostitution, Stanley. That's why I was runnin'. My time had come. I overheard Birdie makin' arrangements t' send me t' London. He was gonna get a bloody high price for me cause I'm . . ." She chewed her lower lip as she considered the look of surprise on the butler's face. "Cause I'm still a virgin."

Stanley shifted uncomfortably but made no response.

"They'll whip me," she stressed again. "Then they'll ship me off t' London and make me a whore. Could y' live with that on yer conscience, Stanley? Could y'?"

Stanley, looking horribly uncertain, sank back in his seat as he watched the countryside roll by.

"Warwick will never know," she pressed. "Just let me out here and I'll disappear, Stanley, I swear it."

His brow creased in a frown, Stanley closed his eyes and appeared on the verge of some monumental decision when the driver called out, "Whoa!" Startled, Bonnie leapt for the door and looked out. Caldbergh, cold and gray, lay sprawled across the valley floor before her like some dead, rotting animal. She was certain she could smell the stench of fear and neglect from here.

"I'm sorry, lass," came Stanley's voice. "Had you informed me of the situation sooner . . . had you discussed the matter truthfully with his lordship . . ."

"It wouldn't have made the slightest bit of difference," she replied softly. Then throwing Stanley a sideward glance, Bonnie shoved open the door and sprang from the coach. She hit the ground running, but had taken no more than a half dozen strides before a pair of burly arms were around her, wrestling her to the ground as she kicked and thrashed and did her best to bite the hand that had clamped like a vise against her jaw, shoving her face into the damp, gritty earth.

"Here now!" Stanley cried. "Take care how you treat this child!"

"Child?" came Smythe's voice, freezing Bonnie with cold dread. "There is little that is childlike about this one, my good man. I wondered how long it would take his lordship to grow weary of her tantrums and return her to her rightful place. I warned him she was trouble, did I not, Timothy?"

The oaf restraining Bonnie shoved her face harder into the dirt and replied, "Aye. Me bloody face is still throbbin' from the butcherin' she give me."

Bonnie was yanked to her feet. Her world spun uncontrol-
lably for what seemed like minutes as she was dragged toward Smythe's quarters. Through the buzzing of blood in her
head she could hear Stanley arguing heatedly with Birdie, but
she knew, even as the door was thrown open and she was
shoved hard enough into the room to send her facedown on
the floor, that Stanley's protestations would do no good.
Smythe had her exactly where he wanted her. The worst was
yet to come.

They came for her an hour later.

Bonnie, her back to the wall, her fists clenched at her sides,
glared into Birdie's small black eyes as he ordered Timothy
to "fetch the unfortunate little bitch."

She was to be made an example of to the others. She knew
that. It wasn't, after all, the first time she had found herself
in such straits with Smythe. But no disobedience that she had
ever committed had been this serious. Still, Bonnie had decided that if there was to be an example made, she would
make one of courage and pride and dignity. She would not
let them break her in front of the others. If she could stand
up to Smythe and his cohorts' cruelties, then perhaps the
others could too, when their time came.

She did not resist as Tim grabbed her arm and dragged her
out the door and into the yard where the other unfortunates
of Caldbergh awaited. Through the lingering fog their un-
emotional faces looked ghostly, their eyes dead. Their spirits
had been broken long ago, and Bonnie knew that if she remained here, she would eventually become one of them. She
would shuffle through each day, grinding stone into powder
from six in the morning until six in the evening, until her
mind ceased to function and she simply existed. Or she could
give in to Smythe's demands, go to London and become a
whore, submit to indignities that far surpassed Caldbergh's.
She'd decided that black rain-swept night weeks ago that she'd
rather be dead. Thanks to his high and mighty lordship she
wasn't.

The sudden thought of Warwick shot through Bonnie as
painfully as Tim's grip on her arm. Too late for regrets, she
reminded herself. Much too late.

Smythe stood to one side of the onlookers, his leather strop swinging at his side. His dark eyes regarded her as Tim led her to center circle and released her. He smiled, revealing pointed yellow teeth.

"Take off your clothes," Birdie told her.

She did so, slowly, dropping her shirt and finally her breeches to the ground. Smythe's eyes narrowed. His tongue snaked out to moisten his lips. Wiggling one finger at her, he ordered, "Peel out of that gauze, if you please. Come now. Don't be shy. There is nothing hidden there that I have not already visualized in my mind." Again his eyes raked her naked form, lingering over the narrow waist, slightly rounded hips, and dark hair at the apex of her slender thighs. "Carry on," he stated. "Or perhaps you would rather Timothy removed the bindings . . . ?"

Doing her best to keep her emotions firmly in check, Bonnie slowly reached for the bindings. How many years had she hidden her identity—her femininity—in those yards and yards of cotton gauze? What good had it done her? Smythe had easily seen through the farce. There was nothing she could do to disguise the delicate contours of her face, the swanlike neck or the outrageously long eyelashes that exaggerated the width of her blue eyes.

The dingy gauze fell to the ground.

For a moment there was silence as Smythe studied her. When he finally spoke again, his voice was hoarse. "It is a shame to have to mar such breathtaking perfection. I might reconsider your punishment were you to beg my forgiveness."

"Never in a thousand years," she replied, "would I ever go t' m' knees before a piece of offal like you."

"Then you may offer me your back."

She did so, bracing herself as the first whoosh of leather vibrated through the air.

Bonnie discovered that if she balanced just so on her knees, bringing her body into perfect alignment, the pain across her back, thighs, and buttocks was not nearly so excruciating. But she could hold that position for only so long. The skin of her knees was already abraded. Soon she would have to fall again to all fours, which she hated. It made her feel like some helpless wounded animal whimpering for pity.

Never once had she cried. Even as Smythe's leather strop bit into the tender skin, she had gritted her teeth, closed her eyes, and visualized pleasant memories. There was her mother kissing Bonnie's finger after she'd pricked it on a rose thorn. There was her father swinging first Bonnie, then Bonnie's mother, 'round and 'round in greeting after a hard day of working the mines. He'd always smelled sooty and sweaty and a little like the ale he'd downed before trudging up the hills to home. That's where the good memories had ended, and almost desperately she had searched for others—anything— to keep her mind off her pain. Then *his* face had appeared: Warwick's. Green eyes taunting, ridiculing; mouth twisting in disdain, sarcasm . . . humor. How she had tried to hate him. How she longed to hate him now. He had sent her back here after all. Then she reminded herself that her own stubbornness had led her back to Caldbergh. Perhaps if she had explained . . .

A melon-colored sun was setting beyond Caldbergh before Smythe returned with Timothy. They each took one of her arms, helped her to her feet, and managed to dress her. They marched her toward the cellar door at the base of the building, and once there, stopped. Her world careened as Bonnie stared down at the pitch-black hole. All the old fears came rushing back, fears of blood and madness and dark, confined places. Her knees buckled, and as she was shoved down into the hole the past closed in around her like a cold, wet mist. Curling her knees into her chest, forgetting the awful condition of her back, she finally closed her eyes and wept.

Sunlight spilled across Bonnie's face as the hellhole door was thrown open. She blinked, remotely wondering where she was. Then the face above her materialized into Smythe's, and she cringed. How long had she lain there? One day? Two? The hunger in her stomach had turned into a numbness that, little by little, had spread throughout her body during the infinite confinement. It hurt now to move.

She had little choice, however. Smythe, after grabbing her sore arm, jerked her out of the tiny, closeted prison with little ceremony and began dragging her toward his office. She fell repeatedly from the lack of circulation in her legs. She felt as if a thousand pins were pricking the bottoms of her feet.

By the grace of God she made it as far as Smythe's office before collapsing completely. Smythe stepped over her and walked to his desk piled high with correspondence. The door opened and closed behind Bonnie as Timothy joined them.

"The wretches are restless today," came his voice.

"Aye. It's thanks to her, I wager." Smythe motioned toward Bonnie.

"We'd best get her out of here soon or there'll be trouble."

"My thoughts exactly." Birdie flipped through numerous papers before looking back at her. "I see no reason why we should not carry on with our original plans for the young lady, do you, Tim? The gentleman in London was most eager to have her. Eager to the tune of a hundred quid, as I recall."

" 'At's a lot of money, sir."

"Seems virginity has become a highly profitable commodity in London, Tim. I understand there are gentlemen of the realm who will pay five times that for the opportunity of deflowering a young woman. And the younger the better, I understand."

Bonnie closed her eyes as the words floated through her consciousness. Somehow, through the fog in her mind, a last thread of a plan took shape, and slowly she opened her eyes and stared at the ceiling.

"Y're too bloody late," she stated quietly.

Both men turned and stared at her. Smythe came out from behind his desk and squatted on his haunches beside her. Bonnie turned her eyes toward him and grinned.

"His lordship did it t' me already. He come t' my room and raped me. When I threatened to reveal him, he tossed me out."

Smythe's face turned white.

Bonnie closed her eyes and began to laugh.

Nine

Damien stared at his reflection in the mirror, noting the strain around his eyes. He hadn't shaved in two days and he stank of ale. Only last night Marianne had again threatened to leave him and return to London. That had sobered him up in a hurry. He wasn't ready to trek to London, and the thought of remaining here with only Miles for company had been too damnably horrible to consider. Of course there was his uncle, but Richard was about the countryside most of the day, checking on properties and tenants. Or he was popped up on his port and sleeping it off in his room. Twice Damien had discovered him walking the gallery at night in his dressing gown, mumbling about the mess he'd made of his life and if he could only have a second shot at it, things would be different. Once when Damien had mentioned riding out to Gunnerside Mine, Richard had suffered such a severe state of the vapors that Damien had considered calling the surgeon. Richard had his own problems, no doubt about it.

Since the guests had all departed two days ago, Damien spent the long, dreary hours staring over Braithwaite's grounds, waiting impatiently for further word from Vicksburg or Parliament. The inactivity and isolation were driving him insane. Work had been a constant force in his life these last years. When he wasn't working, he was doing something with his employees or neighbors, whether it be barn raising or fishing on the Mississippi. But this solitary existence was maddening. It allowed too much time to think, which was what he was trying his best to avoid doing. Obviously he had done too much thinking the last two days. He hadn't been able to make love to Marianne since the morning of the hunt, and for some reason she found it amusing.

She'd even begun teasing him by calling him Harry, which hadn't helped matters.

Turning from the mirror, Damien found Stanley standing in the doorway. The butler's eyes were also strained, as well as condemning. Never in Damien's life had the servant regarded him in such a way. Not that such behavior would normally be allowed by an employer, but after thirty-five years service the butler had become part of the family. It had been Stanley's shins that Damien, as a babe, had first stumbled against when learning to walk. It had been Stanley's arms that Damien had fallen into when, as a boy of ten, his horse had thrown him and fractured his ankle. Stanley had been the last to embrace Damien when, heart shattered, he had left Braithwaite for America.

"Yes," he said to Stanley. "What is it?"

Stanley strode across the room and handed Damien an envelope. "This just arrived from America."

Damien recognized the handwriting immediately: Charlotte Ruth Montgomery. No doubt she was going to try one last time to finagle a proposal out of him. Ah, well, he thought. Why the hell not? Marry the girl and get the world off his back. Give Richard the great-nephew he wanted so he could eventually die happily pickled in his port. Set Marianne up as a respectable mistress for those times when Damien ventured back to England, which he would be doing more often now that Braithwaite was his. Charlotte was pretty, if empty-headed. They would have beautiful children together. Besides, the joining of the two plantations—should the South survive the war—would make for the grandest, most productive properties in Mississippi.

Dearest Damien,
With a heavy heart I must inform you that I have married Tom Dickenson of Long Willow Farm. I have come to care for him deeply during your absence and hope you will understand and forgive me.

Sincerely,
Charlotte Ruth

Damien began to laugh.
"Is something funny?" Stanley asked.

"Yes. It's frigging hilarious, Stanley. My imagined intended has married someone else." Shaking his head, Damien tossed the envelope to the floor. "This calls for a celebration. Fetch us both a brandy. In fact, fetch us an entire goddamn bottle of it."

"But, sir—"

"Don't 'but sir' me, my good man. I said to get the brandy and two glasses. I order you to have a drink with me, and that's my final word on the matter."

"It is highly inappropriate, my lord."

"Right. Get the brandy."

Stanley did so. In the lavender drawing room they sat down before the fire and drank. Damien was working on his second refill before he spoke again.

"Do you realize that this is the first time the two of us have sat together and enjoyed a drink in the entire thirty some years you've worked here?"

Stanley, sitting stiffly on the edge of his chair and looking thoroughly ill at ease, gazed reflectively into the fire for a long while before responding. "Yes, sir."

Damien laughed. "Relax, Stanley. You look as if you expect my father or Randolf to saunter in at any moment. I'm in charge now, whether I like it or not, and I happen to enjoy your company. My overseer in Vicksburg joined me for supper and drinks every night, you know."

"Highly peculiar," Stanley responded.

Damien watched the butler's face closely as he said, "Tell me the truth, Stanley. What is it about me that women find so distasteful that they turn to another?"

"That would not be for me to say, sir."

"Cut the crap."

"Very well. You have the tendencies of an ass."

"Ah. And what, pray tell, do those tendencies happen to be?"

"Take the urchin from Caldbergh for instance."

"Aha! Now we get to the crux of your agitation, I think. You, and everyone else abiding in this mausoleum, is pissed because I sent her back to Caldbergh."

Stanley drank deeply of his brandy for the first time, then pursed his lips. "My lord, it is a dreadful place. I saw that for myself."

"No doubt, but they are better equipped—"

"Balderdash, sir, if you don't mind me saying. The atrocities the lass spoke of—"

"I don't want to hear it." Damien tossed back another drink. "It was all lies anyway, no doubt."

"But if you would only listen to—"

"No." Damien left his chair. Leaning against the Carrara marble mantel, he attempted to pour himself another drink, sloshing brandy over the crystal rim of his glass and onto his hand. "I don't want to hear it," he said more softly, more to himself than to Stanley. "She was going to leave me—us—too. She didn't like us. She hated us. She was trouble. You know that. I know that. It was written all over her beauti— her face. It was in those damned blue . . . eyes." *Ah, God, those eyes. They were* haunting *him*. "Anyway. She's gone now, back where she came from. Our lives can return to normal."

There was silence. When Damien looked up, Stanley was watching him with a sad but understanding expression. "I believe we all became quite fond of the lass," the butler said. Then he added, "Even you, my lord . . . didn't you?"

"Aye," he replied without hesitation. At long last it felt good to admit it.

Sitting forward in his chair, Stanley frowned. "We could get her back."

Damien drank his brandy.

"The old place could use some livening up," Stanley said.

"I can't deny that."

"Think of the company she'll be once Lady Lyttleton leaves."

In that moment the door opened behind them. Jewel, her wide eyes locked on Stanley as he tipped up his brandy glass, opened and closed her mouth several times before managing to speak. "M'lord, I think y'd better come."

Damien blinked sleepily at the jittery maid before replying, "What is it, Jewel?"

Stepping further into the room and lowering her voice, Jewel said, "It's the urchin, sir. Bonnie. She's back."

Stanley came out of his chair. Damien stood upright.

"She's back," Damien repeated.

"Aye. And she ain't alone. There be two men with her, and they want t' see you, m'lord.''

Damien exchanged glances with Stanley before the butler set his glass on a table and took Damien's decanter and glass from his hands.

"She's come back, sir," Stanley said in a choked voice full of anticipation.

Damien nodded, stunned by the feeling of elation that was sweeping more swiftly than the brandy through his system. Without a second thought he moved past the servants and strode as gracefully as possible, considering his inebriated condition, down the long gallery to the foyer.

Bonnie stood between Smythe and the giant with the scarred face. The sight of her made Damien's step falter. How tiny she seemed. Smaller even than he remembered. Her hair had again been tucked under her knitted cap, exposing her white throat, exaggerating the hollows in her cheeks and the size of her eyes. Then he realized that her eyes were naturally wide anyway. They were two huge, glassy pools of violet pain, and even as their gazes clashed he saw the light from the overhead chandelier reflect off her tears. Still, her small chin rose a degree as she faced him. Damien caught himself on the verge of a smile.

In that moment Marianne entered the room, her exhalation of surprise and pleasure at seeing Bonnie most audible. As Damien remained rooted to the floor, Mari hurried past him, held her arms out to Bonnie, and hugged the girl against her.

"Oh, Bonnie, how wonderful to see you again. Isn't it, my lord?"

Damien slid his hands into his breeches pockets and allowed Bonnie a slight nod.

Smythe stepped forward, drawing Damien's attention. The mutinous look on the girl's features did not bode well. The fact that the rodent-faced Caldbergh manager was hovering about her like a slavering jackal did nothing to appease his sudden wariness.

His thin lips parting in a smile, Smythe said, "I trust when you've learned why I have come here, my lord, you will not seem so eager to welcome the girl. Do you think we might have a few moments of privacy?''

"Is it absolutely necessary?"

"Alas, I think so."

Damien considered the threesome again before turning and walking back down the gallery to the library. He took his place behind the desk and was seated by the time the others arrived, Smythe closing the door behind them. They then looked skeptically at Marianne as she stood at Damien's right.

"Be you Lady Warwick?" Smythe asked.

"I am not," she responded, her tone unusually autocratic.

"Anything you have to say can be told to both of us," Damien informed Smythe.

"Very well, my lord." His hands behind his back, Smythe walked up to the desk. "My lord . . . the girl has told me of the heinous crime you have perpetrated against her."

Damien frowned. "I beg your pardon?"

"I must confess, m'lord, to have been stunned by such an abominable act on your part."

Damien sat back in his chair, his gaze straying to Bonnie. Her face looked frighteningly white. Her lower lip actually trembled. She was terrified and looked ready to bolt for the door at any moment. "Bonnie," he said softly, "what is this all about?"

"What this is about," Smythe said, stepping between them, "is the little matter of rape."

Rape.

Damien didn't move. He didn't blink as he attempted to make sense of the statement. He stared into Smythe's eyes for a long, silent minute before calmly speaking. "Are you accusing me of raping the girl, Mr. Smythe?"

"*She* has accused you, my lord."

Damien sat for a moment longer, Smythe's words having left him suddenly stone-cold sober. Very slowly he rose from his chair, shoving Mari's hand from his arm as he rounded the desk. A half a head taller than Smythe, he stared down at the shriveled little man before turning on Bonnie.

She felt him, though she could not look at him. He stood there, towering over her like some dark, ominous cloud threatening to explode. She felt ill and dizzy, not only from her fear, but also from the last three days of pain and deprivation. She felt herself sway slightly toward Warwick, and the memory of his holding her that night by the window, moonlight spilling onto his ruggedly chiseled features, became confused with the present reality. Turning her face up to his, she searched despairingly for the same kindness, the same compassion, the same understanding. They weren't there. He only stared at her with blistering anger, and when his hand came up and caught her face, his fingers biting painfully into her cheeks as he tipped back her head, forcing her to face him more fully, she wanted to die.

"What is it you want from me now?" Warwick asked, more to Smythe than to Bonnie, though he continued to regard her as if she were some loathsome, slimy creature that had just crawled out from under a rock.

Smythe said, "Obviously you are well respected in Middleham, my lord, as well as in London. I wonder what your peers would think if they were informed of your actions against this poor helpless child?"

A cold smile turning up the ends of his mouth, Warwick asked in a silken voice, "Are you attempting to blackmail me, Mr. Smythe?"

"Blackmail sounds so unseemly, my lord."

"How much?"

Silence.

"I said, how *much!*" he thundered.

"Five hundred quid . . . ?"

"Done." Damien dropped his hand and turned for the desk. After jerking open the desk drawer, he slammed the accounts ledger on the desk, dipped the quill in ink, and wrote out a letter of intent. "I shall have the money delivered to Caldbergh no later than noon tomorrow, on one condition."

"And that is?"

Raising his head, Damien fixed Smythe with his green eyes and said in a soft, savage voice that froze Bonnie to the very marrow of her bones, "The chit stays with me. And if you approach me again on this matter, I will see you and your mud-faced cohort buried so deep beneath Caldbergh it would take every miner in Yorkshire a year working twenty-four hours a day to dig you up. Do we understand each other?"

"Aye," Smythe stated, his disbelieving eyes still on the letter Damien was thrusting toward him.

''Now get out of my sight,'' he ordered, ''before I change my mind after all.''

Within seconds Smythe and Timothy were gone. The sudden silence and tension-charged air seemed to reverberate against Bonnie's ears like a thunderclap.

Warwick remained behind the desk, tall, thinner than she remembered, but so very, very virile. Dressed in black breeches that outlined his long, muscular legs to perfection, and an open-necked, white linen shirt that made his shoulders look all the broader, he was every bit the aristocratic, devil-may-care earl his servants and friends professed him to be. But there was that aura of power and forcefulness about him that, as it had since the first moment she saw him, made her grow weak with dread and . . . something else. She trembled with it. Grew flushed with it. It burned her cheeks like fire, and made her want to scream out in anger.

For the first time since entering the library and taking her place at Damien's side, Marianne moved around the desk and stopped before Bonnie. She caught her chin in her fingers and forced her to face her completely.

''Why?'' she asked. ''Bonnie, why have you done this to Damien after he virtually saved your life?''

''Don't bother.'' Damien sneered, his sarcastic drawl cutting Bonnie to the bone. ''It's obvious what she's done. She and Smythe were in this together all along. They set me up, Mari. God knows how many other unsuspecting men they've pulled this stunt on.''

''Is that true, Bonnie?'' Marianne asked.

Her eyes going to Warwick, Bonnie shook her head.

Warwick turned away and walked to the window.

''Now the dilemma,'' he said, hands planted on his slender hips as he regarded the gardens stretching out before him. ''What do we do with you now, urchin? Hmmm?'' He looked back over his shoulder at her, his face like a mask. ''I could turn you in to the authorities, I suppose, but I find the threat of more scandal unacceptable. And there is the minor matter of five hundred quid I'm out. Considering that is as much money as I pay to this entire staff over a year, I estimate that you would spend the next twenty years on your knees scrubbing Braithwaite's floors, should you be inclined to repay me.'' His tone promising terrible consequences, he added,

"And you *will* be inclined to repay me, baggage. One way or another."

Marianne spoke again. "Really, Damien, I hardly think this is the time to discuss the matter. We should wait until our tempers have cooled so we can come to some sort of rational decision. Bonnie obviously needs rest, and you need a drink. So do I. I'll see Bonnie to her room and meet you on the veranda in ten minutes."

Smiling, Mari put her arm around Bonnie's shoulders. Bonnie, still wretchedly sore from Smythe's flogging, flinched and stepped away.

Misinterpreting her response as dislike for her, Marianne frowned. "Very well," she said. "You may go on your own if you prefer, Bonnie."

Bonnie remained for seconds longer, her eyes still locked on Warwick. Now that Smythe was apparently out of her life for good, her earlier fear had abated somewhat, replaced by the growing agitation over his high and mighty's attitude. No one had exactly held a gun to his head and made him pay Smythe five hundred quid. He hadn't even denied the accusation of rape, as she had expected he would. Why? So he could spend the next twenty years making her life a miserable hell?

"That will be all," Damien said. "You are dismissed."

"Is that bloody right?" Bonnie snapped.

"Aye, it is, chattel. You're mine now. Bought and paid for. If you so much as look as if you want to disobey me, I will see that you and your cutthroat partners in crime spend the next twenty years in York prison."

"But I didn't—" Bonnie bit off her response as Warwick approached her.

"Yes?" he asked. "Carry on."

"Y' don't bloody scare me," she said, knees knocking the closer he came.

"No?"

"No."

"Well," he drawled, "we'll just see about that."

Bonnie stepped away until the desk caught the back of her legs. Instinctively her fingers closed around an object beneath her palm, and she lashed out, making a wide arc with her arm so the gleaming edge of the letter opener she wielded sliced the tension-charged air with a soft *whoosh*. She regretted the move the moment she made it. But suddenly she couldn't control all the fury, pain, and frustration that were raging through her. She had been backed into too many corners to curl into a ball and escape into her mind again.

Damien danced back a second too late. The tip of the weapon sank into the flesh of his forearm and ripped. Marianne screamed in surprise, then cried for Stanley. Bonnie gaped in shock as Warwick clutched his arm and bent at the waist, his groan of pain like a lance cutting into her. When his head tipped up again, his eyes were like two burning forest fires, and his handsome mouth was pulled back against his teeth.

"You little bitch," he growled.

She tried backing away again. Impossible. She raised the blade in preparation for another attack.

"Go ahead and try it," he invited, taking one more menacing step toward her.

She was defeated and knew it. The sight of the blood seeping through the fine lawn shirt, along with the sweaty flush of anger and pain on his features, triggered the terrifying memory of her father lying facedown in a puddle of blood. Closing her eyes, she cried out and swung with the knife again. This time he was ready. Warwick captured her wrist and wrenched until she screamed and hurled herself against him, driving her free fist as hard as she could into his chest.

"Bastard!" she cried. "I hate you! I hate you!"

Gritting his teeth against the abuse, he wrenched her wrist again, feeling the delicate bones grate from the pressure. The bloody knife flew from her fingers to the floor, and he kicked it away. She continued to struggle until he had bound his arms tightly around her, holding her squirming body against his.

"You know what I think?" he shouted in her ear. "I think you're in desperate need of a good hiding, lass, and I'm just the man to do it."

"No!" she wailed, as he dragged her toward a settee against the wall. Dropping onto it, ignoring Marianne's cries of distress and, by now, Stanley's noisy protestations, Damien yanked Bonnie's baggy breeches down over her buttocks . . . and froze.

"Jesus God," he heard himself mutter. Damien stared

down at the young woman draped over his lap, her shoulders shaking, her hands making ineffectual movements as she tried to cover her bloody, blistered back and buttocks from further abuse.

"No," she wept. "No, no, no. No more. Please, God, no more. I'll be good. I won't do it again. Please, don't hurt me anymore. *Please!*"

"Oh my God," he repeated. As Damien realized what he'd been on the verge of doing, the fury died within him, replaced by disgust, not only at himself but also at the scum who had beaten the girl so mercilessly. Christ, it was no wonder she had responded to him as she had. She had been turned into an animal *by* an animal.

He did his best to replace her clothing as gently as possible. Then he gathered her in his arms. "Bonnie," he soothed her. "Ah, God, Bonnie, I'm sorry. Don't cry, love. Don't cry. He can't hurt you any longer. I won't let him. Ever. Understand? I won't let him, Bonnie."

He looked at Marianne, whose eyes were glassy with tears. "Help us," he whispered raggedly.

She whirled toward Stanley. "Send some salve and bandages up to Bonnie's room. Have Jewel prepare a pot of tea and fetch my powders from my valise. They'll help her sleep."

With Bonnie still trembling in his arms, Damien gathered her against his chest and left the settee. He carried her to her room (odd how he had come to think of it as Bonnie's room) and placed her gently on the bed. He tugged the hat from her head, releasing her hair. He smoothed the sweat from her brow, pressed his fingers against her forehead, determining whether or not she had a fever. He didn't relish the idea of calling Dr. Whitman back to the house, but he would if necessary.

Her eyes flickered open and centered on him. She blinked sleepily.

Damien did his best to smile.

"Yer arm," she said.

"I'll live."

"Yer fault."

"Not entirely."

"I—I still hate you."

The words stung, more than he cared to admit. "I'm sorry you hate me. I hoped we could be friends."

She turned her face away.

"I'm sorry I sent you away," he whispered, meaning it from the bottom of his heart.

She closed her eyes.

A storm moved in just after midnight. Damien rolled restlessly in his bed, the slashing rain against the window rousing him from troubled dreams. The image of Marianne flashed through his groggy consciousness, and foggily he recalled she had retired to a room closer to Bonnie's in case the girl needed her during the night.

The girl. He must have been out of his mind to let her and Smythe get away with their scheme. Why had he paid the money? He, who didn't give a damn what his peers thought about anything, had turned over five hundred quid for Smythe's silence just like that. And for what?

He tossed beneath the bedcovers and punched his pillow. He knew for what. He'd jumped at the first opportunity to get her back. Fool. She'd stabbed him in the back with her lie about rape—after all the care he'd taken to keep his hands *off* her—then she'd jabbed him in the arm with a letter opener. She hated him, and he'd paid a small fortune for the opportunity of allowing her to smear that fact in his face every time she got the opportunity.

Well, he'd see about that. He'd see that the ungrateful little brat rued the day she ever thought to ruin him with her and Smythe's plans. He'd make her life miserable. He'd have her on her knees scrubbing Braithwaite's floors for the rest of her life, and if she ever hissed at him again like a viper, he'd dump her back into Smythe's lap so fast she'd wonder what hit her.

God, he was glad she came back.

It'd saved him from having to go collect her himself, which he'd been on the verge of doing even before Stanley had suggested it—out of guilt, of course. *Not* because he'd missed her.

He dozed. As thunder rumbled above the house, he opened his eyes when he realized he wasn't alone. A soft whimpering came to him, and a body, warm and soft and small, curled up against him.

In one smooth move he jumped to the floor. Holding his throbbing arm against him, he did his best to make out the shadowed intruder in his bed. Cautiously he walked around the bed until he stood over the form, then, carefully, he pulled the sheet from over her head.

Bonnie?

She trembled as she slept. Her knees, curled up to her chest, gave her the appearance of a sleeping child. But there was something far from childlike in the tear-streaked features that were reflected in the occasional flash of lightning through the window. Damien was struck by the pale, porcelain perfection of Bonnie's face, a face framed by flowing, coiling strands of ink-black hair and the delicate edging of white lace on her gown. In the stillness her breathing was both visible and audible, and he was swept with such intense primitive hunger he was alarmed. The tiger was in him, and he felt his heart race as if he'd run a mile. Yet, within him rose a fierce need to protect her. From what? The horrible secrets she kept locked in her dreams? From Smythe? He'd paid five hundred quid in an effort to do that.

It was not Smythe who posed the danger to Bonnie now.

It was himself, and as he stood by her side he felt it in the hot core of his aroused body, and acknowledged it fully for the first time.

He wanted to bury himself inside her.

She embodied everything he had ever imagined himself possessing. With Bonnie he could shrug off the stifling cloak of restrictions his position in society pressed upon him and be a man, no better or worse than any other, judged not for whom or what he was, but simply for himself. He revered unconventionality—he always had—and Bonnie embodied just that.

As a second roll of thunder shook the house, she cried out again.

Despite his earlier irritation, Damien slid down on the bed beside her, brushed the hair back from her face, and whispered, "Bonnie, you're dreaming."

She stirred, but her eyes never opened. Her arms came up and captured him, wrapped around his shoulders as she rolled against him and pressed her small body into the naked length of his. Damien, his breath catching in his throat, closed his eyes as her legs entwined with his, as his knee slid between her legs and his thigh pressed against her arousingly warm center of femininity. He groaned, and as he caught himself sliding his arms around her to pull her even closer, he stopped.

He sweat where her flesh pressed against his, and to his horror he felt his lower body responding, growing uncomfortably tight and achingly rigid. The idea occurred to him that perhaps this was just another one of her and Smythe's devious plans; perhaps she would scream rape for a second time. But the tears had been real. So were the marks on her back. So were the terrifying nightmares that had driven her to his bed.

Reluctantly, his arms closed around her again, and as he rolled to his back he carried her with him so her body was stretched against his, opened to his as one leg slid over his hips and her pelvis nestled against his.

"It's all right," he whispered, kissing her brow, her cheek . . . the corner of her mouth. There he hesitated, feeling the disconcerting ache rush more hotly through his body. His mouth drifted again over hers, brushing it, covering it so he kissed her fully and completely. He tasted her lips' sweetness, felt not only their softness but also the entire closeness of her body: her fragility, her weakness, her gentleness.

"Damien?" came the soft voice from the door.

He tore his mouth away from Bonnie's and replied, "Yes." He squeezed his eyes shut, aware his voice was tight and hoarse, knowing Marianne would recognize what it revealed.

A moment passed before she asked, a little too smoothly, "Is Bonnie . . . all right?"

"Yes."

He waited for her final response, then realized she was gone.

Bonnie, at last, rested peaceably against him.

Damien buried his hands in her hair and, closing his eyes, said, "Ah, me bonny Bonnie, what are you doing to me, lass? Regardless of everything, I want you. God help me, I *want* you."

With that admission he shoved her away angrily and rolled from the bed.

Ten

The soft *sushing* of the horsehair scrub brush on the floor outside the room was the only sound, aside from the singing of a bird beyond the window, to disturb the silence in the library. While Damien did his best to concentrate on a letter from his sister, his uncle stood at the window, enjoying a cigar and his fifth glass of port. Miles browsed the shelves of books, finally deciding on *The Rise and Fall of Attila the Hun*. Damien watched his half brother leaf through the pages before saying, "You'll find that an adequate reference book, Kemball. I'm certain you'll discover the Hun rather timid, however, should you compare him with your own ideals."

Richard choked on his port.

Miles only turned his hazel eyes on Damien and smiled. "Oh, that's very good, Dame. Very good. It is not I, however, who has Bonnie on her knees scrubbing Braithwaite's floors. Nor do I have her shoveling horse dung from the stables or raking pig slop. I could almost swear you've taken out some sort of personal vendetta against the lass. What, in God's name, has she done to rile you so? Never mind. I, more than anyone, should know it doesn't take much to upset *your* apple cart. I have never known a man who so loved to hold a grudge."

"Why don't you do us all a favor and go visit your mama in Paris?" Damien replied. "Surely you must be growing bored with Braithwaite by now."

"Actually I'll be leaving this afternoon for York. There are a few business matters there in which I'm involved."

Damien laughed. "Don't waste your time. After the mess

142

you made of the Warwick mines, I would think you'd stay as far away from business as you possibly could."

"You're still brooding because our father took the responsibility for the mines away from you and gave it to me, aren't you, Dame? That was a real blow to your pride, wasn't it? It's not as if I begged the old man to do it, you know. I really could not have cared less."

"But you sure as hell raised a stink when he pulled you out and put Richard in charge."

"You convinced him to do it. I know you did. I overheard you talking one night. You told him I wasn't cut out for the responsibility, that I didn't get along well with the miners—"

"You didn't."

"I sure as the devil did a better job than him." He pointed at Richard.

Damien looked back at his sister's letter as silence filled up the room.

Turning from the window, Richard cleared his throat and asked Damien, "How is our Kate?"

"Still childless."

"Not for lack of trying, I imagine."

Damien smiled and agreed. Kate's husband, Lord William Bradhurst, had been one of his closest friends before he'd left for America. During their days of "scouting" the fairer sex, William had been known among the lads as William the Conqueror. His conquests were far-reaching and greatly envied among his peers—until he set eyes on Damien's sister, Kate.

Damien suddenly found William's womanizing not so humorous any longer. Never before their marriage vows were spoken did he allow Kate and William more than five minutes alone together.

"Kate is considering a visit to Braithwaite," Damien said. "I should like to see her again."

"She is a lovely creature," Richard replied. "Much like my own sister, I declare."

Damien smiled at the mention of his mother.

"Your mother was one hell of a woman, Damien," Richard added.

"Aye. That she was."

"She had the heart of a saint."

Miles slammed the book back on the shelf, causing Damien and Richard to look around.

"Something wrong?" Richard asked.

"The dung is getting rather deep. I fear I should excuse myself before I'm overcome by the fumes."

Richard appeared surprised. "Have you something on your mind, lad? Then say it."

A humorless smile twisting his mouth, Miles shook his head. "Far be it for me to blast the saintly Countess Clarissa."

"I should think not. She devoted sixteen years of her life to raising you."

"Indeed."

His face red, Richard squared his shoulders in obvious agitation. "I am perplexed by your attitude and always have been. When your own mother deposited you on this doorstep, Clarissa took you in. Had you been a babe, she would have offered you her breast for nourishment. No one else could have proven a worthier parent."

"Aye," Miles snapped. "But she did not love me. She did it only for my father's sake."

"Are you certain, Miles?"

"It was always Randolf and Damien first. You cannot deny that. That left no room for me, and I was the eldest. The old man didn't even have the decency to legally change my name to Warwick."

"Because you *aren't* legally a Warwick," Damien added. "And for your information, as I understand it, it was my mother who insisted you be allowed to live here. Although I'm not certain whether it was because she felt Father owed it to you or because she decided your presence would be the best reminder to him of what misfortunes happen to one who is unfaithful."

"Do tell," Miles said. "From my understanding, our father had little choice but to stray. Clarissa was like a dead mackerel in bed and—"

Damien was halfway around the desk before Richard could stop him.

"Someday"—Damien pointed one finger at Miles—"there will be no one to stand between us, Kemball. Then you are sorely going to regret that you were born . . . if you don't already.''

Miles stormed from the room, leaving the door open and nearly tripping over Bonnie. On her knees, a brush in one hand, water dripping from the other, she stared at Damien as if she'd just caught him pulling the wings off a butterfly. Damien glared back.

Bonnie dropped the brush into a pail of soapy water and wiped her hands on her breeches. ''I've finished the bloody floor . . . again,'' she told him. ''Is there aught else I can do for his friggin' lordship while I'm at it?''

Richard turned back to the window as Damien walked to the door, his sour mood made all the more surly by the look of blatant dislike on Bonnie's soot-smudged face.

''Let me think,'' he said. ''Have you studied your lessons like a good little girl?''

She nodded and stood.

Damien looked skeptical.

''Wanna hear 'em?'' she asked.

''Why not?''

Bonnie cleared her throat. ''Braithwaite is divided int' four servant zones—the butler's, who is Stanley; the cook's, who is simply called Cook; the housekeeper's, who is Jewel; and the laundrymaid's, who is Miss Gretchen Peabody. The steward, housekeeper, and cook eat in the steward's room, along with the head gardener, the senior lady's maids and valets, when they are so employed, which they ain't right now.''

''Aren't,'' he corrected.

''The upper servants have breakfast and tea in the housekeeper's room, eat the main courses of dinner and supper in the servants' hall, and retire t' the housekeeper's room t' eat their puddin'.''

Damien, leaning against the door frame, crossed his arms over his chest and nodded. ''Very good, urchin. Continue.''

She scratched her nose with the back of her wet hand and blew a tendril of hair off her cheek.

''The housekeeper is in command of the housemaids, one of which is apparently me. Jewel is responsible for cleanin' the house and lookin' after the linen. She also provides, stores, and prepares tea, coffee, sugar, preserves, cakes, and biscuits. Her central territory consists of her own room, the stillroom, storeroom, and closet. Stanley rules over the footmen and any other indoor menservants, except for the valets, which you ain't got right now.''

''Haven't,'' he amended.

''He's in charge of the plate, drink, and table linen, and his many responsibilities include—by way of footmen or groom of the chambers—furnishin' all writin' tables and polishin' the mirrors. He sees that the footmen brush the clothes, clean the shoes, clean the knives, and trim, clean, and fill the oil lamps.''

''I'm impressed,'' Damien said. ''You've obviously paid close attention to Stanley and Jewel. And, I might add, you've done a fairly respectable job on the floor.''

''Am I excused?''

Damien pursed his mouth as he contemplated the look of poorly guarded insubordination on Bonnie's features. Two spots of hot color on her cheeks clearly defined her annoyance. She'd done well the last days to hold that fiery little temper. He was curious to see how far he could continue to push her before she exploded.

''Not just yet, I think.'' He pointed at his boot. ''There is a spot of mud just there. Would you mind, baggage . . . ?''

Her mouth set, Bonnie stared down at Damien's foot. As her head came up slowly, the knot of hair on the back of her head slid from its coil and spilled soft and black as nightfall over her shoulders. His smile—indeed, his entire body—hardened at the sight, a rather frequent, disgusting, and humiliating tendency it had taken on of late, despite his continuing anger at her over the ordeal with Smythe.

''Well?'' he prompted.

''Eat dirt,'' she said, smiling icily. ''That's the bloody footman's job.'' Then she yanked up her bucket of soapy water and sauntered out of the gallery. Damien threw back his head and howled with laughter.

For the second time that day Bonnie filled her pail with kitchen swill and started down the path toward the hog pen. She did not hesitate until she was certain she was far enough from the house that no one would notice her slipping off the pathway. She dropped onto the marble bench she'd shared with Miles what seemed like a lifetime ago, and placed the bucket between her aching feet.

Never had she felt so tired and generally fed up. Not just weary of bone, but weary of heart. She couldn't quite put her finger on the cause of it, but it was there, growing more uncomfortable every day that she remained here. Which was another problem.

How long did she intend to stay here and allow his high and mighty Warwick to treat her so shabbily? She had her pride, after all. Still, she reminded herself that it was better than the workhouse or Smythe's London alternative.

For a moment she imagined what her life might have been like had her parents not died. By now she might have married some sheep farmer and set up housekeeping in a thatched-roof cottage on the Pennines. No doubt she'd be bouncing a bairn on each knee and waiting patiently for the love of her life to sweep in from the fields, smelling like hay and ale and sunshine. Those were Sunday smells. Her da had always smelled that way on Sundays because it was his only day off. They'd attend the church down the lane, then picnic on the moor, weather permitting. She'd sit on a rock and watch her parents frolic together like children. She'd suspected, even then, that secret "things" went on between them. She'd seen the yearning on their faces, heard the rustling of bedclothes at night, the moans, the passion, the sighs and words of love that drifted occasionally to her sleepy ears. After her mother died, there had been only the soft sound of sobbing from her father in the darkness. Then one horrible, stormy night, he was gone and her life had become an unending nightmare.

"Don't think about it," she told herself.

Shaking her head, disgusted by the tears that had formed in her eyes, she swiped them away with the back of her hand and kicked the bucket. Bloody hell, she was tired. Sometimes she wished she could just close her eyes and never wake up. But she wanted, just once more before she died, to experience peace and happiness. She wanted to feel loved. Was that too friggin' much to ask of God? Was it?

Yawning, Bonnie sleepily eyed the marble bench on which she was sitting. A few minutes' rest was all she needed. The nights were so long and lonely. The sudden storms that had been shaking Braithwaite throughout the dark hours had left her rattled and sleepless or tossing with nightmares. Once, she had actually dreamed that she woke up in Warwick's bed. Imagine his high and mighty allowing that. Ha!

She lay down on the bench, cradled her cheek in the crook of her elbow, and watched an ant scurry along a bush branch near the tip of her nose. "Feedin' pigs?" she asked the insect aloud. "Emptyin' his high and mighty's chamber pots? He'll have y' doin' it if y' don't watch out."

Rolling to her back, Bonnie stared through the lacy canopy of tree limbs overhead and laughed. And drifted. Her eyes closed, and Warwick's dream words swirled back to her.

"Ah, me bonnie Bonnie, what are you doing to me, lass? I want you. God help me, I *want* you."

"Bonnie! Gum, lass, I've been lookin' all over. How long have ya been sleepin' there? His lordship is shoutin' for his tea, has been for the last hour."

Blinking sleep from her eyes, Bonnie struggled to sit up. Jewel, her plump hands plunked on her ample hips, scowled in displeasure.

"He won't be pleased y' be lollygaggin' about."

"Then don't bloody tell him," she snapped.

Jewel clicked her tongue. "Y'd better hurry, lass. He and Lady Marianne are wantin' their evenin' tea."

"Is that right?"

"Aye, and he's wantin' you to serve it."

"Me!"

"He won't take no substitutes, lass, and he's tol' me to tell y' that ye're t' get yerself cleaned up before servin'. He says y' smelled like a pig sty when he saw y' last."

Bloody hell! For the last days she'd been forced to take up his stupid tray of tea and biscuits, lugging the damned thing up and down those stairs 'cause Warwick and his tart acted as if they'd been stricken with the pox and couldn't bloody get on their feet. If that wasn't bad enough, they were usually reclining in bed, half clothed, the lady looking agitated and *him* looking like a tom cat with cream on his whiskers.

Well, she thought, we'll see about that.

Bonnie stormed back to the house, entering through the kitchen. The tray was ready, the china teapot sweating with heat, the fresh-baked biscuits placed decoratively on several plates that matched the teapot. There were doily napkins, of course. Jam pots, teacups, milk, and brown sugar. It was all Bonnie could do to lift the lot, but she did, gritting her teeth and balancing the burden on the palms of her hands.

She took the back stairs, like a good servant. Her legs were aching by the time she reached the top. She drew in several deep breaths before continuing down the hallway.

Their voices stopped her first.

"Harry can be so inconvenient at times. Imagine returning to London on such short notice. It can't be helped, I suppose. Will you be traveling with me, darling? I'm certain Harry would love to see you again. He sends his best wishes, you know. Damien, are you listening to me? For heaven's sake, I may as well be in London already for all the good the last few days have done me here. I certainly hope, for your sake, that you fight your way out of this ennui soon."

Marianne looked up from where she sat sewing in her chair as Bonnie rounded the corner. Damien, sprawled lazily over the bed, his shirt unbuttoned and a cigar in his mouth, stared at her through a ring of smoke as she struggled to place the tray on a table.

"You're late," he told her in a heavy voice. "Tea was to be served an hour ago."

Bonnie whipped up a napkin and tossed it in his lap. She turned for the door.

"You may bring me my tea," he drawled sarcastically. "And my biscuits."

Bonnie froze, then slowly turned back for the tray. Her hands were shaking as she poured the tea. She carefully heaped it with sugar, added a dash of milk, and took it to him.

Gripping the cigar between his teeth, he said, "Don't forget the biscuits."

She returned to the tray, piled a plate high with the crumbly confections, and returned it to him.

"And the jam."

"Oh," she said. "Y' want jam, do y'?"

"Please."

She retrieved the pot of raspberry jam and carried it to the bed. "Where would y' like it, milord?"

"Anywhere you like."

Bonnie smiled. "Very well, milord." And with that she turned the jam jar upside down over his bare chest.

Marianne screamed with laughter as Damien came up off the bed. Bonnie stood her ground, fists clenched as the jam rolled down his belly and plopped onto his shoeless feet.

"Y' can take yer bleedin' biscuits and jam and red-haired tart and go straight t' hell. I ain't yer housemaid and I ain't yer slave!"

"Is that so!"

"That's so! I've had it, and I ain't doin' no more . . . Lord Stud." She sneered it, but as his face turned dark, Bonnie backed away. She wasn't sure what had done it—the refusal to obey him or her calling him Lord Stud—but the wicked twinkle in his eye was suddenly gone, replaced by pure, un-bridled rage.

"Damien," came Marianne's voice. "Damien, I think you should calm down. Bonnie was only having a little fun. Weren't you, dear?"

Bonnie cut her eyes to Marianne, then back to Warwick, centering her sights on the sugary red splotch matted in the crop of black hair on his chest. For some odd reason the need to laugh assailed her. She did so before catching herself.

"Something funny?" he asked silkily.

"Aye." She giggled again. "Y' could use a scrubbin', I think."

"Odd that you should mention it, baggage. Just before you arrived I had Stanley prepare my bath. I was thinking, how-ever . . ." He advanced.

Bonnie backed away, not liking the look in his green eyes.

"I was thinking," he repeated. "Seems you could do with a washing yourself."

"Not me." She shook her head and looked for the door.

"Marianne was just saying she thought you might be pass-ably pretty were you washed up—"

"Forget it."

"—although I doubt it. I highly suspect it would take a pickax to chisel away that grime on your face. But I'm more than willing to give it a try. What do you say, Bonnie? Shall we give it a go?"

He made a grab for her arm, but Bonnie was quicker. She whirled for the door, took no more than two long strides before she was caught by the waistband of her breeches and yanked off her feet. Arms and legs swimming in air, she screamed, "Put me down! Y' can't do this!"

"Nonsense," came his calm voice. "I own you. Remember? I can do anything with you I bloody well like."

Before she could respond he had hauled her up against him, locked his arm around her middle, and was out the door. She fought him the best she could, but to no avail. The servants came running from their chores as she screamed "Help!", but they only watched, stupefied, as Warwick threw open the door at the end of the corridor and descended a stairway Bonnie never knew existed. It was darker here, and damper. Once reaching the bottom, she was given the impression that they had left the main house and entered an outbuilding of sorts, connected to the main house by a system of sconce-lit corridors that were walled in mortar and brick.

"My lord!" Stanley's voice echoed down the stairwell behind them. "Will you have your usual brandy with your bath?"

"No!" he shouted, then stepping into a marble-tiled room with soaring ceilings supported with marble pillars, he slammed the door behind him.

"Bloody hell," Bonnie cried. "Yer gonna murder me; y've brought me t' a friggin' mausoleum!"

"Wrong, urchin. It's what is known in polite society as a plunge bath. It may not be as modern as they come, but it more than adequately gets the job done." He pointed to the first icy looking, marbled-sided pool and said, "That one's cold. This one, however . . ." He kicked a door open and steam rushed around them, stinging Bonnie's eyes and snatching away her breath. "Fortunately Braithwaite is built over a natural hot spring. Hot water is much better for cutting through all that dirt. Believe me, you're going to enjoy it."

She took a swing at him and missed. Before she could regroup, he had lifted her in the air and dropped her. She hit the water with a mighty splash. As the water closed over her head, she was forced to scramble to find her footing. She jumped up, finding the water was hip level. Her soaked hair spilled down over her face and nearly suffocated her before she could clear it away.

Breasts heaving, she glared up at a smirking Warwick and sneered, "You bloo-dy—"

"Careful," he interrupted, "or I might be forced to come in there and help you wash behind your ears."

"Over my dead body."

"That"—he smiled—"could be arranged. After being blackmailed out of five hundred quid, I might be sorely tempted to take you up on that threat."

"No one forced y' t' pay it!"

His mouth thinned. With his toe he kicked a bar of soap into the water. "Wash," he told her.

"You can—"

"Wash!" His voice was louder, echoing off the tiles and the gilded dressing stand, basin, and ewer where he apparently shaved. Sinking in the water, Bonnie fished for the soap, caught it, and stood again.

Damien walked to the end of the bath. Overhead, rain spotted the skylight and filled the room with a steamy, gray illumination like fog. Bonnie thought he looked a little—a lot—like a devil swathed in smoke and shadows. A twinge of fear sluiced through her at the sight. Or was it excitement? She suddenly discovered that it was getting ever so much harder to differentiate between the two.

Turning the soap over and over in her hand, Bonnie glanced about the chamber, noting with fleeting curiosity the wall inset lined with pillows. Then she looked toward the door leading from the room. Could she make it out of the bath, through the door, and up the stairs before he caught her? She eased closer to the edge of the bath, took a moment to judge it, then leaped.

He was nearly on her by the time she stumbled to her feet. She hurled the soap at him, realizing in the instant she threw it that it would have as much effect as spitting on the walls of Jericho and expecting them to come tumbling down. The next instant he was against her; she stumbled backward, grabbing a handful of his shirt to keep herself from falling. The effort was futile. He tumbled into the bath with her, sending water to the four corners of the room and nearly drowning Bonnie.

She surfaced, sputtering and gasping so hard for a breath that she hardly realized Damien was laughing. It was a rich sound, yet boyish, arresting, strong, and warmly cordial. She stood with the water lapping at her hips and stared into his dark face, mesmerized by the sight of him. A frisson that might have been fear or excitement tingled along her nerves. She couldn't move. Neither could she speak. A disconcerting heat had begun dancing in the pit of her stomach, and with color suddenly burning her face she acknowledged the yearning for what it was.

Slowly, his laughter died, and for long minutes he seemed to watch her from under his wet black lashes, as if sensing her body's upheaval. The impulse to flee again touched her briefly, then was gone as his masculine presence assaulted her senses. Never had she felt so helpless, so out of control of her emotions. No longer could she deny to herself that her feelings for this man were ambivalent. Far from it. She had lain in bed at night and dreamed of his arms around her, fantasized that he would see her as more than a Caldbergh urchin. She had yearned to reveal the young woman she'd tried so hard to disguise these many years, all so he would . . . what?

Love her?

A heated flush swept to her hairline as her mind and heart acknowledged the illusion. Suddenly she felt naked and vulnerable in his eyes, and foolish. So foolish. He would mock her again and remind her she was little more than baggage. Chattel. A nuisance who had cost him much in money and aggravation. Feeling hot tears gather behind her eyes, she was struck with the overwhelming ache to show him how wrong he was. But she wouldn't do it. He could—would—never desire her that way. Never!

She turned away.

He grabbed her arm.

There were many things she should have done: screamed out her denial, her false hatred, or perhaps torn herself from his grip and escaped. Yet she didn't. She only closed her eyes and felt the heat from his hand sluice through her like a fire, making her gasp in silent anguish and desperate, desperate need. Her body had turned traitor on her, and there didn't seem to be anything she could do about it. She wasn't certain she wanted to.

She raised her eyes to his. His dark gaze searched her

features, coming to rest on her mouth; he lifted a hand to touch her face, and a tremor ran through her. His warm fingers trailed over her cheek, her jaw, and ran slowly down the length of her throat as if he were memorizing each detail, as if he had suddenly discovered her for the first time and found her fascinating and irresistible. Never had she felt so gentle and intimate a caress. It weakened her, made her quiver with an odd need to have done with the tedious and burdensome yoke of girlhood and get on with her life.

Damien watched Bonnie's eyes close as he slid his fingers around the back of her head, massaging her nape, squeezing and releasing, the pressure enough to bring her head back so her curtain of hair poured over his arm like a waterfall. What had happened? Moments ago she was fighting and clawing and now . . . now she was purring in his hands and looking for all the world like a woman caught in the throes of desire. With a gut-wrenching realization he thought he could refuse the child-urchin from Caldbergh—but this woman before him now was something altogether different. He noted the slow rise of color suffusing her cheeks, then his gaze drifted downward, over the soft material of her shirt where it clung to her breasts.

He hesitated. She was as beautiful as he had imagined, high and rounded, perfectly shaped and flushed with heat. To touch her would mean an end to his denial of her. He knew that, yet . . .

How often had he imagined taking her?

He wanted her. God help him, he did, and the dreamy look on her features told him she felt the same.

To hold her just once. That's all it would take. It was the curiosity over the forbidden that was tempting him. Perhaps just a kiss. To experience her kissing him back would satisfy the beast in him. What could she know of lovemaking after all? He would no doubt find his desire dampened by her childish ways . . .

He closed his hand over the taut fullness of her breast, and saw her tremble. He heard himself whisper, "God, you're lovely. But then I knew you would be." He buried his hand in her tangled, wet mass of black hair and eased back her head. He thought of the many times he'd ached to hold her, the many times he'd resisted . . . then he kissed her.

For an instant she stiffened and struggled; he held her head forcibly with his hands, allowing her no escape as his mouth searched hers, gently at first, then fiercely as her lips parted and warmed under his. She went still, then limp as he teased the soft corners with his tongue, brushing the sweet fullness with unhurried enjoyment. Soft murmurings of protest sounded in her throat, yet he ignored her, deepening the kiss until he felt the tenuous control over his need begin to fray. His mind cried out a warning, yet his body ignored it. The last thread of denial was swept away like flotsam in a hurricane as he realized that she had swayed against him and was kissing him back with equal passion.

He raised his head. Her hair, gleaming with dancing beads of water, framed her face, giving Bonnie the appearance of some mythical sea nymph. Frozen, she watched him, her eyes dark with turmoil, her mouth full and red from the pressure of his kiss. Damien allowed his eyes to linger on her parted mouth, then they slid back down to her breasts, noted the increased rise and fall of her bosom beneath the misty veil of water and material. Easily, he slid the garment from her shoulders.

Very slowly he took off his shirt.

Bonnie felt her knees grow weak. In the early hours of morning, awakened by her dreams, she had lain in bed and imagined what loving him would be like, but her imagination had never aroused these feelings inside her. They were unsettling, slowly stripping away rationality, possessing her body with uncomfortable yearnings. In truth, she didn't feel like Bonnie Eden. She felt as if some hot-blooded, restless animal had taken over her body.

Instinctively Bonnie knew what he wanted. She wasn't ignorant of how it was with men, not having spent the last five years at Caldbergh where rape was a weekly occurrence for the girls who weren't so nimble of foot as Bonnie. But there were also the girls who never fought it, but enjoyed it, sneaking the boys into their bunks at night where they rolled about for everyone in the room to see. By no means was Bonnie naive, nor had she been totally unmoved by the lusty spectacles. But nothing had made her body feel so unsettled as this.

Damien tossed his shirt onto the edge of the bath. As his

gaze wandered over her, he murmured, "You're exquisite. But I'm certain you've been told that numerous times . . . ?"

Her look became mutinous. "No. I haven't."

"How remiss of your lovers."

"I haven't had any lovers."

His look darkened. "I'm supposed to believe that from a girl who blackmailed me—"

"I had nothing to do with Smythe's scheme!"

"No? He came up with the idea of rape on his own?" He caught her chin and forced back her head. "Tell me the truth or by God I'll thrash you."

"Aye. I told him you raped me. But that was only because he was about t' sell me off t' some procurer in London who specializes in supplying virgins t' his clients. I believed if he thought I was no longer chaste he would forget the idea. I didn't *know* he would confront you, milord. I didn't realize he would be that stupid."

Damien regarded Bonnie's upturned face, the way her body trembled.

"Your virginity can be easily proven or disproven," he told her, then slid his hands down her sides and released her breeches.

With a queer sense of detachment, almost as if this ordeal were happening to someone else, Bonnie felt his hands move down her back. She felt helpless and tottering on some threshold over which, once crossed, she could never return. In that moment she didn't care. For Warwick was holding her, caressing her, fulfilling her every fantasy, making her feel safe and secure and loved—that's all she needed, wanted for now: just one moment of splendor today, and to the devil with tomorrow!

There was tenderness in his eyes. The same tenderness she recalled from her dreams, the same that had greeted her each time she had roused herself from her feverish state and found his face looking with concern into hers. Was it too much to hope that he cared for her—the way she cared for him? Dare she admit those feelings to him? She couldn't. She was too inept with words. But she could—would—show him how she felt . . .

His arm slid around her waist, drawing her closer until her body was molded to his. She curled her arms around him, ran her slick palms over his back, exploring the curve of muscle over his shoulders. His eyes grew warmer, more intense. He brushed her damp cheek with his fingertips and tilted her head back further until she was bending at the waist. His lips gently brushed her own as lightly as air, scrambling her resolve until sensations inside her burst open like spring buds under a hot sun.

Often she had dreamed of such a kiss, of being touched and caressed by a kind man with clean hands, a man who loved her. But this surprising tenderness from Warwick made those insubstantial fantasies seem like the dreams they were. Warm and wet, his lips covered her own, pressing easily, parting, probing, growing more insistent as he demanded the response she could no longer deny him. As she touched the tip of his tongue with her own, he groaned, tore his mouth from hers, and buried his lips in the soft curve of her neck and shoulder. Her head fell back, her heavy hair spilling over the water, shimmering like pale silver in the ghostly glow of the rain-kissed sunlight from overhead. And when he lifted his head once more, his eyes were black and burning.

"Do you understand what I want to do to you?" he asked.

She nodded.

"If you want to walk away now, I won't stop you."

"I—I want it as well," she confessed.

An hour from now there would be regrets, self-condemnation, anger. He knew he should back off, now, before it was too late. But he couldn't. His need for her had been like a fire burning inside him for too long. He lifted her easily in his arms. With little effort he left the bath by way of the curving steps at one end.

She sank into the softness of the pillows she had noted earlier. They felt damp and clung to her skin, but it didn't matter. All that mattered was Damien. He stood over her now, his features dark and misty and almost frightening. For a moment they reminded her . . .

No! Not now, she thought. Not ever again.

She closed her eyes, forcing away those nightmare images of menacing features cloaked in mist and fog. They had nothing to do with this man. Nothing!

She felt his hands move over her, removing her shoes, peeling the breeches down her legs until she lay before him naked and trembling. Then his fingers were on her, sliding between her legs, forcing her thighs open until she was fighting to cover herself from his eyes.

"Don't," he commanded her. "Don't ever hide yourself from me."

She closed her eyes and succumbed to the magic he was spinning inside her, a heady swirl of dizzying sensations that coursed through her like a maelstrom, sweeping away all lingering thoughts of denial. Oh God, she wondered, what was he doing to her?

"Do you know how long I've wanted you?" he whispered huskily. "Do you know how long I've ached to have you, Bonnie?"

She groaned his name over and over in incoherent, ragged tears of sound that seemed foreign to her own ears. She knew she should stop him, but she couldn't. His hands were too wonderful in their caressing motions, his fingers sliding rhythmically inside her, tantalizingly until the pleasure became a frantic heat that thrummed in her veins like quicksilver.

He left her, stood on his knees above her, his long fingers forcing the staining material of his breeches from around its buttons. Bonnie gasped as his body, swollen and throbbing, sprang free of its constrictions. Somehow she managed to shake her head and utter a cry that was barely audible to her own ears, and as his body moved over hers, the reality of her actions hit her reasoning like a stone.

"Oh," she whimpered. "Oh no . . ."

He covered one sweetly aroused nipple with his mouth, laved the small, sensitive bud with his tongue while his hands gently stroked the flesh of her stomach, to entangle again in her downy black hair and part the quivering moist skin of her inner lips. Threads of blistering heat shot through her, radiating from the bud of desire he had discovered buried there where his fingers thrust. The movement of his hands melted the ice of fear that had momentarily assailed her. Her lower body began to throb and swell until she realized she was losing control. Her body was his, and he played with it as he so desired, building the sweet, delicious torture inside her until she was writhing and whimpering for some surcease she could not even name.

"Tell me you want me," came his words in her ear.

Bonnie groaned and thrashed her head.

His finger buried more deeply inside her, making her cry out, not from pain but with need.

"Say, 'Damien, I want you.' "

She shook her head and beat his shoulders.

"Say it, damn you!"

"Yes! Yes, God help me, I want you!"

"Not . . . good . . . enough."

Reality ebbed away as the feel of his hard maleness pressed against the soft opening of her body. Raising her arms around his shoulders, she sank her nails into his back, making his fists, now buried in the pillows by her face, clench in pain. "Yes," she hissed. "I want you."

A look crossed his features. Anger? Fear? Chagrin? Surrender.

With a low growl and curse, he sank onto her, into her. Her eyes flew open as a sudden pain possessed her. She flung her arms out with a violent effort to throw him off as, once again, his hips came down on hers, pressing the full weight of his strong body against her and inside her. She was suddenly excruciatingly full of him; she could not help but cry out. No one had warned her. No one . . .

He shifted again and the discomfort forced her to spread her legs further, to bury her small fists against his shoulders as if by bracing herself away from him the pain would cease. She could feel the sinews of his powerful arms standing out like cords as he supported his weight off her.

Meeting his eyes with her own, she said, "Please don't go on. I— I don't think I can stand it."

Damien turned his face from her. In a moment he shook his head. "Too late. It's too late for us both, m'love." He looked at her again, his face moist with sweat that trickled from his temples and down his cheeks. A hesitant smile turned up one side of his mouth. "I'll make it good for you."

"This can never be good. It's too bloody painful."

"Perhaps this once. Never again."

He kissed her then, tenderly, his tongue teasing the corners of her mouth as he ever so slowly withdrew his body almost but not quite out of hers. He eased into her again, and again, and with each impalement the burning lessened. The pain turned into pleasure, and Bonnie began to move as well, forward and back until the rhythm took hold of her completely and swept her away on a surging tide of oblivion she had never imagined existed.

"Bonnie," he groaned. "Bonnie."

As their bodies slid together, meshed with sweat and water, the glory grew. As he filled her again and yet again, straining and climbing and pounding his way as far as he could inside her, the intensity became unbearable. They were one. And in the dim corner of Bonnie's mind that was still rational enough to reason, she knew that it would never be this way with any other man.

A bliss, bright and blazing, burst upon her in that moment, unendurable, shattering. It happened for Damien too. Throwing back his dark head and breathing heavily, he let his eyes meet hers. He tensed, then shuddered, and as Bonnie's body stiffened and tightened around him, she felt his body stretch and throb and fill her with a wet heat, unbearably sweet. She arched against him and closed her eyes as the spiraling sensation picked her up then let her fall. Locking her legs around him, she forced him to remain inside her until the end, until he lay against her, relaxed, his breathing falling more normally along the side of her face.

Finally he raised up on his elbows and gazed down into her eyes.

She touched his cheek.

For a moment they did not speak, neither knowing what to say, each somehow sensing that something very special had just taken place, something frightening and magical and confusing.

Almost reluctantly, Damien slid his body out of Bonnie's. For a moment he left her. Then he was back, gently pressing a dry linen between her legs. When she looked at him in surprise, he said, "There's always some bleeding after the first time. It's like the pain. It won't happen again."

He rolled away and yanked his breeches up over his hips. He looked at the linen, smeared with blood, before closing his eyes and shaking his head. Reality had reared its ugly head, as he knew it would; reason washed over him like a tidal wave. All the old obligations—Vicksburg, Parliament, Braithwaite—leered at him from the shadows. Even more sobering was the look on Bonnie's face. She shone with all the radiance of a young woman in love. Normally that realization would have sent him running from the room with a thank-you-but-no-thank-you tip of his hat. So why did he want to throw himself onto her again, burying himself inside her and remaining there for the rest of his life? Why, in that moment, did he not give a damn about Vicksburg or Parliament . . . or anything but Bonnie?

Lying beside her, he reached for her so her head rested on his shoulder. He stared at the ceiling. What an inutterable mess. What the hell was he supposed to do now? He had actually believed that by making love to Bonnie he would assuage this hunger for her; had convinced himself that she would become a temporary fancy.

Yet something had happened here that was totally disarming. He wasn't altogether certain he wanted to understand its meaning. She had become a weakness, a flaw in his armor, and if he didn't stop it now . . .

Dear God, she was so young.

So beautiful.

He could so easily . . .

He raised himself again and looked down at her. Her bright eyes carried the faintest hint of a smile.

He wanted her even more than he had before making love to her.

"This can't happen again," he stated quietly, determinedly, doing his best to convince himself of the words, to ignore the closing off of his throat as he spoke. "It should never have happened in the first place. I take full responsibility for it and I'm . . . I'm sorry, Bonnie."

The lie made him sick.

She sat up. Her face looked white as she repeated, "Sorry?"

"What happened between us must never happen again. A man of my age and position should have known better—"

Slowly she got to her feet, never for a moment quitting him with her eyes, which seemed to penetrate his very soul. She jerked on her breeches and snatched up her shirt, putting it on. "What are you doing?" he asked. "We have to talk, Bonnie."

"I don't want t' talk t' you." Her voice was venomous.

"I hate y'! I can't think what made me do such a horrible thing with y'!"

Damien made a grab for her arm. For a moment they were frozen in place and time, and in her eyes he saw a reflection of himself: a man on his knees, his face tortured with emotions he could not even guess at, least of all admit.

Stunned, he released her and she spun away. He ran after her, the cold of the plunge bathroom stinging his flushed skin like a sudden slap of winter.

She was halfway up the stairs when Stanley threw open the door. The sight of Bonnie barreling at him out of the dim-lit chambers set him back on his heels. She skirted past him, slamming the door behind her.

Upon seeing the butler, Damien stopped short, aware of his own partially unclothed state and how the situation must appear. Then Stanley's eyes were drawn to the linen in Damien's hand. The servant's gray eyebrows shot up.

"Is there anything I can do?" Stanley asked.

"Yes," Damien snapped. "You can keep your mouth shut about this."

"Of course."

"That will be all."

Stanley bowed and quit the room.

Damien hurled the linen to the floor.

Eleven

Perhaps he understood now how Richard felt. Odd how a dependency could so quickly take a grip on the mind and body and drive a man beyond good judgment, even sanity.

Damien stood in the stark room surrounded by sheet-draped furnishings, feeling the cold and damp seep through his clothes and make him, despite the fire in his body, shiver as if with fever. Who was he kidding? Shutting himself off in some closed-up wing of Braithwaite was not going to make this hunger for Bonnie go away.

Only time and distance would do that. Or would it? There was no point in denying his attraction to her any longer, so why continue to refuse the notion that she had become a very important part of his life?

He paced.

He should put this matter into perspective. She was a challenge, and he enjoyed nothing more than that. It kept life from being dull and kept him from becoming dim-witted. She was a diversion. He needed a diversion now with problem upon problem being heaped upon his shoulders.

He shook his head.

There were simply too many conflicts in his life to allow him to become attached to anyone, however briefly. Even if Bonnie had been gentle born, he could not risk the chance of involvement. He would be leaving England soon. He would be forced to take up arms if this war escalated. He might even be killed.

It wasn't as if he loved her, certainly. He was fond of her, but . . .

What had taken place between them had been merely physical need. She was a beautiful young woman. She was at that stage in life where love and desire were easily confused. They'd both made a mistake. If he remained here another night he'd only compound the problem by taking her again, somehow, someway.

Damien walked to the window and stared out at the dark, rain-drenched countryside. The walls were closing in on him. If he didn't get out of here soon he was going to do something he would regret . . . again.

He left the room.

Marianne sat up in bed as he dragged a valise from the wardrobe and began stuffing it with clothes.

"Going somewhere?"

He nodded.

"I suppose it's too much to hope that you've decided to travel to London with me."

He nodded again as he crammed a third pair of breeches into the case.

Marianne yawned and stretched before regarding him thoughtfully. "Judging from the fact that you are already dressed and packed, do I assume that you are leaving Braithwaite tonight?"

"Yes."

"Rather sudden, don't you think? Had you even planned to tell me good-bye?"

"Certainly." He shut the valise and smiled at her. "Good-bye."

Tossing aside the covers, Marianne slid from the bed. She poured herself a glass of water. "Correct me if I'm wrong, but you're running away again, aren't you?" When he didn't respond, she drank the water and placed the glass on the table. She turned to face him. "I won't bother to ask what went on between you and Bonnie earlier. You would no doubt refuse to answer or you would inform me that it's none of my damn business. You might even stand there and try to deny to yourself that what happened between you was nothing more than a momentary, uncontrollable passion, and that it won't happen again."

Damien frowned.

Marianne approached him, her features hard. "I won't try to second-guess why you did what you did. I don't believe for a moment you would even admit to yourself your true reasons. But I do know what this lust of yours has cost Bonnie. There is very little in a woman's life that she can truly call her own. Her virginity is one of those things, and it is a treasure that, if offered the choice, she will give only to the man she loves."

He laughed. "Someone forgot to tell Louisa that."

Marianne smiled. "To quote Byron: 'In her first passion woman loves her lover. In all others, all she loves is love.' I'm certain Louisa must have thought she loved him, whoever he was."

"But I was her betrothed. Where the blazes was the passion she showered on half London and not on me?"

"Since the Warwicks and Thackerays were such close friends, you were a part of her life since the moment she was born. I suspect her feelings for you were deep, but hardly passionate. When she was introduced to London and suddenly found herself desired by half the male population, the thrill was overwhelming. Don't forget, she was little more than a country girl, having been raised totally in Yorkshire. Coming out must have been like walking into a fairy tale."

He grabbed up the valise. "Louisa is a dead issue."

"But Bonnie isn't. For your own peace of mind—and hers—please consider your motives."

"I don't need you to dictate what I should think or feel, Mari. I know what I'm doing and why." He left the room, slamming the door behind him.

The dark engulfed him. The distant chiming of the case clock told him that the hour had grown late. If he left now . . .

He moved quietly down the corridor to the top of the stairs. He looked first to the foyer below, then toward the distant bedroom door. Bonnie's door. The valise grew heavy, the air thick. He closed his eyes and pictured her again, white limbs stretched out beneath him, eyes glazed with desire, lips abraded from passion. The heat of her body had been both heaven and hell.

"Get out now, before it's too late," he told himself. Yet he walked directly to her door and put down the valise. She deserved a good-bye. He owed her that much. He'd explain the reasons why a relationship between them just wouldn't be possible. Besides their coming from two different worlds, besides their age difference, there was Bent Tree, and the war, and . . .

He shoved open the door. The sitting room was dark. Through the open doorway of her bedroom dim candlelight shone. Her bed, though rumpled, was empty.

Wearing a white flannel gown, she stood at the window staring through the black, rain-spattered glass. Her hands were splayed over her breasts, and despite the chill in the air, her face appeared moist with perspiration.

He might have spoken; he couldn't be certain. He couldn't be certain of anything but that he wanted her. He wanted her more in that moment than he'd ever wanted another woman. She looked around, appearing almost frightened. Her pale face, with its large dark eyes—haunted eyes—regarded him. Her lips parted. Her hands clenched into fists.

Somehow he managed to open his arms, never expecting her to comply.

She ran to him, threw herself against him, and he closed them around her, tight.

"Bonnie." It was a broken whisper. "Ah, God, Bonnie."

He tunneled his fingers through her hair, buried them along her scalp, and forced back her head. "I want you," he growled. "You're a sickness inside me, and I want you."

He kissed her and she trembled. As his tongue raked the inside of her mouth, she whimpered and struggled against him. He knew the feeling, the valiant fight to deny the desire, the shattering of the soul at the capitulation. Her small hands beat against his chest even while her body responded by pressing closer to him.

"I hate you." She gasped. "I hate you."

"Don't. Bonnie, please, don't hate me." He kissed her eyes, her nose, her throat. "Just love me," he said. "I need you to love me."

He carried her to bed. Slowly, he sank with her onto the down-turned covers and wrapped his arms around her, though she continued to struggle halfheartedly against the attempt. Gradually, gradually, she allowed him to hold her. Her body warmed against him until her breath fell along the base of his throat like gentle fire.

He knew what was happening, and he couldn't stop it. He

didn't want to. She had fast become a fever inside him; he knew it. He had been on the verge of running from the desire to make love to her again. Whatever madness had gripped him, he simply was not strong enough to fight this over-whelming need to be inside her. No matter how many times he'd told himself he was a bastard for even imagining—fantasizing—overtaking her.

He caught the hem of her sleeping gown and slid it upward, until the lace edge barely covered her sex. Her thighs shone pale in the darkness. The dark triangle of hair was as potent as any aphrodisiac. She gasped as his fingers briefly, gently, slid into then out of her. Her face looked flushed and her eyes glittered with dark and light. He flipped open the buttons of his breeches, released himself, and moved over her.

"No," she whispered. "No." Yet she opened her legs.

He drove into her instantly.

Bonnie turned her face away, closing her eyes as he rocked back and forth inside her. Her hands twisted into the sheet beneath her, and she groaned, raised her legs high over the small of his back, locking them together tightly before rising to meet his every thrust.

It had never been like this for him. Ever.

She was so tight, so wet, so astoundingly hot he felt as if he was dying. But it was more than that. In one mad moment there had been such a rush of feeling through him he wondered if he had finally lost his mind and succumbed to insanity. Lost. That's all he could think. He was lost, out of control, frantic with desire and rage, wanting all of her—her body, her soul . . .

He rolled to his side, taking her with him, burying his hands in her wild hair and forcing her lips to his. He kissed her with his mouth, his tongue, forcing her head to be still under his as he gripped her hair in his fingers and continued to drive himself inside her, until she was clawing his shoulders and back and arms and struggling to breathe. Until a flush suffused her face and neck and she went rigid with a woman-in-ecstasy cry.

Still he continued, allowing his own climax to build and build, until he was making low animal sounds in his chest and throat, and his body was slamming against hers with an urgency he couldn't control. Suddenly she was crying out again, twisting beneath him, whimpering, "Yes, yes . . ." and groaning with the spasmodic relief for a second time. He felt the flood inside her, the heat that bathed him in wet and fire. Desperate to find it himself, he went on loving her, harder than he had ever loved anyone. Until it seemed his entire life's energy was spent inside her and all he could do was collapse against her.

She lay very still beneath him, arms and legs tangled with his, hair like a fine dark web around them. Rain whispered against the windowpane as silence settled into the shadows. Then Bonnie turned her face up to his, stared at him with those eyes that had given him not one moment's peace since she had stumbled into his life. Who was she? Where had she come from? He felt a sudden desperation to know.

"Who are you, Bonnie? Why were you at Caldbergh?"

"M' parents are dead."

"Who were your parents, and where did you come from?"

She tried to roll away. He pulled her back. "In your dreams you cry out for your father. How did he die?"

"Let me go."

"How did he die?"

"He—he was killed."

"How? When?"

"I don't remember!"

"The hell you don't." He pinned her to the bed with his body. "The least you could do is tell me your last name."

She thrashed beneath him.

"I have a right to know, Bonnie."

"Just cause I was fool enough t' give y' liberties with m' body don't mean y' own me."

"I want to help you."

She turned her face away, refusing to look at him. He lowered his head and flicked his tongue over the thrumming pulse in her throat, ran his mouth down her neck to the base of her collarbone, and inhaled her scent of arousal. He grew hard again, and slid inside her.

"I can't get enough," he groaned. "God help me, I can't get enough of you."

The candle sputtered and went out, but Damien continued to sit in a chair near Bonnie's bed, watching her sleep. The decision had been made. In his present state of mind he could not live in the same house with Bonnie without having her. Time away should remedy that. It had with Louisa, and he'd been in love with her . . .

He closed his eyes.

This wasn't love . . . it wasn't. It was lust, pure and simple. To acknowledge it as anything else would be a foolish mistake.

Still, Marianne had been right. His insatiable desire to have Bonnie had cost her her virginity. He owed her for that. After all, she might meet some sheep farmer someday and want to marry . . .

He smiled. Christ. A sheep farmer. What kind of existence would she have as a sheep farmer's wife? She was beautiful, fiery, and spirited, but soon a life of such hardship would wear her down, weather her, perhaps even kill her.

Damien left the chair and stood by the bed, rubbing a tendril of Bonnie's hair between his fingers. "You deserve better than that," he said.

He stood at his uncle's bedside for several minutes before coming to a decision. "Richard," he said. "Wake up."

Richard grumbled and opened his eyes. "Wh—what the blazes, Damien?"

"I'd like to see you in the library as soon as possible."

Richard sat up in bed, rubbing his eyes. "Good God, it's black as pitch outside."

"No doubt, but business is business."

"Business, is it?"

"In a matter of speaking." Damien walked to the door and in a more authoritative voice added, "I'll expect you in five minutes."

"Of course, my lord."

By the time Richard arrived at the library Damien had settled in his chair. Rearing back, he brushed his lower lip contemplatively with his finger and said, "I want the girl investigated."

"Meaning Bonnie."

"I want to know who she is, where she came from, and why she was at Caldbergh. I want to know who her parents were, and her grandparents. I want the finest investigators in England on the job, and I don't care how much it costs me.''

"Why don't you simply ask her?''

"I tried. I could get more information out of a rock.''

Richard grunted in agreement. ''Am I overstepping my limits by asking *why* you want Bonnie investigated?''

"Yes.''

Richard nodded in understanding. ''Very well. I know a man in York who is more than qualified. I shall query him this very morning. Will that be all?''

"No.'' Damien left his chair and moved to the window. ''I'm leaving Braithwaite for a while.''

"Have you been summoned to London?''

"I'm not traveling to London.''

"No? Then where?''

"I don't know.''

A heavy silence followed. Finally Richard asked, ''Might I ask *why*, Nephew?''

Damien closed his eyes. ''I wish you wouldn't, Richard. I'm not certain I know myself.''

"Restless.''

"Yes.''

Richard poured himself a port before addressing Damien again. ''What do I do with Bonnie while you're gone?''

"Search out the finest tutors in Yorkshire. I want her educated.''

"I see.''

"It's the least I can do.''

"Do you intend to refine her as well?''

"I have someone in mind for that task.''

"What if she refuses? Need I remind you that she does not seem overly fond of Braithwaite? We cannot keep her here if she chooses to leave.''

Damien crossed his arms over his chest and replied, ''That is debatable.''

Richard moved up behind him. ''What do you have in mind, Nephew? Or dare I ask? You have that damnable Warwick tilt to your jaw that can only bode ill. I repeat, you cannot keep the lass here against her will, unless . . . Good God, you cannot think to take legal custody of her.''

"You'll make the arrangements with the magistrate, of

course. I'm certain once you've explained Bonnie's circumstances, the courts will approve. However, unless you can help it, tell Bonnie nothing about my taking guardianship of her until I return.''

"She won't like it, Damien."

"No, I dare say she won't.'' He turned from the window and met his uncle's inquisitive eyes. His brow creased with concern, Richard returned his look without blinking before stepping back and, for the first time, assessing Damien's appearance. When Richard's faded eyes returned to Damien's, there was a knowledge there that set his teeth on edge.

"So," Richard said. "It seems Smythe's accusations have turned into prophecy."

"Hardly," Damien snapped. "I should like to think I am above rape."

Richard turned away angrily. Crossing the room, he drove his fist against the desk before spinning to face Damien again. "You idiot."

Damien walked to the line of decanters and poured himself a whiskey.

"Was she a virgin? Turn around and face me like a man. Have you no conscience, Damien? No concern for another person? My God, man, have you forgotten whatever morals you once possessed?''

Damien regarded his uncle for a long moment before tossing back his drink in one quaff. He slammed the glass down and filled it again. "Obviously I have no morals."

"Obviously. You're just like your father and that black sheep half brother—''

"Careful," Damien snarled, "before you overstep your limits, sir."

"Wasn't it enough that you have one woman in your bed already? You use Marianne as if she's some—''

"No more than she uses me."

"If you grew bored with the woman, you might have gone wenching in Middleham and left the *child* alone. This insatiable lust—''

"Lust has nothing to do with what happened between me and the girl." The admission shook him.

Richard's eyebrows arched in surprise. "No? What do you

call it then? Well? Answer me, Nephew, and assure me that the fruit of my dear sister's womb is not a total reprobate.''

Damien's mouth thinned and his hand tightened around his whiskey glass. He stared at some point over Richard's head before replying evenly, ''I intend to do right by her.''

''I suspect her virginity will cost you dearly, my lord. Not only in money, but also in reputation.''

Damien laughed and brought the glass to his mouth. ''Ah, reputation.'' He drank the glass dry, then walked over to his uncle. ''As you recall, my reputation was spoiled some years ago, thanks to Louisa. Leaving England with my tail between my legs, then returning to plead the South's cause over a war Her Majesty wants no part of, hasn't exactly endeared me to my peers.''

''But what about Bonnie? She's young. She'll want to marry . . .''

''With a large enough dowry to accompany her into matrimony no one will question, or care, whether she's virgin or not.''

''Ah. So that's why you intend to educate and refine her. You're going to marry her off to the first bloodsucker who offers for her.'' Richard slapped a hand on Damien's shoulder. ''My boy, I congratulate you. I'm certain Miles will be thrilled that you have finally sunk to his level. I'm certain he was extremely lonely down there.''

''Go to hell,'' Damien said softly.

A look of surprise, then regret, swept Richard's face as the two men stood toe-to-toe. Dawn light poured gently through the window into the room and over their shoulders.

Less emotionally, Richard said, ''Will you see her again before you leave?''

''No.''

''May I ask why not?''

Damien thought a moment, conscious of the ache that seemed to flow through him at the very idea of facing Bonnie again. He couldn't trust himself. Recalling those moments of half-fierce, half-gentle urgency in her arms; of her clinging to him in fear, then in passion; of her body twisting and meeting his—dear Jesus, the sweet taste of her on his mouth— he felt his lower body grow full and heavy with desire. He hurt with it. But what frightened him most was that he had never—*never*—felt so strongly about a woman. Not Louisa. Not Charlotte Ruth . . . not Marianne. This burning desire was only Bonnie's. Her name was like a brand searing into his brain . . . driving him mad with need and . . .

"Damien."

He looked into Richard's eyes. Experience and understanding stared back at him. Almost as an afterthought, his uncle said, "I see." Then he added, "Well. Rest assured that during your absence Bonnie will be taken care of. Have you some idea how long you will be gone?"

Damien moved toward the door, thinking *as long as it takes to sweat this need for her out of my system.* "None whatsoever," he replied. "I'll write and let you know."

"I shall give your regards to Bonnie."

Damien stopped and looked around. "You do that," he said.

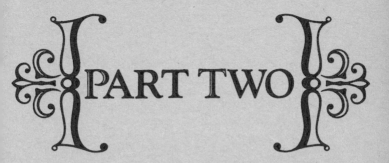

PART TWO

I hate and I love. Why I do so, perhaps you ask. I know not, but I feel it and I am in torment.

—CATULLUS

Twelve

Bonnie rolled a ball of yarn across the floor, laughing as the kittens tumbled over each other in an attempt to catch it. Then she looked toward the door. Richard stood there watching her, his eyes hooded and his face pinched in concentration.

"Hullo," she said, then grinned. "Do y' like the way I said that? That's the way Philippe says 'hello.' "

He nodded, giving Bonnie the impression that he hadn't even heard her.

Bonnie glanced at the letter in his hand. Her heartbeat quickened. "Have y' heard from his lordship?"

"Aye. He'll be home any day."

She turned back to the kittens, her excitement at seeing Damien again soaring then plunging with her mood. She frowned. "I've a good mind t' bugger off before he gets here."

"I wouldn't advise it."

"He don't—doesn't—deserve any better. He didn't exactly offer m' any good-byes before he left."

"There wasn't time. His business was urgent."

Richard's voice was thick, causing Bonnie to forget the kittens and center her attention on him. He'd been drinking heavily again. His eyes were bloodshot, and his nose was red. She could smell the sweet scent of port from across the room. "Is anythin' wrong?" she asked.

He shook his head slowly. "For a moment you reminded me of someone." He slid the letter into his pocket. "How are the lessons coming along? Is Miss Crandall, your new governess, working out?"

Bonnie thought for a moment. At first she had been surprised when informed that Damien had decided to educate and refine her. Then she'd been angry, believing it was his way of making up for his sneaking off in the middle of the night without a fare thee well. She'd rebelled by making the tutors' lives as miserable as possible.

"I can't say as I like her any more than the others."

"Do you enjoy your lessons?"

"Sometimes. I'd rather be out ridin' with Miles."

"You two have grown rather thick. Damien won't like it."

Before she could respond, Richard left the room. She was still watching the door when Jewel entered with Bonnie's tea. Hands shoved in her pockets, Bonnie walked across the floor and dropped into a chair. She kicked a footstool before saying to Jewel, "Ever'one is always sore at Miles. He ain't—hasn't—been so bad t' me."

Jewel poured tea into a cup and handed it to her. "Just keep yer guard up and he's harmless enough. It's when ye ain't expectin' his mischief that he pulls it."

"What did he ever do that was so bad?"

Jewel glanced toward the door, then lowered her voice. "He were always causin' trouble for our lad—Damien. Once, Damien went ridin' and the girth bust on the saddle, spillin' him t' the ground s' hard his ankle was broke. 'Cept on closer inspection the groom discovered that the girth didn't break, it was cut. Another time they was grouse huntin' and Miles's gun went off, supposedly by accident. The bloody bullet missed our lad's head by an inch. I'm tellin' y', lass, stay clear o' that one. There'll be trouble if y' don't. I'd stake m' job on it." With a bob of her head and a sniff, Jewel bustled from the room, her starched skirts rustling in the quiet.

Bonnie drank her tea and considered Jewel's warning. No doubt Miles was a troublemaker—she'd seen enough of them at Caldbergh to recognize the signs. But she understood that people did things occasionally that they didn't really mean. Sometimes they struck out in anger or in pain, or because they wanted attention. She'd been guilty of those pranks herself the last years. Her attack on Damien with the letter opener was proof of that.

Damien.

Bonnie shoved the cup and saucer onto the tray and left

the chair. He would be home soon, and then what? Upon awakening and finding him gone from Braithwaite she'd been assailed with conflicting emotions. She had actually allowed him to make love to her, and more than once. He had come into her room, into her bed, and she had welcomed him with open arms, knowing it wasn't love that drove him, but desire. Just moments before his entering her room the same needs had driven her from her bed with shameful yearnings and memories of his body doing strange and wonderful things inside her. She must have suspected even then, though she hadn't admitted it to herself until days later, when she kept coming up with reason after reason why she couldn't leave Braithwaite.

She was in love with Damien Warwick.

Imagine that. In love with his high and mighty. After scoffing at all those silly fairy tales, she'd found herself swept up in one. The problem was, this high lord didn't love her in return.

She couldn't blame him. Who was she, after all? Just a village girl whose mother and father had done their best to teach her right from wrong. They'd taught her to read and write, how to cook and sew. They'd instilled in her a faith in God and mankind, and enriched her life with love and happiness.

She couldn't quote Shakespeare or Byron or Coleridge. She didn't know who the devil Aristotle was.

Her grammar was atrocious, her elocution disastrous— or so claimed the tutors who had trooped in and out of Braithwaite.

She didn't know one end of an etiquette book from another, and she refused to wear a dress.

But what if . . . ?

What if she *could* quote Shakespeare and Byron and Coleridge? What if she learned who Aristotle was, improved her grammar, and worked on her elocution? She'd overheard Miss Crandall telling Richard that Bonnie seemed very smart, and if she'd cease being stubborn for stubbornness sake, she might even prove to be bright and passably presentable.

It was certainly something to think about.

* * *

"En garde, mon ami, and take care. My prize today may well be your heart."

"Never," Bonnie replied, laughing. "My heart belongs t' me, sir, and no other. I shall not bestow it for anything less than love."

Miles smiled while positioning his sword tip high off the ground. "My thoughts exactly," he parried. "I think it is high time we discussed this matter."

"Yer a bloody rogue," Bonnie teased. "And a scoundrel. I shouldn't trust you as far as I could toss you with one hand."

"Alas, it's a Warwick's fate, I suppose. Watch your stance. You're off balance."

Sunlight glanced off the hilt of Bonnie's sword as she raised the tip of her rapier to touch his. Then, with no warning, she dropped her arm to her side and turned back for the blanket spread beneath a horse chestnut tree. She fell onto it with a sigh and stared up through the branches at the threatening sky. "I don't feel like fencin' today," she told Miles.

"You didn't feel like studying your text either. Miss Crandall is at her wit's end, I fear. Do you intend to send her trotting down the road in a hail of books like you did the others?"

"They bore me. I told Richard: leave the books and I will study 'em in my own good time. I don't like bein' judged by uppity old spinsters. They all think I'm a horror anyway, just because I wear breeches and don't *speak correctly.* "

Miles eased onto the blanket beside her. His curly hair fell over his brow as he laughed, and Bonnie smiled. Despite what the others said, he had been a great companion since Damien's departure, perhaps because, like her, he was somewhat of a misfit at Braithwaite.

Bonnie rolled to her stomach and, propping up on her elbows said, "Tell me again about Paris."

"I've told you about Paris a dozen times."

"Is it beautiful?"

"Occasionally."

"Are the men handsome and romantic?"

"No more than I." He wiggled his eyebrows at Bonnie, and she laughed.

"Tell me about your mother."

He looked surprised. "My mother!" Rolling to his back,

he thought for a moment, his face pensive. "My mother is a whore," he said. "Occasionally she sings opera, but mostly she earns her living on her back. Not flagrant prostitution, mind you. She's more subtle than that. She allows herself to be kept, however, which boils down to the same thing. I really don't like her much, but I see her now and again, for the lack of anything better to do."

"Do you think she loved your father?" Bonnie asked.

"Perhaps. I imagine she thought she did. That's why I wasn't aborted when she learned she was pregnant. She told me once she thought she could win Joseph back if she had his child. Obviously it didn't work. When she realized it, she bundled me up and sent me off to live with dear papa. I was eight at the time. I didn't see her again for six years. Not even a letter."

"You must have been very unhappy," she said.

"Yes. I suppose I was."

"Are you still unhappy?"

"Sometimes."

"And yer lonely too, I suppose. I feel like that, not havin' a home and anyone who truly cares for me."

Miles shifted to his side. "I have a confession to make. Once, I thought to become your friend just to infuriate Damien."

"And now?"

"I sincerely like you."

She smiled, and before she could react he had grabbed her up and turned her over, pressing her flat against the ground. His broad shoulders blocked out the sky as he smiled into her laughing face. "Scoff, will you? I've a mind to show you just how fond of you I've become."

Bonnie squealed with laughter as Miles playfully attempted to kiss her. With a well-planted knee against his stomach she shoved him away and grabbed up her sword. By the time he stumbled to his feet, she had taken her stance, back ramrod straight, arms and knees in position.

"*En garde,*" she said. "Prepare to defend yourself, you ravisher of young maids. You will sorely regret having trifled with Bonnie of Caldbergh—"

"I regret only that you have brought out the gentleman in me, lass. I should have seduced you long ago."

''Try and y'll feel the tip of my sword all the way to yer—''

Bonnie closed her mouth as, beyond Miles, a coach appeared on the horizon. Her heart took an unexpected leap at the sight. Shielding her eyes against the sun, she reasoned aloud, ''It's only a coach. This road is well used. It could be anyone.''

Miles looked around; his face became dark.

''Is that a Braithwaite coach?'' Bonnie asked.

He didn't respond, but drove the tip of his sword into the ground.

''It is!'' she cried. ''Is that Damien, do you think? Of course it is! Miles, Damien has come home!''

Before Miles could respond Bonnie had thrown her sword to the ground and hurried toward the horses grazing nearby. In horror and frustration she watched the skittish animals gallop away. With little recourse, she began running over the heather-topped moor back to Braithwaite.

The wind whipped her face, blistering her cheeks. It teared her eyes and raked her hair. Time after time she tripped in some hole hidden within the grass; her breeches caught upon the sharp edges of the stone walls that she was forced to climb over. She began to sweat.

By the time she rounded the house the coach had arrived. Servants were congregated outside the door. Within the group stood Damien, his back to Bonnie as he spoke to Stanley.

Bonnie froze.

She was not prepared for the shock of feelings that swept through her upon seeing Damien again. For days she had imagined their meeting. She had blundered through her greeting until every word flowed as correctly as any high-stocking's could hope to. Now, as she stood hidden behind a rowan tree, her eyes fixed on Damien's tall frame immaculately encased in a coat of navy blue broadcloth with gold buttons, buckskin breeches, and highly polished Hessians, all the strength left her. Would he think less kindly of her if she ran full-out down the path and threw herself in his arms, as she had that last night at Braithwaite?

Just as she stepped out from around the tree the group of servants parted. Bonnie stopped, her surprise like a fist driven hard into her chest.

A woman stood at Damien's side: a beautiful woman, delicate and demur, her skin like pure cream and her short curly hair like a soft black cloud around her face. Her eyes sparkled up at Damien as she bestowed upon him a generous smile.

Bonnie closed her eyes, a rush of fury and sickness turning her dreamy state into a flood of bitter disgust. She had pined for his return, wanting nothing more than to please him, hoping he might acknowledge the differences in her and see, not the filthy-faced urchin from Caldbergh who had denied her femininity out of fear and desperation, but the woman she longed to be, or could be . . . if he would only care.

But he had returned to Braithwaite with another mistress.

"Fool!" she cried to herself. "Silly, stupid little fool!"

"The transformation has been amazing. Amazing! The lass is a genius, Damien. Never in my fifty-three years have I ever encountered a mind as quick as Bonnie's. And she's quite congenial, you know, aside from running her first two governesses away in a fit of vapors. She has the servants wrapped around her little finger. We've all grown fond of her since you've been away."

Amused, Damien listened to his uncle while he nursed a glass of water.

Richard stopped pacing and regarded Damien in return. "You've lost weight, Nephew, a stone at least. You haven't been ill . . . ?"

"No."

"Ah. All that late night carousing, I suppose. You look positively gaunt."

"Thank you."

"You're welcome."

"Is Miles still about?"

"Of course. He and Bonnie have become quite close."

The drink halfway to his mouth, Damien looked up. "I beg your pardon?" he said.

"Oh, yes. Like Damon and Pythias, those two. You rarely see one without the other. I dare say she's made him forget his unsavory ways and turn over a new leaf."

Damien sat back in his chair and tried to imagine Bonnie and Miles squaring off, but the only image that came to mind was of her stubborn chin tipped in defiance and her magnificent sapphire eyes flashing up at him in anger . . . and passion. That same image had driven him from his bed night after sleepless night. It was no bloody wonder he looked gaunt.

Shoving his drink aside, he asked, "Have you informed her that I am now her guardian?"

"No need. Bonnie's been content."

"She wasn't upset over my leaving?"

Pursing his lips, Richard pondered the question a moment before answering. His hands behind his back, he responded, "She hid her distress well enough. As I recall she said only 'good riddance.' "

"Indeed." Damien glanced through the piles of correspondence stacked atop his desk. There was nothing yet from London. And nothing from Vicksburg. He glanced at Richard again and found his uncle gazing at him rather smugly. Once again he sat back in his chair and stretched his legs negligently before him.

"Obviously you have something on your mind . . ."

"It's Bonnie."

Damien closed his long legs at the ankles and raised his glass of water to his lips. "Carry on."

"She's become quite the young lady, has our Bonnie. Aside from her riding astride and daily duels with swords, she has tamed considerably. And her appearance has become very nearly radiant! Why, if I were a younger—"

In that moment the library door was thrown open. Bonnie stood on the threshold, her hands clenched at her sides, her hair damp with sweat and tangled from the wind. Her shirt and breeches were an ungodly mess of mud and straw, and her face was little better.

Richard, his cheeks pale with shock, looked at Damien in utter horror. "Great Caesar's ghost!"

Leaving his chair, Damien grinned. "It seems," he drawled, "that you've never learned to knock. I'll have to speak to Miss Crandall on that matter."

"Y' can take that old battle ax and—"

"Careful, love. I would hate to have to wash your mouth out with soap so soon after my arrival."

She stormed across the floor like a small whirlwind and

planted herself before his desk. "I'd like to see y' try," she snapped.

"Is that a dare?" he replied dryly.

Bonnie squared her shoulders and refused to respond.

Damien gazed down at the girl standing so bravely, irately before him, at her blazing eyes, at her mutinous mouth that always, even in the throes of anger, quirked up at both delicious pink corners, and he wondered if Richard had finally imbibed too frequently of his port. There was nothing remotely ladylike about Bonnie. To call her congenial was an absurd stretch of the imagination. Yet . . .

There *was* a difference. The smudge of dirt across her cheek seemed a little out of place now. The hair flowing so wildly about her face and shoulders was lush with cleanliness. Her once pallid complexion now glowed with vibrant health. And though she looked as if she had spent the day shoveling out the stables, there was the slightest scent of soap teasing his nostrils.

His first rush of anger having dissolved, Damien relaxed, swept her stormy blue eyes and obviously trembling figure with a glance, and wondered why he was besieged by this all-consuming ache to possess her, to tame her without breaking her spirit.

"What do you want?" he asked more softly.

"I'm leavin'," she said.

"Oh?"

"Aye. This very minute. I've just been waitin' for you t' come home because . . . because . . ."

Damien crossed his arms over his chest.

". . . because I wanted t' tell y' myself that yer the most ill-mannered bad-tempered ass in all of England. Yer arrogant too. And yer rude. Just as soon as I pack my few meager belongin's I'm leavin' Braithwaite forever."

Bonnie turned on her heel and started back toward the door. She stopped abruptly as Damien replied in a droll voice, "Impossible."

She partially turned and looked over her shoulder at him, then at Richard.

"Impossible," Damien repeated. For the first time since Bonnie's unexpected entry, Damien glanced at his uncle, who had been viewing the spectacle with something short of amazement. "Would you care to explain to Bonnie *why* her leaving Braithwaite is impossible?" Damien asked.

Clearing his throat, Richard took a stance at Damien's side. "Because, my dear young lady, you are now bound by document to his lordship. He is now your legal guardian. He is responsible for you until you turn twenty-one, unless, of course, you decide to marry before then. In such a case you would need his lordship's permission, of course. Until that time he will provide you with all the amenities necessary to make your life at Braithwaite as happy and fulfilled as possible, including home, food, clothes, education, travel and, at the time of your marriage, a dowry as handsome as any young woman of good birth could offer to her new husband."

Pausing, Richard shuffled through the papers on Damien's desk until he located a sheaf of documents. "There are a few technicalities that must be cleared up. First of all, according to Caldbergh's files, you have never divulged your last name, where you are from, or your date of birth. The magistrate was somewhat lenient here, since this action is not, in all actuality, an outright adoption. He also recognized the importance of removing you from Caldbergh. For the record's sake, would you care to tell us your last name?"

Her eyes burning into Damien's, Bonnie shook her head.

"We know you are from West Yorkshire, but exactly what township in West Yorkshire?" Richard waited for Bonnie's response. It didn't come. "I see. Well, will you at least give us your exact age? For the record we estimated your age at fif—"

"Eighteen."

A deafening silence seemed to implode in the room as all eyes turned to Damien. As Bonnie began to smile, his face turned a slow, burning red. Idiot, he thought as he frantically searched Bonnie's appearance for some truth to her words. He had driven himself half mad because he'd actually believed Bonnie to be some innocent babe he had seduced in a rutting fever. Idiot. He could see it now. During his absence she had put on much needed weight. Her shirt fit snugly across her breasts, her hips were more rounded. Idiot.

Bonnie, having faced Damien fully, asked in a voice quavering with rage, "Does this mean I'll be expected t' call y' *father* from now on?"

The implication drove home like a battering ram. "Good God," he breathed aloud, "no."

"My feelin's exactly. In fact, there is nothin' in that document that can force me t' stay here if I desire t' leave. Which I do. And if you wish t' drag me kickin' and screamin' before that bloody magistrate, I will be more than happy t' inform him of every *intimate* detail about my life at Braithwaite." Bonnie spun back toward the door so suddenly, so swiftly, that her hair flew in a stormy, black cloud around her shoulders.

"Come back here!" Damien ordered.

When she didn't respond he came out from behind his desk and in three long strides caught up with her at the door. He grabbed her arm and jerked her around.

"Let me go!" she cried. "Y' cannot force me t' stay here!"

"Can't I? Try me. And while you are defiling my name to the court, I will be there to add that you and Smythe defrauded me out of five hundred quid!"

"Ohhh!" she screamed. "I did absolutely nothin' of the sort!"

"Right." He smiled. "And who do you think the courts will believe? There are servants all over Braithwaite who witnessed your stealing my pewter and food. Your character, pet, leaves a lot to be desired."

Bonnie tried once more to extricate her arm from Damien's grip. Finding it impossible, she glared at him and hissed, "I have no intention of stayin' in this house again while you parade yer mistress about these halls as if this was a friggin' harem."

"Mistress? What mistress?"

"Marianne. And now that *other* one. Don't deny it. I saw her arrive with y'." With a toss of her head, Bonnie looked away, centered her attention on the massive walnut-banistered stairwell, and added, "She is very pretty, yer lordship. Younger than the red-haired tart by numerous years. I would not have taken her for a trollop had I met her on the street."

Unable to believe what he was hearing, Damien laughed aloud. Aware the house was ominously quiet, therefore assuring him that the entire staff was no doubt congregated behind some door listening to every word that passed between him and Bonnie, he lowered his voice to just above a whisper. "You're jealous, aren't you?"

Bonnie's head jerked around. Her eyes were wide, and the angry flush staining her cheeks literally drained from her face. "Jealous!" She almost choked. "Don't be daft!"

"No? Not even a little?"

"Of course not. Why should I be?"

He relaxed his grip on her, ran his hand tenderly up and down her arm as if the action would remind her of another time, when anger had turned to desire and then to passion. Then realizing the foolishness of such a gesture, he stepped away, dropping his hand to his side with a reluctance he loathed admitting even to himself.

In that instant the front door opened. Damien's guest stepped in, her midnight hair sparkling with drops of rain that had just begun to fall from the dreary sky. Her arms were full of fresh cut flowers. They, along with her apricot dress, gave her creamy complexion a radiant glow that was almost breathtaking. She exclaimed, "Damien, darling, the flowers are absolutely heavenly!"

Bonnie, white to her lips, looked up at Damien with eyes that were as dark and wet as the approaching night sky. Without speaking, she turned and ran up the stairs, ignoring him as he called out her name. She marched to her room and slammed the door behind her. She hurried to the wardrobe and dug out a valise she had hidden there upon first learning that Damien had left Braithwaite.

"I should've gone," she stormed aloud. "But no. I had t' wait for him t' flaunt another bloody mistress in m' face."

There came a knock at the door.

"Go away!" she shouted.

The door opened and Jewel peeped in. "I've brung ye a present from his lordship," she announced.

In the process of stuffing a shirt into the valise, Bonnie hesitated, frowning. "A present?"

"Aye." Jewel nudged the door open further and offered the parcel. Bonnie eyed it suspiciously. "Go on and take it, lass. It won't bite."

"I-I don't want it."

"O' course ye do. He says he brought it all the way from York."

Jewel placed the package on the bed, and smiling, quit the room. Bonnie chewed her lip and tried to remember the last time anyone had ever given her anything. Not since her father had died, that was certain. Still, she didn't want it. He only brought it to assuage his own conscience for treating her so shabbily, for foisting another mistress on her after she'd pined for his return . . . after she'd imagined she'd actually fallen in love with him . . .

She turned her back to it and focused on the valise. Or tried to. Her attention kept being drawn back to the parcel wrapped in bright pink paper and a white satin ribbon. Tears burned her eyes, and angrily she snatched up the package and said, "Y' bloody bastard, how dare y' make a fool out of me. How dare y' make me think for a minute that y' really cared."

She raised her arm to hurl the box across the room. But she couldn't do it. Instead, she tore the ribbon and paper away with trembling fingers, occasionally swiping the tears from her cheeks with the back of one hand. She opened the tissue-lined box and withdrew the gift.

"Oh," she whispered. "Oh my."

It was a music box. Once released from its wrappings, the porcelain couple, dressed in courtly attire and smiling into each other's face, began a slow pirouette to the tinkling, lighthearted music that filled up the silence. But it was the card Damien had attached to the dancers that broke her heart. He had signed it: "With love."

Thirteen

"Damien, you should have told her I am your sister," Kate said. "The poor dear was absolutely beside herself with fury."

"She didn't give me the chance."

"Somehow I doubt that. Really, Damien, at times I think you take pleasure in irritating the world. Why is that, do you think?"

"I really haven't given it a great deal of thought, chooch. I suppose it's because the world seems so intent on irritating me."

Damien smiled at his sister as they sauntered down the flagstone path toward the rose garden. A breeze stirred the leaves of a tree under which they were passing, scattering raindrops over their shoulders. Coming to a wrought iron bench, Damien removed his jacket and placed it on the bench so his sister might sit and relax after their grueling journey from York. She thanked him with a fond smile before saying, "Bonnie is a beautiful young woman."

"Do you think so?"

"Highly unusual. I imagine that had she been gently born, educated, and properly prepared for society, she would have been the rage of all London during her Season."

Knowing Kate continued to regard him in amused curiosity, Damien slid his hands into his pockets and gazed over the rose garden, doing his best to ignore her. She had a way of seeing right through him which had, through their years of growing up together, allowed him little privacy of thought or feeling.

"Is that why you've brought me here?" she asked. "Do

you want me to refine her?'' When Damien didn't respond, Kate added, ''Are you in love with her?''

He looked around in surprise. ''In love?'' He laughed. ''With the urchin? Good God, chooch, don't be ridiculous.''

''You've dragged me back to Braithwaite for some reason, and I highly doubt it's *only* because you wish for us to 'become reacquainted' as you mentioned. I suspect we did that while you visited with William and me at Bradhurst.''

''I've missed you, for God's sake.''

''Missed me? You wrote me exactly twice the entire six years you were in Mississippi, then it was only to say hello, how are you? I'm fine and good-bye. Honestly, Damien, you never could lie worth a damn.''

Arching one eyebrow, Damien glanced askew at his sister and said, ''Since when did you learn how to curse?''

''Since I married your best friend. And don't change the subject.''

The bushes by Damien's leg began to rattle. Then the water-heavy leaves parted and a kitten leaped out, pounced upon his leg with all the ferocity of a young lion on a kill, and sank its claws into his boot. Kate burst out laughing as Damien raised his leg, caught the kitten by the scruff of the neck, and lifted it to eye level. It stared at Damien with one eye ringed in black, the other in white.

''How very adorable,'' Kate said. ''Is it a pet?''

''Bonnie's.''

''What's his name?''

''Her,'' he corrected. ''And it's Winkin. Or is it Blinkin?'' Damien dropped onto the bench beside Kate, allowing the frisky oat to crouch on his lap. Occasionally it would stretch one paw up and bat at Damien, making Kate break out again and again in a fit of giggles that eventually brought tears to her eyes and a scowl from Damien that made Kate laugh that much harder.

He would never be certain where the confession came from or why he made it. But suddenly it was there on his lips and he couldn't stop it.

''I've made love with her, Kate.''

The laughter stopped.

Tossing the kitten to the ground where it scampered into the bushes, Damien took a breath and admitted, ''She was a virgin and I took her. I seduced her. And the night before I left Braithwaite I did it again."

Unblinking, she stared at Damien in horrified amazement. "Oh dear," she finally managed.

Her small hands twisted together in her lap, and her face turned a burning hot pink as the implication gradually took hold of her mind and senses. Then, very slowly, she left the bench and Damien knew, before she opened her mouth, that he was in for a tongue-lashing of the worst degree.

"You hot-blooded young ram!" she cried. "Do you realize what you've done?"

Damien opened his mouth to respond, but wasn't given the opportunity.

"You hypocrite! You, who threatened William within an inch of his life if he dare lay a *hand* on me, much less anything else . . . *you,* who would not allow us alone together for five minutes for fear it would somehow taint my reputation . . . *you,* who continually reminded William of the virtues of cherishing a woman's chastity until marriage, have ruined that helpless young woman!"

Damien negligently crossed his legs and laughed harshly. "Helpless," he drawled sarcastically. "She's about as helpless as a wild she-cat, Kate. She might have stopped me, you know."

"Would it have done any good to try? No doubt, in the throes of panting ecstasy, you mumbled something stupid and typically male like 'I can't wait, darling, I've wanted you for all of my life and I will make it good for you if you will only *let* me,' or some such stuff."

"Careful, chooch," he said in a silky, threatening voice. "I repeat, she might have stopped me. I was not totally out of my mind and senses. I was still rational."

A brief flare of amusement replaced the anger in Kate's eyes. "Well, it's quite obvious why she didn't; she's enamored of you, Damien."

Damien left the bench in one smooth motion. He walked partially up the path before turning angrily to face her again. "My sweet, naive sister, I beg to differ. She loathes me and tells me so with every other breath she takes. I have a scar on my arm where she set upon me with a letter opener to prove it."

"There is a fine line between love and hate."

Damien regarded his sister, her obstinate chin, her flashing eyes. He had always admired her spirit, her slight unconventionality that set her apart from her peers. Now, however, as he noted those very assets he so admired about Kate, he realized it was those same quirks of personality that made him now think of Bonnie, imagining her standing there dressed in London's finest satins and silks, shaking her fist in the face of convention.

Without speaking to Kate again, Damien turned on his heel and walked up the path, brushing against water-heavy roses as he went. Once, he closed his hand around one, shredding its tender petals from the stem until they bunched like so much confetti in the hollow of his palm. Stopping at the top of the path, he opened his hand and rubbed the dew-kissed petals between his fingers, annoyed that the fragrant, velvety texture of the flower reminded him of Bonnie, of the smoothness of her cheek beneath his fingers when he kissed her. Then a wind whipped up from the moor, cool and smelling of musty heather and rain, and scattered the petals over the pathway at his feet. Damien glanced once at Bonnie's bedroom window, then entered the house.

Bonnie was standing by the window, her head partially down so she appeared to be watching something in the garden. The wind stirred her hair. Sunset cast a blush upon her features not unlike the rose blooms he had earlier stroked. She gripped the music box to her breast.

She must have sensed his presence there, at the door, for her head slowly turned and she regarded him with stormy eyes full of light and dark. Her hair was loose and appeared windblown. It gave her a wild look, stirring the savage within him. It hit Damien full force. As he stood there, his height and shoulders filling the big door, he felt weakened, like an alcoholic too long without drink, a babe too long without nourishment; he shook with it, this need to touch her, to bury himself inside her, to have her wrap her arms around him and breathe her warm breath against the moist skin just behind his ear. He'd been fooling himself by thinking time and distance would kill this hunger for her. He must have been insane to think that by becoming her guardian he would

somehow see her as something other than the desirable creature who'd made him burn with need.

"I meant wot I said," came her voice, sounding abnormally heavy in the encroaching shadows. "I'm leavin'."

He watched her fingers tighten around the music box, and
he said, "Don't you like your present?"

She gripped the porcelain piece a second longer, then put
it down on the windowsill, refusing to look at it again. "I
don't want it. If y' think buyin' me trinkets'll make up for
wot y've done, yer wrong. I'm leavin' and nothin' y' say or
do is gonna change m' mind."

Damien took a breath and released it. "Where do you intend to go?"

"York."

"What will you do there? Scrub floors?"

Her lower lip quivered a little. Silence dragged on while
Damien thought, *Go then, and good riddance. Get out now,
you odd beautiful haunted child, and leave me in peace. I am
weary of denying and fighting this unnatural desire for you.*

"Nothing you say can make me stay," Bonnie replied, and
Damien wondered if it was fear or something else that made
her voice quaver.

He walked through the room and stopped at the foot of the
bed. An unfamiliar valise was placed there, and he wondered
where she'd found it. Then it moved, as if its sides were
nudged from the inside. It rocked back and forth and finally
spilled onto its side. The taffy-colored kitten rolled in a small,
furry ball over the bed and landed with a thud on the floor
by his feet. He bent over and scooped it up in his hand.

Bonnie stood rock still before the window, the light now
like a blaze of fire over her shoulders as she fixed him with
her frantic eyes, questioning his intent.

"Why do you look at me like that?" he asked softly.

"I wasn't stealin' her," she said. "Y' gave her to me."

Damien scratched the kitten behind its ears and felt its
warm belly vibrate against his hand. He walked to the window and noted that he could just see the bench in the distance, and Kate. Without looking at Bonnie, he said, "Will
you have dinner with me, Bonnie?"

She shook her head, spilling her soft black hair around her
face.

He smiled. "Ah, but I insist. There is someone I want you to meet. Besides, it may well be your last decent meal for some time."

Her eyes still on the kitten, Bonnie chewed her lower lip in concentration.

Tucking the kitten in the crook of his arm, Damien turned back for the door and, once reaching it, stopped. "Perhaps over dinner we can discuss the custody of the cat, among other things. Is that agreeable?"

With some reluctance, she finally nodded, and Damien left the room.

Stanley was just entering the vestibule as Damien descended the stairs. Dropping the kitten into the servant's hands, he said, "Have someone round up the other two kittens. I think you'll find them in the rose garden."

"What shall we do with them once we've found them, my lord?"

"Hide them."

Stanley's eyebrows raised. "Hide them, sir?"

"Correct."

"Might I ask *why,* your lordship?"

"Certainly," he said. "We're holding them hostage, Stanley."

Jewel's reflection beamed at Bonnie in the mirror as the servant skillfully brushed her hair and plaited it with ribbons that cascaded over her shoulders with her hair.

"There ain't been no lady's maid at Braithwaite since her ladyship died," Jewel said. "She were a fine mistress, was Damien's mother. She were blessed with a heart of gold." Jewel stepped away from Bonnie and, plunking her hands on her hips, nodded with grave satisfaction at her handiwork. "Seems I still got the touch. Them ribbons bring out the blue in yer eyes, fer sure. D'ya like 'em, lass?"

Bonnie gazed at her image and brushed the satin smoothness of the bright blue ribbons with her fingertips before smiling. "'M' mum wore ribbons," she said. "Her hair was long and black, and she would gather it away from her face and tie it with a bow on the back of her head. M' da would buy her ribbons for her birthday and Christmas because they were her favorite gifts, and because he really couldn't afford anything finer. Mum lost one once and cried for a week. On his only day off work Da walked ten miles t' the nearest Gypsy camp t' buy her a new one.''

Bonnie lowered her head, embarrassed because her eyes had filled with tears. In a softer voice, she said, ''Da was like that. He seemed a little gruff most of the time, and sometimes he frightened me. But he was gentle as a lamb with me and m' mum. I remember how she would stand just outside the door of our house and watch for him returnin' from work. She'd wait until he walked through the gate, then he'd place his lunch pail on top of the stone fence surroundin' our cottage and he'd brace his legs apart and open his arms. She'd run down the path with her hair flyin' out behind her and throw herself int' his arms. He would be covered with black soot and his face would be streaked by sweat, but it didn't matter t' her. He'd always laugh and say 'Careful, darlin', or ye'll spoil yer pretty clothes,' and she'd say, 'So I'll wash 'em. Just kiss me, m'love.' And of course he would, right there in the garden for all the world and God t' see. They would laugh then, and spin around. Their laughter would echo all the way down the moor.'' Bonnie sighed. ''When I dream of love,'' she said, ''that's what I imagine it's like.''

She didn't realize until then that Jewel had placed a comforting hand on her shoulder. She was surprised to look in the mirror and see the woman's eyes as tear-filled as her own.

''You should know, lass, that we've come t' care deeply for y'. I wish y'd reconsider leavin' us.''

Bonnie placed her hand over Jewel's and squeezed it affectionately. ''I've been horrid and I'm sorry. For so long there was so little t' trust in or t' hope for and so much t' despise. It's very hard t' forget all that and t' learn how t' dream again, t' trust, and even t' love. Love is unsettlin' when you've been so long without it.''

Bonnie left her chair and smoothed her hands over her shirt, making certain it was clean and tucked neatly under the waistband of her breeches. She checked her shoes for any spot of mud she might have missed, then smiled at Jewel. ''I 'spect his high and mighty is waitin'. Think I'll pass inspection?''

''Aye, lass. I've never seen a young lady look so lovely in breeches.''

"Right then," she said. "Let's go."

On the way down Bonnie did her best to prepare herself for her final meeting with Damien. Her chest ached so badly she could hardly breathe.

The others had gathered in the gold drawing room adjacent to the dining room. Bonnie remained outside the door as she waited for her racing heart to slow and her breathing to become normal once again. She noted Richard first, then Miles who stood with his back to the door as he gazed out the window.

The woman sat in an armchair near the fire, gazing into the flames. She was smiling, perhaps laughing at something Damien had just said to her.

Her heart in her throat, Bonnie forced her gaze up to Damien's and was startled to find that he was watching her from his place next to the woman. There was a ruthless nobility about his dark features. He seemed so inordinately tall and intimidating, his shoulders filling out the impeccably cut lines of the black dinner jacket he wore. As Damien raised his glass of champagne to his lips, he continued to watch her. She felt swallowed by his eyes, by the implacable authority that radiated around him. She suddenly could not breathe. Her hand flew to her throat and clutched the collar of her shirt closed. She desperately wanted to hide. Perhaps she should leave now, before all the memories of his loving her tumbled in on her and made escape impossible.

"Bonnie!"

It was Richard, snapping her from her reverie. Then the woman looked up, so beautiful Bonnie felt sickened by her own lack of sophistication. She felt foolish for ever hoping and dreaming that the lord of this manor would see her for something other than his "urchin." For she could never *ever* be anything but that, she suddenly, regrettably realized.

"Stop hovering there like a timid bird," Miles said. "Come in."

She started to, but the woman left her chair and was suddenly gliding toward her. Bonnie stared at her dress, thinking she had never seen anything so fine or extravagant. It was all she could do to stand her ground, to summon the pride that had never deserted her the entire five years at Caldbergh.

Taking a breath, she looked the woman in the eyes and . . . smiled.

"M' lady," she said. "I am honored t' make your acquaintance."

"Oh my," the woman said. "How very proper. Damien, will you please introduce us so we can forget all this tedious formality?"

Damien drained his glass and put it on the mantel. Bonnie raised her chin as he moved in all his catlike grace toward her, absently adjusted his sleeves over his cuffs and shifting his shoulders inside his jacket. His mouth had taken on that rakish, lopsided smile that made Bonnie's blood warm. Briefly closing her eyes, she steeled herself for the overwhelming effect his nearness always had on her senses.

"Hello, Bonnie," Damien said.

She opened her eyes and felt her knees turn to water. She managed to take a breath, but barely.

Damien slid his arm around the woman's waist and pulled her closer. "Bonnie, I would like you to meet someone very special to me. Lady Katharine Bradhurst." His devastating mouth turned up even more as he finished. "My sister."

Stanley entered the room and announced dinner.

Richard set his port aside and left his chair.

Miles hurried across the room and offered his hand to Bonnie. "May I see you to your chair?" he asked.

Bonnie stared down at his arm in a sort of daze. Sister. Bloody hell, the woman was his sister.

She felt Miles take her arm and wrap it over his. Then she was moving toward the dining room, followed by Damien and his . . . *sister?*

Miles escorted her to the far end of the mammoth table where all five place settings had been set. She was seated between Miles and Damien, Miles being to her immediate left, Damien, at the head of the table, to her right. Richard and Katharine sat across from her.

The food was served, but Bonnie couldn't eat. She was far too conscious of Damien, the way his long tanned fingers gripped the heavy silverware or lightly caressed the delicate stem of his crystal wineglass. His hair had been earlier brushed into place, but now it tumbled over his brow, dark and shiny as a raven's wing as it reflected the light from the chandelier. She memorized the way his straight dark lashes looked against his skin as he concentrated on his meal. She watched his mouth as he drank his wine, and she recalled how hot and wet and hungry it felt moving on her own.

"Bonnie," Katharine said, "Damien tells us you're leaving Braithwaite."

Damien looked up, straight into Bonnie's eyes. Her face burning, she quickly directed her attention to Damien's sister and nodded in response.

"I'm terribly sorry to hear that. I was so hoping we could become companions during my stay here."

Surprised, Bonnie said, "Why would you care t' be companions with me?"

Equally surprised, Katharine responded, "Why not?"

"I ain't exactly yer peer," Bonnie said, a bit of her old sarcasm returning, challenging the young woman who looked only a few years older than Bonnie.

"Oh, that doesn't matter at all. One of my very dearest friends throughout my childhood was the daughter of one of my father's tenants, until she married a young man from Leeds and left Middleham. We still correspond. As I recall she had quite a crush on Damien. She very nearly swooned each time he rode by on one of his hunters. He winked at her once, and she fainted to the ground."

Bonnie couldn't help herself; she smiled in understanding.

"When do you propose to leave?" Richard asked.

"Tomorrow mornin'," Bonnie said.

Miles, having remained silent for the majority of the meal, placed his knife and fork on his plate and looked sternly at Bonnie. "Well, I for one, am in total disagreement with this arrangement. I don't want you to go; it's simple as that."

Damien, having raised his wineglass nearly to his mouth, paused and stared at Miles over the rim. There was something threatening in the way his fingertips suddenly gripped the fragile crystal.

Bonnie, her heightened senses detecting the sudden oppressive tension, glanced at Damien, then at Miles who, by now, was leaning close to her, his arm slung familiarly over the back of her chair. His smile was rakishly appealing as he said to the others, "Bonnie and I have become the best of friends. I should miss her terribly if she left."

Richard cleared his throat, and in an attempt to alleviate the growing tension, bantered, "No doubt. We all will, I'm certain. Especially Miss Crandall. She will be devastated by the news."

"Whom shall I ride with every day?" Miles continued. "Who will duel with me beneath chestnut trees on lazy, sunny afternoons?" More closely, so his words were but a soft breath against her ear, he added in a whisper, "And who is the most alluring young creature ever to fill out a pair of breeches?"

Damien placed his glass on the table with a thunk. "If Bonnie wishes to leave Braithwaite, then Bonnie may leave Braithwaite. We certainly don't want to keep her here if she isn't happy."

Her head snapping around, her eyes wide, Bonnie stared at Damien with the words, *But I am happy. Very happy!* on the tip of her tongue.

"Do you still plan on going to York?" Katharine asked.

Bonnie looked at her plate without responding.

"Although my husband and I have a town house in London, our permanent home is just outside York. You'll be welcome to visit any time."

"What time did you wish to set off?" Damien asked.

"I—"

"There will be a coach at your disposal whenever you're ready."

Her head came up. "A coach?"

He smiled at her lazily while swirling the claret in its glass. "Surely you didn't think I am so ungracious as to allow you to *walk* to York."

She could not sit there a moment longer and hear them all discuss her departure as if it meant nothing to them. Slowly she left her chair and quit the room. She was halfway to the vestibule when Damien's voice stopped her.

"Bonnie."

She turned. He stood in the shadows of the hallway, his weight resting on one leg, a white linen napkin trailing from the fingers of his left hand. "The coach will be ready at dawn."

"Y' just can't bloody wait t' be rid of me, can you?" she cried. Then realizing how weak and foolish and hurt she must have sounded, she spun and ran for the stairs, taking them two at a time. She was nearly to her room before he had caught up to her. She reached for her door and he grabbed her, spinning her around to face him, his fingers biting into her wrist like the jaws of a trap.

His face flushed with wine and heat and anger, Damien tipped his dark head over Bonnie's and sneered, "It's what you wanted! You wanted out so you've got it. So what the hell is wrong with you now?"

"Yer hurtin' me," she said through her teeth.

Gradually, he released her. But as she made a quick turn back toward the door, he was suddenly blocking her way, his right arm slammed against the doorjamb like a fallen oak. "The least you could do," he said, "is say good-bye."

She tried and the word stuck in her throat.

"Come, come," he drawled, "since when have you been without words, Bonnie? Or perhaps you're saving them all for Miles. Perhaps you are wishing he was standing here instead of me."

She tried her best to step around him, to duck under his arm, but to no avail. When she thought to back away, his left arm came around her, pinning her in her tracks.

"Not so fast," he said icily. "There are a few things still to be said."

Bonnie's breath froze at his nearness. They stood only a fraction of an inch apart, he towering above her like some furious pagan god with eyes as green as bottle glass. The large, hard hand placed firmly against the small of her back felt like a firebrand burning her skin; his clean, starched-linen scent, mixed with the faintest hint of the claret he'd been drinking, made her mind reel with frightening confusion. He was standing too damnably close. If she didn't move now—

Then his hands were on her shoulders, gripping her tightly, lifting her to the tips of her toes. For a moment she thought—

"Why must you continually fight me?" he demanded. *"Why!"*

His mouth was just above hers, his breath hot against her lips. She heard herself groan and say, "Please . . . oh don't, please . . ."

"I did everything I could to make you happy, Bonnie. I

was willing to share with you my home and wealth and whatever respect my name could bring you, yet you throw it back in my face, preferring poverty!''

''Y' don't understand . . .'' Bonnie closed her eyes, wincing at the hard bite of his fingers in her flesh.

''Look at me, damn it, and explain. I'm willing to listen, Bonnie. Just tell me, for God's sake, so I *can* understand.''

They stood that way for what seemed like minutes. Then Bonnie opened her eyes.

Something deep in Damien's chest turned over. Suddenly he had a distinctly queasy feeling. She was immensely vulnerable, and her vulnerability was becoming his own. He should let her go, send her on her way, and say to hell with it.

He forced himself to release her and step away. ''Should you change your mind and decide to stay at Braithwaite, you are more than welcome. My protection comes with no strings attached. What happened between us . . . won't happen again, Bonnie, if that's what you're afraid of. I promise you that. It should never have happened in the first place, considering your dislike for me. I took advantage of you and I'm sorry. I'll do my damnedest to make it up to you if you'll let me.''

There. He'd said it. He tried to take a breath, but it wouldn't come. There was only Bonnie, with her questioning eyes and her silent pride that unnerved and unmanned him.

He stepped around her and walked away, stopping as he reached the top of the stairs. Bonnie remained where he'd left her, awash in shadows, her face pale in contrast to her dark hair and eyes. Damien felt the unwelcome, disconcerting stirring inside him again, then turned and descended the stairs.

Fourteen

That night Bonnie prayed for rain and got it.

Jewel said she hadn't seen such a deluge since four summers ago. Bonnie remembered the time—storms had raised the river Cover well above its banks. The waters had rushed in a torrent down the muddy fells, toppling turf and trees and cottages. But this rain was worse. Far worse. The crash of thunder that shook the ground and house seemed like a rending of the entire earth and sky, jarring her from her half-conscious state as she lay dreading the coming of dawn, when she would be forced, by her pride, to leave Braithwaite as she had threatened.

For the next half hour she sat upright in bed, holding the cherished music box, trying to convince herself that his reason for giving her such a gift was only to soothe his conscience, not because he really cared for her. And it wasn't as if he'd really asked her not to leave Braithwaite. Was it?

She closed her eyes as the memory of his making love to her in this very bed shook her as explosively as the thunder overhead. Drawing her knees up to her chest, she clasped them tightly with her arms and rocked back and forth, damning the tears that surged into her tired eyes and spilled down her face. He actually believed she disliked him. Bloody fool, did he think she'd allow him to make love to her if she hadn't felt something for him? Now he had signed that horrible contract of guardianship that tore asunder any hope she might have secretly coveted of his ever loving her in return.

It was a bitter pain, like a yawning black hole that stretched bleakly and forever before her. There was no one to love except a few scrawny kittens . . .

* * *

Damien also lay awake in his bed, listening hard after each crack of thunder for Bonnie's cry, dreading it, knowing he dare not enter that room again to hold her and soothe away her nightmares. He had taken on the role of her guardian—yes, to make certain she would never want for anything in her life, but mostly because he actually hoped he would come to see her in a different light. But he'd known since the moment that afternoon when she stormed into the library, her hair wild as a moor wind and her face streaked with dirt, that his hunger for her had not been dampened the last weeks. The surcease he'd found in other women's arms the past weeks had been far from satisfying, leaving him with a deeper, darker, more despairing ache.

Throwing back the covers, Damien left his bed and stood in the darkness while the draft through the distant open door of his bedroom raked his naked flesh like icy breaths. His lower body felt full and tight again. Miserably so. He paced, forward and back across the room, to the window and back to the bed, to the highboy against the wall and back to the chair before the hearth. He reached for a cigar in the carved ivory box on a low table by the chair, but didn't light it. He flung it into the hearth with all his strength and cursed. Then, out of desperation, he did something he had never done before. He purposefully called up the image of Louisa and her lover together, every minute detail. How she had looked with her long white legs thrown open wide to receive him; the look of mindless ecstasy on his face as he slid inside her. Damien forced his mind to picture it over and over, everything—her gasp of pleasure, her lover's groan of desire—over and over until the image began to blur and distort like watercolors on paper.

Leaning against the back of a chair, his head down, his body damp with sweat, Damien opened his eyes. A concerned voice called out in the quiet, "My lord!", and he realized that Stanley had been standing there for some time, trying to get his attention.

Without looking at the servant, Damien took a breath and released it. "What is it?" he asked.

"It's Bonnie, sir . . . I fear she's gone."

Damien stood upright. He looked at the servant, noting his

tousled gray hair and fine silk dressing gown. Stanley stepped closer, unperturbed by Damien's state of undress.

"I was up to light the fires for Cook, sir. I found the front door open. I took the liberty of checking the girl's room; she isn't there."

Damien grabbed for the trousers he had thrown over the back of a chair. Stanley reached for a shirt, holding it up and open for Damien to slide his arms into it.

They turned in unison for the door. He took the stairs two at a time and hit the vestibule floor running, sliding on the rain-slick marble, nearly losing his balance. He threw open the door and ran into the stormy night just as a bolt of lightning ripped through the clouds and exploded in a shower of fire and sparks against some ancient crooked tree on a distant fell. Damien cried out, "Bonnie!"

The rain drowned the sound of his voice as he ran down the drive, calling and calling until his throat turned raw and hoarse, until he thought he would drown from his inability to capture even a single breath through the deluge. Beyond him the tree fire blazed, casting contorted light that writhed with the wind and rain. The wood of the old tree groaned as if it were dying, its hard wood snapping and cracking and hissing long tongues of steam into the boiling air. Shielding his face with the crook of his elbow, Damien did his best to see down the river of water that had been the road, then he heard his name being called.

Stanley, his hair plastered against his head and his dressing gown clinging to his body, waved his arms frantically and pointed toward the rose garden. Damien struck out in a run, bogging up to his bare ankles in mud as he leaped over a hedge. Still he ran until he reached the flagstone pathway, then he paused, searching the darkness.

He ran down the path until he saw her. He plowed through the rose bushes, vaguely aware of the thorns stabbing and slicing his arms. Another bolt of lightning struck the earth nearby as he bent and swooped her off her hands and knees and into his arms. She clung to him as he turned back for the house, burying her face in his chest for protection against the needlelike rain that was driving furiously against them.

Stanley waited by the door, a blanket uplifted to wrap around Bonnie as Damien entered the house. Damien then hurried her to the library, where a fire had already been started. He fell into the wing chair before the hearth and gripped Bonnie to his chest.

"Jesus Almighty Christ, Bonnie, what in the name of all that is holy did you think you were doing?" He pulled the blanket more tightly around her as she began to shake. "Jesus," he repeated, rocking a little as he held her tighter. "You might have been killed, you little idiot. And for what?" He grabbed her shoulders and sat her upright. He shook her and demanded, "Will you tell me for *what?*"

Her face looked bloodless. She blinked spiky black lashes at him and said so softly he hardly heard her, "My cats."

"Your what?"

"I looked in the stables, and they weren't there. I checked the laundry house and the conservatory. I thought they might be in the garden, and I—I was afraid they would drown."

Holding her small face in his hands, he shook his head in disbelief. "Cats? You were looking for your damn cats?"

Her head moved up and down, spilling rain from her hair over her brow, onto her cheeks. Damien began to grin. Then he wrapped his arms around her and fell back into the chair, hugging her close and rubbing his hands roughly up and down her arms to warm her. He laughed so hard that his entire body shook; he laughed until the cold ache in his chest melted into something warm and pleasant and glowing.

"Cats. And here I thought you'd decided to strike off for York in this weather just to spite me."

He felt her smile against him. "I might be dumb," she said, "but I ain't stupid."

Long minutes ticked by, yet he continued to hold her until her shaking stopped and her body warmed and relaxed against him. Her head came up as Stanley entered the room with a basket in his hand. He placed it at the foot of the chair. The lid popped open, and the kittens spilled onto the floor. Grudgingly, Damien released Bonnie as she slid off his lap and dropped to the carpet. He regarded her for some time before looking back at Stanley.

"Bring us a warm drink, please," Damien requested. "A brandy for me. A toddy, perhaps, for Bonnie."

Stanley, who had changed from his drenched dressing gown into his customary black suit, brocade waistcoat, and starched white shirt, nodded and added, "Perhaps I can get his lordship something dry to wear . . . ?"

"Later."

Her arms full of kittens, Bonnie looked first at Stanley, then at Damien, and asked, "What's a toddy?"

Damien dismissed the servant with a brief lift of his hand. "A toddy is a mixture of hot water and an alcoholic beverage. A dash of sugar is added and a touch of cloves. Little old ladies drink it by the buckets back in Vicksburg. Because it's sweetened with sugar they consider it hardly stronger than lemonade, and therefore perfectly acceptable." A space of several minutes passed before he spoke again. "Bonnie, about your leaving . . ."

She had buried her face into Nod's furry belly. Now she looked up. Color had returned to her cheeks, brushing the smooth almost translucent skin like rose dust. Her lips were red and moist.

Damien looked toward the fire. He cleared his throat. "Considering the weather . . ."

"Yes?"

"I don't think it would be feasible for you to leave for York in this downpour. Do you?"

"Probably not." The words were muffled. She had pressed her face against the cat again, gripping it so closely that it squirmed and batted her temples with its snow-white paws.

"No doubt the roads will be out," he added.

"And the bridges."

"Aye," he agreed, smiling.

Stanley returned with the drinks. Bonnie accepted hers with thanks and brought it to her mouth.

"Slowly," Damien told her, and she obeyed him, taking sips of the pale gold liquid until her glass was drained and placed beside her on the floor. She had been leaning back against his chair as she enjoyed her drink and continued to play with her pets. Now, however, the warming effect of the toddy had subdued her. She rested against his leg, her head placed tenuously upon his knee as she stared into the fire. He watched her lids grow heavy and close.

Damien touched her hair lightly with the tips of his fingers. The soft black curls, still damp from the rain, wound in shadowy coils around his hand. "Actually," he said in an aching voice that sounded strangely unnatural to his own ears, "I thought those damnable dreams had driven you from your bed again."

Her eyelashes fluttered open, briefly, then closed again. "No."

He tilted his head to better see her face. He watched the light play over her sleepy features before saying, "If you would care to tell me about the dreams—about what happened to your father—"

"I don't."

Gripping one long strand of her hair in his hand, Damien settled back in his chair and continued to gaze into the fire.

Damien checked his watch as he walked down the gallery to the lavender drawing room. Outside the door, he stopped. Since his return to Braithwaite he'd found himself straying this way more and more throughout the morning hours.

Miss Crandall, attired in a somber brown dress, her gray hair pulled atop her head in a knot, stood behind Bonnie tapping a flat wood stick against her skirts, and said, "Repeat, please: the Prince of Wales eats crumpets in jail."

"He's a daft bugger, ain't he?" Bonnie giggled.

Damien grinned.

"Repeat," Crandall ordered more forcefully.

"Can't y' come up with aught more int'restin'?" Bonnie asked. "I'm gettin' bloody tired of sayin' that over and over. Why don't we talk about sheep? I like sheep. How about, Sheffield sheep shiver at shavers?"

Miss Crandall's shoulders went rigid. She raised her stick.

Bonnie's eyes grew large. "If you rap my fingers with that stick again, you'll be sorry."

The governess lifted one brow. "Very nicely spoken. Your pronunciation was perfect. You see, you can speak correctly when you so desire."

Bonnie smirked and glanced toward the door, finding Damien. He smiled back.

"Read from your text, please," Miss Crandall ordered.

Her cheeks suddenly flushed, Bonnie gazed down at her open book. She moistened her lips. For an instant she appeared flustered and uncertain. Her voice quivered slightly when she spoke.

The words poured out perfectly, and with a strange sense of melancholy and surprise Damien noticed the subtle changes that were gradually shaping Bonnie into a new woman. Since he'd dragged her in from the rain three nights before, they had gotten along remarkably well. She seemed happy and content. Where was his urchin who hurled dishes and sent the servants scattering as if a demon were in their presence? He could have coped with the rough-talking hellion who spit and clawed each time he approached her. Then perhaps he could convince himself that she was unlikable and unacceptable, and that his life would be better off without such trouble. He'd done that while in York, hadn't he? He'd assured himself that by making love to her he'd satisfied his curiosity and his hunger. So why the hell was he standing here like some dumbstruck schoolboy with his body growing uncomfortably hard in his breeches?

"Well, well, look who we have here."

Damien looked around.

Miles smiled. "What brings you here, as if I didn't know."

Damien stepped away from the room before responding. "I thought you'd ridden to Leeds for the day."

"I changed my mind. Besides, Bonnie and I have an assignation. In case you didn't know, I'm teaching her chess . . . among other things."

Damien shoved his hands in his pockets.

"Before you know it she'll be as polished as Kate," Miles said. "Then what?"

Before Damien could reply, Bonnie had joined them, her books nestled against her chest, her eyes watchful as she looked from Miles back to him.

Miles bowed, took her hand, and kissed it. "A beautiful reading. Wouldn't you say so, Dame?"

"Very nice," he replied dryly.

"Are you ready for your chess lesson, Bonnie?" Miles asked.

She nodded. Miles hooked her arm through his, and without looking at Damien again, escorted her down the hall. His eyes on Bonnie, Damien felt his chest tighten. He wasn't certain whether it was over seeing her with Miles, or because, little by little, Miss Crandall and Kate were changing her

from a hoyden into a young lady . . . and the sickening realization suddenly occurred to him that he didn't like it.

Kate sat before the fire, concentrating on each delicate
stitch she applied to the needlepoint pillow cover she would
use to decorate her own settee back at home. Damien glanced
toward her frequently as he continued his discussion with
Richard.

"Surely Investigator Bradley has something by now, Uncle. How difficult can it be to trace a girl like Bonnie?"

Frowning, Kate looked around. "I suggest you keep your
voices down. Bonnie will be joining us at any minute for her
stitchery lesson."

"If she can tear herself away from Miles and his chess
instruction." Damien poured a glass of water from a Water-
ford pitcher before relaxing again in his chair. He stretched
his legs negligently before him and forced a bland expression
upon his features as his sister continued to regard him.

"Really," she said, "if you're so perturbed by Bonnie
spending time with Miles, you could try and spend some time
with her yourself. This horrid rain shows no sign of letting
up; use this opportunity to become better acquainted with
her."

He stared at Kate without blinking. Her only response was
a lift of one delicately arched brow.

"Bradley is doing all he can," Richard said. "He has all
but tortured the truth out of Smythe. It's obvious the man
knows little more than we do. She was caught by a farmer as
she was attempting to filch a ham from his smokehouse. She
refused to speak, even after she was turned over to Caldbergh. According to Smythe, she refused to utter a single
word to anyone for six months. Then one day she walked
into Smythe's office and announced her name was Bonnie,
her parents were dead, and she could not remember her last
name or where she came from."

"She remembers," Damien cut in. "She remembers everything else about her family." Knowing his sister was oc-
cupying the room next to Bonnie's, he asked, "Have the
nightmares recurred?"

Placing her needlepoint aside, Kate shook her head.

Richard said, "Smythe never bothered to get the name of

the farmer who turned Bonnie in to Caldbergh. Our investigation now is focused on finding that man. Doing so will narrow the area of the search considerably.''

The only sound to intrude on the heavy silence in the room was the muffled drone of the continuous rain against the window. Then somewhere in the gallery outside the library, Bonnie's laughter rang out. The light, melodious tones rebounded through the room like music, filling every nook and cranny, warming away the damp and cold as assuredly as sunshine. Kate's expression was wistful as she glanced toward Damien. He looked at Richard and discovered his uncle was smiling dreamily.

"I say," Richard remarked. "In all my years of visiting this house I cannot remember ever having heard anything as gay as that ring out in these halls."

"Nor can I," Kate replied softly.

Damien closed his eyes and tried to force that very thought from his mind. Reluctantly, it surfaced anyway from someplace deep in the warm hollow of his chest. "Nor have I," he murmured.

The library door was thrown open and Bonnie entered. Suddenly the air smelled of fresh rain and clover and sweet, wet hay. Her hair was riotously curly around her face. Her cheeks were bright red and damp from the rain as she swept them all with a smile.

A prolonged silence filled the room as Damien, Katharine, and Richard waited with heightened anticipation for Bonnie's first words. Somehow they always succeeded in throwing open the doors for animated conversation, and this time was no exception.

Catching sight of her muddy shoes, she exclaimed, "Bloody hell, would y' look at that. What a nuisance I am." Hopping up and down on one foot, she pulled off her right shoe, then her left. She turned and plopped them into Stanley's hands as he entered the room behind her. "Be a love," she told him, "and drop those out the back door. I'll be along directly to clean 'em up a bit."

"I'll see they are taken care of, Miss Bonnie," the servant responded.

"Y'll do no such thing. I'm perfectly capable of cleaning m' own dirty shoes." She hurried to the chair facing Kate, dropped into it with a huff, and folded her slender legs underneath her. Looking back at Stanley, who had paused at the door to allow the entrance of Bonnie's bounding three kittens, she added, "Tell Cook I'll drop by in about an hour." To the others she added, "I promised Cook I'd share my mum's secret for puddin's. Mind you, there's nothing wrong with his puddin's that a little milk couldn't help. That's the secret, really. M' mum used milk instead of water."

"I never cared for puddings," Richard said, smiling over his glass of port. "I find them rather tasteless."

"Y'll like mine," Bonnie stated matter-of-factly. "I promise." She slapped her knees, and the kittens scrambled up on the chair and curled together in one big furry ball in her lap. Once they were settled and purring contentedly, she smiled at Kate. "Sorry I'm late for m' lesson. We were watching the horses being exercised down at the enclosed arena."

"We?" Damien asked.

Bonnie looked directly at him for the first time since entering the room. He slouched in his chair. His white shirt was open partway down his well-muscled chest. His dark eyes regarded her openly as he waited for her response.

"We," she said, "meaning me and Miles."

"This must've been after your chess match," Damien said in a low voice that sent tingles of apprehension down Bonnie's spine. She scooped up a kitten and tucked it into the crook of her arm before replying.

"I beat him at chess for the first time t'day. He promised me a ride on Gdansk if I ever bested him." She watched Damien and Kate and Richard exchange glances. Damien's chair creaked as he stood and walked to the long line of crystal decanters on a table next to the wall. He did not turn to face her again before responding.

"Gdansk was not bred for pleasure riding, Bonnie. If you must ride, there are plenty of mares—"

"But I don't want t' ride the mares," she interrupted.

"Gdansk is out of the question, Bonnie, and that's the end of the matter."

"But—"

"Enough!" He slowly turned to face her. For what felt like an eternity Bonnie sat perfectly still, doing her best to remain calm in the face of Damien's obvious irritation. "I have given you a direct order," he continued. "You stay away from that horse, from those stables, and . . ."

"And?" she demanded hotly.

He didn't respond, just slammed his drink down on the table and quit the room. Stunned, Bonnie looked at Kate. Kate looked at Richard. Richard only smiled and followed Damien out the door.

Relaxing against the chair, Bonnie released her breath. "Bloody hell, what's got int' him?" she said.

Kate smiled and picked up her stitching. "I can think of a number of things, none of which will bear repeating among young ladies such as ourselves. I imagine the least of his problems is boredom."

"Then he should find somethin' t' do."

"My thoughts exactly. I told him only this morning that there is absolutely no reason why he should remain at Braithwaite if he doesn't wish to be here."

Bonnie glanced down at her own needlework, noting the haphazard stitches that didn't look remotely similar to Kate's. Placing it aside, she studied her companion's face, noting how the ice-blue satin of Kate's gown exaggerated the porcelain quality of her skin. Studying the threadbare knees of her own breeches, Bonnie chewed her lower lip before saying, "I displease him. Every time he looks at me he grows angry."

Kate smiled without looking up.

"Do y' think he would be less angry if I were more like you?"

Kate's hands paused in their sewing, and this time her green eyes raised slowly to meet Bonnie's. "I'm not certain, Bonnie. Are you so concerned about what Damien thinks?"

She shrugged.

"Damien has a great deal on his mind, you know."

"And my presence makes matters worse."

Placing her sewing aside, Kate sat back in her chair, folded her small hands in her lap, and regarded Bonnie for a long moment before speaking again.

"I am going to tell you something in confidence, Bonnie, that you must never mention to anyone ever again. I tell you this because I sense you care for my brother, and, in his own rather cynical way, I believe he cares for you. Damien was in love once. Very much in love with a young woman called Louisa Thackeray.''

Bonnie blinked and said, ''Oh.''

Kate tilted her head and studied Bonnie's reaction closely. Bonnie did her best to concentrate on the kitten on her lap and not on the growing hysteria she could feel edging up her throat. ''Perhaps I don't want t' hear this after all.''

''No, I suppose you wouldn't. It isn't easy accepting the fact that we might not be the first love of our men's lives. It leaves us feeling a little insecure and inadequate perhaps. When I think of the many women in my husband's life before he met me, I very nearly weep. But then I remind myself that he didn't marry *them*, he married me.''

Kate gazed at the fire. ''The Thackerays were our close friends. We grew up with Louisa.'' Her mouth curling in a hard smile, she added, ''She was one of my dearest friends as we were growing up. She was very pretty, and having spent her life in Yorkshire and not London, she was unaffected by her position in society and totally unaware of herself as a beauty. You were as likely to see Louisa riding bareback or skipping stones over water as you were to find her sitting prettily beside a fire reading poetry. Being the type of man who abhorred affectation of any sort, Damien naturally was charmed by her vulnerability and innocence. But she was young, and though it was understood between the families that Damien and Louisa would marry, everyone concerned agreed that she should have her Season in London.''

Shifting in her chair, Kate looked pensive before continuing. ''All of London was charmed by Louisa's free-spirited nature, as well as by her loveliness. Within a month of having arrived in London, she was sought after by dozens of men, some far wealthier than my brother. She changed. She enjoyed the attention men flaunted on her, and the more we all tried to keep her in line, the more she rebelled.

''Then the rumors started. She was spied with a duke here, a marquis there. Damien suspected she was seeing others, but the old adage holds true: Love is blind. He chose to ignore her peccadillos and shrugged it off as harmless coquetry, assuring family and friends that as soon as they were married she would again become the girl we all once knew and loved. He insisted on continuing the plans for the wedding, as did her parents, although on more than one occasion she voiced her disapproval over it. On the eve before their wedding he found her in bed with another man.''

Bonnie stared down at the taffy-colored kitten, the image of the Damien she knew today—hard, cynical, angry—blurring into one who was gentle and vulnerable enough to love and be hurt by a woman.

''I truly believe,'' Kate said quietly, ''that Louisa intended him to discover her tryst. I feel it was her only way of stopping the marriage once and for all. But I pray to God that I never see Damien so shattered again. I was not aware, until then, that men could experience such intensity of emotion. They are so staid, aren't they? Even when my mother died, my father never wept. Not once. But there was something about Louisa's betrayal that was more painful than death for Damien. She had stolen his manhood from him. She robbed him of his pride. She murdered the man Damien was as assuredly as if she had stabbed him in the back. He will never again be the boy who spent hours entertaining his baby sister because there was no one else for her to play with. Nor will he be the young man who gave up his nights with the lads to act as chaperon each time I had a gentleman caller.'' Kate shook her head. ''She turned him into a bitter stranger, Bonnie, and for that I will never forgive her.''

Damien had not entered this part of the house since his return to Braithwaite. It had been his father's domain. It smelled of leather and tobacco. The walls glowed with dark rosewood, and the Oriental carpets muffled the footsteps of all encroachers.

The door of the smoking room was open. Damien stood just inside the threshold, recalling the first time he had ventured here alone. He'd been no more than four or five, but the image was still so vividly ingrained on his mind that it might have been yesterday. The trophy heads were just as he remembered. There were stag and bear and a tiger from India. Joseph had taken great pride in his kills. Aside from his children they were the only true evidence of his manhood. He loved to entertain his guests with each gory detail of the slaughters. Once, he'd caught Damien, only five at the time, weeping over the brown-eyed doe his father had just mounted on the wall. Joseph had removed him from the room and boxed his ears, told him to act like a man and never embarrass him again.

Miles, who now sat watching Damien from a chair before the hearth, raised the double-barreled hunting rifle he'd been polishing and aimed it at Damien's chest. He squeezed the trigger, and the clap of the hammer against the empty chamber reverberated through the room.

Miles smiled. "Should you care to remain, we can try for barrel number two. It may or may not be loaded." He raised the gun and, squinting one eye, peered through the sights as he aimed the barrel at Damien's head. Damien felt the fine hairs rise on the back of his neck as Miles slowly squeezed the trigger. As before, the hollow clap rang sharply in the silent room.

"Bang," Miles said. "You're dead."

Damien didn't move, and Miles laughed, lowered the gun, and placed it across his lap. "Not even a flinch," he said. "Very nice. Our father would have been proud, though God knows, had he found himself in a similar situation, he would have run from the room in a state of mild hysteria with Randolf hot on his heels. Would you care to join me in a drink?"

"No."

"Ah. Then you've come for some other reason."

"Stay away from Bonnie."

"So that's what has your hackles raised. I knew there was some reason. Jealous, old boy? Don't tell me you have finally woken up and 'smelled the roses,' if you'll pardon my lack of originality. It always did take you a long time to come to your senses where women are concerned . . ." Miles laughed as he loaded the gun. He raised his hazel eyes to Damien's again, and grinned. "You were saying about Bonnie?"

"I don't think I need to repeat myself."

"Come now, Damien. Bonnie is adult enough to choose her own friends. Or did you think that by becoming her guardian you could control her completely—even her choice of admirers? Knowing Bonnie as I do, I don't think she would approve."

"And you know her so well," Damien snarled softly.

"We've become close. I won't deny it." Reaching for an

oilcloth on the table, Miles shook his head. "You were always an arrogant son of a bitch, Dame. Thought the world owed you something just because you were born in the bed instead of under it. Well, your blood may be blue, dear brother, but when you bleed it's the same color as mine." He polished his fingerprints off the barrel of the gun before looking at Damien again. "Did you expect her to pine away during your absence? If so, you have again miscalculated your effect on a young lady, I'm sorry to say."

Damien moved further into the room, stopping short as Miles swung the gleaming gun barrel his way. "Have you bedded her?" Damien asked through his teeth.

"What do you think?"

"I'll kill you if you have."

"Strong words. I suspect that if you had the guts to kill me you would have done so already. Or perhaps you've developed a spine since moving to Mississippi?"

Willing back his increasing fury, Damien warned, "If you so much as touch her, Kemball, you will sorely regret it." Then he turned for the door.

The cold *click click* of the gun's double hammers froze him in his tracks. He didn't have to look to know the barrel was pointed at his back. He felt it.

"Have *you* bedded her, Damien?" came Miles's voice.

"Go to hell," he replied, and left the room.

Fifteen

The weather finally broke. A warm but reluctant sun edged through the clouds and ushered in summer weather. Even so, nothing more was said of Bonnie's leaving Braithwaite. The idea had been completely dismissed.

Bonnie had just joined Kate for breakfast when Miles strolled in, dressed from head to toe in riding gear and carrying a crop. He offered them a gentlemanly bow before saying, "I'm in desperate need of a riding companion on this sunny morning. Come join me, Bonnie."

Bonnie and Kate exchanged glances. Dusting the scone crumbs from her fingers, Bonnie shook her head. "No, thank you."

"What? Young woman, have you looked outside? There isn't a cloud in the sky. This weather is just begging for a vigorous romp on horseback across the moor. Besides, I've already taken the liberty of having a mare saddled—"

"I won't ride one of those squat, lazy little ponies," she interrupted. "And since his high and mighty has ordered me not to set foot near Gdansk again, a gallop over the moor won't be possible."

"Ah, but you'll change your mind once you've seen Ashanti."

Kate, on the verge of drinking her tea, stopped and regarded Miles in surprise. "I don't recall our owning a mare called Ashanti."

"Of course you don't. She only arrived this morning. Come along," he coaxed Bonnie. "Come and see for yourself."

Kate grabbed Bonnie's arm hard enough to slosh tea over

the edge of her cup. "I think you should wait until Damien returns from Middleham," she said in a panicked voice. "You know what he said about those horses."

"He said she wasn't to ride Gdansk," Miles declared in a flat no-nonsense tone that sat Kate back in her chair. "If you wish to run tattling to big brother, then be my guest. You will find us down at the stables."

Before Bonnie could respond, Miles had dragged her from her chair. She was out of the room and down the gallery before looking back. Kate stood at the door, her eyes wide and her mouth pinched in worry as she regarded their departure. However, any irritation Bonnie might have felt over Miles's abruptness disappeared the moment they stepped through Braithwaite's door. It was a glorious morning! The air smelled fresh. The gardens were a great splash of colors that took her breath away.

Miles said nothing else as he hurried her to the stables. There was a sense of anticipation about him that was contagious, and by the time they reached the barn she could hardly contain her curiosity.

"What's this all about?" she asked him.

"You'll see for yourself." He escorted her through the stable door and stopped. "Well, lass, tell me what you think."

She stared at the sleek black mare, a smaller replica of Gdansk, and could hardly believe her eyes.

"Well?" Miles laughed. "Do you approve, Bonnie?"

"She's beautiful."

"And spirited. She and Gdansk will make magnificent foals together." He caught Bonnie's hand and urged her toward the horse. Then he grabbed her around the waist and easily lifted her into the saddle. "So tell me, Bonnie: What do you think?"

Bonnie ran her hands down the animal's glossy black neck and along the well-groomed mane before looking down at Miles. His eyes were bright with excitement.

"She's beautiful," she told him. "The most beautiful horse I've ever seen."

"Ha!" Miles shook his fist at the ceiling, then grabbing her hand in his, he announced, "She's yours, Bonnie."

Bonnie frowned.

He laughed again. "I'm serious."

"But—"

"No buts. It's my way of saying thank you. You've made my return to Braithwaite a delight that would otherwise have been a debacle. You've given me something to look forward to each day, lass, and for that I will be eternally grateful."

Bonnie continued to stare down into Miles's eyes, unable to believe what she was hearing.

Miles's head fell back in laughter. Then he caught her hand where it lay on her thigh and gave it an affectionate squeeze. "God, girl, you're beautiful. I would gladly give you ten of these horses if you would stare at me that way each time."

"You-you're serious," she said.

"I vow it with my life, Bonnie. She's all yours to ride until your heart is content."

Chewing her lip, she considered the extravagance of the gift before saying, "Have y' done this t' spite Damien? 'Cause if y' have, Miles, I don't want anythin t' do with it."

Miles stepped away and for the first time considered his true reason for buying the animal for Bonnie. A month ago he might have done the deed to goad Damien into insensibility, but now? He didn't think so, and the realization made him smile.

"Damien had nothing whatsoever to do with it," he said.

Bonnie closed her eyes, the surge of emotion enough to make her giddy. Slowly she began to smile, then to laugh until the stable rang with the melodious sound and several stable hands eyed her with curiosity.

Finally catching her breath, she said to Miles, "I don't know what t' say."

" 'Thank you' should be sufficient," he replied.

"Oh, sir, thank you is hardly sufficient. She is a grand beast and deserves a grand show of appreciation. But I have nothing—"

"You have your friendship," he interrupted. Holding her hand more tightly, he stepped closer to Bonnie and said more softly, "It gets pretty damn lonely being the black sheep in the family. Just be my friend. That's all I ask."

She reached out without thinking and placed her hand against his cheek. Then his arms were around her, and she was sliding out of the saddle. Miles held her against him, hugging her so fiercely she could hardly breathe. She laughed again and hugged him back, relishing the embrace and the warmth of his proferred friendship. It had been so long. So very, very long . . .

The force hit them both so suddenly that Bonnie cried out in surprise. The next thing she knew she was on her back in the dirt while the frightened mare pranced nervously to one side. Shoving away the stable hand who had rushed to her aid, Bonnie scrambled to her knees and watched in stunned amazement as Damien lifted Miles by the lapels of his jacket and threw him against the stable wall.

"Stop!" she shouted. "Why are you doin' this?"

"Indeed," Miles said in a steady voice to Damien. "Have you taken leave of your senses, my lord?"

"I have," he responded evenly, almost calmly, though his voice seemed abnormally deep in the quiet stable. "I warned you a fortnight ago that I would kill you if you touched her again."

Bonnie rose slowly to her feet. Dust stirred in the air and in the hazy shaft of sunlight that sliced through the shadows.

His eyes on Damien's, Miles smiled. "So, you intend to kill me now."

"I do."

"In front of the girl?" Miles's gaze shifted to Bonnie and Damien glanced around.

"Leave," he told Bonnie. "I will deal with you later."

"I will *not* leave," she told him. "Not until you take your hands off that man and tell me why you have done this."

"Bonnie!"

She looked around as Kate and Richard hurried into the stables. Richard stopped short upon seeing his nephews. Kate hurried to Bonnie's side.

"Come away from here," Kate said.

Bonnie shook her head, walked cautiously toward the men. Damien, his long legs spread slightly, still pinned Miles to the wall with his fists, his knuckles white where they gripped the fabric of Miles's jacket. The thought occurred to her that only one other time in her life had she ever witnessed such anger in a man—the night her father had been killed.

"Please." Her hand trembling, she touched Damien's arm.

"Don't. Please don't do this. If you don't want me t' have the mare, then I won't take it."

Damien's head snapped around, and he stared at her with such fury that Bonnie almost quailed. "Are you pleading for this bastard's life?" he asked. When she failed to answer immediately, he looked past her to Kate and ordered, "Get her out of my sight before I do something twice as stupid as killing him."

Kate hurried to Bonnie and took her arm. "Come along. We cannot stay here."

Stubbornly, Bonnie planted her feet apart, her eyes still locked on Damien. "It's only a horse, m'lord. A bloody horse. I will give it back—"

"Get out!" he shouted.

"No! I won't get out as long as you are like this!"

Richard intervened by stepping between Bonnie and the others. He regarded her sternly, and in a voice that was uncharacteristically harsh said, "Leave here at once, girl. I'll see that my nephews come to no harm. Now off with you quickly, Bonnie; you're only making matters worse."

Kate whispered, "No harm will come to Miles, I swear. My uncle won't allow it."

Miles? Bonnie frowned as she looked into Kate's worried eyes. She understood now how Damien had misconstrued her concern. They all thought her worry was for Miles, and while it should have been, she supposed—he was her friend, after all—Bonnie realized that her fear had been for Damien.

"Come away," Kate repeated.

With some reluctance, Bonnie backed away, her eyes still on Damien and the fury she could still see on his face, in the body trembling under the stress of holding his immense anger in check. Finally she turned with Kate and quit the stable, the image of Damien and Miles still stamped vividly on her mind's eye. They did not speak again until they entered the house, and then not until they were in the lavender drawing room with the door closed to all eavesdropping ears.

Bonnie sank into a chair while Kate paced the floor, her small hands clasped at her breast as if she were praying. Bonnie watched her for several minutes before saying, "I cannot believe they would truly harm each other. They're brothers."

"So were Cain and Abel." Kate stopped and faced Bonnie directly. There was no denying the worry in her eyes; Kate looked older suddenly. Her usual angelic features had taken on an angry mien so unlike the Kate Bonnie had come to know that Bonnie's concern grew sharper.

"You know that Miles is our half brother," Kate said. "Legally he should not even call himself Warwick, but he does."

"But it's wrong t' condemn him for his birth," Bonnie argued. "He cannot help being illegitimate any more than I can help bein' orphaned and poor."

"No one condemns him for his birth. I think you know us better than that," Kate returned.

Bonnie looked away.

"Since Miles's mother dumped him on our doorstep, it has been Miles's own twisted sense of spitefulness that has made him an outcast. Because he was my father's firstborn son he felt the right was his to usurp Randolf's and Damien's place in this house. And he went to it with a vengeance. Randolf, of course, was just like my father—if either of them experienced an emotion other than pride I never saw it. Their response to Miles's ploys was no more than a lift of an eyebrow and an appropriate glide from the room. Damien, however, was cursed, as was I, with my mother's and Uncle Richard's temperaments. Damien spent more than half his life being antagonized by Miles in one way or another, but unlike Randolf, who showed no signs of having let Miles get to him, Damien retaliated. And because of that the animosity between them grew to such proportions my mother and I actually feared for their lives. My father's reaction was not to put Miles in his place—*his* behavior was understandable, considering the circumstances—but to dress Damien down with the reminder that *he* was of gentle birth and therefore above such actions."

"Rivalry is to be expected," Bonnie argued. "But they are grown men now. Surely they can put their childish jealousies behind them."

"Damien tried . . . once. When my mother's health began to fail, he did everything possible to ease her fears over his and Miles's animosities. As my mother lay in the very bed in which she later died, Damien stood before her and offered his hand in friendship to Miles.''

"And did Miles accept?''

Kate's eyes turned hard. "He took it,'' she said. "For the next year, even after my mother died, there seemed to be harmony between them. But then, Miles was rarely around. He'd found a new way to do his dirty work. He discovered charm and actually began to worm his way into society. He certainly found a way to my father's heart. He threw himself into the Warwick businesses with a passion that set even Randolf aback. He accomplished his goal so subtly that we didn't even realize at first—we were too thankful that he had ceased making trouble. I should have known that something was up when my father requested that I return to Braithwaite. After all, I had just married and moved to York. Damien was forced to take leave of the businesses he was overseeing and return to Braithwaite. When we had all congregated in my father's office, he informed us that he was turning over the running of all the Warwick businesses to Miles.''

Kate sank into a chair before Bonnie's. "You can imagine our shock. Damien had been groomed for most of his life to step into that position. For Damien it must have felt as if he had been disinherited. After all, Randolf would come into everything upon our father's death. Other than a yearly allowance, Damien would have no income except the wage he earned by overseeing the businesses.

"Outwardly Damien appeared to take the news well. And perhaps, knowing my brother, there was a thread of relief underlying his immediate disappointment. He was never one to relish the burden of ancestry, I fear. It was the idea of what our father had done that chaffed Damien most. His pride was terribly bruised. Had it been anyone but Miles . . .''

Kate relaxed in the chair. She gazed down at the fire in the hearth, and her eyes became sad. "I suppose you're thinking that we're all a group of ninnies for fretting over inheritances and the like when you have nothing.''

"I haven't thought that,'' Bonnie replied softly. "But I do think it sad that two grown men cannot put their differences behind them. After all, it seems everything has worked out. Damien has fallen heir to Braithwaite due to your older brother's unfortunate accident. He also controls the businesses. Your father must have reconsidered . . ."

"Oh, yes. He did reconsider in time. Just as long as it took Miles to nearly bankrupt us." Kate frowned with some thought. She looked again at Bonnie. "What is he to you?"

"My friend," she responded.

"Is that all?"

"A close friend."

"How close?"

Shaking her head, Bonnie came to her feet. A hard knot of disbelief was working up the back of her throat; she tried to swallow it down.

Kate also left her chair. The same height as Bonnie, Kate looked at her directly and said, "Were you forced to choose between my brothers, whom would you pick?"

"Unfair!" Bonnie cried. "Y' cannot expect me t' answer somethin' like that."

"You may well be forced to, if I know Damien."

"But Miles did nothin' wrong. Perhaps his gift was too extravagant—"

"Damien gave Miles strict orders to stay away from you."

"Damien has no right!" Angrily, Bonnie left Kate and walked across the room. "Miles has never harmed *me*, and I doubt he ever would."

"So he *has* charmed you. Bonnie, I thought you too wily for that."

She raised her chin. "He's shown me friendship and kindness. That's more than his bloody lordship has done."

"Oh?" Her eyes flashing, Kate joined Bonnie where she stood by the desk. "Who has paid for the tutors you've sent flying out of this house in a state of the vapors? Who's fed you and housed you? Who lies awake at night unable to sleep for fear he won't hear you should you call out in your nightmares?"

"But he hates me!" Bonnie cried.

"Hates you!" Kate grabbed Bonnie's shoulders and shook her. "Open your eyes, Bonnie. Damien is in love with you!"

The confession rocked them both.

Bonnie shook her head, silently cursing the rise of tears in her eyes. She shoved Kate's hands aside and backed away. "I never thought you t' be cruel, m'lady."

"I'm not cruel, Bonnie."

"Y' are! Yes, y' are t' even suggest such an outrageous thought! Warwick cannot abide me and tells me so each chance he gets."

"Does he? What does he say?"

Bonnie opened and closed her mouth. Again she shook her head, more adamantly this time.

Kate smiled. She picked up a paperweight from the desk and turned it over in her hands. "He won't admit it, of course. In truth, I suspect he doesn't realize it himself."

"The very idea is absurd," Bonnie declared.

"He thinks so too, I dare say."

"I'm not of his class, y' know."

"That's a problem, I confess. It would take a rare woman to overcome the stigma of class separation that comes to such ill-matched marriages."

"I'm not even passably pretty."

"Yes, you are and you know it. With a little polish you could shine bright enough to blind Prince Albert himself."

Bonnie turned away, ashamed for Kate to see her cry. With tears rolling down her cheeks, she said with a touch of her old rebelliousness, "All the same, it's a ridiculous notion. His lordship hardly grants me the time of day. He blames me for all his problems and would like nothing better than t' see me back at Caldbergh. It's only due t' his bloody conscience that he hasn't already returned me there."

"So it would seem. Or so he's convinced himself. Men are funny that way. They are usually the last to realize when they've fallen in love."

"Stop sayin' that." Bonnie angrily wiped her nose with the sleeve of her shirt. "He don't love me, Kate. He don't even like me."

"And what about you? I suppose you care nothing for him as well."

"Not a bloody whit. He's a stupid pain in the butt, if yer askin' me."

"If you hate him so much, why are you still here?"

Bonnie covered her mouth with the tips of her fingers, foolishly believing they could somehow hold back the sob rising in the back of her throat.

"Well?" came Kate's words. "Why are you here, Bonnie?"

Without responding, Bonnie turned on her heel and ran for the door. Throwing it open, she ran straight into Damien, who locked one hand around her arm and pulled her back into the room.

"Excuse us," he told Kate in a voice that brooked no refusal.

Bonnie struggled for release as Kate glided across the floor and from the room, closing the door gently behind her. Bonnie was then shoved so hard toward the chair before the fire that she landed with enough impact to nearly topple the chair backward. Coming upright, her cheeks burning with fury, she cried, "Y' bloody bas—"

He turned on her so suddenly that Bonnie's words died in her throat.

"Shut up," he said coldly. "Just shut up, Bonnie, or I swear to God . . ." Damien paced toward the window where he raked his fingers through his hair before facing her again. His face white with anger, he demanded through his teeth, "Do you want him? Well? Stop staring like a goddamned mute and answer me!"

Before she could respond, he crossed the room, grabbed her up by her arms, and kicked the chair aside so forcefully it spilled toward the fire.

"Y-yer hurtin' me!" she cried.

"I want the truth, if you're capable of it. Have you *been* with him?" He shook her painfully, his fingers digging like vises into her flesh. "Have you? Answer me, dammit!"

She struck out with her fist, connecting against Damien's cheek and mouth with enough impact to rock him backward. When he turned on her again, his fist raised as if he meant to strike her, she tossed back her head and said calmly, "Try it."

Time hung suspended as Damien outwardly grappled with his fury. Blood had begun trickling from the corner of his mouth as he stared down into Bonnie's cold face. Gradually lowering his fist, he wiped it across his mouth. He glanced at the red smear on the back of his hand before looking at her again.

''You haven't answered my question,'' he said in a hoarse voice.

''It does not warrant a response.''

''Do you want to go with him?''

''He's leavin'?''

''Aye, he's leaving and good riddance. I should never have allowed him here in the first place.''

Bonnie backed to the door, her eyes on Damien's dark face and the smear of blood on his mouth. ''I cannot believe y' can be so cruel as t' turn him out. This is his home, and he has done nothing more than be a friend t' me. What crime is there in that? Rather I leave Braithwaite than see him dismissed because of me. Without a place t' call home, one has nothin'. How can y' be so heartless?''

Without waiting for a response Bonnie turned for the door.

''Bonnie!''

She threw it open and left the room.

''Go on!'' he shouted behind her. ''You deserve each other! Bonnie! . . . Damn you, Bonnie!''

She turned down the gallery. Kate stood there, her hands at her sides buried in the folds of her blue gown. Her worried eyes met Bonnie's as she approached.

''Are you going with him?'' Kate asked. When Bonnie refused to respond, Kate roughly grabbed her arm and said, ''Because he appeared to offer you friendship you think he is noble, that Damien has no right to accuse either of you of misconduct.''

''He hasn't! Miles has been a gentleman—''

''Miles was the man Damien found in bed with Louisa the night before their wedding.''

Bonnie froze.

''If my brother does not care for you, as you believe, why would he be so upset because you might have bedded Miles?'' Kate released her. Without speaking again she hurried down the gallery, pausing only once to look back.

In a state of numbness Bonnie turned back down the hall. Miles stood before her, a half smile on his face as he noted her surprise.

''Yer leavin','' she said.

''I have little choice. My brother . . . requests that I depart, at least until he has returned to London.''

As he raised his hand to touch her face, Bonnie backed away. More quietly she said, "Is it true what Kate tells me?"

There was a long silence before he responded. "It seems they've pulled out the heavy artillery."

"Then it *is* true." Bonnie closed her eyes and shook her head. "I would not have thought it of y'. How could y' do such a wicked thing?"

"I have no excuse."

"And the horse? Y' did that to hurt him, too, didn't y'?"

"No."

"Yer fools," she said. "I'd give m' soul to have a family, and here are the two of you tryin' yer best to destroy what little family y' have left."

Without speaking again, Miles moved down the hall. Finally she looked up and called, "Miles!"

He stopped and looked back.

"Godspeed," she told him.

Kate was standing at Damien's side as Miles walked to the library door. "In case anyone is interested, I'm leaving for the time being."

"Good," Damien snapped.

Miles started to turn away, then stopped. "Just for the record, I haven't slept with Bonnie. And something else. The night you found me with Louisa was the first time I'd bedded her. She came to my flat uninvited, Damien. She *asked* me to make love to her."

"You might have resisted," Kate joined in. "But then, it was another way of hurting Damien, wasn't it?"

"Perhaps. But I think the idea of a woman as lovely and desirable as Louisa acting as if I really meant something to her went to my head. After all, I always made do with second best. You can't deny that. And if you must know, I had always admired Louisa, perhaps fantasized a few times that she threw you over for me. I realized the moment you walked in the bedroom door that she had used me to hurt you. She knew, because of our stormy relationship, that I would be the logical choice to make you the angriest."

"That's no excuse for what you did," Kate said.

"No, I suppose it isn't. But in defense of Louisa, you must admit that she'd already done everything in her power to call off the wedding. She wasn't in love with you, Dame, but you kept insisting, didn't you?"

Damien turned away.

Miles shifted his valise from one hand to another. "Adieu," he said.

Damien did not look at Kate again as she quit the room. Alone, he contemplated his past, and his present. What could drive him, in the blink of an eye, to lose grip on his sanity? He might have killed Miles had Richard not intruded. Louisa. It had to be. He was still plagued by her deception. Jealousy was a hidden emotion inside him that, for a fraction of a second, had upended his reason.

He looked at his hands. They were shaking.

Was his reaction over seeing Miles holding Bonnie due to any lingering feelings—anger or love—for Louisa? Had he been wrong these last years to believe he no longer cared for her?

Could he be confusing these troubling feelings for Bonnie and some lingering love for Louisa?

He felt caught in a dilemma that was also a flux of indecision; it was almost palpable, a force driving him into a future he did not want to acknowledge—he would not acknowledge.

Of course his reaction had been due to Louisa.

It had nothing remotely to do with Bonnie.

Sixteen

Bonnie carefully laid out the selection of dresses on her bed, then stepped back and eyed each one critically. Kate had given her the frocks with the excuse that since marrying she had put on weight and could no longer wear them. It seemed a lame excuse, and Bonnie told her so. Still, Bonnie had accepted with a grace that would have made her mother proud. Until now, however, she had not grown brave enough to try them on. They were so beautiful, much too fine for a commoner like her. She might even begin to think that she belonged among these people and that Damien would find her attractive enough to fall in love with her.

Flights of fancy, she thought.

There was one gown in particular that caught her eye. It was a peculiar shade of pearl-gray silk with a luminescent mist green sheen among the folds of the skirt. Bonnie ran her hands over the shimmering material, thinking she had never seen a gown of such richness, such elegance. After all, her mother had done well to clothe herself and Bonnie in simple calico. Carefully, Bonnie picked up the dress and held it against her, then turned to view herself in the cheval glass.

"Gum, but ain't you luvely!" came Jewel's voice behind her.

Startled, Bonnie spun. The servant's round face and bright eyes beamed her an appreciative smile.

"Bloody hell," Bonnie said. "Y' frightened me out of my wits. Have a care, Jewel, and whistle before y' sneak up like that."

Jewel chuckled and nudged the door open further with the

tray in her hand. "I've brought ye a bowl of cobbler and a glass of milk, just like ye asked."

Momentarily forgetting the dress, Bonnie tossed it on the bed with the others before accepting the tray and placing it on the writing desk at the window. She wasted no time in dropping into the chair, retrieving a spoon, and digging in.

"Y've certainly developed an appetite of late," Jewel said. "That's the second bowl of cobbler y've downed since noon."

"Aye, and second glass of milk. I've a cravin' for it lately."

"It'll do y' good."

"It'll make me fat. I swear it has already. I can hardly get into my breeches any longer."

"All the more reason y' should try wearin' one of them fine dresses Lady Katharine's given ya." Jewel swept up the gray dress and spread the skirts over her arm. "I'm sure 'is lordship wouldn't mind seein' ya in this one."

With her mouth full of cobbler, Bonnie looked around. "His bloody lordship don't know I'm alive these days. He's still mad at me for befriending Miles. He hasn't spoken— nay, looked—at me since Miles left."

"Mayhap he needs somethin' to grab his attention from all them business worries. This'd do it for certain."

Bonnie swallowed. "I'm not certain I want his attention."

"He's only broodin'. He were always a bit of a brooder, was our kid. He gets over it in time. Wot d' ya say, lass? Shall we give it a go? Won't do no harm and might do worlds o' good."

Grinning, Bonnie stirred her cobbler with her spoon, her eyes still regarding the dress Kate had given her.

Her voice a mischievous whisper, Jewel added, "I could scare up a ribbon or two that might match the dress. We could pull yer hair back and tie it with a bow."

"Yer dreaming now," Bonnie told her.

"He were askin' about ya earlier."

"Oh?" Bonnie looked back at her cobbler.

"He come into the drawin' room where I be dustin' and asked, 'Where's Bonnie?' "

"More likely where's the brat or the urchin or baggage . . ."

"Naw, he don't say them things no more. He's calmed down now that Miles is gone."

"He's certainly made himself scarce."

"Beggin' yer pardon, lass, but it's you who's made herself scarce. Y've closed yerself up in this room, comin' and goin' when yer certain his lordship ain't about. If yer expectin' him t' come knockin' on yer door, yer in for a disappointment. Men's got their pride, lass. The sooner y' realize that the better."

"And women don't?"

"Sometime y' got t' compromise yer pride just a bit t' get wot y' want in life."

Bonnie put her bowl on the tray. "Are y' saying that I want his lordship?"

"Are y' sayin' y' don't?"

Bonnie looked out the window. "There are dreams; then there are fantasies, Jewel. I am old and wise enough to know the difference."

Jewel spread the dress out once more, and as Bonnie looked around the servant smiled and said, "It would be a shame to waste opportunity when it's offered. It's a right nice dress, don't y' think?"

Bonnie looked the dress over again. "Aye." She sighed. "Too fine for me."

"Nonsense. First we'll start with a bath scented with rose-water. We'll braid yer hair so there'll be nothin' t' take away from yer luvely face and this magnificent dress."

Bonnie couldn't help but laugh. The idea of spending the afternoon in this manner seemed far more appealing to her than whiling away the hours pouring over the texts Miss Crandall had left behind when she'd resigned in a huff of exasperation. Thinking of the woman, Bonnie's face colored. Having been cracked across the knuckles by the governess for swearing, Bonnie had yanked the stick from her and swatted her back. Crandall had reported the incident to Damien, and he had responded, "Good God, woman, you deserved it."

Bonnie smiled. What harm could come from trying on the frock? It had been a fantasy once, when she was a child, to dress like a princess and be swept off her feet by a prince.

Right, she thought. But I'm definitely not a princess. And Warwick is far from being some gallant prince.

* * *

A half hour later Bonnie was soaking up to her chin in rose-scented bubbles. Her head resting against the brass tub, she closed her eyes, feeling pampered and luxurious and just a little decadent. After all, Jewel had poured enough rose-water into her bath to have lasted Bonnie's mother a year. Jewel had even bathed her, taking such pleasure in the chore she had begun singing loud enough to bring several wide-eyed servants into the room to join in on the effort.

The door opened again and Jewel breezed in, her arms full of various and sundry articles that Bonnie could not recognize. Her eyes widened as Kate followed, her face shining with excitement and her hands full of ribbons.

"How wonderful!" Kate exclaimed. "How simply wonderful! Oh, Bonnie, this will be such grand fun. You won't regret your decision, I promise!"

Bonnie sank further into her bubbles and thought, Bloody hell.

She was rinsed with warm scented water, towel-dried by Gretchen, who had stumbled into the room with her arms full of clean laundry. Bonnie was then wrapped in a frilly white peignoir with Watteau pleats, which also belonged to Kate, and plopped in a chair before the cheval glass. Kate stood behind her, her green eyes twinkling as she instructed Jewel in the arrangement of Bonnie's hair.

The tresses were drawn back from Bonnie's face and up to the crown of her head where they commenced in a very tight braid that succeeded in lifting the outer corners of Bonnie's eyes slightly. "You'll get use to it," Kate assured her, but Bonnie wasn't so certain. She thought the hair at her temples would be pulled out by the roots, and told them so in no uncertain words. Kate only laughed, Gretchen tittered, and Jewel chuckled so heartily that her entire plump body bounced up and down.

An hour later the thick black braid, interwoven with pearl-gray ribbons, hung down Bonnie's back. Kate then stepped between Bonnie and the mirror, took Bonnie's chin in her hand, and tipped up her face. Without turning to Jewel, Kate held out her hand and said, "My rouge, *s'il vous plait.*"

Bonnie watched from the corner of her eye as Jewel placed a tiny milk glass pot of French carnelian rouge in Kate's hand. "What's that?" she asked suspiciously.

"Only a bit of color. We add it to your cheeks and perhaps very faintly to your eyelids. Done properly, and with a light hand, no one will ever know it's not natural. Sometimes we add it to our lips as well, but in your case it won't be necessary. Your lips have beautiful color already. Now give me the powder,'' she instructed Jewel. Bonnie's face was then dusted lightly with rice powder.

When Bonnie tried to see around Kate to the mirror, Kate moved before her and shook her head. "Not yet. Not until the dress is on.''

Kate moved Bonnie from the chair to the foot of the bed, where Jewel waited with a contraption that stopped Bonnie in her tracks. "It's a corset,'' Kate explained. "You are more than thin enough, but to be fair to the dress it is absolutely imperative that you wear it.''

"What about what's fair to me? It looks like a bloody torture device!''

"And well it may be. Regardless, it is de rigueur and must be tolerated. You'll grow accustomed to it with time. Now suck in.''

Bonnie did and Jewel wrapped the corset around her. The steel busk cut into Bonnie's tender skin as the servant adeptly fastened the hooks down the front, then stepped away.

"The stockings,'' Kate instructed.

The servant rolled out the pale silk hosiery with a flourish, along with garters decorated with silk rosettes that would hold the finery in place. Bonnie was gently nudged down on the bed by Kate while Jewel eased the filmy stockings up her slender legs and secured them with the garters. Bonnie was still staring and considering how long and shapely they made her legs appear when Kate announced, "Now the petticoats!''

Before Bonnie could refuse she was pulled up from the bed, the dressing gown was removed, and she was smothered by a petticoat of lawn, then a second, and finally a third of taffeta with a lace- and ribbon-trimmed hem. Before she could gasp for breath the dress was lifted over her head and eased onto her shoulders. The necessary adjustments were made as the skirts spilled to the floor. The many tiny buttons up the back were fastened while Kate produced a pair of soft kid slippers that fit Bonnie almost perfectly. Then Kate and her assistants stepped back.

Jewel's eyes were wide and sparkling as she said, "Gum, but would y' look at that. I wouldn't've believed it if I ain't seen it with me own two eyes."

"It's bloody miraculous," Gretchen added.

"I knew it!" Kate exclaimed. "Didn't I tell you? Didn't I tell them all?" Grabbing Bonnie by the shoulders, Kate turned her toward the cheval glass. "Behold the fairest maid in all of Yorkshire!"

Bonnie's eyes took in each elegant detail of the dress, from its modestly cut décolletage with a ruching of off-white ribbon and a frill of lace, to its long full sleeves ruched in bows and demi-revers at the elbow, which allowed the undersleeves of fine lace to show. The double skirt stopped just below her ankles with a deep flounce that was also edged in lace. Very slowly her gaze went back to her face, and Bonnie wondered if this were a dream or whether she had somehow become truly lost in her fantasies. The image of the lovely, sophisticated woman whose blue eyes shone like bright gems in her face could not be her.

But it was, she realized.

Covering her face with her hands, she burst into tears.

Damien dropped the papers in Richard's trembling hands. "I have just returned from Middleham," he said. "While there, I spoke with Carlton Ashbee."

"Good God." Richard's double chin quivered as he choked, "Ne'er-do-well swore he wouldn't approach you. How much did he hit you for?"

"Twenty-five hundred pounds." Damien paced before stopping. He glanced at his uncle. Richard's face was bloodless. "Why?" he demanded.

His voice barely audible, Richard replied, "A run of bad luck at White's."

"So it would seem. Have there been others?"

Richard dragged a kerchief from his coat pocket and blotted the sweat from his brow. When he didn't respond, Damien moved back to the desk, flipped open the ledger, and slammed his fist against it. "Dammit! You've been taking money from the business to pay off your debts—"

Richard blinked in shock.

"You don't even deny it?"

"How—how can I?"

Damien turned away, focused his eyes on empty space, and did his best to control his anger. Richard dropped into a chair and cradled his face in his hands. "What do you intend to do?" he asked.

A moment passed before Damien could bring himself to say, "The only thing left to do. I'm removing you from your position, Richard."

"Damien, please . . . "

Swinging around, his frustration apparent in the tight sound of his voice, Damien implored, "How could you think to steal money from your own flesh and blood? Had you come to me or Randolf—"

"I tried!" Richard left the chair. "I spoke to Randolf the very morning he was killed, but he refused. I couldn't come to you, Damien. I was too ashamed. Surely you can understand that."

"I could understand that more than I can accept the fact that you've been robbing the Warwicks blind for the last two years!"

His face suffused with color, Richard clenched his fists. "The hell you say. As far as I'm concerned the Warwicks owed me that money for tolerating the lot of them for forty years."

"I think we've been pretty damned lenient, considering the mess you made of your life."

Richard, his eyes bulging with fury, leaped at Damien so suddenly that there was little time for response. Savagely gripping Damien's coat, he slurred, "Goddamn you to hell. I have loved you like a son and you turn on me like a dog!"

Too stunned to speak at first, Damien stared into his uncle's face, the sweet smell of port filling his nostrils so strongly that he could hardly breathe. Then he slowly raised his hands and took hold of Richard's wrists. "Remove them," he ordered quietly.

Richard, realizing what he had done, released Damien and stumbled back. He turned away and fell again into the chair. "Forgive me. My hellish temper gets away from me occasionally. Dear heavens, I never meant to let it happen with you.''

Damien smoothed down his lapels, then ran his hand through his hair. He had witnessed his uncle's temper directed at other people, but rarely at himself. The encounter left him shaky. He forced himself to breathe normally.

Richard looked up. "Did I hurt you?"

He shook his head.

"It's this damned drinking. It does things to me, Damien. I'm truly sorry.'' Sitting more erect, he twisted the kerchief in his hands and sighed. "I ask—beg—you to give me one last chance. I swear I will leave off the port. I won't come within a mile of a gambling establishment.''

Damien was a fool for agreeing. He knew that, yet he couldn't stop himself. "One last time, Uncle. If you slip up again—"

"I won't."

"And there is the matter of twenty-five hundred pounds you owe me, not to mention the sums you have taken from the accounts. Have you any idea how much that would be?''

Richard tugged at his shirt collar. "Not offhand. I have a few properties in Wales and Scotland. They may take some time to liquidate, but you'll get your money, Damien, I promise you.''

Jewel's voice interrupted from the doorway.

"M'lord, the post has just arrived. Letters from London.''

He took the letters from the servant and stepped from the room. Flipping one envelope over, he stared down at the parliamentary seal. So, it had finally arrived. He had actually managed to put the dreaded confrontation with Parliament out of his mind the last weeks while he worked diligently to unravel the botchery Richard had made of the ledgers. He could leave now, put Braithwaite and everything she stood for behind him . . . *if* that's what he desired.

Damien looked uncertainly down the long corridor to his left and right. "Too late now for second thoughts,'' he told himself. Taking a long, slow breath, he pulled the letter from its envelope.

The tea things had been arranged on a table beneath a chestnut tree in the south courtyard. Bonnie stood at Kate's side while Stanley added an arrangement of cut flowers to the table, then a small plate of petit fours. Bonnie didn't miss the appreciative glances the old servant threw her as he hurried to place the silverware and china on the table.

"This seems like an awful lot of trouble t' go to just for a cuppa tea," she said to Kate.

Kate looked back toward the house and frowned. "Damien is late as usual. Have you seen him, Stanley?"

"He was recently in the library with your uncle. They were discussing business, I believe. Shall I remind him of your appointment?"

"No, thank you. I suppose he'll be along soon enough."

As Stanley moved away, Bonnie said, concentrating on her pronunciation (it simply wouldn't do to talk like an urchin when she was dressed like this), "Y'—you—didn't tell me *he* was going to be here."

"I didn't tell Damien that you would be here either. There was no point in giving either of you the upper hand." Kate glanced critically about the table and chairs. "I think you should sit there. The red roses compliment your dress better than the yellow ones, I think." Kate moved Bonnie around the table and seated her in a chair. "Perfect. Now remember. Don't cross your legs. Spine away from the back of the chair and hands folded gently, palms up, in your lap."

Bonnie rolled her eyes. "And how am I supposed to drink this bloody tea if my hands are folded gently? Lap it from the cup like a cat?"

"On second thought, forget that for the moment. Perhaps at first you should appear to be doing something . . ." Kate glanced about and, spying the bench where she had earlier been reading while waiting for Bonnie to make her appearance, she hurried over and picked up the book. "Perfect."

Bonnie groaned. "Not another bleedin' book—"

"A novel." Kate opened it to where she'd marked the page with a ribbon. "Of course you'll be so absorbed in the book that you don't hear him approach. When he speaks to you, you will look up surprised, making a soft moue with your mouth." Kate affected the pout as an example.

"Bloody hell, if I will. You look as if you've just bit into a green persimmon."

They both looked around as Damien appeared at the top of the walk.

"Oh my," Kate cried softly. Facing Bonnie, her eyes alight with excitement, she giggled and fluttered her hands. "Oh, do something. Quickly! He's coming! Oh dear, I may swoon from the anticipation!"

Bonnie raised the open book before her face and fell back in the chair.

"Sit up! Sit up!" Kate whispered.

She sat up.

"Put the book down. He cannot see your face."

"I'm readin'!"

"No one holds his book up like that to read!"

"*I* do!"

"Since when?"

"Since now!"

They both burst out in a fit of giggles until Kate said, "Shh! Here he comes."

Hidden behind the book, Bonnie closed her eyes and held her breath. She could hear him walking down the flagstone path, his footfalls heavy and fast as he approached. She tried to swallow and discovered her mouth had gone bone-dry. The corset had somehow squeezed every breath of air from her lungs, and she could not seem to retrieve it.

"Sorry I'm late," came his deep voice, vibrating through Bonnie and making her dizzy. She swayed a little before catching herself.

"That's quite all right, Damien . . . *Bonnie* and I were . . . were just discussing the book we are reading."

There was a long silence, and Bonnie knew he was looking at her. She lowered the book slightly and peered at him over the top of the page.

Damien stood at ease by his sister; the slight breeze ruffled his dark hair, and his features were relaxed . . . until their gazes met. Only then did she notice the strain on his face, the tight lines etched around his mouth and eyes.

Upon seeing Bonnie, Damien narrowed his eyes almost imperceptibly, and his broad shoulders within his white lawn shirt became rigid. She briefly wondered if the responses were due to any lingering animosity he held for her or to surprise over her appearance. She lowered the book slowly, closed it, and placed it on the table. Never had she felt more conspicuous. She had the frightening notion that once he recovered from his shock, Damien would burst into gales of laughter and ridicule her for her silly attempts to look the lady.

But he didn't laugh. He continued to regard her in silence, surveying Bonnie with slow care from her head to the lace-trimmed hem of her dress, and the toes of her slippers underneath.

Kate cleared her throat before asking, "Do you intend to stand there all day or will you join us for tea?"

Damien pulled out his chair and sat down.

Kate poured the tea, first Bonnie's, then her own, and finally Damien's. "As I was saying, Bonnie and I were just discussing this wonderful novel."

He looked at Bonnie. "What is it?"

Bonnie glanced at the book, then back at him. "*Jane Eyre.*"

"Isn't that a romantic novel?"

"Highly romantic," Kate joined in. "It's about a poor governess who falls in love with her wealthy employer, and he with her."

Damien smiled as he picked up his teacup. "Sounds more like fantasy to me. Why do you women like to read that drivel?"

"We have to take romance where we can find it. Were we left to get it from our husbands, I fear we would starve."

Raising one eyebrow, Damien laughed. "Is the honeymoon over, chooch? Should I speak with Lord Bradhurst on the matter?"

"You will mind your own business. William and I had enough of your interference during our courtship."

Silence again. They all sipped their tea and nibbled their cakes. Or tried to. Bonnie could not force even a crumb past her lips. The stays beneath her dress were cutting sorely into her flesh, and the petticoats beneath her skirts were making her itch. She felt ill. And foolish. She had believed, hoped, that her new appearance would affect Damien in some positive way, but it seemed not to have impressed him at all.

"Were you and Richard discussing anything of importance?" Kate asked.

"As a matter of fact, yes. I have finally received a letter from Palmerston." He stirred a second spoon of sugar into his tea. "I am to meet with Parliament two weeks from to-day."

Kate clumsily placed her cup on the saucer. Her cheeks were suddenly pale as she gripped the edge of the table for support. "That means you'll be leaving Braithwaite for London."

"Yes."

"And when you've completed your business in London, you'll leave for America."

Bonnie's heart turned over.

"Yes," he answered softly. Kate turned her face away and appeared to study the roses. Damien reached over and took her hand. "You knew it was inevitable."

"That doesn't mean I have to like it." Her voice quavered. When she turned back to Damien, her eyes were bright with unshed tears. "Don't go back. I beg you! Why become involved in that awful war? I've seen the papers; thousands of men will die!"

"I have a home to protect, Kate."

"This is your home!" Leaving her chair, she stared at her brother as tears rolled down her cheeks. "Braithwaite is your home. Why must you deny it?"

"Kate—"

"Don't you 'Kate' me! You have damned and defied the world for most of your life, Damien, and while it was rakish and appealing when you were a young man, now it is not. You are no longer young. You have responsibilities to this land, and to me. Y-you and Richard are all I have left of my family; if you return to America, I know I will never see you again!"

Standing, Damien took Kate in his arms an ' gently rocked her as she wept against his chest. Occasionally his eyes drifted to Bonnie, and for a space of time they regarded each other in silence. Finally Bonnie looked away, unwilling to permit him to see her own worry or the feelings for him that would surely show in her eyes.

"Hush," she heard him whisper. "Let's not spoil our tea party. After all, the table is so pretty . . ."

"Just the table?" Kate murmured against his shirt.

Bonnie looked up. His eyes were on her, warm and yearning, as he said, "The ladies, my love, are beautiful."

Bonnie thought she was beginning to understand Damien more, why he sometimes acted and reacted the way he did. He was a man with a great many responsibilities. And with responsibilities often came problems, and disappointments.

She could remember her parents worrying over money, such as how would they afford to fix the wagon and still have the funds to buy the new milk cow they so desperately needed. She could recall her father becoming angry and frustrated with his inability to solve the dilemma, but her mother had been there to comfort him. Damien's problems were much greater, and there was no one to soothe his brow and take his mind off his problems after the lights went out.

Her presence at Braithwaite had not helped matters. He had no doubt returned here in hope of reacquainting himself with his ancestry, perhaps preparing for the upcoming confrontation, not only with Parliament, but also with the war in America, a war, according to others, that he wanted no part of. And here *she* was, defying him at every turn, denying every consideration he showed her, all because her childish pride was on the line.

Bonnie stared a long moment at the dresses in the wardrobe and briefly reached out to touch the pearl-gray creation that, for a time, had made her feel like a princess. Then she forced herself to shut the door, walk to the bed, and retrieve the valise she had earlier packed. It contained little: a brush, a clean shirt, several ribbons Kate had given her, a garter, and the pair of stockings she had worn that afternoon. And, of course, her cherished music box. She left the room.

The hallways were dark. She crept soundlessly to the stairs and descended them carefully, thankful upon reaching the vestibule that no lights were burning. Without looking back—she dared not or she would surely change her mind—Bonnie walked to the front door and found it unlocked. She left the house.

It was a rare night sky in Yorkshire that was not covered with clouds. Stars spattered the velvety-black backdrop in what seemed like a million pinpoints of pulsating light. As Bonnie stood on the top step and looked out over Braithwaite's gardens and the road drenched in moonlight beyond, she was swept with such a deep sense of loss she was forced to sit down until the debilitating weakness left her.

She turned her face into the rose-fragrant breeze and thought on the many days and hours she had sat among those flowers and glades, reminiscing on her childhood before Caldbergh, daydreaming of the present, and fantasizing over her future. She wanted nothing more than to return to her room, to awaken in the morning, head for the kitchen, and proceed to tell Cook how to cook, Gretchen how to better starch their laundry, and Stanley how to relax. But she'd made the decision. Damien had enough problems in his life. Why add to them by forcing her presence on him any longer? Besides, he said himself he would soon be leaving England. The idea of standing on some dock waving him good-bye was just too painful for Bonnie. The idea of spending the next years of her life, surrounded by *his* servants and *his* house, waiting for some letter to arrive announcing *his* betrothal to another, seemed to Bonnie like some long and lingering death. Better to nip it in the bud now, while the good-byes were on her terms. She could better deal with it that way. Still . . .

She rested her forehead on her knees, doing her best to force back the nagging need to cry. She was doing that often lately, over the least little things . . .

Damien emerged from the shadows and sat down beside her. "Going somewhere?" he asked quietly.

She looked at him, surprised.

He smoked a slender black cigar as he stretched his long legs down the steps and crossed them at the ankles. His curious glance shifted from Bonnie's face to the orange fire of his cigar as he said, "Nice night for a walk. Would you care to join me?"

She looked guiltily toward her valise.

"You may bring it if you wish. Perhaps you'll need it and perhaps you won't." Damien stood up and offered her his hand. She accepted it hesitantly, catching her breath as his fingers closed around hers. With some effort, she stood.

They walked together down the drive. Finally Damien strolled down the zigzagging flagstone garden path that shone in the moonlight. Bonnie paused, telling herself that to dally any longer would be folly, yet as he stopped and looked back she was compelled to follow.

A rowan tree stood at the foot of the path, a pair of ornate iron chairs beneath it. Damien leaned against the twisted and gnarled tree trunk and continued to smoke as he looked back at Braithwaite Hall. Bonnie sat in the chair farthest from him and clutched her valise to her stomach as hard as she could.

Finally Damien spoke.

"I have known only one other person who was apt to steal away in the middle of the night without saying good-bye."

"And who was that?" Bonnie responded.

"Me."

"Oh." She smiled and tried to relax.

"Will you answer me something?" he asked.

"If I can."

"I have offered you everything money can buy—home, food, education—yet you spurn it for poverty. Why?"

Bonnie looked through the darkness at him. A grim smile moved across his face as he regarded her in return.

"You have offered me a house," she said, "not a home. There is a difference. And while food and education may be sustenance for the mind and body, they do not feed the soul, in my opinion. I had a roof over my head and some form of food at Caldbergh, but little happiness and certainly not . . ."

Bonnie looked away. "When I was very young I wished on a star every night that I would someday be married to a king and have all the money in the world. My mother heard me. She told me that I may have great wealth, but if I did not have someone I loved and who loved me, with whom to share those riches, I may as well have a castle filled with rubbish. If you will pardon my saying so, m'lord, I did not truly believe that until I came here."

His eyes on her, Damien stood unmoving for long, tense moments. Abruptly he gave a sharp laugh before looking away. As he took a deep drag from his cigar, firelight momentarily brightened his features. Then he said, "So in your infinite wisdom you have deduced that Braithwaite is sorely lacking happiness." His mouth curled up again before he added, "How very astute." He tossed the cigar to the ground and crushed it out with his boot heel.

As the night's stillness settled upon them, Bonnie forced her eyes away from Damien's dark form and looked one last time at the gardens. The moon's gleam was pale upon the roses and hedges. The night wind gently shifted a few strands of hair that had escaped her braid and brushed them against her cheeks. Lifting her hand, she tucked them behind her ear. She took a deep breath against the tightness gathering in her chest, then reached for her valise.

"Tell me," came his voice, "do you remember which star it was that you wished on when you were a child?"

Pausing, Bonnie said, "Certainly. I wished on it this night. Just because one ceases to be a child does not mean one must also cease to dream."

"Odd words coming from a girl who vows she doesn't believe in fairy tales." He grinned.

Bonnie felt her cheeks warm. Standing, she placed her valise aside and stepped from beneath the tree limbs to better view the sky. Damien moved up behind her, and for several moments stood at her back, his hands placed lightly, warmly on her shoulders. The effort to concentrate on the endless constellations and not on Damien's nearness was almost more than she could accomplish. The touch was both painful and arousing. She wanted nothing more than to turn and bury herself against him this one last time, but she dared not. Not now. They were too close to good-bye.

"There," Bonnie said. She pointed to a star that was slightly separate from the others. "It is directly above Braithwaite's northernmost gable. It shines brighter than any other star. Do you see it, m'lord?"

"Aye," he said, "I see it."

"Now close your eyes. Are they closed?"

He squeezed her shoulders gently in response.

"Star light, star bright, brightest star I see tonight, I wish I may, I wish I might, have this wish I wish tonight . . ."

A sigh of wind broke over the moor, the only sound in the silence.

Finally Bonnie stepped away from his hands and picked up her valise. Very slowly, her heart drumming in her throat and her eyes burning with tears, she turned back to face him. His hands were in his pockets. His eyes were dark, and his face looked hard with some hint of his old anger.

"Good-bye," she said.

He did not respond.

Forcing herself to turn away, Bonnie started up the walk. So much for wishes, she thought.

"Bonnie."

She stopped and looked around very slowly. Damien stood like a shadow on the walk, his eyes slumberous and unreadable, his face stern with his thoughts. A pulse began a frantic beat in her throat as she awaited his next words.

"Please don't go."

The enormity of his request pressed in on her. She knew what it had cost him to say it.

"Come to London with me and then . . ."

"And then?" She held her breath.

"We'll work something out."

She hugged the valise to her chest while the next minute clipped by like eternity. She moistened her lips with her tongue before saying. "I have been trouble enough. I wouldn't wish to burden your journey to London—"

"You won't."

"It might seem improper . . ."

"Kate will companion you. You may stay at her and William's town house."

She nibbled her lower lip before responding. "But York—"

"Has been where it is for hundreds of years. It will still be there should you decide to return."

Bonnie looked toward the silver ribbon of road in the distance. It was long and bleak amid the craggy moorland. She thought the road seemed a little like herself, a bright existence for the moment but with a future that stretched into an abyss of dark uncertainty.

She focused again on Damien and lifted her chin. "Do y' *want* me t' stay, m'lord?"

A heartbeat passed before he answered. "Yes. I would like that very much."

Bonnie locked her arms around the valise and began to head back up the pathway. Damien remained where he stood, hands in his pockets, the light wind ruffling his hair as he regarded her.

"Where are you going?" he finally called out.

"T' bed, sir, t' rest for the journey to London. I imagine that tomorrow will be a long and taxing day."

As he started to smile Bonnie turned up the walk. She threw one last glance toward the brilliant star in the heavens as his final words came softly through the darkness.

"Good night, m'love."

Damien returned to the library and found Richard and Kate sitting before the fire. A paper in his hand, Richard looked worried.

"It seems you have forgotten to mention this letter to me and Kate," Richard said. "When did it come?"

"With Palmerston's."

"According to your President Davis, the war is escalating."

"That is hardly news."

"Now it is quite apparent that the deep South will not go unscathed by artillery. Tell me, Nephew, do you intend to enlist?"

Damien gazed into the fire before replying. "I don't know."

Richard handed him the letter as Damien sat in a chair. Damien read the note from Davis again. According to the Provisional Confederate President, the month of May had seen an increase of activity. General Benjamin F. Butler had advanced Federal troops into Baltimore without official authorization, and continued to hold the city. North Carolina had assembled a convention at Raleigh, voting for secession, and Confederate Provisional Congressmen had elected to relocate the Confederacy's capital to Richmond, Virginia. Only three days later, Virginia had approved secession. However, the western portion of the state remained clearly pro-Union and was now contemplating a formal break with the rest of the state.

But perhaps the most important and startling fact of all was the announcement that the first Union combat fatality of the war had occurred during the Federal occupation of Alexandria, Virginia. Elmer Ellsworth, head of the eleventh New York regiment, died in an attempt to remove a Confederate flag from a hotel roof. The man who shot Ellsworth, the hotel keeper James Jackson, was then shot by a Union soldier. "It seems the North and the South now have their first martyrs for their respective causes," Davis wrote.

Damien looked at the blazing fire in the hearth, then at his uncle. Richard said gravely, "There will be no turning back for either the Union or the Confederacy. The lines have been drawn."

"So it seems."

"Tell me, Nephew. Do you think you could kill a man over a cause in which you do not stalwartly believe? Can you imagine what it might do to your soul to look into a man's lifeless face and know you had killed him? Would you ever manage to forget him as you lay in your bed at night and tried to sleep?" Richard shook his head, his features haggard. "I think not. You would wonder about his life, his family, his friends. You would agonize over the future he might have had." His voice shaking, Richard whispered, "Don't do it, Damien. For the love of God, don't do it."

As Richard left his chair and quit the room, Damien neither moved nor spoke. Finally he tossed the letter into the fire and watched as it went up in flames.

From the shadows, Kate said, "What about Bonnie?"

"She is traveling to London with us."

"Why?"

Elbows on his knees, he buried his head in his hands. Suddenly Kate was on the floor at his feet, her concerned face turned up to his. "This prolonged good-bye will only hurt her more. Send her to York or allow her to remain here, but don't put Bonnie through this hell of watching you sail out of her life, never to return. Let her go!"

"I can't." He left the chair and moved away so suddenly that there was no time for Kate to stop him. "I . . . can't," he repeated, hating the tortured sound of the words even as he spoke them.

"Why, for God's sake? Will you finally admit to yourself that she means something to you?"

He gave a humorless laugh, but he did not look at Kate. "I told you, chooch. I owe her. I spoiled her for another man, so it's up to me to remedy the situation."

"You can hardly restore her virginity." Leaving the floor, Kate moved up behind him. She asked softly, "Will you go through the remainder of your life being afraid of commitment? Of loving a woman for fear she won't care for you in return?''

He smiled derisively and shrugged off the hand she had placed on his shoulder. ''I don't have a life to commit, Kate. I poured it all into Bent Tree.''

''Then all the more reason why you should let Bonnie go.''

''I will.'' He raised his brows, and a self-mocking humor touched the firm line of his mouth. ''When I'm ready.''

Seventeen

They traveled from Braithwaite at dawn. Although a train ran from York to London, Damien decided they would take the coach. He thought Bonnie might enjoy the countryside, and besides, he was too restless to be cooped up in the stifling quarters of some railway coach. Therefore, Bonnie and Kate had the coach to themselves, while he rode horseback with the outriders ahead of them.

Bonnie had slept little during the night. An hour before their departure she'd called up Jewel, and the two of them had carefully packed the dresses Kate had given her, opting to leave her breeches at Braithwaite. For traveling Bonnie had chosen a gown of pale blue tulle with a single skirt whose hem was edged with a wide band of antique-white lace. The sleeves were short and rode slightly off her shoulders. She'd tied a wide band of matching velvet ribbon around her neck. Upon seeing it, Kate had hurried back to her room and returned with a pendant of blue china centered with a white cameo. She'd applied the pendant to the ribbon, and it lay exquisitely at the hollow of Bonnie's throat. Jewel had then brushed out Bonnie's hair. But instead of braiding it, she simply pulled it back from her face and tied it behind her head with a ribbon.

Bonnie, Kate, and Jewel had been disappointed to learn that Damien had already struck off on his journey just moments before they boarded the coach. "Ah, well," Kate had said, "we'll see him eventually."

While Kate continued reading her Brontë novel, Bonnie peered out the coach's open window at the passing countryside. The sweet smell of moorland grass filled her senses.

The road paralleled the river Cover for some time, and Bonnie took pleasure in following its meandering path. As the sun rose higher in the sky, the water glistened with flashes of silver, bubbled under the humpbacked bridges they were forced to cross, and eventually coiled out of sight as it headed eastward, and they continued south.

Bonnie then concentrated on the towering slopes and barren grassland that spread out around them. Richard had informed her that the distance from Middleham to London by way of the main coach road was two hundred fifty-one miles and six furlongs. It was said that the pass through Coverdale was one of the most rugged coach trips. Richard had also laughingly informed her that no traveler of circumstance would ever think of undertaking the journey without previously having arranged his worldly affairs. Which was no doubt why Richard had declined the journey to London for the time being, and why Damien had chosen to ride horseback.

At midday Damien sent one of his outriders back to the coach to inquire whether the ladies would prefer to stop at the Horsehouse Inn and take lunch or whether they cared to continue traveling while they ate the meal Cook had packed in the basket riding at Kate's elbow. They opted for the latter, once informed that if they did not stop they would reach Grange Inn by dusk. Kate spread a fine lace and linen cloth on the seat and laid out pork pies, sausage rolls, and tarts. Cheese followed with a great loaf of crusty white bread and a bottle of wine. They ate the food but did not uncork the wine until the afternoon sun had begun to heat the stuffy confines of the coach uncomfortably.

"At least it's not raining," Kate said. Turning her second glass of warm red wine to her mouth, she added, "Yet."

Bonnie smiled, drank her wine, and continued to peer out the window.

"What do you find so interesting out there?" Kate asked.

"The world. Before coming to Caldbergh I had never left the town where I was born."

"And that was . . . ?"

Bonnie momentarily considered revealing her past to Kate, then reconsidered. Despite the warm bond she had developed with the Warwicks, she simply could not force herself to convey the gruesome, terrifying details of her father's murder, not as long as the possibility existed that the killer could still find her. Besides, the nightmares had returned less and less frequently during the last weeks. Why dredge them up again when she was so close to putting all that fear and pain behind her?

"I consider all of the Pennines my home," she said. "Those distant fells may well be where I played as a child. At least they are very much like them. They are beautiful, aren't they?"

Kate pursed her lips in consideration before replying. "Once you've seen one fell and dale you've seen them all."

"Not so, m'lady."

Bonnie pointed to the nearest fell, a steep slope with patches of dead bracken that looked almost scarlet against the dark green grass. "Do you see those deep grooves on yonder hillside? Do you know what they are? They are called 'hushes.' Hundreds of years ago the first miners of these hills would dam up streams in order to uncover veins of lead. That was before shafts and levels were used. And do you see those faint lines running horizontally along the sides of the fells? They are footpaths once used by the first men who worked these mines. Did you know that Swaledale provided roof lead for French abbeys as far back as the twelfth century? And for the King's castle at Windsor as well. Many Roman cathedrals have lead roofs from the remotest Yorkshire mines. The Romans were the first miners here, after all. A pig of lead was actually found with 'Adrian 117—138' stamped on it. And many believe that mining here went back even further than that."

"Really!" Kate stared at Bonnie in amazement, then looked back at the countryside. "I've lived here all my life and never knew."

"You wouldn't. Your life was never touched by mining the way . . ." Bonnie bit off her words and gazed again out the window.

"When the miners of today come across signs of their ancient predecessors, they say 'T'owd man has been here before us.' They say a prayer for those long-lost people, and for themselves, before delving further into the black tunnels. Do you know that when the industry was at its height, Swaledale and Arkengarthdale between them produced five to six thousand tons of lead every year? Now, when one walks the high dales, they come upon the dark openings of deserted shafts, and they cannot help but think of the men who worked as far as four hundred feet down in the earth. Most who work the mines die before seeing forty years. The air somehow poisons them.''

Sitting back in her seat, Kate watched Bonnie closely before saying, ''That's very sad.''

''Aye,'' she responded softly. ''It isn't enough that life itself is hard. Each day that the miners face the mine they know it could mean one day less to live. It isn't enough that most are forced to walk six or seven miles to work, but their wages are also meager. Many who are not married live on nothing but porridge and brown bread, and that has to sustain them during the long hours of working in the black pits.''

''The harshness of their lives must be unbearable,'' Kate said. ''They must suffer great unhappiness.''

Bonnie watched the green countryside, the zigzagging dry stone walls with their occasional nest of wild birds fixed firmly among the gray stones, the empty rolling miles of browns and greens and yellows, and the occasional bog pools like dark mirrors under fringes of swaying reeds. In the distance a farm house stood bleakly against the blue sky, its windows like staring eyes, its chimneys eeking thin streams of black smoke in the air. Fleecy white sheep dotted the farm's fields, and their bleating brought memories to Bonnie's mind that she had not recalled in years.

''They aren't unhappy,'' she responded quietly. ''Despite the hardship, the gangs of miners often sing as they trudge over the fells to their labors. And they sing on their way home as well. They're proud of their work and of their dales. Aye, the dalesmen are fine men.''

''They must be. Tell me, Bonnie, did your father die in the mine?''

''No, he . . .'' Frowning, Bonnie looked hard at Kate and said, ''I never said my father was a miner.''

''You didn't have to.''

Bonnie sat back in her seat. They continued their journey in silence.

* * *

The coach arrived at Grange Inn by dusk, just as Damien had predicted. The aged accommodation huddled in a hollow of the Whernside moor, along with several dark stone houses whose windows glowed with welcoming yellow light.

The inn appeared to be a popular stopover, not only for weary travelers, but also for the locals. As Bonnie and Kate gratefully stepped from the coach, the patrons' boisterous laughter echoed all the way over the moor, or so it seemed. Bonnie and Kate exchanged amused glances before laughing themselves.

Predictably the tavern was crowded and warm, the few open windows offering too little breeze to cool the low-ceilinged room. Bonnie and Kate had no more than stepped into the tavern when they were approached by Damien. By all appearances he had arrived a good while before them. Already having shucked his jacket, he looked little different from the common men who were crowding the long tables. His white shirt was dusty and clung to his chest and back with sweat. His hair and face looked damp as well. Stopping before them and planting his feet slightly apart, he threw back his head and quaffed his tankard of ale. Then he wiped his mouth on the sleeve of his shirt before greeting them.

"Ladies, have you had a pleasant journey?"

"Pleasant enough," Kate replied with a lift of one brow. "And you, my lord?"

"Aye. The ale in this place makes up for the rigors of the trip. Grange had the finest ale in all of Yorkshire when I was a lad. It still has, I'm happy to say."

"Is that why we were driven to do without lunch? So you could ease your aches and pains in Grange ale?" Kate affected a slight pout as Damien grinned in response. "You are a cad, Damien. And a drunk, I fear. Careful, Bonnie, I suspect he is on his way to being caught in his cups. As I recall, the near vicinity is no place for a young woman to dally if Damien is drinking. He does not hold his ale well."

Damien looked at Bonnie directly for the first time since she had entered the tavern. There was an arrested expression on his strong features. As on the day before, he said nothing about her dress or the way she wore her hair, but his eyes appeared black in the smoky room—fathomless, filled with dangerous, shifting currents that no doubt had more to do

with the ale he had consumed than with his feelings, Bonnie
mused. Still, she could always hope . . .

"I've had hot water and food sent up to your room. I
assure you it is quieter there than it is here. You should have
no problem resting."

Kate glanced around the tavern again and was about to
respond when Damien was set upon by a buxom wench with
frizzy red hair and a face full of freckles. The woman
snatched his empty tankard and replaced it with a full one,
sloshing ale over his sleeves and down the front of his shirt.
She appeared to fall against him and he, in turn, wrapped his
free arm around her, both stumbling backward as they attempted to regain their footing. Then the woman's arms were
clinging to his neck, dragging down his head until she could
cover his mouth with her own. Bonnie could not draw her
eyes away from the spectacle; her face grew cold despite the
sweltering heat in the room.

Hearing Kate call her name, Bonnie forced herself to look
away. Kate, along with their coachman, was headed toward
the stairs at the far end of the room. Bonnie followed, but
not before looking back at Damien once more. He stood half
a head taller than the men surrounding him. So close-fitting
were his brown leather breeches that she could plainly see
his narrow hips and the flex of his thigh muscles as he walked
with the woman. Bonnie looked quickly away, aware of an
angry, painful heat in her chest and stomach as she remembered his kissing the hussy.

They were shown upstairs by a pleasant woman who Bonnie deduced was the innkeeper's wife. Cordially she referred
to both Kate and Bonnie as "m'ladies." It seemed disconcerting to Bonnie to be addressed in such a way, but since
Kate made no attempt to correct the error, Bonnie let it go.

The room was small but adequate for their needs. A double
bed took up one wall. A crude table, topped with their dinner, took up another. In the center of the rugless, rough-hewn
floor was a tub filled with hot water. Another five pails of
steaming water waited alongside.

Drying her wet hands on her apron, the innkeeper's wife
said, "Soon as one's finished with 'er bath, just give us a
ring and me girl'll empty the tub and fill it with fresh water.

As you can see, I've brung up yer dinner. It ain't fancy, but it'll fill yer belly and stick to yer ribs.''

"It smells wonderful," Kate said. "You're most kind."

"It ain't often we gets such fine folk into the Grange, ma'am, though we can remember yer brother easy enough. He stopped by frequent-like in years past. Him and his lads were real roof raisers, as I recall. Weren't a safe wench for miles once they got boozin' on me Jimmy's ale.''

Kate smiled. "No doubt. He seems to be in fine form already tonight.''

"Aye, he were a fine lad, and he's grown into a handsome man. He were generous to a fault was our Damien. Oh, I do beg yer pardon, ma'am, I mean his lordship. We always did find difficulty in rememberin' he was gentle bred.''

"Understandable since he finds it difficult as well," Kate replied. She thanked the proprietress again and showed her to the door. "By the way, in which room is my brother staying?''

"Directly across.''

Kate closed the door and sank against it with a laugh. "I'll flip you for the bath,'' she told Bonnie.

Bonnie lay on her back, staring at the ceiling and listening to the distant commotion from the tavern. The hour must be well after midnight, yet Damien had not returned to his room.

She dared not close her eyes for fear of seeing him again with the tavern wench. Had it been her imagination or had he really made a point of kissing the woman in front of her? She didn't want to think it. After all, he had invited her to come on this journey. He'd *admitted* that he wanted her to come. Still . . .

Bonnie rolled from the bed. She couldn't lie there any longer and imagine his being with the woman. Why would he want to be with the wench if the woman meant nothing to him? If Kate was right, if Damien did care for her, why didn't he search *her* out? It seemed so nonsensical to her that anyone would care to make love to someone he didn't know, much less care for.

She paced, convincing herself that believing Kate's admission that Damien loved her would be a mistake. A dreadful mistake! She would be setting herself up for a great fall by allowing herself to believe, even for a moment, that his feelings stemmed from anything more than guilt and responsibility. Yet, he had asked her to come on this journey. He had admitted he didn't want her to leave him . . .

Hidden by midnight's shadows, Bonnie stood at the bottom of the stairs and searched the tavern for any sign of Warwick. The crowd had thinned somewhat, yet a cloud of tobacco smoke still hovered near the beamed ceiling, and the acrid smell of sour ale made breathing next to impossible.

A group of six men crowded a far corner, taking turns at darts, while in another corner a man lay facedown on a trestle table, an empty tankard in both hands as he attempted to sleep off the ale's effects before venturing home. Several more men were scattered throughout the room, some in pairs, some alone, but Damien was not among them.

Bonnie was about to turn back to her room when the sound of a woman's voice stopped her. There was no mistaking the abrasive laughter of the wench who had accosted Damien earlier. With a heart pounding in dread Bonnie looked down the wall nearest to her, to the far corner of the room. She could just make out the white of Warwick's shirt in the shadows, then, as she focused harder, she saw him resting back against the wall as he lounged on a bench, his long legs stretched out before him, propped on another bench and crossed at the ankles. The wench sat beside him, one hand dragging his shirt open and off his shoulder while the other hand explored his bare chest and stomach, all the way to the waistband of his breeches—and further.

"Yer a real man," she heard the wench say. "We don't get many like you through here. For twopence I'd give y' a tumble y' won't soon forgit, no sir. Wot d' ya say, m'lord? Will y' go a round upstairs with ol' Rita?"

Damien raised his tankard and drank deeply. Bonnie held her breath, as much from anger as from concern that he would actually agree to the proposition.

"Tell y' wot, m'lord. Yer a fine specimen f' certain. Wot say we forgit the twopence and just enjoy ourselves f' the rest of the evenin'?"

Damien smiled as the woman ran her hand urgently over

his breeches and planted her palm none too gently on his groin. "Perhaps I should charge you," he said.

"And maybe I'd pay it. Like I said, we don't get the likes o' you through here. Yer stiff as a shepherd's staff, I'll wager." The woman giggled and added, "Just about as big as one too, by the feel of it."

A burst of laughter from someone on the far end of the room caused Damien to look up. Perhaps he sensed Bonnie standing there in the smoke and shadows, because his head slowly turned and suddenly she was staring down into his dark eyes and heat-flushed face. A moment passed before he dropped his feet to the floor and sat up. Looking back at the wench, he shoved his tankard into her hand and said, "Get me another."

Rita sat back in surprise. Then she saw Bonnie. "Lud, that ain't yer wife—"

"No," he snapped. "She's not."

"Yer fiancée—"

"No. Just shut up and get me the ale."

Without speaking again, the woman left the bench and headed for the bar. Bonnie followed her with her eyes before looking back at Damien.

He was staring at the floor between his boots. His elbows were on his knees, and his dark hair had spilled over his forehead, nearly to the bridge of his nose. Even from this distance she could tell he was angry. But no more than she. Bonnie shook so hard with fury it frightened her. She could no more control it than she could force back the words.

"Yer bloody disgustin'."

He came to his feet so quickly that the bench skidded backward and banged against the wall. With his shirt sagging off one shoulder, he pointed a finger at Bonnie and said through his teeth, "And you have no right to stand about shadows and watch me. What I do and with whom I do it is no business of yours."

She said nothing, just fixed him with her stare and summoned a courage she didn't feel. It wasn't easy. Aside from her fury and the odd sense of betrayal she felt in her heart over his interest in the wench, her body was responding to a different upheaval that was even more disconcerting than his behavior.

"Stop looking at me like that," he demanded.

With a note of constraint in her voice, she asked, "How am I lookin'?"

"Like a damned kicked puppy. I won't have it, Bonnie. I want you to stay away from me. Just stay completely away from me and leave me alone."

"Yer the one who asked me t' stay!" she replied more angrily. "Yer the one who wanted me t' go t' London."

The wench returned, but he shoved her away and approached Bonnie. "That does not give you the right to sneak about shadows and spy—"

"I was not spyin'!"

"You were spying."

Bonnie opened and closed her mouth. Aware the room had gone silent as the tavern's patrons regarded them, Bonnie slowly turned back for the stairs. She was halfway up them when Warwick's voice came booming at her from below.

"Come back here!"

"I think not," she replied.

"Bonnie!"

She topped the stairs and started down the corridor to her room. Then Damien hit the stairs behind her and Bonnie broke into a run. She'd barely reached the threshold of her room before he moved up behind her and caught her wrist, spinning her around.

Bonnie stared up into Damien's disturbingly handsome face, noting some undefinable emotion flicker in the depths of his eyes. His presence bore down on her, and his fingers dug painfully into her arm, yet the look that washed over his features in that moment was like no anger she had ever seen. She sensed the war of control he was fighting, not only of the mind but of the body; she was suddenly fighting it herself.

"I see I'm going to have to speak to my sister," he said in a tight voice. "By now I would have expected her to teach you how to better respect your elders, Bonnie. You do *not* turn your back on a man who is talking to you."

"What yer sayin' is that one of the lower class should not turn away from one of the upper class—"

"Stop putting words in my mouth."

"But that *is* what y' meant. *Ain't* it?"

His dark eyes fixed momentarily on the curve of Bonnie's bare shoulder, very slowly shifted to her throat, then moved very gradually to her mouth. "No," he said more softly. "It is not. In truth it has been difficult the last two days to recall that there ever was an urchin from Caldbergh who stumbled in my door."

Bonnie was extremely aware of the warm hand still on her wrist, gripping less forcefully now but surely harder than need be. She became conscious of a great many things—the faint odor of tobacco and ale that emanated from him, the powerful body that pressed against her more closely than polite society would approve. She could feel his breath stirring the hair on her temple, brushing her cheek, warming her blood so it rushed to her head like quicksilver and made her dizzy.

Looking again at Damien's face, Bonnie became lost in his eyes, and her heart began thudding in thick, painful strokes as she said, "Is the urchin so easily forgettable, m'lord?"

He gave a strangely bitter laugh and murmured, "She is when she is swallowed by yards of lace and ribbons. In truth a man would be hard-pressed to remember his own name when confronted by a woman of such extraordinary . . . loveliness."

Bonnie sank back against the wall as his free hand traced the contours of her face and nestled against the curve of her throat, where her pulse beat like a hummingbird's against his palm. She did her best to swallow before saying, "I am hardly lovely . . ."

He laughed bitterly again. "Charming humility, but I doubt it will last long once we reach London and you gain an audience of admirers—I've seen it happen before, after all. I wonder who is the bigger fool: me for taking you there or you for going? Whichever, I fear we will both suffer for it in the end."

"I cannot imagine how."

With his thumb he tipped up her chin. Breathless, Bonnie stared at the black hair that fell rebelliously onto his forehead and at the eyes that were filled with a fire and passion that stole the last remaining strength from her knees so she was forced to twist her fingers into Damien's shirt or she would surely have fallen.

He wanted her, she could tell. He *did* care for her! She

could see it in the angry set of his jaw, in the scowl of his heavy black brows, and in the mouth that was taut with suppressed emotion. All the dreams she had recently dampened seemed to rise up from ashes in her heart and glow hot with new hope.

What sense of courage drove her to rise on her toes and press her open mouth against his, she would never know. It was something she had only fantasized as she lay unable to sleep deep in the night.

Damien groaned and, releasing her wrist, plunged both hands into her hair while he held her head against the ferocity of the kiss that followed. His tongue moved in and out of her mouth as his body had once moved in and out of hers, driving her to moan and wrap her arms around his neck, to kiss him back with equal passion.

When he finally tore his mouth free of hers, Damien's chest rose and fell raggedly as he ran his hands slowly up her arms to her wrists and dragged her hands from around his neck. "God help us, but I want you," he said roughly. "If I ask you to come to my room, will you do it?"

Searching his eyes, she said, "What about the woman downstairs?"

"Had I wanted the silly bitch, I would have taken her."

Tilting her head, Bonnie lowered her lashes, knowing what she wanted to answer but not willing, in that moment, to admit it even to herself. She saw a slow smile turn up one side of his mouth before he said, "Coyness becomes you, girl, but I'm too hard and drunk to appreciate it much. Will you come to my room or not?"

"But Kate—"

"Is a heavy sleeper as I recall." He backed to the door of his room, his fingers still gripping her wrist. She hesitated for a moment, then followed, feeling slightly dazed by the hunger in his eyes and the need palpable around him.

He dropped her hand and opened the door, then stood to one side, allowing her to make the decision to enter on her own. He was not going to force her; she wished he would. As her mind and body combatted each other, she could not move, but stood where he'd left her, staring beyond him at the distant bed and feeling her body flush with heat as the memories of their previous meetings assailed her.

The sound of heavy footsteps on the stairs jarred Bonnie from her thoughts and without raising her eyes to his she entered the room, walked to the foot of the bed, and stopped, unable to turn and face him. It wasn't nervousness. It wasn't even shame that gripped her in that moment. She realized it was the love she felt for him, the happiness that she could at last face him without the barrier of anger and hate between them.

He moved up behind her. Then his hands were on her shoulders, nudging down the neckline of her dress, fingertips lightly brushing over the exposed portion of her breasts. As he wrapped one arm around her waist and pulled her against him, Bonnie could feel the heat and sweat of his body burn through the material of her dress and set her afire with a longing that was as hot as it was consuming.

She turned to face him, gasping as his hands moved over her breasts, holding them momentarily before sliding up to cup her face. His palms were hot and his eyes were blazing. His voice sounded raw as he said, "Kiss me."

Again his fingers tunneled through her hair and gripped her scalp. He angled her head back and moved his mouth onto hers, searing her with his tongue as he stroked and explored and ravaged her with his own. Until she felt consumed. Until she felt as if she were drowning and out of control.

Finally he moved back very slightly, but still so close that his lips brushed hers as he demanded, "Look at me."

Her lashes fluttered open. His face, so near, was damp and flushed. A single drop of sweat beaded at his temple, and Bonnie was tempted to catch it with her tongue as it trickled down the side of his face. But she didn't. She was helpless to do anything but stare into his piercing eyes and wonder what he meant to do. Then it occurred to her that he was waiting for *her* next move, as he had at the door. She reacted from her heart.

Cradling his face in her hands, she said, "I love you."

For a moment he did not move. Neither did he speak. Then, very slowly, Damien backed away.

Twisting her hands together, Bonnie smiled unsteadily and added, "I think it's wonderful that we've gotten this out in the open. Don't you?"

His face expressionless, Damien turned away, walked to the chest of drawers against the far wall, and stared at his image in the mirror. Bonnie moved up behind him, hesitantly wrapped her arms around his waist, and pressed her cheek against the hard plane of his back. She breathed deeply, finding that the musky scent of him made that core of need inside her grow even hotter and brighter, if that were possible. A soft groan of arousal worked up her throat before she could stop it.

When Damien turned back to Bonnie, his face looked harder, his eyes darker. Caution called out to her briefly as he closed his hands over her shoulders. He kissed her again, driving her head back with brutal force, until she was clinging to him, breathless with fear and anticipation. When he raised his head and looked at her once more, he said in a steely voice, "Never mistake this for love, Bonnie."

"If not love, then what is it?"

"Lust. When the fire is between your legs and not in your heart, it can't remotely resemble love." He backed her to the bed even as his hands moved down her dress and closed over her breasts. "You don't love me," he said. "You love this."

Her eyelids fluttered closed as his hands roughly pulled down her bodice, exposing her breasts and imprisoning her arms next to her body. Then the bed met her thighs and she floated backward, assisted by his hands that laid her gently onto the soft bedding.

As his palms closed over Bonnie's breasts, her eyes flew open. As he bent his head and nuzzled her hard, rosy nipples with his face, she gasped. As he took them in his mouth, first one then the other, she cried out and arched her back in such wanton need that she surprised even herself.

His dark head came up and he smiled that crooked smile that made him look both roguish and boyish. "I'm drunk, but not too drunk to think I must have been crazy for thinking you were a child. I'm not too drunk to suspect I should carry you back to your room and tuck you into bed with my sister. But I'm too goddamn drunk to do it." He shoved himself off the bed, swayed a moment before using one leg to ease open her thighs. Bonnie tried to sit up, but he nudged her back down and eased her pantaloons off, dropping them to the floor before wedging himself between her legs, spreading his own so that she lay open to him.

He pulled his shirt from the waistband of his breeches. It slid from his shoulders and he tossed it to the floor. He flipped open the buttons on his trousers one by one, until the leather gave way to expose darker, thicker hair than was on his chest. Then bending over her slightly, he eased his hands under her shoulders, took the material of her dress, and rent it down the back; arm muscles flexing and face determined, he tore it completely from her body and threw it aside.

She lay exposed to him in every sense of the word. Yet she didn't care.

Damien moved his gaze over her body, slowly, deliberately, as if memorizing each detail in his mind. His chest rose and fell sharply, his breath sounding harsh between his parted lips. Then he slid his breeches partway down his hips, releasing his manhood into his hand. Bonnie felt the breath leave her in a painful rush as she watched his fingers close around himself and slowly pump.

"I have lain in my bed many nights telling myself that my memory was playing tricks on me," he said, "that you could not possibly be as beautiful as I remembered. I've lost count of how many times I imagined storming into your room and taking you so I could quench the fire you've put inside me here." His hand slid to the end of his shaft, then drew back again. His eyes closed, and the cords in his neck became taut. He murmured in a low voice, "I'm too damned tired and drunk to fight it again tonight. I want you so badly, girl, that it hurts."

Very slowly Bonnie sat up. She buried her face against his stomach, breathing hotly against his skin before dropping back her head and looking at his face.

"It's what I've wanted as well," she told him. "And no matter what you think, I do love you."

"Don't. You don't—"

"What must I do to convince you?" She ran her hands over his hips, and he groaned.

"Careful," he whispered huskily. "I might show you."

"I'm more than willing to learn."

He looked down into her eyes, and for a moment his face lost the anger and despair that had twisted his features. "And you will learn. Someday. I've taken your virginity already. I would not rob you of your innocence entirely. There must be something left for . . ."

A shadow seemed to pass over his face, and suddenly he seemed angrier. His hands became rougher as he forced her back on the bed. He kissed her mouth, her throat, her shoulders. He teased the tips of her breasts with his tongue and teeth until Bonnie sensed her control shattering.

With a wild and hungry urgency he moved down her stomach, nipping with his teeth, dipping his tongue into her navel until she was gripping the sheet under her and panting his name aloud. Then his head was moving down again, and his breath was beating hotly against the equally hot and sensitive flesh between her thighs.

"No. Oh no," she cried, realizing only afterward that the words had been no more than a dry sob in her throat. She tried clutching his hair, his shoulders, then fell back on the bed and covered her face with the backs of her hands.

His tongue slid inside her like a hot, wet flame. Again and again he pressed into her, thrusting and withdrawing, searching out the intimate folds, each flick and jab splintering her body into tiny pieces. Then the pressure began, rippling in flashes through her arms and legs and centering where his tongue worked so feverishly inside her. She writhed and twisted against him, pleading not only for the sweet surcease she knew he could bring her, but also for his body to move inside her, deep inside where she ached for him most.

Rising up over her, he positioned the tip of his smooth, thick shaft against her, then in one long, slow stroke, embedded himself inside her, so deeply and completely that their bodies seemed as one.

Damien's head fell back and his sweat-glazed chest rose as if he were in pain. "Oh my God," he groaned. "Sweet God, I didn't imagine it."

Bonnie raised her legs and locked them around his waist. She whispered, "Please . . ." then rocked her pelvis against his.

He moved with her, hesitantly at first, then more boldly, sinking and withdrawing, stoking the fires inside them until the air became impossible to breathe and each was lost in a storm of such sweet agony that the world around them ceased to exist. She reached for Damien as he did for her, hands touching, grasping, fingers entwining. He pressed her down in the bed, her arms outstretched and hands gripping his.

"Look at me," he demanded raggedly. "I want you looking at me when you come."

She did; their eyes locked.

Their bodies moved together.

"Hold on," he whispered. "Hold on, and don't let me go."

The next moment reality ceased for them both. The release beat in Bonnie's blood and vibrated through her body. She was vaguely aware of crying out words of passion, of love, incoherent murmurings that she could no more control than the responses of her body. Then his hands were gripping her hips and his body was throbbing inside her, spilling inside her a hot liquid rush that made him grow motionless and rigid for a long, heart-stopping moment.

Gradually, the world ceased its spinning, and their bodies relaxed. Bonnie held Damien tightly to her, enjoying the weight of his body on hers, in hers. She stroked his hair, finding it damp at the nape and slightly curly. When finally he raised up on his elbows and looked down at her, she smiled.

Damien smiled back. "Well," he said. "I'm not drunk any longer."

"No?"

"Stone-cold sober."

He eased his body from hers and helped her further into the bed. He peeled off the rest of his clothes before joining her, then he stretched out against her, one leg thrown negligently over hers as he ran his hand over her cooling flesh. She shivered a little and he paused. His hand went slowly to her thigh and slipped gently between her legs. He stroked her with his fingers, inside and out, before asking, "Are you all right?"

Moved to tears by his caring, Bonnie nodded.

Finally, and with a deep breath, Damien lay back on the bed. He stared at the ceiling for a long while before looking back at her. She rested partially against his chest. Her hand ran idly over his shoulder as he said, "Your name suits you, you know. You're a bonny lass."

Bonnie smiled.

Damien touched her face with his fingers. "So much for innocence," he whispered thoughtfully. Then he slid both hands around her head and kissed her mouth, lightly stroking her lips with his tongue. When finally he backed away, he confessed. "I want you already. What have you done to bewitch me so that I can't control my feelings?"

He kissed her again, more passionately this time, while his arms drew her closer against him. When he finally pulled back, it was Bonnie who spoke.

"The fire is still burning, m'lord."

His hand slid to her thigh. She caught it and moved it up, pressed it against her racing heart. "The one here," she told him, "is burning ever brighter."

Bonnie's soft breathing was the only sound to disturb the hush in the room. Damien watched the gentle rise and fall of her breasts as she slept. She looked beautiful. So beautiful. Her innocence of heart made him feel vulnerable and unmanned, and he hated himself for the weakness.

He hated himself for what he would do to her. But he'd made his decision before leaving Braithwaite, and he wouldn't back down. Bonnie may *think* she loved him now, but the fire in her heart would soon be extinguished by new experiences—and new men—when they reached London. Besides, as fond as he was of her, there was no room in his life for extra baggage. There was Parliament to face, then a war to endure.

A soft rap at the door jarred Damien from his morose thoughts. He rolled from the bed and tossed a loose sheet over Bonnie, covering all but the crown of her head. Swiftly he pulled on his breeches and buttoned them as he crept for the door. He opened it a little and looked down into his sister's stern face.

"Is Bonnie here?" Kate demanded.

He nodded.

Kate looked away. Even in dawn's gray shadows he could see she was furious.

When she looked at him again, she said, "Will you at least see her back to her own bed before people are about?"

"Of course."

"See to it now while I keep watch."

Leaving the door slightly ajar, Damien retraced his steps to the bed and tried to rouse Bonnie. She only groaned and snuggled deeper into the pillow. Finally he was forced to tuck the sheet around her and lift her in his arms. With her head resting on his shoulder and her hair trailing beyond his knees, he carried her to the door, waited as Kate slipped across the hallway and opened her own, then he carried Bonnie to her bed and eased her onto it. Her eyes opened sleepily and she smiled.

"I've carried you back to your room," he whispered.

"Ummm. Must you?"

Damien grinned. "We have your sterling reputation to consider."

"Me mummy used t' say, 'Y' never miss what y' never had.' "

"I'm certain your mummy was a wonderful woman."

"Aye. She would have approved of you, m'lord."

"I'm not so certain of that, lass." He kissed her forehead as she drifted off to sleep again. He returned to his room, where Kate was pacing.

She waited until he had shut the door before demanding, "How could you?"

Dragging his hand through his hair, Damien closed his eyes. "My head hurts like hell. I wish you would lower your voice."

"I am speaking barely above a whisper."

"That's still too loud."

He walked to a ewer and poured himself a glass of water, swishing the liquid around in his mouth before spitting it into a brass cuspidor on the floor. He ran his hand over his beard-stubbled jaw before facing his sister again.

"How could you take advantage of her feelings, knowing you have every intention of marrying her off to the first man who asks for her hand?"

"Not necessarily the first, Kate. I want her well taken care of. You know that. And there damn well better be some affection for Bonnie, or I won't agree to the alliance."

"Oh, I am quite certain there will be no bounds to the affection the gentlemen will feel for Bonnie, especially to the tune of one hundred thousand pounds—that is the sum Richard told me, I believe. I'm also certain Bonnie will be more than pleased that you place such a high value on her happiness." Kate walked to the door and opened it before looking at Damien again. Her eyes were bright with tears as she said, "I never thought to feel such disappointment in you, my lord." Then she slammed the door.

Eighteen

William and Katharine's London town house in Park Lane was pleasant and relaxing, even on so dreary an afternoon. After the grueling journey from Middleham, Damien was more than ready for a bit of relaxation. He was going to need it before facing the grim tasks before him.

He took one last glance out the window at the rain-drenched street and the hansoms and buses that crowded it. Kate and Bonnie's coach had no doubt been held up by the rain and traffic. And judging by the looks of the sky, or what he could see of it through the sulfurous fog choking the city, more rain was imminent.

Damien turned away from the window and watched his brother-in-law pour them each a brandy. Then he dropped into a Queen Anne chair before the fireplace and smiled his thanks as William handed him the drink.

William, his tall frame dressed casually in a loose white shirt and snug black breeches, remained standing, his curious brown eyes regarding Damien. "Word is out, my good friend, of your return to polite society. I'm certain when you arrive at your house in Mayfair you'll be greeted by numerous salutations and invitations. The young ladies are all atwitter with the news. As are their mothers," he added, smiling. "I'm certain their mouths are literally drooling over the idea of dangling their daughters before you, Dame. How many teas and sweet cakes will you enjoy during the next few weeks while the young ladies bat their pretty eyes at you? I wager you can hardly wait."

Damien grinned and sampled his brandy. "I'll try to contain my enthusiasm," he replied dryly.

271

"No doubt you'll be making a few appearances at White's as well."

"Certainly."

"Of course you realize you've set the tongues to wagging over why you've returned to London."

"I'm not surprised. I'm certain they will be wagging even harder by the time I leave."

"There has been a great amount of debate over the stand you're taking. I spoke with Palmerston only this morning, and I have to tell you, the news is not good. Palmerston and Lord Russell, our Minister of Foreign Affairs, say there are many members who are highly agitated over the possibility that Parliament may actually agree to see Madison and Slidell."

Damien considered the comment a moment before responding.

"President Davis himself has appointed James Madison and John Slidell as commissioners of the venture. Madison is a well-respected planter from Virginia and a presecession United States senator who served as a chairman of the Foreign Affairs Committee. Slidell has had an equally enviable political career in statecraft. He is also socially well connected, being the brother-in-law of the South's General Pierre Gustave Beauregard. Slidell is a leader in Louisiana society, which should certainly gain the favor of imperial Paris. Both men have a great deal of experience in dealing with people and government. They cannot help but have impact on Parliament's decision."

William met Damien's eyes with some reluctance. "You know I'm helping you with this because of my love for you and your sister. I mightily respect you, Dame, and always have, but I do not respect this war. You know England's feelings on slavery. Why, only last month, Her Majesty's own Negro subjects were kidnapped and sold into bondage while their ship was docked in New Orleans, taking on cargo. Recently one of our most esteemed naval captains was tarred and feathered while in Charleston, just for allowing a Negro to eat at his table. Quite frankly, knowing the kind of man you are, I'm surprised you tolerate slavery."

"The slavery issue has little to do with the war," Damien replied, "but everything to do with the continuation of the

South as we know it.'' He drank his brandy before going on. "Speaking for myself, I find slavery abhorrent and do not practice it. I pay my workers well and threat them fairly. But I'm also far wealthier than other planters who rely totally on their crops to make ends meet. But like them, I am also a Southern planter, and even now I have cotton rotting on the docks due to the Union's naval blockades.''

"The *Economist* will shoot that excuse full of holes,'' William replied.

"Not only will our textile industry here in England eventually suffer from the cutbacks of Southern exports, if the war continues, but as you well know, cotton is not the South's only resource on which England relies. Tobacco, sugarcane, rice—''

"You've made your point,'' William said, cutting him off.

"Then surely Parliament can understand why we should all wish to see the war over soon as possible.''

Taking a chair across from Damien's, William nodded. "When are your commissioners due to arrive?''

"As soon as Parliament agrees to see them I'll write President Davis and he'll set our plans into action. Madison and Slidell will board the armed steamer *Nashville* out of Charleston. She's a blockade runner Davis has appointed for the mission. They'll sail for Havana, a neutral port, and from there catch a British ship for London.''

Taking a long moment to consider this information, William asked, "I know you're here to pave the way for the Confederate representatives, but what then?''

Damien stared into his brandy before bringing it to his mouth and drinking it completely. Finally he said, "I return to Mississippi and, if necessary, take up arms to safeguard my home.''

William appeared stunned. "Have you spoken to Kate about this?''

He nodded.

"I trust she didn't take the news well.''

"No.''

"I must confess to being somewhat surprised myself. Marching into battle is hardly our forte, my lord.''

Damien smiled. "I expect our forefathers are tossing in their crypts at that comment. Do you forget that it was their defense of their kings that landed them the properties and wealth we enjoy today? I'm certain old warhorse Earl of Warwick didn't think twice about defending what was his.''

"They were bred to fight, Dame. We were not. And, yes, that old warhorse Warwick may be rolling in his crypt, but I'll warrant it's not over my comment but over the idea that his offspring would turn his back on his heritage and swagger off to some other country and get himself killed for a cause with which he is not in total agreement.''

A racket from outside brought the conversation to an end. William left his chair and went to the window. "The ladies have arrived,'' he said.

Damien stood and they both walked to the front door, William opening it with a flourish and striding down the brick walk to meet Kate. Damien followed more slowly, wondering if Kate had yet cooled down enough to speak to him again. Noting the belligerent look on her face as she stepped from the coach, he decided she hadn't. Then Bonnie emerged and Damien stopped.

William opened his arms as Kate ran to him. Lifting her off the ground, he spun her around, upsetting her bonnet and making her laugh. "I've missed you,'' he said. "It's been a hell of a long time without you.''

"And I you,'' Kate replied. They gazed into each other's eyes for a long moment before Kate managed to look away. She turned back to Bonnie, who had also halted the moment she saw Damien. "William, this is Bonnie. Isn't she lovely?''

Damien noted the look of surprise and appreciation on William's features. His friend took Bonnie's gloved hand in his and raised it just short of his mouth before saying, "Extraordinary. Bonnie, may I welcome you to our home. Did you enjoy your journey?''

"Not likely,'' she responded bluntly. "We baked the first half of the trip, and the last day and a half we were bogged up t' our bloody axles in mud. M' backside feels as if it's been flogged.''

William appeared momentarily stunned. Then his head fell back in laughter before he managed, "Good God, and I thought they exaggerated your honesty. Seems I owe them an apology.''

"Who is 'they,' m'lord?''

"Why, Fitzpatrick, Millhouse, and Newton, of course. They all returned to London infatuated with you, I think. They could not stop talking about what a delight you are. They'll be extremely pleased to learn you've come to London with Damien, and will no doubt be anxious to show you the town. As are Kate and I, of course."

"Not until Bonnie's rested," Kate said. Taking Bonnie's arm, she planted herself firmly between Bonnie and Damien and escorted her up the walk.

William and Damien watched them go. William called out, "Darling, aren't you going to speak to your brother?"

Without looking back, she replied, "No!"

Though she wanted to, Bonnie dared not look back to either of them as she hurried with Kate up the walk. She wanted Damien alone so she could press him for his reasons for avoiding her during the last days. While she could understand Kate's distress over what had transpired at Grange Inn, and her demands that the two of them spend no unchaperoned moments alone together, Bonnie simply could not understand why Damien had chosen to ignore her completely.

They were met at the door by a rotund maid with sparking blue eyes and a cheerful smile. "Welcome home, my lady. I've tea brewing and cakes fresh from the oven. I knew you and Miss Bonnie would be weary, so I've taken the liberty of warming you each a bath and turning back the bed covers in case you'd like a nap before dinner."

"Edna, you are a treasure," Kate replied with an exhausted smile.

Bonnie stepped inside the town house and stopped. The furnishings were much finer than anything she had imagined. Finer even than in Braithwaite. For while Braithwaite was grand and certainly beautiful, its character was in its heritage and the belongings that were often centuries old and hinted of more masculine tastes. This decor, however, truly suited Kate's personality, stylish and graceful, full of pastels and delicate swirls and curves that showed in everything from the carved white moldings near the ceilings to the legs of the polished, cherry-wood furniture.

"Which room has been readied for Bonnie?" Kate asked.

"Lord Bradhurst requested the blue room for the young lady," Edna replied.

"Splendid!" Kate caught Bonnie's hand and ushered her upstairs. "You mustn't look so terrified," Kate teased.

Bonnie shook her head. "I wasn't aware that London was so very . . . large."

"Some three million people live here, and the city is growing every day."

"But how do so many find work?" Bonnie asked.

"I fear they don't," she replied softly.

Upon finally reaching Bonnie's room, Kate stood aside and smiled. "Tell me what you think."

Speechless, Bonnie gazed about the roomy apartment, noting the carved cream-colored moldings along the ceiling that complimented the pale blue walls. The oak floor was covered with a beautiful tapestry rug, and on one wall a cheerful fire blazed beneath a Georgian mantel displaying a quintet of eighteenth century Staffordshire figurines. Ivory-colored damask drapes dressed the deep windows, giving the matching Queen Anne chairs and Chippendale settee before the hearth an added elegance.

But it was the tester bed that held her fascination. Yards of the sheerest, most delicate ivory lace swagged from the bed's overhead frame and spilled to the floor.

Perhaps sensing Bonnie's feelings, Kate walked to one of the windows and looked out briefly before turning back to face her. Her cheeks appeared slightly flushed, and her eyes were bright as she said, "You'll get the morning sun. You will also face the garden, which is nice this time of year. As you can see, the roses are still blooming, and on sunnier days you can smell them like heady perfume."

Kate approached Bonnie and took her hands. "I hope you'll be happy here."

"I'm certain I will be, m'lady."

"And please, you must cease addressing me that way. I'd like very much to be your friend, Bonnie, and not, in any way, your superior. I fear I'm like my brother in that respect. The idea never quite sunk into our heads that we were supposed to be better than anyone else, much to our father's regret. I hope to learn a great deal more about you, and from you. In turn I suspect there will be a great deal you will learn from me. Hopefully we will both wind up better people than we were before. Now, I trust you'll want to rest before dinner. I'll send Edna up to wake you half an hour before we eat."

Bonnie waited until Kate reached the door before speaking.

"Kate?"

She turned.

For a moment Bonnie stared down at her hands, knowing what she wanted to say but not sure if she could. Taking a deep breath, she looked up and said, "It's been a very long time since I've had a friend . . . thank you."

"Oh, Bonnie." She smiled. "You are so very welcome."

The hour having grown late, Damien retired to the study of his Mayfair town house, took up a pen and paper, and wrote to Investigator Bradley concerning Kate's conversation with Bonnie. There was every reason to believe that Bonnie's father was a miner, and that he may possibly have worked at one of the mines in Swaledale or Arkengarthdale. It was a long shot, but at this point, with Bradley running into dead ends, it might help to narrow his area of investigation considerably.

Dropping the pen on the desk, Damien sat back in his chair and rubbed his eyes. He'd dismissed his servants for the evening, yet for whatever reasons he could not make himself climb the stairs for bed. He felt caged and restless. Funny how the silence had never bothered him before. Back in Mississippi he would sit for hours on the porch in the dark, listening to the whirring of night creatures and watching the flashing of fireflies in the trees. And, at times, when he just couldn't face another night of solitude, he would ride over and sit with Charlotte on *her* porch and listen to the whirring of night creatures and watch the fireflies in the trees. Not much change, but at least he hadn't been alone.

Damien left his chair and walked to the window. Staring out at the gaslit street, he tried to recall the many nights he'd spent in London as a young man. Some he could remember; many he couldn't. Most had been filled with endless hours of chicanery that ultimately resulted in strict reprimands from his father or a sermon from one or more of his tutors when he returned to the university. Professor Corocan, his history teacher, had once strolled through the lecture room with his hands behind his back, his eyeglasses perched on the end of his nose, and stopped before Damien, Philippe, Freddy, William, and Claurence and announced, "This highly distinguished fivesome takes the lead in every disgraceful frolic of juvenile debauchery." The others in the class had stood and applauded.

Thinking of his friends, Damien frowned. Upon returning to England he'd considered them all a lot of rousers who'd never grown up, who'd never known a moment's responsibility, worry, or pain. Now, however, with the threat of war tapping him on the shoulder, with Braithwaite's obligations demanding every free moment, he almost envied them. How nice it would be to drink himself into oblivion and not have to worry about anything more important than waking with a headache the next morning.

He thought of Bonnie and the questions in her eyes as she emerged that afternoon from the coach. It had been all he could do not to march down the walk and sweep her into his arms, as William had Kate. But he couldn't. They were in London now. The plan was in motion. He would keep his distance. Soon she would be so enthralled with her new life that she would discover her feelings for him had been little more than infatuation. He could return to Vicksburg with a clear conscience and the knowledge that he had done everything feasible to see she was happy.

That *was* what he wanted . . . wasn't it?

Cursing under his breath, Damien returned to his desk and sifted through the stacks of correspondence that William had so adeptly predicted would be awaiting upon his arrival home. There were calling cards, letters, and invitations to soirees, and banquets, and teas. He supposed he should respond to them, but the task seemed too overwhelming at the moment.

He threw the letters down just as a knock at the front door sounded. Grateful for the interruption, he hurried to answer it.

The tall, broad-shouldered figure on the step was swallowed by shadows. Then snickering came from behind the visitor, making Damien laugh despite his earlier aggravation.

Stepping into the light, Philippe raised one blond brow and

said, "Knew it was us immediately. No doubt it was Freddy who gave us away."

"No doubt," Damien replied. "What the devil are you about at this time of night?"

Freddy followed Philippe through the door. Then came Claurence, who regarded Damien with his usual aloof expression.

"Waited about at White's, certain you would come up," Philippe said.

Freddy snickered again and added, "The whole place is wagering you ain't got the stuff to come in. Says you've abandoned your peers for barbarians."

"Oh, Dame," Claurence said, affecting a sigh, "say it ain't so."

"To be frank, my good man, I've placed a rather sizable wager in the book that I could convince you to join the old gang at the club before midnight." Philippe crossed his arms over his chest and, being the only one of the three who stood as tall as Damien, looked at him levelly and grinned. "I've taken an embarrassing beating of late. I do hope you'll help me out."

"I'd say embarrassing is an understatement." Freddy winked and poked Claurence in the ribs. "Shall we tell Dame about the water wager with Mr. Wilde?"

"Do," Claurence said.

"Philippe wagered one thousand pounds against Mr. Wilde that a man could live twelve hours underwater. Wilde went and hired a low fellow who was willing to give it a try for the money. They put him on a ship and sunk the ship."

"I'm afraid to ask," Damien said, "but what happened?"

"Philippe's bet was lost!" Claurence and Freddy announced in unison, then both burst out in laughter.

Damien waited until Freddy and Claurence had controlled themselves before saying, "I'm almost afraid to ask about the low fellow . . ."

"Oh, he bobbed up." Freddy snickered again before finishing, ". . . eventually."

"So you see now why you simply must do me this favor, my lord." Clapping Damien on the shoulder, Philippe said to Freddy, "Fetch his lordship's coat. I'm not about to lose five hundred guineas because he's turned into a Beau Brummell."

"I have not," Damien argued.

"Oh, yes you have. Watch him, boys, or he'll be planting himself in the bow window at White's and despising everyone he sees."

A coat was produced and slid onto Damien's shoulders. Without further discourse he was shuffled out the door to one of the two cabs waiting at the curb. He thought of refusing, but the idea of pacing the house unable to sleep seemed totally unappealing. Besides, a few hours with the lads would keep his mind off other things.

He entered a cab with Philippe, and both sank against their seats as Freddy called out in the dark, "St. James's at the top of the street! A guinea's in it for you if you make it by ten!"

"I fear I've been shanghaied," Damien said.

Philippe grinned and adjusted his coat sleeves over the cuffs of his shirt. He flicked away an imaginary piece of fluff from the knee of his trousers before replying.

"Has it occurred to you, Dame, that you have come to take life too seriously?"

"Occasionally."

"You act like a man shackled by a marriage vow. Relax and enjoy yourself while you can. Soon you'll return to Mississippi and no doubt die of pox or something, or be skewered by one of those red-faced savages who creep about the dark and rob people of their hair." He affected a shiver, making Damien laugh.

"It's not as bad as that," he replied. "The Indians near us are quite harmless, really. And it was the French who started the practice of scalping by doing it to the Indians."

"I wouldn't put it past 'em, bloody frogs that they are. So tell me, how is our Bonnie?"

Damien looked out the window, watching the old, familiar landmarks pass by. "Bonnie is well," he finally replied. "I've taken guardianship of her welfare. She'll want for nothing for the rest of her life."

"Ah."

Damien looked again at his friend and found him smiling.

"And she's come to London with you?" Philippe asked.

"She's residing with Kate."

"How convenient. I'll drop by first chance I get. If you have no objections, perhaps I'll take her out and buy her something pretty."

"Such as?"

"A bonnet perhaps. Or perhaps we'll chance an outing to New Bond Street. Madame Rachel's has imported bath crystals from Arabia that are scenting every stylish woman in London. Or perhaps she'd like Magnetic Rock Dew Water of the Sahara. My own mama swears by it, as does my sister. It'll make Bonnie feel like a new woman, I understand."

Damien frowned at the twinge of irritation he felt over Philippe's interest in Bonnie. "That's very generous of you."

Philippe shrugged, smiled, and replied, "Yes, it is."

Their cab rolled down St. James's Street, passing both Brooks's and Boodles, which, by the looks of the many hansoms parked along the street, were as crowded as usual. Glancing out the window at Brooks's, Philippe said, "Mr. Thynne retired from the club recently, you know."

"Oh?"

"He was dispirited and fed up. He had won only twelve thousand pounds in two months. It is the ardent wish of the club's members that he never return."

"Understandable. I trust both clubs are lively as always?"

"As lively as a duke's house with the duke lying dead upstairs. The Pelican, now, is a different matter. It is hearsay that not long ago a peer of the realm was accused of throwing a boar's head that laid a peer insensible in the fireplace. When questioned about the incident he responded somewhat indignantly, 'Not me. Can't have been me. I've thrown nothing but jelly all evening.' "

Damien laughed. "That lord would not have been you, would it?"

"Can't have been me," Philippe responded with a wry smile. "I ain't been to the Pelican for a fortnight. I wouldn't have put it past the Marquis of Salisbury, though. Heard tell he was reprimanded lately by the Carlton Club committee for willfully breaking down the dinner boards in the coffee room. That was just after the Duke of Buckingham complained about the unfair way in which members helped themselves to the rice pudding. You know how the duke loves his rice pudding.''

At the top of the street they arrived at White's, or the Great House, as it was affectionately nicknamed by its distinguished members. Joined by Claurence and Freddy, Damien was ushered expeditiously into the club, where he was immediately surrounded by the familiar faces he had last seen here six years ago.

Two hours and two dozen toasts to Warwick's ''return to polite civilization'' later, he and his companions stumbled past the hall porter, Claurence calling out to the upper servant, ''You are dismissed f' the remainder of the evenin', my good guardian.'' Then they wobbled down the front steps and into a hansom. Damien thought, but he couldn't be certain, that he heard Philippe call out, ''Eleven twenty-three Park Lane, Mr. Cabman, and hurry!''

They lined up across Kate and William's parlor, Philippe in the center and Claurence and Freddy on either side. Damien stood behind them, leaning against the fireplace to steady himself.

William, appearing disheveled and bleary-eyed from sleep, regarded them all wistfully, while Kate paced the floor in her dressing gown, hands on hips and mouth pinched in disapproval for not only calling so late, but also for calling while so obviously intoxicated. He'd hear about this tomorrow, Damien thought, and the next day, and the next . . .

Bonnie entered then, having hastily dressed in the same pearl-gray satin gown she'd worn at tea on their last day at Braithwaite. The color brought out the intense blue of her eyes and the red of her mouth. She smiled, and Damien, forcing himself to look away, reached for the port William had poured him. He drank it and shuddered.

The lads, however, stood speechless, their arms at their sides and their mouths gaping. It was Bonnie herself who broke the spell. Recognizing her callers, she dashed across the room and threw her arms around Philippe's neck.

''Good gad,'' he said. ''Bonnie, is that really you?''

She laughed happily and replied, ''Aye. Whom did you expect? Or rather, *what* did you expect?''

''Breeches!'' they all exclaimed.

"Don't you like me in a dress?"

Philippe blinked and slowly raised his hands to her waist. Even more slowly, he closed his arms around her.

William said, "I'm not certain I have ever witnessed Fitzpatrick at a loss for words, Bonnie. Congratulations for accomplishing the impossible."

She spied Damien then, and her features clouded. He looked away, uncertain what bothered him more—the hurt look on her face due to his recent neglect or the sight of her in Philippe's arms. Whatever, the brutal force of feeling that was slamming inside his chest had a sobering, not to mention frightening, effect on his inebriated senses. For an instant he had to physically curtail the instinct to tear Philippe away from Bonnie—as he had Miles—and smash his face.

Placing his glass aside, Damien said, "I don't know about you gentleman, but the night is young yet and as long as I'm out, I intend to reacquaint myself with a few of our old haunts. Are you joining me or not?"

Philippe looked around in surprise. "But it's after midnight."

"That didn't stop you from coming here," he snapped.

Fitzpatrick dropped his hands from Bonnie's waist as if she'd suddenly burned him. He watched Damien cross to the door before saying, "I meant that the only establishments remaining open—"

"William," Kate interrupted, "perhaps you'd better go along—"

"I think not," Damien said. "No doubt you wouldn't approve, chooch." His eyes went back to Bonnie's, briefly, before he again addressed Philippe. "Are you coming or not?"

Philippe appeared to hesitate, then he shrugged. "Why not?" Smiling at Bonnie, he took her hand and squeezed it. "I'd like to drive you through the park tomorrow. What do you say?"

Bonnie looked at Damien, her eyes wide and questioning.

"Go with him if you want," he said curtly. "I'll not stop you." Then without waiting to hear her reply, he flung open the door and walked to the cab they'd asked to wait. When Claurence and Freddy had joined him, Damien called out to the driver, "Kent Street, and hurry up about it!"

Philippe ran down the walk and leaped into the cab as it

swung around in the street. Damien looked briefly toward the house and asked himself what the hell he was doing. His head was already splitting, and he'd discovered while at White's that most of his peers were as obnoxious as he remembered. But he hadn't been prepared to see Bonnie in the arms of another man, even though that man was his friend. The sickening realization hit him—not for the first time—that very soon, should he go through with his plan, he would be returning to Vicksburg to an empty house, to a war, and a life without her . . .

He sure as the devil had no intention of returning home to dwell on the dismal prospect for the next sleepless hours. He would blot it from his mind some way.

Nineteen

Bonnie splashed her face with cold water, hoping it would alleviate the sluggishness that had gripped her since her arrival in London. She reached for a linen and gently blotted the moisture from her face, then gazed at her reflection in the mirror.

Her skin looked dewy and flushed with color. Her hair shone with highlights, thanks to Kate's many fragrant soaps. In truth, she had never appeared so healthy and radiant . . . but something was wrong.

It was nothing she could put her finger on, and at first, upon arriving in London she'd attributed her illness and disquietude to simple confusion over Damien's behavior. The afternoons when she had returned from parading in the park with Philippe or Kate or William, and thrown herself across her bed to weep, were explained away as simple homesickness for Yorkshire and shock over being thrust into a world so expansive and teeming that she did not seem to cope with it.

"It's understandable," Kate had assured her sympathetically.

But Bonnie wasn't so certain.

There came a knock on her door, then Edna called out, "You've a guest, Miss Bonnie, in the garden."

"Thank you. I'll be right down."

Bonnie checked the clock. There was an hour yet before Philippe was due to arrive. And while she had met many people since coming to London, Bonnie could not imagine any one of them calling on her. There was no one else except . . .

She checked herself in the mirror again, making certain every hair was in place. She smoothed the bodice of her tea gown so the folds of her skirt spilled smoothly to the floor.

"Silly girl," she said aloud. "Of course it's not Damien. Don't be a bloody idiot. Why would he show up today? Unless, of course, he's finally come t' his senses and has decided t' apologize for his inexcusable behavior."

Lifting her skirts, she walked to the door, took a breath, then ran for the stairs, not slowing until she reached the lower level where she paused and waited for a momentary dizziness to leave her. Very slowly she walked down the hallway, out through the conservatory, and into the garden. Someone sat at the white wrought iron table amid the roses. It wasn't Damien. Her heart turned over as the woman, resplendent in purple satin, her fiery hair mostly hidden beneath a broad-brimmed hat, looked up at Bonnie and smiled.

"Hello, Bonnie."

"Damien ain't—isn't here," Bonnie replied.

Marianne left her chair and hesitantly approached Bonnie. She held a wrapped parcel in her hands. "I'm not here to see Damien."

"Oh." She blinked. "Then perhaps he's with you. Have you come t' inform me of your and Warwick's impending marriage?"

"Marriage?" Marianne's head fell back in light laughter before she replied, "Oh my, you do have a fertile imagination, my dear. Did Damien not inform you that I am already married?"

"Oh. Then congratulations are in order."

"They would be about ten years too late, I'm afraid."

Bonnie frowned.

Marianne caught Bonnie's shoulders and helped her to a chair. "Sit down, my dear. Aside from looking positively enchanting, you also look ill. Are you all right? I didn't mean to shock you so. Would you like me to leave?"

"Perhaps. But first you might tell me what you're doin' here. To see Kate?"

"To see *you*." Marianne took her seat and placed the gift-wrapped parcel on the table before Bonnie. "I've recently returned to London and was told by friends that you were here.'' Smiling, she motioned toward the gift and added, ''Open it.''

Bonnie carefully tugged on the ribbon, then unfolded the bright paper surrounding the object. It was a book entitled *Habits of Good Society*.

''Everything a young woman should know about etiquette,'' Marianne told her.

Bonnie looked at her hands. ''I see. Thank you very much.''

Ignoring Bonnie's less-than-enthusiastic appreciation, Mari asked, ''Are you enjoying London?''

''Not particularly.''

Smiling, Marianne removed her gloves and tossed them onto the table, along with her reticule. ''What have you been doing with your time?''

''William and Kate have taken me twice to the theater. That was very pleasant. Every other day I ride in the park with Philippe Fitzpatrick, and that's very nice too.''

''Philippe is charming. Do you like him?''

''Of course. I wouldn't agree t' ride with him if I didn't like him.''

''What a silly question.'' She crossed her legs. ''How is Damien?''

''I wouldn't know. I ain't see him since he brought me here.'' Realizing her anger had almost gotten the better of her, Bonnie took a deep breath and looked out over the garden. ''He's busy with Parliament, Kate says.''

''So I understand. I hear there are a few in Parliament who are giving him fits about this dreadful war business . . . Bonnie, if my coming here has distressed you—''

''No.'' Closing her eyes, she did her best to force back the unreasonable tears that threatened to fall. ''Truth is, I could do with some conversation. The days are sometimes very long . . . Kate is very busy. She's involved with a great many organizations, and William, of course, spends most of his hours with Damien at Parliament.''

''But London is such a grand city in which to occupy your time, Bonnie. Why, a young lady could spend days going from one couturiere to another. Certainly Kate has made some arrangements for fittings—''

''Oh, yes,'' Bonnie said, cutting her off. ''But I really

wasn't interested.'' She tugged at her corset, frowning as she added, ''These dresses she's given me should do me fine while I'm here. Afterward . . .''

Marianne raised one eyebrow and smiled. ''Afterward?''

''When Damien leaves . . . when Damien leaves . . .'' Bonnie swallowed, and feeling her control shatter, she covered her face with her hands and let the tears fall.

Suddenly Marianne's arms were around her, comforting her while Bonnie buried her face against Mari's shoulder and wept.

''There, there,'' Mari whispered. ''Has he made you so unhappy, Bonnie?''

''He don't never come to see me. He ain't even written. He just told Kate t' buy me anything I wanted or needed, but I don't want them things. I don't!''

Marianne pulled a handkerchief from the sleeve of her dress and pressed it to Bonnie's face. ''Men. They can be such unfeeling oafs. They gad about the world in their tight-fitting breeches as if they own womankind. I learned early on, Bonnie, that women will die of old age before they get what they need or want from men. As long as women sit by docilely and prettily, accepting what men shovel out, they will continue shoveling until we are suffocated by the refuse. They are primitive creatures who are driven, not by intelligent reasoning, but by physical urges. Therefore, women must learn to deal with them on that level. That's why God made woman both beautiful and sexual. That's why he gave them breasts, for heaven's sake, as well as brains.''

Bonnie blinked away her tears and looked at Marianne in surprise. ''I thought He gave us breasts t' feed babies.''

''If that were the case He could just as easily have given us udders.'' Mari sat down again. ''Bonnie, what's good for the goose is good for the gander. You must simply demand more of men, then more and more until, one day, they look up in surprise and wonder what's hit them.''

Bonnie considered Marianne's words before asking, ''And how does one do that?''

Mari smiled. ''Damien's case shouldn't prove difficult. Unlike most men, who are controlled by their pride as well as their loins, Damien is ruled largely by heart. Granted, a mixture of pride *and* heart can be dangerously combustible, but the results can be gratifying if you're willing to chance it.''

Marianne reached for her gloves and purse before looking at Bonnie again. ''Judging from the fighting spirit I saw in you when you first arrived at Braithwaite, I think you are up to the challenge. That would depend, of course, on how much you want him.''

''Why are you tellin' me this?'' Bonnie asked.

''Because I know Damien better than he knows himself. I know his needs and desires, and I know how damnably stubborn he can be.'' She slipped on her gloves before adding, ''Because I do not wish to see him return to America and get himself killed in that dreadful war. But most of all . . . I want to see him happy. You, my dear, innocent, beautiful child, could make him happy indeed.''

''I don't see how. I could hardly be an asset, considering my background. His peers would never approve.''

''I am his peer. So are Philippe, Freddy, and Claurence. We like you.''

''But you hardly make up the aristocracy.''

''Believe me, Bonnie, if there is one thing aristocrats love, it's having the opportunity to show how charitable they can be. They will become so caught up in their own philanthropy they will actually forget that you aren't one of them. And when they suddenly wake up to the fact, they will already love you so dearly it will no longer matter.''

Frowning, Bonnie said, ''Well, so far I've seen no signs of that.''

''You will . . . now that I'm back in town.'' Marianne swept up her reticule, skimmed the wide brim of her hat with her fingertips, then threw back her head with a laugh. ''Damn, but this is going to be great fun,'' she said. ''I simply can't wait to get started!''

The invitations began to arrive the next morning. Kate burst into Bonnie's room with a look of such excitement on her face that Bonnie temporarily forgot her own queasiness and grabbed Kate, fearful that she might actually faint.

''Whatever has happened?'' Bonnie asked.

Kate thrust the numerous envelopes into her hand and

cried, "Marianne's done it. She's actually done it, Bonnie! Will you look at that monogram?"

Bonnie studied the envelopes carefully before glancing back at Kate. "They all look the same t' me."

Kate grabbed the top envelope and raised it to the tip of Bonnie's nose. "*M* for Marlborough, Bonnie. This note is from the Duchess of Marlborough!"

"So?"

"So? So! Open it, for heaven's sake!"

Bonnie tore open the seal, removed the note, and quickly skimmed it. "It says she will be in the area and would like to drop by at teatime this afternoon to make my acquaintance."

Kate's face turned white, and her eyes appeared to glaze. "This afternoon? *This* afternoon? Oh my. Oh dear. This afternoon." Without warning she dashed to the door. "Edna! Edna, come quickly! The Duchess of Marlborough will be taking tea with us this afternoon. Look through my files and check her preferences. I think she enjoys India tea and not China. Sweetmeats! She loves sweetmeats: sugarplums, bonbons, but no strawberries. Oh my, she breaks out in hives at the slightest mention of strawberries—"

"No strawberries!" Edna echoed as she hurried down the stairs.

Kate ran to the top of the stairs and called out, "She adores daffodils as well. See that the house is filled with them!"

"I'll do my best, ma'am!"

Kate spun back toward Bonnie, grabbed her arm, and propelled her into her room where she was plunked unceremoniously down at a davenport, given a pen and a piece of stationery, and told to write exactly what Kate dictated.

"But I don't write too good!" Bonnie cried breathlessly.

"That doesn't matter. Do the best you can, Bonnie."

"You do it!"

Her eyes wide with disbelief, Kate shook her head. "Good heavens, no! The duchess knows my handwriting, and besides, it is considered poor etiquette not to answer one's letters oneself. Now write, 'To the Duchess of Marlborough, I would be highly honored to receive your company at teatime today and look forward to making your acquaintance. Respectfully, Bonnie . . .' " Kate stared at her until she looked up. "Well?" Kate said. "What do we call you?"

"Anything you like," she responded.

"Bonnie, you must have a last name!" Bonnie set her chin, and Kate sighed. "Very well. Sign it simply 'Bonnie' and be done with it."

As carefully as possible, Bonnie wrote out the note, Kate slipped it into an envelope, sealed it, then sent it on its way by a courier.

The duchess arrived with all her entourage at straight up four o'clock. She was a short, stout woman with iron-gray hair, piercing brown eyes, and a mouth so rigid Bonnie thought her face would surely crack if she smiled.

Taking a chair across from Bonnie, the duchess fixed her with an unblinking stare and said in a high-pitched voice, "Lady Lyttleton tells me you are an orphan. How simply dreadful for you, my dear."

Bonnie opened her mouth to respond, but was not given the chance.

"Marianne tells me that Earl Warwick has accepted you into the bosom of his home and family, that he has taken over guardianship of your welfare. It was the very thing his mother would have done, God rest her soul. Clarissa was a fine woman, and we all miss her. Tell me, child, is it true that you were virtually starved and dying of congestion of the lungs when his lordship saved you?"

"Well, he—"

"Absolutely," Kate responded for her. "Poor dear child was a shadow of the beautiful young woman she is today. Why, she told me only this morning that her goal in life is to compensate Damien for all the kindness and compassion he has shown her. Not only that, but she plans to educate and refine herself so she might capably explain the problem of the homeless to those who are more fortunate and in a position to help."

I did? Bonnie thought.

"How very commendable!" the duchess exclaimed.

Refreshments were served with a great flurry of activity, the duchess's own servants pouring her tea, heaping it with sugar and only a touch of milk, then stacking a small china plate with what seemed to Bonnie enough sweetmeats and petit fours to feed half the dying urchins at Caldbergh Workhouse.

As Kate had instructed, Bonnie did not speak until the woman had devoured every crumb on her plate and gulped down her tea. Her servants rushed back to collect the china, to dust the crumbs from her lap, and gently dab the tea-moist corners of her mouth with her napkin. Then she settled back in her chair to study Bonnie.

"She is very pretty, isn't she, Kate?"

"Very."

"Tell me, Bonnie, do you like living at Braithwaite?"

Bonnie considered her response. Finally, concentrating on her speech, she said, "It has its good points and its bad points."

"But surely it is better than that to which you were accustomed."

"It is much finer than Caldbergh Workhouse, where I spent the last five years of my life. But I cannot truly say it is any better than my home where my parents raised me. Of course it is much larger; our house would have fit nicely into Braithwaite's ballroom. And the furnishings are pretty and certainly expensive. But it is not comfortable. It does not welcome guests with warmth and cheerfulness the way our cottage did. Why, the folks from nearby towns would walk a mile out of their way for the opportunity to stop in and say hello to my mother. Sometimes they would stand for an hour at the cottage's half door, leaning partway into the kitchen while my mother chopped potatoes for stew or kneaded dough for our bread. If there was any man without employment, she would gladly slice him a bit of pie or bread or fetch him a bowl of porridge if he stopped. I loved that door because it allowed the sun and stars to trace patterns on the kitchen floor all the way to the fireplace. That's where I mostly stayed because it was my favorite place in our house. We always gathered there in the evening while my father played his fiddle or sang my mother a song."

Bonnie smiled. "My da said once that as long as the hearth burned brightly, the hearts of its tenders would never grow cold. But if the fire went out, the soul went out of the people of the house. It's true. The night my mother died in my father's arms he wouldn't let her go. He held her into the morning, and the fire died. My father's soul died too; he was never the same. His last words to her were, 'Ah, Mary, you was lovely and fair as the rose in summer.''

For a long moment the duchess stared at Bonnie without speaking. Then, very quietly, she said, "I wish I had known her."

"I'm certain she would have been honored to know you, ma'am."

"My dear child, I cannot imagine why."

The duchess lifted her hands, and her attendants hurried to help her from her chair. She moved to the front door before turning to address Kate.

"Perhaps a weekend at Blenheim would be beneficial. Expect an invitation within a day or two."

Smiling, Kate curtsied slightly and said, "That is very gracious of you, your grace."

"Poppycock!" The duchess looked at Bonnie, and her stern mouth turned up in a smile. "I look forward to it with great anticipation . . . Charming, my dear, absolutely charming."

She swept from the house with a flourish, leaving Bonnie standing by her chair, her hands gripping her skirts as she decided that she must have said something terribly wrong for the duchess to have so abruptly up and left.

As Kate closed the door and leaned against it, Bonnie said, "Bloody hell, I really bogged that one, didn't I?"

"Bogged it? Bonnie, do you realize what you've just done? The Duchess of Marlborough has invited you to Blenheim Palace. Every door in England, as well as on the Continent, will be open to you now. Only an invitation from the Queen herself could surpass this honor. Tell me: *How* do you do it?"

"Do what?"

"Manage to make the world love you so."

Twenty

The invitation to Blenheim Palace arrived the next day, as did fifty others, all to dinners, teas, and for rides in the park. Kate sat at Bonnie's elbow, telling her which invitations she should accept and which she should decline.

The next two mornings they spent on their feet as Bonnie was measured for the wardrobe she would take on her weekend to Blenheim. There were elegant costumes in velvet or silk that she would wear for breakfast, tweeds for lunch, elaborate silks with crinoline underskirts for tea, and satin and brocades for dinner. When Bonnie questioned Kate over the enormous cost of any particular article, Kate only smiled and responded, "Damien won't mind."

Damien. The sound of his name weighed heavier on Bonnie's heart every day, and spoiled the happiness she should have felt over the upcoming events. It seemed she spent her days and nights hoping for that knock on the door or listening attentively as William related the hours he'd spent with Damien in Parliament.

On her rides through London or the park she was continually searching the crowds, hoping for some sight of him, yet knowing the chances were so remote as to be ridiculous. Little by little the realization set in that he had no intention of ever seeing her again . . . until she overheard Kate ask William if Damien had received an invitation to Blenheim Palace. His affirmative response sent Bonnie's hopes soaring, and for once she actually looked forward to the upcoming weekend.

It was a Wednesday afternoon as Bonnie joined Kate and Marianne in a carriage ride through the park. The brisk temperature was a sure sign that summer was ending, yet the sun was bright and the sky was a cloudless blue. It seemed a perfect day, and the park was unusually crowded with carriages and gentlemen and ladies on horseback. Their own conveyance was forced to slow to a snail's pace due to the congestion, but it gave Bonnie a chance to watch the scenery and the people more closely while Kate and Marianne chatted about the week's upcoming activities.

The awareness that she was being watched came over Bonnie slowly. Tipping her head, she peered from beneath the velvet brim of her navy-blue bonnet at the gentleman who rode horseback beside them.

He wore a black frock coat over a white lawn shirt and black waistcoat. Unlike most men, he did not wear a hat, allowing his light brown hair to blow in the gentle breeze. He boasted a fawn-colored silk cravat about his neck, and tight trousers that were covered from the knee down by black Hessians. His wide mouth smiled at her rakishly, and Bonnie smiled back.

To her surprise he eased his horse closer to the carriage. Bonnie looked swiftly toward Kate and Marianne. Kate appeared surprised as Marianne threw up her gloved hand and cried, "Trent Halford, you rogue! What are you doing about the park?"

"Looking for the loveliest of ladies, of course," he replied. His dark eyes scanned the carriage before again focusing on Bonnie. "Seems at long last I am in luck."

"Indeed you are, sir. Would you care to tie your horse to our carriage and ride with us a way?"

"I was hoping you would ask."

As the driver pulled up the bays and Halford tethered his horse to the rear of their carriage, Kate glared at Marianne and said in a whisper, "What can you be thinking, Mari? Trent Halford is a notorious rake."

"The worst," Mari replied. "And other than your brother and Philippe Fitzpatrick, he is the handsomest *eligible* rake in London. He is also one of the wealthiest."

"You know Halford was Damien's biggest rival for Louisa's hand. My brother detests him!"

"And he detests your brother."

"Damien will be furious."

"I certainly hope so."

Bonnie looked from Kate to Marianne, then back to Kate as the women regarded each other in silence. Then Halford climbed aboard and settled into the seat beside Marianne and across from Bonnie. Bonnie forgot the women's curious conversation as Halford fixed her with his gray eyes and smiled.

"You must be Bonnie," he said. "Now I understand why all of London is abuzz with your name. I am honored to make your acquaintance, my lovely young woman."

Bonnie blinked and said, "You are?"

"Absolutely." He turned to Kate. "Hello, Katharine, and how is your brother?"

"Very well, thank you."

"I understand he is rattling Parliament's roof these days. Or is it Parliament's pockets? He has the conservatives and liberals positively snapping at one another's heels. I understand her majesty is becoming piqued over the ordeal. Imagine. The fine Warwick reputation which has spanned centuries is about to be obliterated all because the earl has taken the side of a people who believe in enslaving a part of the human race with whips and chains."

"That is not the case at all," Kate argued hotly. "But he does believe in the South's right to secession, if that's what it desires. And he does believe that if the South is to survive this war it will need England's help."

Halford shrugged nonchalantly and looked back at Bonnie. "I can't understand why we should become involved in a war for a country that, as a whole, fought like a bunch of rabid dogs to be independent of us. But enough of that. Tell me, Bonnie, are you looking forward to your weekend at Blenheim?"

"Very much," she said.

"I trust you will be there, Trent?" Marianne asked.

"I had not decided yea or nay . . . until now." His mouth curved in a smile. "I would not miss it for a queen's ransom, I think."

Bonnie spent the next hour in animated conversation with Halford, finding him witty and charming and highly complimentary. He seemed genuinely interested in her opinions, praising her forthrightness, applauding her candor. He made her blush as he leaned toward Marianne and said, "I could spend the better part of my days hearing her laugh. Do you think I might convince Bonnie to attend Astley's theater with me this evening? I have tickets to a Shakespearean play she might enjoy.''

"That won't be possible," Kate said.

"Oh? Why not?''

"Because I am not available to chaperon, that's why.''

"That is easily remedied," Marianne said. "I have no plans for this evening.''

He looked at Bonnie and smiled. "Would you like that, Bonnie? Perhaps we could dine at Chatelin's in Covent Garden afterwards.''

Bonnie searched her memory for the appropriate response. Buried somewhere in the midst of her etiquette manual had been the proper way in which to answer this invitation, but for the life of her, she could not recall it. So she simply smiled and said, "I would enjoy that very much, thank you.''

"Hello!'' came the cry.

Bonnie looked around and froze, her heart seeming to pause in its beating as her eyes locked with Damien's. At his side William raised his arm and waved as they rode up to the carriage.

"I thought to find you here," William said. Then sitting a little straighter in his saddle, he looked directly at Halford and added, "This is a surprise.''

"No doubt," Halford responded. His eyes shifted to Warwick's, then back to William. "I have been acquainting myself with your beautiful houseguest, my lord. I have just asked Bonnie to join me for dinner and the theater tonight, and she has accepted.''

Bonnie sat back in her seat and did her best to breathe. She dared not look at Damien again or—

"Tonight?'' William asked. "But that's why I've come looking for you," he said to Kate. "Damien and I had decided to escort you and Bonnie to the reopening of the Astley Theater. It promises to be quite an event.''

"I fear you are too late, my lords," Marianne replied. "At least where Bonnie is concerned. I, however, could benefit with an escort, as my husband is indisposed.'' Clapping her hands together, she cried, "What an excellent idea! We could all meet at the theater and afterward go to dinner together.''

"Together?" echoed Kate and William.

"Won't this be positively cozy?" Marianne said.

Halford smiled at Damien. "You'll join us, won't you?"

Damien slanted Bonnie an appraising glance, taking in the gown of deep Prussian blue and the hat cocked jauntily on her head. Her hair spilled from beneath it in loose coils and ringlets that brushed her shoulders. Since he had ridden up to the carriage she had refused to look at him. Instead her eyes were uncharacteristically veiled by demurely lowered lashes, and her chin was tilted just enough to emphasize the stubborn line of her fine jaw. Watching her closely, he couldn't tell exactly how she was feeling about seeing him again, which was disconcerting. She was becoming extremely practiced in hiding her emotions.

In truth, this fashionably attired femme fatale, who only resembled his urchin of a few weeks ago, aggravated the hell out of him. Kate was certainly to be applauded in her efforts to transform the girl—if Bonnie could catch Halford's eye the chances of her landing an acceptable husband were good. He should be overjoyed by that thought. So why wasn't he? Instead, he was besieged by an illogical and ridiculous anger. He tried to tell himself that it was due to her being with Halford. After all, Trent had been one of the first men to court Louisa on the sly while in London. Then Damien was swept with the appalling awareness that he would have been equally furious if Prince Albert sat across from her.

Finally his gaze moved to Halford, and he realized everyone was staring, waiting for his answer. Damien smiled coldly and tipped his head in response.

He didn't move until the carriage had rolled away, then he looked at William. "What the hell is she doing with Halford?"

"I don't know."

Without speaking again, William turned his horse and trotted toward home. Damien remained where the carriage had left him long after his friend had been swallowed by the crowds. He couldn't seem to shake the image of Bonnie, beautiful and sophisticated, ignoring his existence. She was hardly pining away for lack of his company. Just like Louisa. She was becoming a bitch like Louisa, and the next thing he knew she would be cutting his heart out—

The noisy traffic around him dimmed to nothing as the awareness of his thoughts struck him full force. Impossible. It would be impossible for Bonnie to hurt him that way. He had been in *love* with Louisa.

Gripping the reins, Damien dug his heels into the horse's flanks and tore off down the bridle path after William.

A virtuous woman should hold a repugnance to excessive luxury in underclothing.

"Kate, have you any idea to what lengths I went to get those tickets?" said William.

A lady never wears too much lace embroidery or ribbons and bows; to wear a garter below the knee is against all rules of taste.

"Do you know to what lengths I went to get your brother to agree to go to that blasted play?"

Night chemises must have long sleeves and reach down to the feet.

"He *loathes* plays, Kate."

When asked to dance, a lady no longer replies, "I shall be happy," but should appear less eager, glance at her dance card, and in a more ladylike manner, reply, "I will give you a dance if you will come for it a little later. I am engaged for the next three," or "I am afraid I have not one to spare except number fourteen, a quadrille."

"Halford, for God's sake! Of all the bloody rakes in London . . ."

On gracefully entering a drawing room— not rushing in head-foremost—a lady should look for her hostess, a smile upon her face, granting an elegant bend to common acquaintance, then accepting the hand extended to her with cordial pressure, rather than shaking it. She then sinks gently into a chair. Her feet should scarcely be shown and not crossed.

"Of course we are going to attend the theater! I'm not shouting! Jesus, you should have seen Damien. He was like a madman. I came to fear for my life, I tell you."

A lady never raises her voice.

"Stop shouting at me, William!"

"I am not shouting!"

"It isn't my fault that Halford happened along when he did!"

A door slammed.

Another door slammed.

Bonnie stared down at her book, *Habits of Good Society,* and tried her best to concentrate. It was no use. She could not forget Damien's expression before the carriage had driven off. She had never seen a look so furiously cold. And he had not even bothered to speak to her. Not once. He'd only sat astride his horse with all the arrogance of a bloody king and ignored her completely.

She lay across her bed until she was forced to dress for the evening.

Damien arrived at half past seven with Marianne. Wearing a forest green frock coat, brocaded waistcoat, and a creamy white shirt with a green cravat at his throat, he was standing at the mantel with a drink in his hand when Bonnie entered the room. She stopped cold upon seeing him, unprepared for his impact on her, though she had imagined the moment a thousand times during the last few weeks.

He seemed grander than she remembered: taller, his shoulders broader, his legs longer. His eyes were not so green as the potted fern on the floor near his feet, but darker and smoky, like a forest on fire. She could not seem to move as those heavy-lidded eyes regarded her. She could not seem to breathe. She could only manage to lift her chin and hope that the efforts to which she had gone would prove fruitful.

He raised his drink to his mouth before speaking. When the glass was empty, he placed it aside and gave her a lazy, amused smile. "You look very pretty. Did I pay for that dress?"

She thought the query odd, but responded simply, "No, it was Kate's."

"Have you been enjoying yourself these last weeks?"

She considered telling him the truth, that, no, she had not enjoyed herself, that her days were filled with agonizing hours of thinking of him, but she dare not hurt Kate's and William's feelings when they had tried so hard to entertain her.

"I have enjoyed myself very much," she replied.

Bonnie took a much needed breath to steady her emotions, then moved to a chair before the window. She sank gently into it, making certain her feet did not show and her hands were placed loosely in her lap. She glanced at Damien again and found him watching her. He stared at her for so long in silence that Bonnie cleared her throat nervously and felt a betraying blush of hot color rise to her cheeks. There was a disturbing expression deep in his gaze as it rested on her features, and her heart raced so painfully fast that she felt certain he could hear it.

Trent Halford's arrival at that moment broke the spell. Upon entering the drawing room with William, he walked directly to Bonnie and presented her with a bouquet of flowers and a box of chocolates. He then kissed her hand.

"I thought I had imagined how lovely you are," he said, smiling, "but you are even more beautiful than I dared think."

Edna hurried to take the flowers and candy while Trent turned to Damien. The two eyed each other warily before Trent smiled and offered his hand.

"It seems a truce is in order, Warwick."

"Really." An insolent smile lurking at the corners of his mouth, Damien said, "I can't imagine why."

Trent lowered his hand. "These jealous feuds cannot last forever. We are hardly a threat to each other any longer. At least where the ladies are concerned. We've grown up, have we not?"

"I have," Damien responded.

Marianne stepped forward. "We'll be late if we don't hurry. Are we all ready?"

Turning back to Bonnie, Halford took her arm and escorted her out the door to his coach. Kate and William followed, then Damien and Marianne. Bonnie prayed Kate and William would choose to ride with her and Halford, but it was Marianne who said, "We'll ride with Bonnie." Bonnie thought she heard Halford groan, but his handsome face showed no signs of distress as he helped her into the coach.

Damien settled into the seat across from Bonnie. His knees brushed her skirts as he planted his feet on either side of hers.

The silence seemed deafening until the coach lurched into motion. Bonnie fixed her eyes on the emerald stickpin adorning Damien's cravat and prayed the corset cutting into her tender skin would not suffocate her to unconsciousness, for certainly she felt in that moment as if she might faint for lack of air. Occasionally she would glance toward Marianne, hoping she would begin a conversation to alleviate the tension, but Marianne only peered out the window with a slight smile on her face.

Bonnie closed her eyes briefly, willing away the rush of heat that seemed to press down on her and make her dizzy. She breathed deeply, then opened her eyes.

Damien gazed steadily back at her. The sight of his firmly shaped mouth, quirked ever so slightly in a smile, made a shiver of pleasure run through her. Bonnie thought, perhaps the evening will not be so bad after all.

Upon arriving at the theater, Damien disembarked first. Next came Marianne, then Bonnie. As he caught Bonnie's hand, her eyes met his and her entire face lit up in a smile. Not for the first time that day he was struck by her beauty.

He watched as Halford took Bonnie's arm and escorted her to the theater door.

"Something wrong, my lord?" came Marianne's voice in his ear. "You seem upset."

He glanced at Mari.

"You don't approve of Halford?" she asked.

"He has no scruples," Damien responded. "But then, you know that, Mari. I have to ask myself why you allowed him to see Bonnie. If this is any indication of how well you and my sister see to Bonnie's welfare, I may be forced to take matters into my own hands once again."

"Do I detect some jealousy on your part, my lord?"

"Hardly."

"Not even a little?"

Without responding, he took Marianne's hand and walked swiftly across the carpeted lobby to catch up with Bonnie. Kate and William were at her side as she was introduced to numerous acquaintances.

Halford looked around. "Thought we'd lost you."

"No such luck."

"You are certainly taking your guardianship seriously, my lord."

"I'm far too aware of your reputation with the ladies, Halford."

"I'm hardly dangerous any longer. Age has mellowed me."

"Not according to what I've heard. I understand that in the past year alone two young ladies of good reputation have been forced to take their Grand Tour early. Aside from that, the very fact that you and Miles are friends is enough to warrant caution where Bonnie is concerned.''

Halford glanced toward Bonnie again before saying, ''She is obviously an innocent. A very beautiful innocent who, apparently, has caught the fond eye of the Duchess of Marlborough. I would not be so ignorant as to ruin my own reputation for something I can attain just as easily down in the East End. Now if you will pardon us, the first act starts in five minutes, and I wouldn't want Bonnie to miss a moment of it.''

Halford excused himself and Bonnie from the crowd and entered the auditorium.

Bonnie wondered if the queasiness and dizziness that had plagued her all evening had anything to do with being so near Damien. Sitting on the edge of her chair in the balcony, she had a perfect view of him and Marianne below—until the lights went down, and she was forced to sit in darkness and endure her worsening sickness in silence. Unable to stand it a moment longer, she removed herself halfway through the second act. Trent stood to attend her, but she motioned him back into his chair with the promise that she would return momentarily.

With a sense of relief she moved as steadily as possible down the stairs to the lower auditorium. Pausing, she peered back through the dark and listened one last time to the actors' performance of *The Taming of the Shrew.* A burst of laughter from the audience made her frown, and not for the first time she wondered what it was they found so hilarious. *She* had been unable to understand a single bloody word all night.

Upon reaching the theater lobby, she sank into a chair next to a towering marble pillar and pressed her cheek against the smooth stone, hoping the coolness would assuage the hotness of her body. No doubt she had just committed some grand faux pas. Tomorrow she would open her *Habits of Good Society* and learn that a young lady faints gracefully in her chair after excusing herself from polite company.

''Bonnie?''

Startled, she looked up to find Damien standing over her. He looked worried.

"Are you all right?" he asked.

As he bent to one knee before her, she did her best to smile. "It's only this bloody corset," she said. "It's pressin' the wind from me, and I can't breathe."

A flicker of a smile touched his mouth. "For the life of me I cannot fathom why you women insist on wearing the silly contraptions. It cuts off your air and compresses your organs, besides being damnably uncomfortable."

"You will have to debate that with Madame Roussaue, my couturiere." She took a breath. "I wouldn't mind some fresh air."

He stood and helped her from her chair.

As they stepped from the theater into the brisk night, Damien offered his arm to Bonnie. She took it as they strolled down the gaslit walk.

"Are you enjoying the play?" Damien asked.

"Not really." She tipped her head and looked up at him. "Are you?"

"Not really."

"Then why are we here, I wonder?"

"Because fashion and politeness deem it necessary, I suppose."

"If being a lady means I must, for the rest of my life, subject myself to the rigors of such fashion and politeness, then I think I will go back to Caldbergh."

Damien laughed. "You don't mean that."

Bonnie smiled.

"Perhaps you do," he said. "Tell me what you think of Halford."

"He's very handsome and nice . . . I like him."

Damien walked on in silence, his eyes strangely bleak and remote.

Bonnie watched several hansoms roll past before asking, "Why have you been ignoring me since we came to London?"

He didn't respond.

"I think I deserve some explanation, especially in light of what transpired at the Grange Inn."

Damien's expression didn't change, except, perhaps, to grow harder. His mouth took on a familiar, sardonic twist before he replied. "That is best forgotten, lass."

She stopped, forcing him to pause as well and to reluctantly face her. "Are y' saying that we are t' pretend it never happened?"

His eyes carefully searched Bonnie's upturned face. He noted the pale complexion, the cheeks dotted with bright color, and the taut curve of her usually soft mouth. He reached out and gently brushed her chin with his fingers. "I am saying that what happened at the Grange Inn and Braithwaite will not happen again . . . ever. Not with me. Not with anyone until after you have married. Do you understand me, Bonnie?"

She backed away, her eyes full of tears as they reflected the lamplight behind him. "It meant nothin' to you," she said. "Nothin'."

Drawing back his shoulders, Damien swallowed his self-disgust. He thought he'd prepared himself for this moment, but the sudden upheaval of feeling inside him made him realize how wrong he was. "Making love to you was a pleasant pastime, sweetheart. But to imagine that it goes any deeper than that would be a mistake for us both."

Her eyes flashing angrily, Bonnie opened her mouth to speak, but Damien stopped her with a lift of his hand.

"Don't say another word. We will only end up saying things we don't mean, as we've done too often. Perhaps someday we'll be able to discuss matters like sensible human beings, but God help me, right now, where the two of us are concerned, I'm not rational. I haven't always been a gentleman with you, as I should have. I'm truly sorry for that. But God knows you can make a man lose his head and do and say things he regrets. I wanted to make love to you at Braithwaite and at the Grange. Heaven help me, if I could I would take you here and now. But desiring someone and loving them should not be confused, and that is where we stand."

Her chin high and her shoulders back, she said, "Then I was right. You don't care for me. This trip to London, the clothes, are all trinkets to soothe your own sense of guilt for robbing me of my virginity."

His face stony, Damien made no attempt to deny her words.

"That makes me little better than a whore," Bonnie said. "How could I *ever* have felt anything more for you than loathing?"

She turned, lifted her velvet skirts, and ran back to the theater. He watched her go, biting back his need to call out to her. With something like shock he realized he'd just burned his bridges where Bonnie was concerned. He supposed he should be glad. Yet the swift and powerful emotions sweeping through him screamed otherwise, and with a vicious curse, he strode back to the theater.

The remainder of the night was torture. The meal at Chatelin's *looked* wonderful, but Bonnie hardly ate it. She was too numb and furious. The sickness she'd felt throughout the evening was exaggerated every time she glanced Damien's way. When he spoke, the sound of his voice was like a poison lance through her heart.

How could she hate him so desperately, yet love him too? she wondered miserably.

By the time Trent saw her back to Kate and William's town house, both her illness and anger had reached a boiling point. She managed to excuse herself politely from her hosts, then hurried to her room.

Warwick had used her.

That thought drummed repeatedly through her mind as she paced. What an idiotic fool she had been to believe, even for a moment, that the great high and mighty earl could see her for anything more than a convenience to use at his whim? Now he was finished with her, so how better to assuage his conscience than to ply her with treasures? No doubt that's what he did with his bleedin' tarts when he was tired of them and ready to move on to another.

Spying the music box, she stormed across the room, grabbed it and, without thinking, hurled it against the wall. Stunned, Bonnie stared down at the precious gift lying shattered across the floor. Hot tears filled her eyes.

"Damn you, Warwick, yer gonna pay!" She wept.

Twenty-one

"Thank goodness, you've finally arrived," Kate said. "I feared you had decided not to make an appearance after all."

Making certain of their privacy before responding, Damien glanced toward Blenheim's closed drawing room door. He reached into his coat pocket, crossed the room to where Kate sat on the edge of her chair, and dropped a stack of papers onto her lap.

"I'm late because I've been battling my way through creditors. Explain these purchases, if you please."

Kate sifted through the bills of sale, her eyes growing round as she noted the exorbitant sums circled at the bottom of each sheet.

"Did you approve the purchase of sapphire jewelry?" he asked.

She shook her head.

"An ermine coat?"

"No."

Damien walked to the window and gazed out over the palace's rolling gardens. "On the bottom of that stack you will find a bill from Madame Rachel's for Chinese Leaves for the Cheeks and Lips, Circassian Beauty Wash, Favourite of the Harem's Pearl White—whatever the hell that is—Magnetic Rock Dew Water of the Sahara and Royal Arabian Toilet of Beauty . . . coming to a rather startling total, including clothes and jewelry, of just under five hundred guineas." He looked back at Kate, whose face had turned chalk white. "Did you approve that purchase?"

"No," she replied weakly.

"No. Then how the hell did she make them?"

"I—I must have given her your letter of promise—"

"Must have . . . ?"

"Oh, well. Yes. She's been so restless the last few days, and when she mentioned that she wanted to ride down to Bond Street alone and do a little shopping—"

"A little? That's like calling Napoleon 'a little' aggressive."

Kate paced the length of the grand room before facing Damien again. "I cannot understand it. Bonnie's changed, Damien, and it frightens me. Since our arrival at Blenheim she has been a different girl. She's gone out of her way to seek the attention of men and has actually flirted with several. Marianne and I have both done our best to caution her, but she doesn't seem to care."

"Where is she now?"

"The last I saw she was running about the lawns playing tennis. That was after she returned from shooting pigeons with several . . . 'lads,' I think is how she put it."

"Has Philippe arrived?"

"Last evening, but she's rebuffed any attempts he's made to seek her out. She refuses even to speak with him."

Damien left the room and walked down the palace's immense west wing gallery, his footsteps echoing on the marble floor. About him the walls of the gallery displayed Marlborough's great collection of pictures, a virtual museum of art by any standard, but Damien paid little notice. His mind was on Bonnie, as it had been constantly since the night at the theater. He continued down one corridor after another, then out through the hall, exiting the palace through the south front entry.

He searched the grounds for another hour before finally locating Bonnie. Surrounded by several admiring young men, she sat on a marble bench atop a hill just beyond Marlborough's Roman bridge.

Upon seeing Damien, she widened her eyes momentarily, then narrowed them. Flashing her followers a smile, she said, "Here is my guardian now, gentlemen. Do say hello."

They all turned to Damien and bowed slightly in greeting.

"Excuse us," Damien responded, and obediently the men departed. He did not speak again until he was certain they were out of hearing.

"What do you call this?" he snapped.

"What?" she asked.

"Don't play the innocent with me, Bonnie. You're not even good at it."

She turned her head, and the sapphires adorning her ears flashed like blue fire in the sun. But they were no match for her eyes; they burned with anger as she responded, "If my innocence is lacking, milord, it is no one's fault but yours!"

"Ah. So that's it. You intend to make me pay for my lack of good judgment."

Bonnie left her seat to face him squarely. Her chin set at a mutinous angle, she replied, "Why not? You used me. You wanted me near you for one reason and one reason only. Well, two can play at that game, my high and mighty lordship. You *owe* me, and I intend to collect!"

His mouth curving, Damien drawled, "I should be very careful, baggage, or you may find yourself 'collecting' from half the men at Blenheim by the end of your visit."

Bonnie's face paled, and without thinking she struck him forcefully with an open palm across his cheek.

As stunned as Damien by her actions, Bonnie stumbled backward and stared, horrified, at the imprint of her hand that was burning his face like fire.

For a long minute Damien watched her. At last he said, "I should be very careful about biting the hand that feeds you, you little vixen, or you may well find yourself tossed back to Caldbergh on your ear. Knowing what has gone on between you and me, Smythe and his cohorts won't be so reluctant to climb between those lovely white thighs next time, and, I assure you, you won't be rewarded with sapphires for your efforts. More likely than not you'll find your belly full of Smythe's brat and a long line of nameless faces outside your door as they each await their turn on you."

"You're disgusting!" she cried. "I hate you!"

The words stung far worse than the previous slap on his face, and without speaking again, he turned and walked away. For the first time since he'd stormed from the palace he realized the extent of his fury. It shook him, yet he couldn't help but question his motives for stalking her down and confronting her before her admirers. It wasn't due to the gifts she'd bought herself. He wouldn't have hesitated a moment to purchase the items, had she asked for them. It was the idea that, for the second time in his life, he was standing by helplessly while a woman he knew, and cared for, turned into a cold-blooded stranger who welcomed the attentions of other men.

For dinner Bonnie chose to wear a gown of plum silk. The short sleeves were garnished with ribbon rosettes, which also decorated the hem of her full skirt. The décolletage was modest in comparison to many of the older women's, but low enough to hint of the fullness and perfection of her white breasts. She had chosen to wear her hair pulled back from her face, looped in a braid atop her head, and secured with Marianne's pearl- and diamond-studded combs.

By the time she reached the hall, the orchestra had begun to play. Dozens of guests gathered in groups, chatting amiably. Bonnie searched for Marianne or Kate or William but saw only a sea of strangers' faces.

"You look lost," came a familiar voice behind her. Bonnie turned to face Trent Halford.

"Have you just arrived at Blenheim?" she asked.

"Only an hour ago. Did you miss me, by chance?"

Bonnie smiled and looked away.

"Are you enjoying your weekend?" he asked.

"Very much. One could spend a month here, I think, and never tire of the scenery."

Trent nodded and looked up at the orchestra on the balcony above them. "I hope your dance card is not already filled."

"No," she said, then on second thought added, "I have one to spare, and that would be—"

"Don't tell me. Number fourteen, which happens to be a quadrille."

They looked at each other and burst out laughing.

"Ah, Bonnie," Halford said, shaking his head. "You are a delight. Your naïveté is positively charming."

"You cannot fault me for trying," she said.

"I would not dream of it."

Dinner was announced. The duke and duchess walked to the door, paused, and looked back at Bonnie. Bending close to her ear, Halford said, "It's your move, darling. As guest

of honor, you follow the duke and duchess to dinner. I trust
you have chosen your escort?''

''Escort?''

''The gentleman whom you chose to sit at your side.''

''No. I didn't realize . . .'' Bonnie quickly scanned the
guests, noting with some consternation that all eyes were on
her. That's when she saw Damien standing with Philippe and
Freddy.

Damien cut a striking figure in a black velvet coat, a black
single-breasted, satin waistcoat, and black trousers. Like his
shirt, his cravat was snow-white, exaggerating the bronze of
his skin and the darkness of his thick hair, worn longer than
was fashionable, by all appearances. With his tall, lithe body
and his hard, handsome features he stood out among the or-
dinary men surrounding him, and despite her earlier anger
Bonnie was tempted to approach him. It seemed that no matter what her head told her, her heart refused to listen. Then
she quickly, bitterly, reminded herself that her heart had gotten her into this predicament in the first place.

Turning to Halford, she smiled graciously and asked,
''Would you do me the honor, sir?''

A soft stir of surprise sounded around her.

Halford himself seemed stunned, but after a moment's hesitation, he responded, ''Of course.''

He offered Bonnie his arm and followed their hosts toward
the saloon. As they passed beneath the grand arch decorated
with carved cherubs playing trumpets, she glanced toward
Damien again. He was addressing a pretty girl with curly
blond hair and delicate features; the girl smiled her thanks as
she accepted a flower from him.

Bonnie did not realize that Halford had addressed her until
he squeezed her hand gently. She looked at him in surprise.

''I dare say you have set the tongues to wagging, Bonnie.
I think they all thought you would ask Warwick.''

''Really? Why?''

''He is your guardian, after all.''

''But not my lord and master,'' she replied more hotly than
she intended.

Halford only smiled.

Dinner was Blenheim's usual lavish affair, starting with
two soups, one hot and one cold, followed by two fish, one

hot and one cold. Several racks of lamb were then carved and served to the guests, then tiny jade bowls of sorbet were passed among them.

That was followed by individual servings of quail, which had been shipped from Egypt and fattened in Europe before being transported to Blenheim for preparation. Dessert was wheeled in on carts, doused with liqueur and set afire, much to the surprise and pleasure of the guests. When that had been consumed, several foursomes of servants reentered the saloon, carrying large pyramids of fruit—peaches, plums, apricots, nectarines, raspberries, pears, and grapes, which they placed among fresh flowers on the table. When the fruit had been eaten and the guests were all chatting among themselves, Halford leaned toward Bonnie's ear and said, "Very impressive, don't you think?"

"Decadent, I would say. Do all aristocracy eat like this?"

"Occasionally, although the fare may not be so well prepared. I was recently taking dinner with the Duke of Buccleuch. Our first course was a sprawling bit of bacon on a bed of greens. That was followed by a serving of two antediluvian fowls and a brace of soles that must have perished from original inability to flounder into the Ark. We were then forced to gnaw our way through the fossil remains of a sirloin of beef. I tell you, the food was very bad."

The duchess left her chair, smiled at her guests, and quit the room. The men stood and helped the women from their chairs.

Halford bowed to Bonnie and said, "Of course you realize that you are to follow the duchess to the library, where you will listen to the orchestra's interpretation of Bach or Wagner or Beethoven for the next hour while the gentlemen enjoy their cigars and port."

"Certainly," she said. "I knew that."

Catching her hand, he bent over it and said, "Remember, number fourteen—the quadrille—is mine."

Chagrined, Bonnie tugged her hand away. "I'll remember."

She hurried from the saloon into the hall, where she was greeted by both Kate and Marianne. One look at her friends' faces told Bonnie what she already suspected.

Falling in beside Bonnie, Kate said, "Do you realize what you've done? You have publicly humiliated my brother."

"I would not go so far as to say that," Marianne replied. "But I wouldn't have given you twopence for your life at that moment, Bonnie. Damien was furious."

"I'm not certain I can convince him to forgive you for that one," Kate added. "He does not take lightly to being slighted before his peers."

"You have certainly given the gossips something to maul to death." Marianne almost laughed before catching herself. "I suppose it really isn't funny, considering Trent Halford's reputation."

"It certainly isn't," Kate agreed.

Bonnie was led into the long library and seated between Kate and Marianne. Bonnie was given the impression that if a ball and chain had been at hand they would have fastened it to her ankle.

For the next half hour the orchestra played, but Bonnie barely heard it. In her mind she was reliving over and over the horrible argument between her and Damien earlier that day. How right he had been the night of the play. It seemed they could not discuss matters like sensible human beings. They *were* destined to say and do things to each other that they didn't mean.

A soft giggle caught her attention. Bonnie looked across the room, her gaze alighting on the young woman Damien had escorted into dinner. In her hands she twirled the flower he had given her, and somewhere deep in her breast Bonnie felt a tightening that robbed her of breath.

The doors were thrown open, and the gentlemen entered. Philippe went first to Bonnie. Taking her arm, he said, "Dancing is starting. I believe you did promise me the first waltz."

She moved with him into the hall and was swept into his arms. Grabbing him for support, she stared up into his immobile face. "Will you slow down? I told you, I cannot dance."

"I'm certain by the end of the evening you will have it pat." Raising one blond eyebrow, he added, "The gentlemen are already lining up to dance with you, or haven't you noticed?"

"Are you angry with me?"

"Should I be?"

"I would hate it if you were."

They danced in silence for a while longer, giving Bonnie the opportunity to search the dancers around her.

"Looking for someone?" Philippe asked.

She shook her head.

"If you hunt for Damien, you will no doubt be disappointed. He is strolling the grounds, I think."

Her gaze came back to his. "Oh? With whom?"

"Does it matter?"

"No," she responded mildly. "It doesn't matter a whit."

By the end of the evening Bonnie's shoes pinched abominably and her head reeled with the effect of too much champagne. She'd smiled so long her face hurt, while inside she felt miserably ill and downhearted.

"May I see you to your room?"

Looking up in surprise, Bonnie smiled at Halford as she accepted his hand and walked with him into the hall. Several servants stood about, each holding a tray on which numerous silver candlesticks were placed. Halford retrieved one of the elaborate candlesticks and handed it to Bonnie.

"It's a Blenheim tradition," he said as she took it. "As I see you to your room I'll explain."

Since the palace's living quarters had only recently been moved to the second story, there were no grand staircases to ascend. Buried further in the bowels of the house, the narrow stairs led up into the shadows, with only a faint light at the top to show the way. Bonnie proceeded as carefully as possible while Halford held her arm. They continued to walk in silence until they reached Bonnie's room. Almost timidly she turned to face him. It was difficult to see his features in the dark, but she thought she saw him smile.

"Show me your candle," he said.

She raised it between them.

With the scrape of a match a fire bloomed between them. Carefully, he touched it to the candlewick.

"Tradition has it that while lighting a young lady's candle her admirer might whisper a suggestion of a rendezvous in the morning. So what say you, my lady? Will you meet me at the stables before breakfast? A ride in this country air will whet your appetite for the feast that will undoubtedly follow.''

Watching the dancing yellow flame of her candle, Bonnie considered his invitation.

His hand touched her face, and Bonnie stepped back in surprise.

"I assure you," he said softly, "there is nothing wrong with an affectionate good night kiss."

Her back against the door, Bonnie looked into Trent Halford's face. His eyes were warm and admiring. His smile was gentle and kind. Unlike Damien's, his features were not harsh or sarcastic or angry. As his hand slipped beneath her chin and tenderly tipped up her face, she did not turn away, but closed her eyes and did her best to calm the frantic racing of her heart.

Halford's mouth brushed hers tentatively at first. It was a questing kiss and did not assault her senses the way Damien's did. She thought it pleasant and was slightly disappointed when he stopped.

"At the stables at seven," he said, smiling. Before she could respond, Halford turned and walked away.

Damien awoke with a surprisingly clear head, considering the amount of champagne he'd drunk the night before. Since the fiasco at dinner he'd made himself put Bonnie from his mind. In truth, he needed this time away from the problems he had encountered—not only with Bonnie, but also with Parliament. Just three mornings ago the London *Times* had screamed its disapproval of England's proposed involvement in the war loudly enough for the Queen, as well as three fourths of Parliament, to hear. The effect had been staggering, setting back the negotiations to a point where he had come to believe Parliament would turn down his request in no uncertain terms.

He bathed and shaved, whistling softly to himself as he recalled dancing the night away with Christina Gosford. She was a demure little thing, timid and quiet as a mouse. Not at all mule headed, fiery tempered, and *spiteful*, like Bonnie.

Damien winced as he cut himself with his razor. Blood trickled down his neck, and he was forced to press a linen to it to staunch the flow. He tried desperately to think of Christina again, but the girl's fairness melted like warm wax into an image of flashing blue eyes and hair as wild and black as a raven's wing.

"Witch," he muttered to himself, and with disgust flung the towel to the floor and his razor into the basin of soapy water. No matter how he battled it, the confrontation with Bonnie the day before tumbled in on him. The picture of her surrounded by other men reared up before him, and the ready anger came flooding back so strongly that he felt sickened. For the love of God, what was happening to him? He had stormed about London the last days like a man in the throes of a jealous temper. He had *never* been a jealous man. Not even with Louisa. Even as she waltzed through her Season on the arm of a different man every night, he'd stood aside calmly and encouraged her to make a fool of him.

No more, by God. There wasn't a woman on this earth worth that kind of misery.

He dressed quickly and left his room, anxious to meet up with Christina. She had hinted that she might enjoy a walk by the river before breakfast. If he hurried . . .

"Damien!"

He looked back over his shoulder and saw Kate hurrying down the corridor. Ignoring her, he continued walking.

"Stop!" she cried.

"No. I have an assignation with a young lady who *won't* claw my eyes out."

"But Bonnie is missing!"

He halted.

Panting slightly, Kate joined him. "I've checked her room, the morning room, the verandas where breakfast will be served. She isn't there."

Damien adjusted the sleeves of his leather coat before smiling at Kate. "I'm certain she's about somewhere. Check Marianne's room."

He walked away.

"Trent Halford is missing as well."

He stopped and slowly turned to face her. Halford, he thought. That son of a bitch Halford . . . "You are absolutely certain?"

"I asked around, trying to be as discreet as possible, of course. No one has seen him this morning."

"Have you checked the stables?"

She shook her head.

Without speaking again, Damien descended the stairs, left the palace by way of the south entry, and hurried to the stables. Upon questioning the liveryman, he learned that Bonnie and Trent had ridden out together two hours earlier. He ordered a horse saddled, then struck out across Blenheim's twenty-five-thousand acres to find them.

He rode hard for the better part of an hour and was on the verge of turning back when the sound of Bonnie's laughter stopped him. Urging his horse through the copse of trees crowding the path, he searched the shadows until he spied their mounts tethered to a bush.

Damien slid from his saddle and moved quietly through the trees until he came to a grassy open glade that sloped to the river. Near the river's edge Bonnie lay on her back, her hair spread across the grass and reflecting the morning sun. Halford lay on his side next to her, smiling down into her face. Damien watched, frozen, as Trent lowered his mouth and kissed her.

She kissed him back, hesitantly at first, then passionately, her slender arms sliding up around his neck, her fingers burying in his brown hair.

At that moment a horse whinnied and Halford looked up; his eyes locked with Damien's. He must have said something quietly to Bonnie, for she rolled away from Halford so suddenly that she almost toppled him. Scrambling to her feet, her face as white as a sheet, she spun around to face Damien. He could not take his eyes from her. Bits of grass clung to her habit, her hair was wild, and her mouth looked red and swollen from Halford's kisses. Her eyes appeared glazed, and he wondered if it was from passion or fear or both.

Halford stood more slowly. He was without his jacket. His shirt was partially unbuttoned. His mussed hair tumbled over his brow as he threw Damien a discomfited smile.

"My lord, you startled us," he said.

"So it appears."

Halford glanced toward Bonnie before making an obvious effort to relax. He brushed grass from his sleeves before looking back at Damien. A long silence followed, interrupted only by a curlew that lifted from a nearby clump of grass and flew away.

Finally, his hands on his hips, Halford said, "For God's sake, there's no need to stand there and stare at us like a damned henchman. Nothing untoward happened. You saw for yourself, 'twas only a simple kiss."

Damien's gaze shifted back to Bonnie, once again taking in her disheveled state and the redness of her mouth. In his mind's eye he saw again Halford's body pressed against hers, his mouth moving on hers, and the new swell of unreasonable fury that rushed through him was almost blinding. He was forced to look toward the river to control himself.

"Mount your horse and ride out of here," he told Halford in a gruff voice. As Halford glanced toward Bonnie, Damien finished, "I'll see the young *lady* back to the palace."

Without speaking to Bonnie again, Halford walked to his jacket and swept it up from the ground. He shrugged it on and moved toward his horse, but before he could pass Damien, Damien's hand shot out and gripped his arm. A flash of alarm came and went on Halford's face as his eyes locked with Damien's.

Very quietly, Damien said, "If you so much as speak to Bonnie again you will sorely regret it."

"My lord," he responded as quietly, "you sound more like a spurned lover than a concerned guardian. Surely the anger I see does not stem from jealousy?"

Damien shoved him away.

Bonnie watched the exchange with growing dismay, but she said nothing until Halford had ridden away. "What did you say to him?" she demanded. "You have no right—"

"Shut up," Damien snapped viciously.

Bonnie stepped back as Damien moved slowly down the slope toward her. His black hair had been tousled by his ride, and the sunlight through the trees behind him created sinister shadows over his features. His eyes looked cold, and the taut line of his mouth told her that nothing short of a miracle could save her from his anger.

"He was a perfect gentleman," she said defensively.

"A gentleman would not have brought a lady here. But then, a *lady* would not have come."

A chill of apprehension shivered down Bonnie's back as she glanced about for some means of escape. "Stay away from me, or I swear I'll scream."

"Go ahead."

Before Bonnie could move, Damien's hand darted out and grabbed her arm in a lurching grip that nearly toppled her. In retaliation and anger she twisted and drove her fist into his shoulder.

"Y' bleedin' hypocrite!" she cried. "Y'd bed me and ruin me and not give a damn. But if another man so much as looks at me—yer hurtin' my arm!" She hit him again and struggled harder. "Trent would not treat me like this . . . he is gentle and caring—he *cares* for me!"

"And I don't, I suppose!"

"No! You don't!"

"You little idiot." He shook her. "Trent Halford cares for nothing but a decent lay, and you would offer yourself to him on a platter."

"You lie. Yer just envious because he's a better man than you!"

The instant Bonnie spat out the words, she longed to take them back. The look of anger that had fired Damien's eyes turned into an icy rage that was terrifying to behold.

The pressure from his hand on her arm became excruciatingly painful as he drew her up close to him, so close his mouth was but a fraction of an inch above hers as he said, "If I thought, even for a moment, that you had allowed him, or any other man, inside you, I think I would kill you both."

"Would y' have me live like a nun for the rest of m' life?"

"Until you are married."

"Oh!" She laughed shrilly. "Then y' won't give a damn when my husband mounts me. How very gracious. Thank God this is not the medieval days or y'd dawdle at my marriage bed and witness the intercourse, perhaps even applaud the consummation."

"Careful, m'love. You push me too far."

"What? Will y' spank me? Lock me in my room? I'm no longer a child. Y' made certain of that, not once, but three times. With yer own body y' taught me the pleasures of makin' love, and now y' condemn me for the feelin's you, yerself, made me groan for." Tilting her head and smiling

invitingly, she leaned into him, brushing her breasts against
his knuckles. "I dare say, if I laid on m' back and opened
m' legs, y'd fall on me like a ruttin' dog."

Grim amusement lit Damien's green eyes as he laughed
softly. "I'm sure you're right, but if you'd care to try me—"

"You disgust me. It will be a cold day in hell before I ever
let you touch me again."

She spun away, but suddenly his hand was in her hair,
yanking her back. She struck out violently with her fists,
pounding his chest and shoulders as he fought to subdue
her. Then his fingers were twisting into her shirt, raising her
up to her toes so his dark head was a mere breath above hers.
Lips curling in a sneer, he growled, "Dog that I am, I can't
be faulted for acting on my baser instincts. You will forgive
me . . . ?"

With a rending of material, he tore her shirt and chemise
down the front and thrust them off her shoulders, baring her
to the waist. The sun beat hotly on her exposed breasts as
she stared, too stunned to move, into Damien's face. His eyes
explored her first, then his hands, his fingers playing with her
nipples until they swelled and hardened. Bonnie frantically
attempted to suppress the wild surge of pleasure that rushed
through her as she saw the desire, mixed with heated anger,
turn his eyes the color of hot green stones.

He buried his hand in her hair, dragging her head back.
"Do you know what seeing you with Halford did to me?"
he snarled. "Damn you to hell for doing this to me, Bonnie.
Damn you, damn you . . ." Jerking her against him, he
covered her mouth with his in a punishing kiss. He felt her
tremble, but he couldn't stop himself. He didn't want to.
Some warning called out in his brain that they could be discovered at any moment, yet he went on kissing her, forcing
open her mouth so he could rake inside her with his tongue,
until she had ceased struggling and was kissing him back.
He wanted to hurt her, to punish her for turning to another
man so easily, yet the sweet pleasure of holding her again,
of tasting her, smelling her, was an assault on his anger.

Closing his arms around her, he lowered her slowly to the
grass, pinning her to the ground with his body, moving his
hips against hers in a sensual rhythm that matched the slide
and thrust of his tongue in her mouth. Her small hands beat

his shoulders and clawed his neck, yet her body responded, pressing against him, rubbing him until the need to take her consumed him completely.

Bonnie shivered and moaned as his knees shoved open her legs, and knowing instinctively what he meant to do, she tried to fight him. No, she thought. No, this couldn't be happening again. She had vowed to hate him. Yet she couldn't. No matter how she willed her heart to deny him, she found herself responding, murmuring soft sounds of resistance, then acceptance as his hands ran over her, awakening the arousing, familiar ache between her legs.

His mouth went on kissing her, bruising her lips, robbing her of breath. His fingers fumbled through the slit of her pantaloons, parting her sensitive flesh and sliding urgently inside her. Helplessly she felt her fury turn into a hotter fire. She groaned and rolled her head from side to side, did her best to push him away as he buried his face into the curve of her throat and growled:

"You're hot and you're wet. Is it for me or for Halford, my love?"

She squeezed closed her eyes as he flipped open the buttons on his breeches. His body moved inside her.

"Ah, God," he whispered. "God help us, Bonnie . . . Bonnie."

Sanity left them in that moment. Bonnie turned her face away and arched to him, feeling her body stretch and fill with him time after time as he thrust and withdrew. The sun's heat beat onto them as hotly as the primitive fire inside her. His body, slick with sweat and her own body's desire, drove inside her until she was twisting her hands into his lawn shirt in an effort to control the sobs of exquisite pleasure that tore from her throat. His face a mixture of pain and desperation, Damien closed his eyes, and as his own climax ripped through him, he gave a guttural growl of satisfaction. Bonnie felt his body throb within her, and with an odd sense of conquest she locked her arms and legs around him as he collapsed against her.

For long moments they remained together, until the passion had cooled and reality closed in on them once more. Damien carefully slid his body from hers, and for an endless second he stared down into her face. An anguished, uncertain expression washed over his features as he said, "Bonnie, I . . ."

He rolled away. Lying on his back, he tunneled his hands through his hair and closed his eyes. "You didn't deserve that. Bonnie, I'm sorry. I never meant to . . . to take you like that."

Drained of all fight, of all hate, she watched numbly as he rearranged his clothes and moved to her side. He tenderly smoothed down her skirts and tried vainly to replace her shirt over her breasts before removing his coat and wrapping it around her. He touched her face, and the hard lines about his eyes and mouth relaxed. "Why is it the only peace between us comes after we've made love?"

"Is that what you call it?" Feeling suddenly used, and furious at herself for allowing it to happen, she laughed bitterly. "How can you call it love, my lord? You don't *love* me, you only desire me. Shall I remind you of your own words? 'When the fire is between her legs and not in your heart, it can't remotely resemble love.' "

She tried to stand, but he grabbed her wrist. "You're wrong. I *do* care for you, Bonnie. Very, very much."

She turned her face away, confused over the tears burning her eyes and threatening to fall. She should feel some sort of satisfaction, she supposed. After all, Damien's confession that he "cared" was the closest he'd come to admitting any feelings at all for her. Still, he hadn't said he loved her. And that's what mattered. It was the only thing that had meaning in her barren life.

Damien walked to the line of decanters on a table near the wall and as steadily as possible poured himself a drink. He stared at the tapestries on the wall depicting the battles of the great Duke of Marlborough. The wealth surrounding him seemed strangely incongruous beneath the heroic forms of dying horses and dead soldiers portrayed on the tapestry. Odd, though, how the bloody scenes suited his mood. He felt like a man who had waged a long, terrible battle . . . and had lost.

Without facing Kate and Marianne, he said in a lifeless voice, "Bonnie is not to be left unattended again with *anyone*

. . . including me. If you must, employ a companion for her.''

"Why won't you tell us what happened?'' Kate said. "I've just left her and she is as closemouthed as you, although it's apparent that *something* has gone on. Her clothes are grass stained, there are bruises on her arm, and her lip is cut. She is shaking as if she has a fever.''

Marianne left her chair and walked to the window near Damien. She gazed out at the grounds while saying, "Damien looks little better. I could swear those are grass stains on his knees.''

Very slowly Kate left her chair, her eyes still fixed on Damien. "Did you find her with Trent Halford?''

"Yes.''

"Oh dear. They weren't—''

"No.'' He turned back to the decanter before adding angrily, *"Halford* didn't touch her.''

There was an intense silence as he refilled his glass and brought it up to his mouth. He closed his eyes as he swallowed the sherry, then said, "When we return to London I want arrangements made as soon as possible for her coming-out ball.''

Marianne turned from the window, surprised. She looked at Kate. "But that's as good as announcing to the world that you want to marry her off.''

"But that is exactly what he intends to do,'' Kate responded. "Why do you think he brought her to London in the first place?''

"But considering—''

"Damien feels that a sum of one hundred thousand pounds will adequately make up for her lack of innocence, as well as her lack of heritage.''

"Damien!'' Marianne gasped. "Is that true?''

"Yes,'' he said. "It's true.''

A moment passed before Marianne said to Kate, "Will you excuse us? I'd like to speak with Damien alone.''

"Certainly. I'll check on Bonnie.''

The door closed. Marianne cautiously moved up beside him, but he did not look at her. She gently brushed a few blades of dead grass from his sleeve, then her hand drifted up and tugged aside the collar of his shirt where his neck burned from Bonnie's scratches.

"Did you rape her?" Marianne asked in an urgent, quiet voice.

He shook his head.

"But you did make love with her."

"Yes." He drank his sherry, and the anger and confusion and disgust he'd felt earlier over his actions reared up inside him again. "I don't know what the hell happened. I saw her with Halford and I . . . lost control."

"Perhaps you were reacting to the time you found Louisa—"

"No." He cut her off. "It was only Bonnie there kissing him. Only Bonnie," he repeated more softly. He lowered his glass. "Mari, what the devil is happening?"

Marianne touched his shoulder. "I think you can answer that, if you only will."

He turned from her and walked away. One hand in his pocket, the other swirling the sherry in the crystal glass, he stared at a French blue opaline clock that was about to chime the hour. Behind him, Marianne said, "Of course you won't admit your feelings—"

"I care for Bonnie."

"You care very much."

"Very much."

"But admitting that your feelings might run deeper than that is impossible because your first obligation is Bent Tree. You have a war to fight in America. I suspect the battle you're waging within yourself will destroy you before a bullet does, my lord. I pray you realize that before it's too late for you, and for Bonnie. Because if you go through with this ridiculous plan of marrying her to someone she does not love, you will not only break her heart, but also your own. It seems such a foolish sacrifice to make just because you no longer trust the wisdom of your own heart."

Marianne quit the room, leaving a vast and terrible stillness in the air that settled on Damien's shoulders, cold as death. He stared at the door, feeling a familiar, unwelcome emotion rise up his throat so that he couldn't swallow. His hand tightened around the glass. Anger at himself, at the weakness of mind and body that had thrust him into this asinine fix, surged inside him until he thought he might explode from it.

"You're wrong, Mari," he whispered. "I don't love her. She's not even of my class . . ."

As if *that* mattered one iota, a voice in his mind called out.

Shaking his head, he told himself all he wanted was to be free of Braithwaite and England . . . of these insane feelings . . . and the girl whose untimely interruption of his life had left him with his priorities—which had once *seemed* so settled—scattering like smoke in the wind.

He did not love her. Other than a certain obligation, a genuine fondness . . . and a desire that engulfed him like fire each time he saw her . . .

He felt nothing for her at all.

Twenty-two

"Gentlemen!" Lord Palmerston raised his aged hands and attempted to quiet the gathered mass. "Gentlemen, please! I suggest that we all remember where we are. Silence, please, and come to order!"

A man sitting in a chair and shelling nuts looked up and cried, "Vote, I say, vote!"

"Here, here!" someone responded.

A rumble of stomping feet shook Parliament's grand walls.

"Gentlemen!" Palmerston pleaded. "We are here to discuss the situation in a sane and rational manner. I have word that Lord Gregory has given notice to recognize the independence of the Confederate States of America. How say you?"

"Yea!" came the immediate outcry.

"Nay!" came another.

A stout man left his chair and, hooking his fingers around the lapels of his coat, declared, "My lord Palmerston, let it go on record that I find your support of Warwick's mission treason. I agree with Brougham's earlier statement. If any Englishman is found aiding the Confederacy by fitting out a privateer, he should be found guilty of piracy and hanged!"

John Russell, Minister of Foreign Affairs, jumped from his chair. "My Lord Chelmsford, there is no need to so sternly voice your disapproval; Her Majesty is not about to call out the fleet at this point. Earl Warwick is only doing his duty as President Davis has requested. He only asks that we speak to Madison and Slidell with an open mind. Warwick has pointed out the sorry state of this escalating war in America. Remember, not only will the Confederacy be blemished by this tragedy, but our own resources will suffer as well. May

I remind you that three fourths of our exports are purchased by the southern states of America?''

The excited din mellowed somewhat as Russell bowed toward Damien and continued. ''M'lord, while I sympathize with your mission, you must understand, England is still reeling from the last damnable war we experienced. Therefore, it is Her Majesty's wish that the Confederacy demonstrate its ability to maintain its position as an independent state before we can allow ourselves to become involved in this war. If we were to help finance it, and the South were to fail, then we could be confronted with another very unseemly situation with the Union.''

He smiled and spread his arms. ''But we are fair. We will see these gentlemen from the Confederacy and speak with them, if only for the sake of favoring the son of one of our past and most influential members of the House of Lords.''

Damien stood and offered the members a bow. ''I thank you, Lord Russell, but it is not my wish to ask favors because of my heritage. I ask on the behalf of humanity and a proud Confederacy that might certainly perish under the heavy hand of the Union.''

Chelmsford stood again, his face red from anger. ''It escapes me, young man, how you have the audacity to tarnish Joseph Warwick's fine name and reputation with your traitorous ideas. Your father was appalled by slavery, as are all *true* Englishmen. What say you, sir? Are you Englishman . . . or Confederate?''

''Here, here!'' many cried.

''Gentlemen!'' Russell shouted. ''The earl's patriotism is not at issue. Now please, let us vote on the matter of the Confederacy and get it behind us. Who of you is in favor of the vote?''

A rumble of feet sounded throughout the room.

Russell turned to Damien, ''Then we will vote. If you will please leave the room . . . ?''

Damien glanced once more at the men, bowed, and exited through a rear door. It was not long before William joined him. William offered him a cigar and watched as Damien paced the long gallery.

"This is a difficult time for you," William said. "Let me assure you that those men are sympathetic to your cause."

Thinking of Chelmsford, Damien studied the glowing tip of his cigar. "It doesn't look good, you must admit. Palmerston has only so much influence."

"It will be close. Palmerston's parliamentary majority was always fragile. However, the issue at this point is not our involvement in the war, but whether or not to meet with Madison and Slidell. I see no harm in that, and who knows. If the Union were to get wind of the fact that we are at least speaking to the commissioners, perhaps they will reconsider future blockades."

"A nice theory. But I suspect they are more likely to do what they can to stop the commissioners from ever arriving in England. For that reason we must do what we can to make certain the Union never receives the information."

They remained silent. Damien stared into space, considering Chelmsford's earlier words—"Are you Englishman . . . or Confederate?"

For a very long time he'd imagined he knew the answer to that. Confronted by it now from one of his peers, he found he was not so certain of his feelings after all. So what had changed? Why, suddenly, did the idea of sailing back to Vicksburg no longer seem so appealing? What had happened to that need to cloister himself from close ties, to expend his energy in building and farming, to spend the long hours of darkness in a huge, rambling house with only a handful of servants for company?

Thinking back, he wondered—truly wondered—why he had gone to America in the first place. Certainly, he had needed to sweat Louisa's betrayal from his system. Definitely he had been frustrated and fed up with the tedious demands his heritage made of him. But mostly—mostly—he'd had to prove that he was his own man; that he wasn't just a Warwick, the younger son of an earl. He was Damien, a man who did not need the money or position his birthright bestowed on him to confirm his manhood. He'd established that beyond any doubt, if not to anyone else, then to himself.

The door opened and John Russell entered. He looked at

Damien before closing the door behind him. "You have taken the majority vote, my lord. We will see Madison and Slidell. I'll make the necessary arrangements to meet the gentlemen in Cuba. My secretary is even now writing to inform Mr. Crawford, Her Majesty's consultant in Cuba, to extend full hospitality to the commissioners upon their arrival in Havana."

Releasing his breath, William slapped Damien on the back. "This calls for a drink at White's. What do you say?"

Damien crushed out his cigar in an ashtray and nodded.

After days of constant rain, the sky had cleared. The streets, however, still stood with stagnant water and morass, some of which was thrown onto the walks by passing coaches, cabs, and buses. Damien and William stayed as far from the street as possible as they took advantage of the clear weather and headed for White's.

After some time of walking in silence, William looked with concern at Damien. "For a man who's just accomplished his objective, you seem subdued. I expected jubilation to a degree. At the least some relief. You look like a man who's just been saved from the gallows but informed he's about to have both arms and legs amputated."

"Am I that transparent?"

"You always were, my friend. Should I take your mood as encouragement? Perhaps you've reconsidered returning to America at this time?" When Damien made no response, William stopped walking. "By God, you *have* reconsidered, haven't you?"

Damien strode on before turning back to face him.

William smiled. "Might I ask what's changed your mind?"

"I haven't changed it."

"But you *are* considering it." William moved up beside him, and they continued their stroll. "Your reluctance to leave wouldn't have anything to do with Bonnie, would it?"

"Good God, you are beginning to sound like Mari." He walked on before adding, "'How are plans coming for Bonnie's soiree?"

"Proceeding nicely, thanks to Marianne. I'm certain that by the night of the ball she'll have Chatsworth Hall looking as fine as Blenheim and Bonnie will know everything there is to know about entertaining. She has accompanied Mari and Kate through the addressing of invitations as well as the writing of dinner cards. Yesterday she made the round of Chatsworth's guest rooms with the housekeeper, spoke with the chef, and approved the menu. This morning she was to sit with Mari and learn the fine art of placing guests for meals. This afternoon she was to meet with Madame Roussaue for the final fitting of her gown.''

''Has Kate explained to her the reason for this ball?''

''Ostensibly, it is to formally introduce her to society. Bonnie did note, however, that there are a great many unmarried gentlemen invited. She showed some concern that you might be upset and suggested we invite more unmarried young ladies. To 'balance things out,' is how she put it.''

''Word is out, I suppose, of the dowry.''

''Like wildfire. Last night three suitors called. The night before there were four, and the night before that they paraded in and out of the house like a troop of ants.''

His hands in his pockets, Damien glanced toward the crowded street, no longer surprised at the irritation he felt at himself for going through with his plan. The image of his waltzing into William's home with the idea of courting Bonnie himself *did* disconcert him, however. It had taken precedence over Parliament, and even Vicksburg, during the last few days. He had woken in the middle of the night with the dream imprinted on his mind and his heart pounding in his head like a drum. ''Has she shown any interest in anyone in particular?''

''None whatsoever.''

Noting William's consternation, Damien asked, ''Is something wrong?''

''Nothing I can put my finger on. In truth, Kate has asked me not to bring up the matter to you, but I feel you should know. Bonnie has not been herself for some time now.''

''Since Blenheim?''

''Before that. She tries hard to appear content, but I must tell you, Dame, she is dreadfully unhappy. I fear her state of mind is beginning to affect her physical well-being. Twice now in my company she has come close to fainting. She no longer eats, and she spends a great many hours of the day napping."

"Have you called in a physician?"

"Kate suggested it once. Marianne argued against it, for some reason. She suspects Bonnie's problem is only a severe melancholy over missing Yorkshire and . . ."

Damien looked at his friend. "And?"

William continued walking, and without responding to Damien's query, said, "When they hear you have finished with your business in Parliament, both Bonnie and Kate will suffer severely. I don't look forward to telling them."

At that moment Damien spied Marianne's coach parked outside Madame Roussaue's establishment. "Perhaps," he said, changing the subject, "we should drop in and say hello to the ladies."

Bonnie considered an assortment of ribbons on a table while behind her Marianne and Kate discussed the final plans for the ball. Madame Roussaue burst through a curtained door, followed by numerous assistants with their hands full of material, chalk, and pins. Taking Bonnie by the shoulders, the couturiere hurried her into a fitting room walled in mirrors and ordered Bonnie to remove her clothes. When she hesitated, Madame looked concerned.

"But you must," she said. "We cannot try on the gown without the removal of the one you are wearing. Quickly! There is much to be done before tomorrow night. *Oui?*"

With the help of Madame's assistants, Bonnie peeled out of her gown. She turned her back to the others, but her modesty did her little good. Her reflection stared back at her no matter where she turned.

Madame Roussaue fluttered about like a butterfly while her assistants helped Bonnie step into several petticoats. Then the ice-blue creation she had designed for Bonnie was eased down over her head and shoulders, over her breasts and waist, and finally her hips.

Madame hurried forward, scattering her assistants as if they were a bothersome covey of guinea hens. She circled Bonnie with a critical eye toward the fitting of the gown. She ran her fingers expertly along the seams of the bust and the tightly cinched waist before stepping back and shaking her head.

"Is something wrong?" Bonnie asked.

Madame's keen eyes met Bonnie's. "Perhaps we need to let out the waist a little. *Oui?*"

"It does feel somewhat snug."

"And the bust as well. It is too tight there too?"

Bonnie nodded.

Madame circled Bonnie slowly, her long fingers running around Bonnie's waist and sliding over her stomach. Then she stepped back and smiled. "Everything else seems perfect." To her assistants, she said, "You may help the mademoiselle to undress." To Bonnie she added, "It is a good thing the ball is tomorrow night, *oui?*"

Bonnie regarded the couturiere curiously until she left the room, then she dressed as quickly as possible, while outside of the dressing room Madame Roussaue quietly spoke with Kate and Marianne, inviting them into her office.

When Bonnie was dressed she continued browsing through the bolts of fabric and the many displays of ribbons near the window. Some movement outside caught her eye, and she looked up.

Damien was watching her, his hands in his pockets. He was smiling lazily.

Unable to move, she stood frozen with the silver ribbons spilling through her fingers like rivulets of water. She wondered if she were imagining him, so still did he remain as he watched her. She was almost afraid to return his smile, but she did, eventually. After all, they had not seen each other since leaving the palace. They had not spoken since the afternoon by the river, an eternity ago, it seemed. Looking now into his eyes, she wondered what was worse—living with him or without him? Each felt like torture.

Damien turned and within a moment was walking with William through the front entrance. Bonnie closed her fingers around the ribbons and did her best to steady her breathing.

"Have you found something you like?" he asked, coming up behind her.

"The ribbons are very nice," she responded politely,

breathless suddenly at the warm quality of his voice. Where was the anger? The sarcasm? He sounded and appeared genuinely glad to see her. "I—I confess to having a soft spot in my heart for them, as did my mother. My father bought her ribbons when he could afford it."

"What color do you like?"

Bonnie closed her eyes, fighting the need to look into his face and confirm what she was hearing. "That would be a difficult choice to make, I think. They are all beautiful."

"Then we'll take a length of each," Damien said.

Bonnie spun around. Her head dropped back slightly as she looked up into his face. "But I was not asking—"

"I know you weren't. Accept them anyway." He smiled again, looking handsome and roguish and just a little sleepy. "Please," he added softly.

Kate and Marianne entered the room. Kate appeared slightly pale. Marianne looked ecstatic. Kate hurried to her husband and said, "You are out early, William."

"Indeed." He glanced toward Damien. "Damien's business is finished. Parliament has voted to see the commissioners."

Kate glanced at Bonnie. Bonnie looked at Mari, then they all stared at Damien. He stood with one hand full of ribbons. His face was emotionless. Apparently choosing to ignore their silent query, he cleared his throat and asked, "Are you bleeding my purse again, ladies? Should I busy myself with obtaining a loan to pay for this spree?" Madame joined them then, and he added, "Please cut Bonnie a length of each of these ribbons."

Bonnie turned away and pretended to watch Madame Roussaue measure and cut the ribbons. In her mind, however, she heard William's dreaded news again and again. *He is leaving . . . He is leaving*, she told herself over and over. Little by little, she felt the life drain from her until her knees trembled and the voices around her were no more than a distant buzz. She gripped the table and prayed the weakness would pass, but as Madame Roussauc placed the ribbons in Bonnie's hand, and she closed her fingers around them, her tenuous control shattered.

"Bonnie!" Mari cried out.

Then there was blackness.

"My name is Dr. Blackstone, Bonnie. Are you feeling better?"

Bonnie tried to nod, but a terrible pain centered in the back of her head brought tears to her eyes.

"You hit your head when you fainted. Is it very painful?"

"Yes," she replied weakly.

"I have some powders that will remedy that."

"Where am I?" she asked.

"Home."

"Where are the others?"

"Waiting outside. They're very concerned."

"May I see them?"

"In a moment." He sat beside her on the bed and took her hand. His smile was kind as he said, "Bonnie, do you realize that you are going to have a baby?"

She turned her head, unable to face him.

"You appear to be at least four months pregnant. Have you felt movement?"

"I think so. I don't know."

"It will be a slight tickling . . . here." He gently placed his hand over the swelling above her pubic bone. In that instant, the child inside her moved.

"Yes." She smiled. "It's like a butterfly inside me."

Dr. Blackstone left the bed. "Does the father know?" he asked.

Still marveling over the movement inside her, Bonnie took a moment to acknowledge the doctor's question. "No. I only recently realized myself."

"Didn't you suspect when you stopped your monthly bleeding?"

"I didn't realize one had anything to do with the other."

He looked concerned as he said, "You did realize that intercourse could lead to pregnancy?"

Bonnie's face turned warm.

"Do you intend to tell the father?" Blackstone asked.

"I—I don't know."

"Is he married?"

"No."

"Then I suggest he be informed immediately. Would you like me to discuss this matter with your guardian?"

"No!" She sat upright.

"He should be aware—"

"No! I—I'll tell him myself. Please, you mustn't inform him."

Dr. Blackstone took up his black bag and walked to the door. He stared at Bonnie for a full minute before saying, "You are not the first young lady to find herself in these straits, my dear, so do not be overly harsh on yourself. But you must consider all alternatives. Marriage to the father is, of course, desirable. If that is not possible, however, there are homes in Europe to which you might retire for the duration of your term. They are affiliated with numerous adoption organizations that can help you place the child with a loving family."

"Do you mean that I should give my baby away to strangers?"

"Consider the alternatives." He opened the door before adding, "I'll drop by to see you next week. Until then, rest and food will help alleviate the symptoms."

He left the room, closing the door behind him. Bonnie fell back on the bed.

So. It was true. Staring at the ceiling, she wondered how she could have failed to recognize the reason for her state. Then she reminded herself that, not ever having had pregnancy explained to her, her ignorance would not be surprising.

"Bonnie?"

She looked around.

Kate smiled from the doorway. "May I come in?" she asked.

Bonnie took a breath and nodded.

Kate crossed the room and sat down on the bed. She took Bonnie's hand. "Damien is speaking with the doctor." Noticing Bonnie's concern, she said, "Dr. Blackstone is very discreet. He won't say anything to Damien unless you asked him to."

Bonnie closed her eyes. "Then you know as well. Does Mari?"

"Madame Roussaue realized when the dress had to be let out."

"Do you think Damien suspects?"

"I don't think so. But he'll have to be told as soon as possible. Plans will have to be made—"

"Plans?"

"For your marriage, of course."

"To Damien?"

"Certainly." Kate's eyes widened. "He *is* the father . . . ?"

"Of course he's the bloody father!" Bonnie cried. "But he don't want t' marry me. He don't love me!"

"Poppycock. Of course he does."

"He *cares* for me, Kate. That ain't love. I won't marry a man who don't love me."

Kate left the bed and said angrily, "If you believe he does not love you, how could you let him touch you that way?"

"Because I love him, and I hoped he would come t' love me as well." Covering her face with her hands, Bonnie said, "If Damien were forced t' marry me, he would surely end up hating me, and that I couldn't bear. It's torment enough knowing he resents my intrusion in his life."

Bonnie rolled from the bed, and the world spun crazily around her. Kate hurried to help her as she walked to a chair. Once seated, she said, "It seems I have held onto the memory of my parents' marriage for too long. While other men regarded their wives as chattel, my father cherished my mother until he died. The fantasy I spun for myself that Damien could love me was only that . . . a fantasy."

"Bonnie, little good can come from trying to second-guess a man who does not know his own mind. Damien must be told."

She shook her head. "I won't have him marryin' me out of duty. He would only end up dislikin' me more than he already does. I've told you, I couldn't bear that."

"Then what will you do?"

"I don't know. Let me think."

"Will you at least see Damien? He was out of his mind with worry when you fainted."

"He was?"

"Of course. He held you in his arms the entire ride home, and carried you up to bed. He remained at your side until Dr. Blackstone forced him to leave."

Sinking back in her chair, Bonnie closed her eyes.

"Well?" Kate persisted. "Will you see him?"

Bonnie thought of the many times she had stood in Damien's presence, trembling from fear or longing. She recalled how easily he shattered her judgment with just a smile, a touch, a look, until her mind and body were no longer her own.

After a long silence, Bonnie said simply but firmly, "No."

Twenty-three

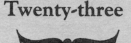

Outside Damien's town house the sounds of London traffic and the hawkers calling their wares were a constant dim drone. Horses and carriages circling Mayfair Place barely intruded on the quiet of his ornate master suite. Damien sat in a chair, his elegant black suit coat open and a cravat hanging loose around the collar of his shirt. His legs were crossed as he stared at the ceiling.

In another hour he would be standing in a crowd of people watching the eligible men of London vie for Bonnie's hand. He should be relieved. He could return to Vicksburg and continue with his life as it had been before she stumbled into it with her saucy tongue and flashing eyes.

No more Bonnie.

An ache sluiced through him so brutally that he clutched his chest with his hand. The pain felt cold at first, like ice. Then the burning began, a slow hot flame that engulfed his heart and made him groan. The idea occurred to him that he was ill. Perhaps the same malady of the heart that had killed his father was now afflicting him.

Leaving the chair, he paced the shadowed room full of overstuffed furniture, books, and knickknacks. He felt oppressed, yet he sensed the feeling had little to do with his crowded surroundings. Something was happening inside him that he couldn't understand . . . or perhaps didn't *want* to understand. The absurd idea had occurred to him that marriage between Bonnie and another man was the *last* thing he wanted. He shook his head and told himself, as he had many times over the last weeks, that he was confusing his feelings for Bonnie with those for Louisa. The anger, the distrust, the jealousy had stemmed from lingering memories of her betrayal. But what of this . . . affection? True enough, the years following his breakup with Louisa, he had fancied himself still in love with her—heartbroken but in love. Was this stirring of emotion inside him some remnant of that? How the devil was he supposed to know for certain? How could he trust his instincts when he'd been so furious, confused, and hurt for so many years?

He stopped pacing. Standing in the middle of the room, listening to the distant outside noises and the pealing of some cathedral bell, he began to slowly tie and tuck his cravat into his shirt. He straightened his coat, imagining Bonnie was now dressing, with Kate and Mari fluttering about her like mother hens. He wondered if her illness had passed. Recalling the fear he'd experienced when she fainted, he frowned. Why had she refused to see him? No doubt she was still upset over the incident at the palace. Yet, for a moment at Madame Roussaue's, he'd believed—hoped—they could put the unfortunate occurrence behind them.

He tugged on the bellpull, and within seconds a servant was curtsying before him. "You called, my lord?"

"Have the coach brought around."

"Yes, milord. Will you be going directly to Chatsworth?"

"No," he replied. "I'll be paying a call on an old friend first."

The maid bobbed again and rustled out the door. Damien reached for his cloak, thrown over the back of a chair, and wrapped it around his shoulders.

A light rain began to fall as Damien stood outside the town house on Regent Street and looked into the servant's face. If she experienced any surprise over seeing him, she didn't show it.

"Earl Warwick to see Miss Thackeray," he said.

She opened the door further, allowing him to step out of the rain into the foyer. "May I take your coat, milord?" she asked.

"No, thank you. I won't be staying."

"Very good. I'll see if Miss Thackeray is in, milord."

Damien watched her go. For long minutes he patiently waited, inwardly convincing himself that he had lost his mind and that seeing Louisa again would be like lancing an old wound. But perhaps that was best. He could finally confront his perplexing emotions and have done with the annoyance once and for all. When facing Bonnie again he would know beyond any doubt that the feelings he had experienced had been confused with those for Louisa.

The servant finally returned. "Miss Thackeray will see you. If you'd like to step into the parlor to wait, she'll join you shortly."

She began to show him down the hallway. He stopped her by saying, "I know the way."

He entered the drawing room alone.

The familiarity of his surroundings felt eerie, as if he had somehow been caught in a whirlpool of memories and sucked into the past. Odd how little had changed. The furnishings were the same. Vases of fresh cut flowers adorned every table, and he reminisced on Louisa's love of eyebrights and sweet williams.

On a saucer near a chair was a partially eaten meat pie and a cup of tea. Damien placed his hand upon the china, finding it warm. He had interrupted her meal. He did his best to imagine Louisa eating alone with only a few preening pigeons on her windowsill to keep her company. Instead, he recalled seeing her surrounded by young men who stumbled over themselves to fetch her a cup of milk punch. Himself included.

"My, how very handsome you are."

Damien looked up.

Louisa stood in the doorway wearing a pale pink dress with a standup collar of starched white lace. Her yellow hair was loose, spilling over her shoulders. She stared at him with something of her old defiance, and he remembered in that instant how once he would watch her from afar and think she was the most beautiful creature to walk the earth. His pulse would race and his brow would sweat with the anticipation of someday cupping her breasts in his hands. Standing before her now, he waited for his body's reaction. There was . . . nothing.

"Hello," he said softly.

She smiled. "I was just taking tea. Will you join me?"

"No, thank you."

He watched her hands twist together, then she moved across the room with a gentle shushing of crinoline petticoats. A slight wave of French perfume washed over him as she stopped before a window and appeared to study the scenery outside the house. Finally she said, "I heard months ago that you had returned to England. I wondered if I would see you."

"It was inevitable, I think."

"I think so too."

She turned away from the window to face him. A shaft of sunlight found its way through the partially drawn drapes and lit one side of her face like soft candlelight. "Why did you come here?" she asked.

"I don't think I know. Perhaps to find out once and for all . . . why?"

She lowered her gaze. "I was young and selfish. But most of all I was too blinded by what I *thought* was important. I had family and friends who loved me, but I hungered for power, for possessions, for wealth far grander than I had ever hoped for. Too late I learned that those cold, inanimate objects could not love me back."

The pigeons outside the window cooed and fluttered their wings. Hooves clacked upon the granite street, and a coachman whistled noisily as traffic became ensnared.

"I was a fool," she said. "I didn't realize until you were gone how much your friendship meant to me. You made me laugh. You understood me as no one else did. You accepted me as I was, not as what society deemed I should be. I hurt you, and I'm truly sorry for that. But I have suffered for my ignorance more than you know, Damien. You see before you an unmarried woman with little likelihood of finding wedded bliss in the near future, therefore little hope for children or for any of those things I once thought I would gladly sacrifice for prosperity."

They stood in silence.

At last she looked at him again. Her pale blue eyes were large and glassy. Her face appeared haggard beyond her twenty-three years. "Do you still hate me very much?"

Damien took a breath and released it as he realized the anger that had burdened him for so long had, at sometime, slid from his shoulders like a mantle of mist. He shuddered in relief.

"No," he replied.

"But you no longer love me, either."

He shook his head. "No."

She gripped her hands together and averted her face. Damien walked to the door before turning back. She stood silhouetted against the light, and for a long minute he searched his heart, giving it one last chance to react.

"Good-bye," he told her, and without glancing her way again, he left the house, his mind, oddly enough, no longer on Louisa but on Bonnie and Chatsworth Hall.

Bonnie could hear the orchestra playing from the room where she had rested throughout the day and dressed for the ball. For the past two hours guests had arrived. Standing at a window she had looked down on the long line of coaches stretched all the way down Chatsworth Hall's drive and out onto the road, and wondered why the people inside them had really come.

She was not so naive as to believe they accepted her. No, it was more likely curiosity, some perversity in their natures that drove them to accept Marianne's invitation to Bonnie's soiree. She was hardly blind to the inquisitive glances, the awkward silences that fell over crowds when she entered a room. She couldn't blame them. As a child she had once happened by the local inn just as a gentleman and lady were stepping from their coach. Bonnie had stopped and stared, curious as to why they were there, fascinated by their manners and spellbound by their wealth. This was no different, and she understood. Still . . .

Bonnie walked again to the mirror and assessed her appearance. The blue skirt of her dress spilled in many tiers to the floor, each tier trimmed in a ruching of ribbons and lace. The pointed bodice fit snugly, and the corset she wore beneath it hid most of her rounding belly. The décolletage, as always, was modest, yet fell slightly off her shoulders. The sleeves hugged her arms to her wrists. She had chosen to wear her hair down, yet swept from her face and tied at the back with ribbons. The sapphires she had purchased during her fit of spitefulness dressed her white throat and ears. Marianne had called her a princess. She didn't feel much like a princess. She felt pregnant. She felt like throwing herself across the bed and releasing the flood of tears and hysteria that had been nagging her for so long.

Fool. Ignorant, silly little fool. She had actually believed that Warwick loved her, and now she was going to have his baby.

His baby. It moved inside her even as she stood gazing at her image in the mirror, even as she pressed her hand gently against her rounding belly.

His baby.

Despite the tears that formed in her eyes, Bonnie smiled.

The door opened and closed. Kate said, "Bonnie, are you ready to go downstairs?"

She nodded.

"Are you certain you won't allow Damien to escort you? He seemed stunned when I told him you had requested William. Bonnie, you'll have to face him sometime."

"Not tonight," she said shakily. "Please . . ."

Without further words, Kate departed, leaving the door slightly ajar. Bonnie listened idly to the comings and goings of the guests. Occasionally she caught bits of conversation. A burst of girlish laughter rang out in the quiet, and curious, Bonnie moved to the door and peeked out. Four young women, no older than Bonnie, had gathered in the hallway. She recognized one of them as Christina Gosford.

"He spent the majority of the weekend with me while at Blenheim," Christina told her friends. "He was to walk with me by the river one morning, but some problem with his ward prevented it."

"Well," another girl said, "you shouldn't have to worry over that much longer. He'll be rid of *her* soon enough, if the rumors prove true."

"Rumors?" a dark-haired girl asked. "What sort of rumors?"

"Haven't you heard?" Christina, her eyes wide, leaned closer to her friends and lowered her voice, though not so low that Bonnie could not hear each horrible word. "Earl brought Bonnie to London to marry her off. He's offering a one-hundred-thousand-pound dowry to any man who will take her off his hands!"

Bonnie's heart seemed to stop. She stepped away, and putting a shaking hand to her mouth, fought back the overwhelming urge to be sick. Her entire body trembled with every conceivable emotion; for a moment she thought she might faint again. She felt strangely numb and cold. As she pressed her hands to her face, her fingers felt like chips of ice.

"Bonnie?"

Lowering her hands, Bonnie looked at William standing just inside the door. Smiling, he walked to her. "You look stunning, Bonnie."

"Thank you," she managed.

"You have a house full of guests waiting downstairs to greet you. Are you ready to receive them?"

She nodded.

He offered his arm, and somehow Bonnie took it. The next minutes clipped by like hours as she descended the stairs and entered Chatsworth's grand ballroom. Almost instantly she was surrounded by guests. Some she had met at Blenheim; others were strangers. She smiled through so many introductions that her face hurt, and all the while her anger mounted.

She was greatly relieved when the dancing started. It gave her a chance to breathe and collect her thoughts, even as she was spun around the dance floor in the arms of a young man hardly taller than herself.

"You look positively enchanting!" he declared with such enthusiasm that Bonnie might have laughed had she not been so furious, not only with Damien, but also with every man in attendance.

Smiling coldly, she asked, "In your estimation, am I worth one hundred thousand pounds?"

He stumbled over his feet, and for the remainder of the dance stared into the air over her head, saying not a word.

The dance ended. He bowed and escaped. She turned to see Trent Halford approaching, a glass of champagne punch in each hand. At first Bonnie was surprised to see him, then embarrassed. She swept the room with a cautious glance before facing him again.

"You look beautiful and thirsty," he said, handing her the drink. Noting her concern, he laughed. "You're surprised to see me here."

"Yes."

"It would have been bad form not to invite me."

"You might have declined the invitation."

"Perhaps I should have, but I wanted to see you again."

"Oh?" She laughed dryly. "My lord Halford, you don't strike me as needing one hundred thousand pounds."

He smiled before sipping his punch. "I don't, I assure you. I have spent that much this year renovating my gardens. My interest is in you and nothing more, Bonnie. I enjoy your company."

She had no more than accepted the punch when she looked up and saw Damien moving through the guests toward her. He looked tall and broad shouldered in a resplendently tailored black suit, and despite the fury and hurt she felt toward him in that moment she was gripped by a painful giddiness as she stared at his hard, dark face.

"We have to talk," he demanded quietly but sternly. She detected a touch of his old annoyance in the words.

"I don't wish to talk," she replied. Forcing herself to smile, she glanced toward Trent and added, "I'm entertaining my guest, as you can see."

Damien looked at Halford. "Have you proof that you were invited here?"

Trent slipped his hand into his jacket and withdrew his invitation.

Damien merely glanced at it before saying, "Must have been an error."

"Regardless, I was invited, and I am here. Unless, of course, you are about to ask me to leave."

"He wouldn't dare," Bonnie replied, diverting Damien's attention to her. The speculation in his eyes caused her heart to thump painfully in her chest. "It is *my* soiree, is it not?" she finally asked.

The orchestra struck up a waltz then, and Damien was forced to raise his voice. "I'd like to speak with you, Bonnie." He caught her arm. "We can discuss the matter while we dance."

"Not possible." She nudged his fingers from her arm and thrust her punch glass into his hand. "I promised this dance to Trent."

Trent handed Damien his glass as well, then escorted her onto the floor.

For several minutes Damien watched Bonnie spin across

the dance floor in Halford's arms. He couldn't take his eyes from her. From the moment she'd glided into the room on William's arm he'd felt upended, as if someone had sneaked up on his blind side and punched him in the gut. Why? Because, whether he wanted to admit it or not, the feelings he was experiencing had nothing to do with old emotions for Louisa. So what *were* his feelings *exactly?* What did it matter? The men were circling her like a bunch of sharks around a kill, and she appeared to be enjoying every moment of it. He had the absurd notion to drag her upstairs and force her out of those clothes and into her breeches, for he suddenly realized how desperately he'd come to miss the spirited, rag-clad girl from Caldbergh who'd thrown her arms around him at the Grange Inn and admitted she loved him.

Philippe, Freddy, and Claurence moved up behind him. "She's a vision of loveliness, don't you think?" Philippe said. "I'm almost tempted to marry her myself."

Freddy snickered. "Not unless you want Dame breathing over your shoulder every time you turn out the lights." Freddy's eyebrows rose as Damien shot him a hot glance.

"Let's place a wager on who takes her," Claurence said. "My money is on Halford."

"Over my dead body," Damien snapped.

"Geoffrey Londonderry called on her twice before tonight." Freddy elbowed Philippe and added, "Rumor has it he'd just lost a thousand pounds at White's when he got news of Bonnie's dowry. He excused himself immediately, and not a half an hour later was seen exiting a florist, flowers in one hand, a box of bonbons in another."

"What a rascal," Claurence said.

"A right bounder," Freddy agreed.

Moving closer to Damien, Philippe slapped a hand on one shoulder and said in his ear, "You're not going to approve of anyone who makes a move on her, Dame, so why don't you save us all a great deal of trouble and heartbreak and marry Bonnie yourself?"

"Smashing idea!" Freddy and Claurence chimed in.

Damien snorted disgustedly and said with an edge, "Imbeciles. I may as well crawl into the matrimonial bed with a pit of vipers."

"So he says." Philippe laughed and said to Freddy and

Claurence, "Personally, I don't think I've ever seen Damien so moonstruck. Not even over Louisa."

"Agreed."

"Absolutely."

Damien's expression was purposefully bored as he regarded his friends. "You have no doubt imbibed too much punch. It has gone directly to your heads. If you're not careful you'll soon be giggling like a bunch of women."

Freddy snickered, and his face turned red.

Philippe shook his head and smiled. "Why not face it, Dame. You're smitten with Bonnie."

"We know smitten," Freddy declared, "and you are smut. You ain't taken your eyes off her since she walked in the room."

"He ain't taken his eyes off her since she arrived at Braithwaite," Philippe observed.

The dance ended. Damien left his friends and pushed through the crowd. By the time he reached Bonnie, however, she was swept into another man's arms, into a quadrille that took her to the opposite end of the room. But not before glancing his way. For an instant they looked at each other, his gaze locked on the willful set of her beautiful mouth, before their eyes clashed in a silent war of wills. Then, with apparent disregard of his presence, she smiled brightly up at her partner and was whisked away.

Three times more he attempted to address her. Three times more she snubbed him. Damien was well aware that heads were beginning to turn his way each time he walked onto the dance floor, and though he did his best to appear calm, little by little his anger was getting the better of him.

The music ended. Damien waited until Bonnie's partner bowed and departed before moving toward her again, a mirthless smile curving his lips as she glanced with wide blue eyes in his direction. Almost frantically she turned away and greeted a gangly blond viscount who approached her. But as the gentleman took up her hand, Damien stepped between them and announced, "I beg your pardon, my lord, but this dance is mine."

"Don't say," he replied and, staring at Damien, stupidly added, "Thought certain it was mine, ol' chap."

"Perhaps later," Damien assured him.

Bonnie did her best to remain outwardly docile, though she was trembling inside like a leaf in a hurricane. As the viscount bowed and quit the floor, she tried to follow.

Damien's arm snaked out and caught her waist. "Not so fast," he said, jerking her back to him. As she glared up into his cold, implacable face, he added, "Be nice. Your guests are watching."

"I don't give a bloody damn about my 'guests,' " she whispered furiously. "And I don't give a damn about you, m'lord. So if y'll kindly let me go . . ."

"No."

The ensuing silence raked at Bonnie's nerves, and it was with a sense of relief that she heard the music begin and Damien swept her into a waltz. Clumsily, stiffly, Bonnie attempted to follow his graceful movements. With a great deal of distress she realized that he was undoubtedly the best dancer who'd held her all night.

Pulling her closer, he solemnly studied her upturned face. "Relax, sweetheart, I have no intention of getting into a duel of insults with you tonight. I only want to know why you've refused to see me since yesterday."

"I find that question ridiculous in light of the many weeks I spent with no word from you."

The quick fire that leaped into Damien's eyes made Bonnie stumble again. His arms tightened around her until she was pressed indecently close to his hard frame. The feel of his hips against hers brought back flashes of memories from that morning at the glade, and the way she had readily and willingly allowed him to take her, despite her anger at him. Dear God, she thought, how could she fight him when his simple touch aroused her to such a humiliating level?

Squirming against him, she demanded, "Let me go. Please! Your monopolizing my company will hardly help to accomplish your goal, will it?"

"What is *that* supposed to mean?"

"Don't play daft," she snapped. "I know about the bloody dowry."

The hand gripping hers tightened for an instant. His face became dark.

Bonnie glanced around her, noting with surprise that many of the guests had stopped dancing and were watching her and

Damien. Nervously, she held him more tightly, and in response he stepped up the pace of the dance. His head inclined over hers as he said in an oddly bitter tone, "So tell me, m'love, have you chosen a husband from your suitors?"

"I?" She laughed harshly. "I rather doubt that *I* will have any choice in the matter."

"I would have you happy, Bonnie."

"Really?" Her head falling back, she looked up into his eyes and was startled at the emotion she saw swimming in their murky depths. At one time she might have foolishly mistaken that look for love. Now . . .

Forcing herself to smile, she leaned closer and whispered, "I assure you, it would take a great deal more than one hundred thousand pounds to entice these men into marrying me now, my lord."

The music ended, but Damien continued to hold her.

She forcibly pushed him away before turning to face their spellbound audience. She smiled and the guests applauded. She then left Damien alone on the dance floor as she hurried toward Trent Halford. He took her hand, and they merged with the crowd.

"You look as if you could use a drink and some fresh air," Trent told her. Without waiting for a response, he scooped up a pair of glasses from a table and a bottle of champagne from a pail of ice. He motioned her toward open French doors at the end of the room, and although Bonnie hesitated briefly, she followed, eager for a chance to calm her senses and catch her breath.

They strolled down a dark, paved path without speaking. Finally they came to a bench placed among neatly cropped hedges and beds of flowers. Water in a fountain tinkled nearby. Halford sat down first and poured the champagne. As Bonnie joined him, he smiled and said, "A toast to our reunion."

She accepted the drink and touched her glass to his.

Halford settled against the bench and watched the water splash in the fountain before looking back at Bonnie. "I missed you," he told her. "I regret the unfortunate incident at Blenheim."

"It wasn't your fault."

"I shouldn't have taken you there alone."

"I shouldn't have accompanied you. I'm as much to blame."

Bonnie drank her champagne and gazed out over the dark grounds, vaguely aware of Trent's arm sliding around her shoulders. In truth, her mind and body were still too numb to make sense of anything but the horrible mess fate had made of her life. Had she truly *wanted* to be rid of Damien, had she *wanted* to become involved with someone else, she could not do it. For even now Damien's child moved inside her like a butterfly batting its wings in flight.

"Happy thoughts?" Trent asked.

Surprised, Bonnie looked around.

"You were smiling," he said, then he touched the corner of her lips with his finger and added, "Just there. It was a very secretive little smile."

Feeling herself blush, Bonnie drank more champagne before saying, "I was thinking about my parents and how happy they were when they learned my mother was pregnant for a second time. I was eight or nine, so they'd waited a long while for another baby." She offered him her glass. He refilled it. "Unfortunately, she lost the child in her fourth month."

"Those are sobering thoughts for a young woman on her coming-out night." His arm wrapped around Bonnie and coaxed her more tightly against him. With a sigh, she closed her eyes and rested her head on his shoulder. "Do you like the champagne?" he whispered in her ear.

She nodded.

"Then drink up. We have an entire bottle to finish before I'll let you return to the dance."

Bonnie turned the glass up and drained it completely. She drank again after he refilled it, enjoying the feeling of lethargy that sluiced through her body.

"This is pleasant," she murmured. "Do we have to go back to the dance?"

"No."

Twisting a little, she looked up into his handsome face and smiled. "You're a true friend to care about me so much."

"I care about you *very* much, *cherie.*"

Bonnie's eyes drifted shut, then opened. Dizzily she tried

to sit up, but Halford's hands pushed her back down. "Wh—what are you doing?" she asked.

"I'm going to make love to you, of course."

Frowning, she watched as he expertly slid the dress off her shoulders and down her arms, releasing her chemise-covered breasts. As adroitly he tugged the filmy material aside. Almost as if she had somehow become detached from her body, Bonnie watched as Halford bent his head and closed his mouth over her exposed nipple. The shock of his tongue darting over the sensitive peak aroused her enough from her inebriated state to try and push him away.

His hands grabbed her wrists and, very slowly, his head came up. A thin smile crossed his lips as he regarded Bonnie in silence.

"Let me go!" she demanded.

"I don't excite you? Perhaps you would prefer my dragging you to the ground and pouncing on you like—how did you put it?—a rutting dog?"

Frozen, the color draining from her cheeks, Bonnie stared at him.

He bent his head and deliberately ran his tongue around her nipple several times before looking at her again.

"You see, I had no more than reached the road after departing the glade that day than I began feeling like a swine for leaving you with Warwick, considering how angry he was. So I went back. I saw it all. You let him mount you, Bonnie, and by the looks of things it wasn't the first time."

His hand inched up her skirt. "I must hand it to the earl. He does have fine taste in women. I haven't witnessed such a hot performance since the last time I bought an East End whore."

Damien watched Christina Gosford smile and bat her pale lashes at him. He supposed he'd better ask her to dance or she would never quit hanging about his coattails.

He'd just put his glass aside when he looked up to find Philippe and Kate bearing down on him, their faces concerned.

"Where's Bonnie?" Kate asked.

"I haven't seen her since she left me standing like an idiot on the dance floor. She went off with Halford, I think."

"Bad news," Philippe said. "I was just playing faro with Greenfells and Aurzon. You'll never believe what they told me."

Damien raised one brow and waited.

"Seems Halford's wagered that he will have seduced Bonnie by the end of the evening. What's more, he seems to be spreading the nasty rumor that you and she are a couple . . . if you know what I mean."

Marianne joined them. "I've checked the house. I can't find either of them."

Damien turned and, as calmly as possible, made his way toward the French doors. Kate, running up behind him, attempted to catch his arm and pull him back.

He shoved her away and exited the house.

The cool night air was like a sharp slap across Damien's burning face. Behind him he heard Kate cry out, "Find William, Mari, quickly!"

Philippe, following at his heels, said, "I strongly suggest we continue the search with a mind to secrecy. We will haul Halford behind the stables and once there, grind his face to a pulp. He will be hard-pressed to seduce a hag by the time I'm done with him."

Damien continued walking while the image of Bonnie and Halford as they kissed in the glade kept flashing before his eyes. He slowed his pace as the path became less visible in the darkness. As he rounded a bend, a noise made him stop. He listened hard. Nothing. Only the splashing of the water in the fountain to his right. Still, some instinct made him hesitate, and once again he scanned the area. The moon cast an eerie glow over the fountain, hedges, and bench, but there was no movement.

Then he heard a sob and the cry, "Take yer bloody hands off me!" and Bonnie seemed to appear from nowhere, crashing through a hedge and sprawling at Damien's feet. The tight hold with which he had kept his fury under control disintegrated as he noticed Bonnie's ripped gown and one exposed white breast.

Halford let out a startled shout as Damien met him face-to-face. He stumbled backward and hit the ground as Damien came at him, his hands doubled into fists and ready to strike.

"Damien, no!" Kate shouted. She threw herself between them and did her best to shove Damien back.

Scrambling to his feet, Halford laughed. "Get out of the way, Katharine, and let him come. He's been itching to go at me since we were lads."

Doing his best to push Kate away, Damien sneered, "You bastard. I should have killed you at Blenheim when I had the chance."

"But you didn't, my lord, because you were hard for the chit yourself. You can't fault a man for wanting a bit of the action."

Kate screamed as Damien leaped for Halford, his attempt thwarted by Philippe, who jumped between them, shoved his heels into the soft earth, and pushed Damien back.

His face sweating and his blond hair tumbling over his brow, Philippe said, "Not here, for God's sake. Not like this. You'll kill him, Dame. Consider! Consider! Have the bastard choose his seconds and meet him at dawn."

Gradually, Damien felt his sanity return. Still staring at Halford, he nodded. "Right. I call you, Halford, to choose your weapons. Are you agreeable?"

"Pistols."

"Then pistols it is. I'll have my second contact you within the hour as to where we'll meet."

Damien turned back to Kate and Bonnie, who was gripping her dress closed and staring at him with startled, wide eyes and a white face. Without speaking, he strode into the house.

Upon returning to Kate and William's town house just after midnight, Bonnie ran to her room and slammed the door, refusing entrance to either of her friends. She paced, her anxiety verging on panic each time the clock chimed a new hour.

At just after three Claurence arrived. Bonnie crept partway down the staircase and listened to him speak quietly with the others.

"He's to meet Halford at Quay Meadow at precisely dawn."

"But you have to stop him!" Kate cried.

"Kate, your brother is determined."

"William—"

"I've done what I can, Kate," William said. "All we can do now is wait."

As Kate burst into tears, Bonnie quietly climbed the stairs back to her room.

Damien poured himself a drink. "If your intention in coming here was to persuade me not to meet Halford, you're wasting your time." He turned to face Marianne and finished, "Go home. Unless, of course, you'd like to come with me upstairs. As I recall you were always at your best about this time of the morning."

"I wouldn't do that to Bonnie," she replied quietly.

Damien raised one brow in mock surprise. "No?" He quaffed his whiskey and plunked the glass onto the table. "Since when did you acquire scruples, Lady Lyttleton?"

Marianne backed away as Damien approached her. "Bonnie's in love with you."

"Certainly. That's why she slinks about the dark inviting men to rape her."

"He didn't rape her."

"He would have." Wrapping one hand around the back of Marianne's neck, he pulled her nearer. "We have two hours. Why not make the best of it?"

Marianne laughed deep in her throat. "You don't want me, Damien. You want Bonnie, and it's past time you admitted it. Think about what you're about to do. For God's sake, Damien, you're about to meet a man on a dueling field, and for what? I cannot believe it is solely to defend her reputation."

Twisting his fingers into her red hair, he yanked back her head and covered her mouth with his in a punishing kiss that made her whimper and tremble against him. He slid his free arm around her waist and lowered her to the settee.

"Don't." She groaned. "I didn't come here for this."

"Of course you did."

"You're in love with her," Marianne persisted.

"Shut up."

"You don't even deny it. Do you think that by making love to me that will somehow obliterate Bonnie's memory from your mind?"

Damien cursed her and rolled away. He returned to the liquor and refilled his glass.

"I don't think you're angry at Trent *or* Bonnie. You're furious at yourself for allowing yourself to fall for her. And you're jealous. You tell yourself you don't want her, that all you want is Bent Tree, yet you die inside every time you imagine her with someone else."

He tossed back the drink and poured another.

"You told yourself there would never be another woman after Louisa. You thought you'd hardened your heart against the emotion. But Bonnie cracked you, Damien. Her innocence and naïveté have been your undoing. For God's sake, look at yourself. You love her so much you're sickened by it!"

He spun and hurled the glass just inches from Marianne's head. It crashed against the wall, spraying shards of glass over the room.

"Get out," he demanded.

Marianne swept up her reticule and left the house.

At just after five o'clock, Bonnie cautiously descended the stairs. Kate and William had retired to their room.

As quietly as possible Bonnie exited the house through the rear door. Swallowed by night fog, she hurried around to Park Lane and stood shivering in the damp and cold for interminable minutes before a cab appeared through the mist. She waved it down, and as she climbed aboard called out, "Quay Meadow as quickly as possible!"

Dawn was only minutes away as Damien, standing at Philippe's and Freddy's sides, regarded the group of men at the far end of the green. Around him patches of fog shifted in the breeze, revealing bare-branched trees with twisted limbs and knobby roots plastered with wet, fallen leaves. The yellowing grass was damp with dew, and somewhere in the distance a lark sang, heralding the morning.

Slowly the dark turned to gray. Halford and his seconds walked to meet Damien and his seconds in the middle of the green.

Curt nods of greeting passed among them. Halford's second flipped open the pistol case and offered the duelists their choice of weapons.

"Name your paces, gentlemen," Philippe said.

"Ten should do it nicely I think," Damien replied lightly. He noted his adversary's eyes widen briefly in his pale face, and suspected that Halford was, by now, sorely regretting his ungentlemanly action toward Bonnie.

"Agreed," Halford replied in a dry voice.

Freddy stepped forward to help Damien remove his coat, revealing a plain loose-fitting dark suit. Philippe leaned close. "He's too damned skittish, Dame. I would look to my back if I were you. He's likely to jump the count."

Damien nodded and for the first time since arriving at the green, looked directly into Philippe's face. "Should something happen to me . . ." He took a breath. "Tell Bonnie . . ."

Philippe waited, his eyes knowing, his features concerned. The idea occurred to Damien that everyone other than himself appeared to be aware of his feelings for the girl. So what the hell had taken *him* so long?

"Backs together, gentlemen," Halford's second called out.

Backs together, they waited as the witnesses moved to the edge of the green.

The count began and Damien stepped forward.

"One . . . two . . . three . . ."

I love her.

"Four . . . five . . ."

But there's Bent Tree.

"Six . . ."

"Too late I learned those cold, inanimate objects could not love me back."

"Seven . . ."

"Little hope for children, or for any of those things I once thought I would gladly sacrifice for prosperity."

"I love you," Bonnie had told him. "I love you . . ."

"Eight . . . nine . . . ten."

Please, God, please.

He turned, aimed, and fired, feeling Halford's bullet rip through the flesh of his arm even as he pulled the trigger.

Damien stumbled from the impact but righted himself in time to see Halford spin and crumple.

"Foul!" Philippe cried, running to Damien. "The damned bastard jumped the count! Foul!"

As Philippe reached him, Damien tossed the gun to the ground and pushed him away. He walked to where Halford lay twisting and clutching his shoulder in pain. "Will he live?" he asked.

"Yes," someone responded.

Turning his back on them all, Damien strode toward his coach, ignoring his concerned friends who tried to help him.

"Leave me alone," he told them.

"But your arm—"

"To hell with my arm," he snapped.

A cab rolled up. The door opened and Bonnie spilled out, her dark hair and cape flying behind her as she ran down the slope toward him.

He didn't stop, just kept walking to his coach until she moved in front of him, throwing her arms around him and pressing her face into his chest. Damien closed his eyes, allowing himself, for a moment, to give in to the stress, the pain that were streaking through his body and mind like splintered lightning. He had won the duel, but the victor was Bonnie. Bonnie, with her guileless ways and her laughter that could turn night into day and winter into spring. Bonnie, who could transform a man's frozen heart into a fire burning out of control . . . who could make the distant dreams of foreign prosperity seem inconsequential. She had defeated him— mind, body, and soul.

Shoving her away, he grabbed his bloodied arm as crucifying pain shot through it. His mind a tumult of conflicting emotions, he snarled into her stricken face—not meaning the words but unable to stop them—"Are you happy now? Are you? Blood has been let because of you, and frankly, *urchin,* you aren't worth it."

Without looking back, he boarded his coach and demanded the driver take him home. The ride was excruciating as each jar and rut they hit sent pain sluicing like fire through his shoulder and chest. Over and over Bonnie's image as she ran down the slope came and went through his fleeting consciousness, and he would try to rouse himself from confusion and agony long enough to call out to the driver to go back.

He'd hurt her again, and he hadn't meant it . . . he'd never meant it . . .

It seemed forever before they reached his town house in Mayfair. Rain hit his face as he stumbled from the coach and made for the house, ignoring the driver's concerned offer to help. He climbed the stairs to his bedroom and slammed the door behind him, barely making it to the bed before his strength gave out completely. With a moan he fell facedown onto the mattress.

He dreamed he was on fire. As the flames surged up around him, he cried out for Bonnie.

"Bonnie will be here soon, my lord. Kate has gone to get her."

Damien forced open his eyes. Dr. Blackstone, his brow creased with concern, wrapped a bandage around his arm.

"You've lost a great deal of blood. You're in shock and have fever."

Rolling his head, he looked about the room. Philippe's image blurred in and out. William appeared to float somewhere near the end of the bed. And the blood. So much blood. He was lying in pools of it. It was smeared over the door and walls . . .

When he opened his eyes again Kate was weeping against William's chest. Damien licked his dry lips and asked, "Bonnie?"

William spoke quietly to the others and waited as they left the room. He then approached the bed and stood near Damien's side. Hesitantly, he lifted a paper in his hand and read softly.

"Warwick,

I am leavin. Had I left long ago, as I intended, none of this terible afair would have ever taken place. I'm sorry. I never meant to make anyone unhappy, but it seems I am doomed to do just that. Please do not try and find me—not that I think you will, I'm quite certain you will be glad to see the back of me—just know that I am a serviver and will make out just fine.

Kate, William, Richard, Marianne, Philippe, and all,

thank you for yer eferts on my behaf. I am not deservin of
such wonderful frendships. I hope that somehow I can repay you. Perhaps someday.

Respectfully,
Bonnie

P.S. I love you.

Damien stared. He rolled his legs from the bed and sat up,
swaying even as he grabbed the letter from his friend's hand
and tried to read it.

Gone. She was gone.

Blood pounded in his temples and shoulder.

Blackness skirted across his eyes.

Dropping the letter, he lunged at William, wrapping his
bloodied hand in his friend's white shirt.

"Find her," he demanded, his voice raspy. "I . . . don't
care what it takes . . . don't care what it costs me . . . find
her and bring her back to me . . ."

The strength abandoned his legs, and with a groan, Damien collapsed to the floor.

Twenty-four

"Welcome to the residuum. 'At's wot John Bright calls us: the residuum. We's the very bottom o' society. Lower even than poor. We's demoralized sods livin' in almost helpless poverty and dependence, the only folk without somebody beneath 'em." Manfred Jones turned his toothless smile toward Bonnie and winked. "Might as well make the best of it and go back to bed, gal."

Bonnie glanced around the foul-smelling, single-room dwelling and cursed herself again for oversleeping. Normally she was up and out on the street by five, but dragging herself from bed the last few mornings had been an almost impossible feat. Even now, as she attempted to rise from her chair, lethargy pulled her back down. She hugged herself against the cold and damp, and shivered. Winter was almost upon her, and she didn't own a coat. Then she reminded herself that she owned nothing but the dress on her back, which was growing uncomfortably tighter every day, and the pile of soot she called a bed . . . and her ribbons. Other than the dress she wore she had taken nothing from Kate's except her ribbons. She'd hid them beneath the mattress.

Her stomach rumbled, and the baby shifted inside her. There would be no time to stop for a potato on her way to work, not that she could afford it. She'd used the last of her wage the night before to purchase a slice of bread and a small tin of coffee. The bread had turned out to be mostly mashed potatoes and the coffee mostly sawdust, but they had dulled the sharp edge of hunger that afflicted her more and more lately.

Again she attempted to stand. Catching the back of her

chair, Bonnie waited for the vertigo to leave her, then she turned for the door.

"Goin' somewheres?" Manfred Jones stepped before her, blocking her path to the door. "Rent was due yesterday," he reminded her.

"I'll get m' wage tomorrow. Y'll get yer bloody money."

"I want it now. Don't forget, there's a few hundred more girlies just like you who'd give a lot more'n three shillings for that bed."

Gritting her teeth against the pain in her fingers, Bonnie shoved her work-swollen hands into her skirt pockets and turned them inside out. "I told ya, I ain't got no money, Jones. Not even t' eat."

He tutted and smiled. "Wot a bleedin' shame. Pretty girl like you with a babe in her belly shouldn't be goin' hungry. I might see my way to lendin' you a penny or two until tomorrow if—"

"I know what y' want, Jones, and y' can forget it."

He reached out a grubby hand and toyed with a strand of Bonnie's hair. "Wish my Lenore were more like you."

"If y' didn't force her t' walk the street, she would be."

"Man's got to do what a man's got to do, lass. 'Sides, she enjoys it. You all enjoy it or you wouldn't be in that predicament now." He poked at her stomach.

Bonnie backed away.

"Wotcha plan on doin' about the babe?" he asked. "How ya gonna feed it? I ain't havin' no squallin' brat ruinin' my night's sleep. Where you gonna keep it while yer workin'?"

She tried to step around him. He roughly caught her arm.

"I know a man who'd take the brat off yer hands once its here. Name's Collin."

"I know the name. Lenore works for him. What does a whoremaster want with babies?"

"He raises 'em to be in the business, o' course."

"That is the most disgusting thing I've ever heard."

"A keeper who knows his business has his eyes open in all directions. His stock in girls is always gettin' used up and needing replenishin'. A maid like you would keep up the reputation of his house well enough, as would yer babes." He pulled her closer and smiled. "You and the babe is gonna be in the business eventually, whether you want to accept it or not.''

Bonnie turned her face away, the likelihood of his words repulsing her as much as the man himself.

''Ye've got until eight o'clock tonight to get me me rent money.''

''But I don't get paid until tomorrow!''

''Four shillin's.''

''The rent is three—''

''It's just gone up.''

''Bastard!'' She wrenched from his grip and didn't stop running until she reached the street. A slow, cold drizzle soaked her hair and skin and clothes. Mud oozed around her shoes, and as she looked up and down the street the distant gas lamps flickered like candlelight in the dark.

She started walking, then running. Thanks to Jones she would be late again for work. Twice this week she had been tardy, and the supervisor had firmly warned her against doing it again, though Bonnie had gladly stayed after hours to make up for the thirty minutes she had missed those mornings. It was certainly better than crouching in the corner of Manfred and Lenore's room watching them go at each other like a couple of dogs in season. It was better than listening to the cries of hunger and sickness from neighboring children, and certainly better than lying huddled upon her mattress while rats nibbled at the hem of her dress. Work made her forget about her hunger. It helped to divert her mind from the memory of Damien and Kate and Marianne, though on these long walks to work they were *all* she thought about.

Did they still think of her? Had they tried to find her the past weeks? Probably not. Damien had no doubt returned to America by now and forgotten her completely. She wondered if Kate had ever told him about the baby. Of course she would have. How would he have reacted? Angrily, no doubt.

Stopping at a street corner, Bonnie waited for the traffic to pass, taking no notice of the mud that was splashed over her skirt and shoes by the lumbering vehicles. Her mind was too occupied on the flat-roofed building stretched out for half a block down the street, its tiny upper windows blackened with soot, allowing only a trace of sunlight into its dingy quarters. She'd been fortunate to find the job of sewing buttons on ready-made clothes, though the hours were long, from five-thirty in the morning until seven at night. The constant pricking of her fingers with needles had turned them sore and raw, but her supervisor had assured her that in a month or two they would toughen up. Bonnie wasn't so certain. They ached abominably and had awakened her several times during the night, throbbing and bleeding. There were steel tips she could buy for her fingers, but they would cost her dearly, and so far she hadn't managed to save a pence from her meager salary. Now with Jones upping her rent, the likelihood of even feeding herself seemed more and more remote.

She hurried across the street and into the factory. A clock on the wall told her she was half an hour late.

"Stop right there," the supervisor's voice rang out.

Drenched and shivering, Bonnie slowly turned to face him.

"Young woman, you are tardy again."

"I—"

He raised his hand. "Enough. The first time I overlooked it. The second time I warned you that if it happened again I would have to release you."

"No!" she cried. "Oh, no, sir, please don't dismiss me. I need this job—"

"Of course you do. But so do a great many others who would arrive on time."

"I promise I won't do it again. M' landlord—"

"You promised me twice before and I believed you."

"But—"

"I'm sorry. I have already given the position to someone else."

Feeling panic rise inside her, Bonnie watched the supervisor walk away. "What about m' wage?" she called out.

"Be here tomorrow evening at seven and you'll get your wage, minus your fines for being late, of course."

"But I need m' money now!"

"I'm sorry."

He closed the door of his office in Bonnie's face, ending the matter.

Gripping her aching hands together, Bonnie left the factory and stood for some time on the walk in the rain. She tried to reason, but her gnawing hunger and the restless shifting of the baby made thinking next to impossible. Somehow, she had to find work. She had to eat. Having consumed only one meal in the last two days, she felt as if she were caving in inside.

She walked.

She tried a bake shop first because the smell of bread had made her dizzy. A bell over the door tinkled as she entered, bringing the baker's wife at a run. Seeing Bonnie huddled in the doorway, she stopped and frowned.

"Here now!" the woman cried. "You're mucking up our floor with mud. What do you want?"

"I need employment, ma'am. I wondered—"

"We don't need anyone."

"I'd be willing t' do anythin'. All I ask is a bit of bread in return."

"Get out!"

Bonnie flinched.

"I said, get out!"

She stumbled out the door and into the rain. She kept walking.

Bonnie couldn't believe her luck when, just before noon, she found a coin lying on the pavement. She grabbed it up, turning it over and over in her hand, then bit it to make certain it was real. It was only a halfpenny, but a halfpenny would buy her a hot baked potato. She ran down the street to the vendor she had passed earlier. Crouching beneath his striped umbrella, he squinted one eye at her and said, "Show me yer money."

She held out the coin. He took it and bit it, then tossed it in his cup. He pitched her a potato and, almost laughing, Bonnie wrapped her hands around it, savoring the warmth and smell as she hurried to an alley where she stood beneath an overhang out of the rain to eat it.

There came a tug on her skirt, and she looked around.

A boy, no more than five or six years of age, stared up at her with weary eyes. He was little more than bones, and his skin was thin and yellow from disease and malnutrition. Closing her eyes, Bonnie turned away and gripped her potato harder.

"Oh, please go away," she cried. "I'm hungry too."

He tugged again.

"Go away!"

Silent minutes passed, and reluctantly she looked around. The boy sat huddled on his haunches next to the wall. He stared with vacant eyes at the street.

It swept Bonnie in that instant that the urchin, half dead from starvation and deprivation, might well be her own son in another few years. The idea rocked her, and slowly she went to her knees beside him. Her hand trembled as she opened his clenched fingers and pressed the food into them. Then she fled.

In another hour the rain had eased, enabling Bonnie to make her way about the busy streets with less misery and effort. She tried numerous businesses and several factories, but their proprietors all told her the same. No job. No food. No handouts.

She wound up on Regent Street. She was loathe to beg. Night after night as she had lain on her mattress, hungry and cold, she had vowed silently that never would she beg like the many thousands of unemployed who wandered the streets. But as her stomach heaved again in hunger, she ignored her pride and approached a woman in fine clothes who waited outside a haberdashery. A well-dressed man stood near her, his back to Bonnie as he spoke with the driver of the cab from which they'd just departed.

"I beg yer pardon, ma'am," Bonnie said quietly. "Do y' think y' could spare a—"

"Bonnie!"

Bonnie's head whipped toward the man at the cab.

Miles Kemball gaped at her in shock.

She spun and ran.

"Someone stop that girl!" Miles cried out behind her. "Bonnie! Bonnie, come back!"

She ran blindly, darting around vendors who had taken advantage of the break in the rain to peddle their goods. She toppled a costermonger, who sent an apple whizzing past her head in fury as he lay sprawled upon the pavement. She upset a pair of distinguished gentlemen who loitered outside a club, rocking them back on their heels as she dashed between them. She ran until the pain in her side bent her double and a cramp in her lower belly drove her to her knees. Gasping for breath, she beat the ground in anger. Why Miles? When the city was packed with millions of people, why had she humiliated herself before Miles? After all her big talk of being a survivor, Damien was certain to find out what a miserable wretch she had become. Damn!

She struggled to her feet and hurried back to her apartment. She would be safer there for the time being, at least until she was certain she had lost Miles for good.

She had learned early to knock before entering Manfred Jones's lair. The door opened a fraction, and Lenore peered at her through the gap.

"Wot you doin' here?" Lenore asked.

"I live here," Bonnie replied.

"Not no more, you don't."

Bonnie swallowed back her panic.

"Mannie's given yer spot to someone else," Lenore said.

"I don't believe you."

The door was yanked open further, and Jones stepped out. Leering down at Bonnie, he said, "Believe it, gal. Now run along like a nice chit and don't make no trouble."

"Y' bloody bastard, y' got no right—"

"Course I do," he interrupted. "Yer late on yer rent. I warned ya—"

"But y' gave me till eight o'clock tonight!"

"Would it make any difference if I gave ya till eight o'clock in the mornin'? You lost yer job, didn't ya? Course ya did or you wouldn't be here now."

He tried to close the door in her face. Bonnie threw her weight against it and demanded, "At least let me in t' collect m' belongin's."

"You got nothin' here, gal."

"M' ribbons!"

"Whose ribbons?"

Bonnie caught a glimpse of Lenore. The hag had tied back her filthy blond hair with several of Bonnie's ribbons.

Lunging against the door, Bonnie cried, "Those ribbons are *mine!*"

"You must be mistaken, gal." Jones planted the heel of his hand against Bonnie's breastbone and tried to shove her back. She retaliated by locking her fingers around his forearm and sinking her nails into his flesh.

"Those ribbons are mine!" she repeated. "Y' can't take 'em. They're all I have left—"

Bonnie never finished the thought, for the next moment Jones struck her so forcefully across her cheek with his fist that she was sent hurling backwards, sprawling in a heap of refuse that dispatched rats in every direction. Afraid to move, she lay there for several minutes, too stunned to cry but hurting so badly that she thought she might die from the pain, praying that she would. Having no money and no place to sleep meant she would spend the next few nights the same way she had spent her first five nights on the street: sleeping in alleys or shivering on the banks of the Thames. In the end she had been forced to sell her petticoats to a peddler on Rosemary Lane for two pennies. For another two pennies she had stripped her gown of its lace and rosettes. She'd sold her kid slippers for another three pennies, and in turn bought a pair of reconstructed shoes for one penny, giving her a profit of two. But she had nothing to trade now.

Not even her ribbons.

Kate planted herself in the doorway and refused Miles entrance into Damien's town house. "I cannot believe you would have the audacity to come here," she said. "If Damien knew you were here—"

"Why don't you leave that up to Damien?" Miles replied.

"What do you want with him?"

"That's between me and him."

"He's not up to visitors."

"This is not a social call, Kate."

"He's not up to business, either."

"I think he will want to hear what I have to say."

"I cannot imagine what news you can have to impart that would even remotely interest him."

"Even if that news pertained to Bonnie?"

Damien stepped from the shadows where he had been watching Kate's confrontation with Miles. As Kate turned toward him, he gently pushed her aside, twisted his fingers in Miles's shirtfront, and dragged him inside. He shoved Miles up against the wall. "What do you know about Bonnie?"

Unblinking, Miles's gaze shifted over Damien's features, his eyes registering shock at his half brother's appearance.

"Well?" Damien demanded quietly. "I'm waiting."

"I—I saw her."

Silence. Damien gripped the shirt in his fingers more tightly. "If this is another one of your pranks, Kemball, I vow to God—"

"It's not. This morning I was escorting an acquaintance to a haberdashery on Regent Street. My lady was approached by a beggar. It took me a moment to realize the girl was Bonnie."

Damien closed his eyes briefly before focusing on Miles again.

"I barely recognized her," Miles continued. More soberly, he added, "Are you aware that she is expecting a child?"

Kate moved up behind Damien and placed a comforting hand on his shoulder.

"I see," Miles said, looking from Kate back to Damien. "She appears extremely malnourished, even more so than when she arrived at Braithwaite."

"Did you say anything to her?"

"I called out her name, but when she saw me she ran. I chased her for several streets, then lost her down some back alley."

"Why are you telling me this?" Damien asked. "To collect the reward?"

"Hardly. Bonnie is worth more to me than a thousand guineas, my lord. She was my friend for a time, as you recall. I would see her safe again and happy. I've heard to what extremes you have gone to find her. In truth, all of London is conjecturing over your relationship with Bonnie. At White's they're calling you the mad earl because of your obsession with finding her, though few fault you for it. Seems Bonnie won the hearts of most of the aristocracy during her tenure in London; they're as eager to bring her home as you are."

"I doubt that." Slowly, he released his grip on Miles and stepped away. He walked to the hall tree and appraised his reflection in its mirror for a long time, barely recognizing the image there. Eyes, red rimmed from fatigue and too many bouts with drink, gazed back at him. His beard-stubbled cheeks were gaunt and his once-fitted clothes drooped listlessly across his shoulders.

Dragging his hand tiredly over his eyes, Damien said, "I

don't know whether to believe you or not, Kemball. You show me no proof of your words . . . Why would you want to help me?''

''I told you; I don't do it for you. I do it for Bonnie.''

''You say she disappeared down some alley. She might have gone anywhere.''

''Perhaps. But I feel certain she was on familiar ground or she wouldn't have eluded me so easily. Doesn't it stand to reason that eventually she'll venture there again?''

Damien looked at Kate. ''I'll send word to William, Richard, and Marianne,'' she said. ''She can contact Philippe. We can all take separate coaches and comb every street in the area.'' Smiling hopefully, she approached Damien and took his hand. ''I know you've given up hope. I know the many heartbreaking disappointments you've experienced during these last weeks. I've felt them as well.''

Damien turned away.

''What if Miles is telling the truth?'' she asked.

''He could be mistaken. You know how many people have declared they have located Bonnie. If I am forced to walk into a morgue again and inspect a girl's body or trudge my way through East End filth—''

''But Miles isn't asking that of you. We simply search the area around Regent Street, where she was seen. It's a place to start.''

Damien considered Kate's words, fighting back the spark of hope that flickered to life in his heart. He took an unsteady breath. ''Get the coach.''

Within the hour they had arrived at Regent Street. A cold rain had begun to fall, and with it came a gray fog so dense that Damien and Kate could make out little as their coach wove through the traffic at a snail's pace. The weather, however, was one twist of fate in their favor, it seemed. For the rain and fog had driven all but the beggars and scavengers indoors.

Having turned up no sign of Bonnie in the Regent Street area, they wound their way into the East End. Pale faces stared longingly at Damien's coach as they traveled up and down the streets. Masses of human flesh huddled together in the alleys and beneath the eaves of buildings as the homeless prepared for a cold, wet, and sleepless night. Their sunken, vacant eyes stared at him questioningly as Damien called out to his driver to slow so he might study each face, hoping to find Bonnie among them, yet praying he wouldn't. When he was certain she was not there, he rapped on the roof, and the coach lurched forward.

Sinking back against the seat, Damien closed his eyes. "This is useless. Attempting to find one small girl in a city of millions is like searching for a needle in a haystack. I should never have agreed to try. After the many weeks I've already searched, I should have known better."

"We will never give up hope," Kate replied quietly.

"If only I could take back those last words—"

"Well, you can't, and there's no point in crucifying yourself for something you said when you were out of your senses with pain."

The coach rolled on, venturing at last into the warehousing center where, at straight up six o'clock, whistles sounded calling for an end of the work day for many. Doors were thrown open, discharging noisy crowds of men, women, and children into the streets, their clothes soiled and tattered, their faces drawn and dismal. Damien noted that many of the children were barefooted, yet they appeared not to notice as they trudged through puddles of rain and slop. More than once Damien's coach was forced to pull up as children darted into the street, and by the time the coach veered out of the warehouse district and into the housing district Damien thought his head would crack for want of silence.

Still, there was little relief to be found along the stone streets. Through the half-open windows of the hovels he could see the wretched rooms within, bare of all furnishings except soiled mattresses heaped about the walls. Masses of dirty children crowded the thresholds as they awaited the return of their parents. They turned their angry faces toward Damien's coach as it passed, and unable to stand it a moment longer, Damien called out to his driver, "Get us out of here!"

Despite the sudden downpour, they were back in the business district within minutes. Damien pressed the heels of his hands against his eyes, doing his best to blot from his mind the horrible images of deprivation and desperation he'd just encountered. But he couldn't. The idea that Bonnie—

"Stop," Kate said.

Damien looked at his sister. Kate was staring fixedly out the window of the coach.

"Stop the coach," she repeated softly.

Damien rapped against the roof, and the driver called out, "Whoa!"

Kate's hand reached for Damien's and gripped it. Breathless, she looked at him. "I think it's Bonnie."

The girl stood with her back to the street, her small shoulders hunched against the rain and cold, her black hair spilling to her hips, lank and lifeless. Her dress was tattered. Once, it might have been blue, but due to its filthy state and the encroaching darkness Damien couldn't be certain.

Even from the coach he could see she was shaking. She lifted one trembling hand and laid it against the shop window that she appeared to be studying. He raised his eyes and read, "Madame Roussaue, Couturiere." He saw the ribbons then, strands and strands spilling like a bright rainbow over the table inside the bay window.

Damien eased open the door and stepped onto the walk. Carefully he moved closer, doing his best to make out the girl's reflection in the glass. He stopped, afraid of making any move that might frighten her. Then the dark eyes mirrored in the glass noted his reflected image.

And he knew.

"Bonnie."

Very slowly she turned, and Damien lost his breath. One side of her face was swollen and black. The other was gaunt and white with smudges of deep purple beneath her eye. Poised for flight, she looked like a frightened, wounded doe come face-to-face with her hunter. Then her mouth formed a silent *oh,* and before Damien could move, she collapsed to the ground.

In three strides he reached her. He tore the cape from his shoulders and, dropping to his knees beside her, did his best to wrap her safely within its fur-lined folds. "Oh, my love,'' he whispered. "My love. Bonnie, can you hear me?''

Her lashes fluttered. Her lips moved. Bending his head nearer, he waited for her to repeat the words.

"My ribbons.'' Tears leaked from the corners of her eyes and ran down her face. "They took my ribbons.''

Twenty-five

Damien sat in a chair by the bed, gripping Bonnie's hand in his. Her cheeks were hot with fever, and her face was ashen. Kate moved up behind him and placed a comforting hand on his shoulder.

"You should rest," came her quiet words. "Damien, you can't continue like this. You need to eat and sleep; you haven't left her side in three days. If Bonnie's condition declines—"

"It won't," he answered roughly.

"No, of course it won't. I only meant you'll need to be strong if . . ." Kate moved away. "The doctor said her lungs are still weak from her last bout with pneumonia. If she does survive, there's a chance the baby won't."

"She won't die. Bonnie's a fighter."

"She hasn't regained consciousness since we brought her home."

"Kate." He closed his eyes. "Leave us alone."

Without speaking again, Kate departed, closing the door softly behind her. Silence filled the room as Damien continued to watch Bonnie sleep. Occasionally the rasp of her lungs disturbed the quiet, reminding him of her last war with death. She had won the battle then . . .

But this wasn't the fiesty, angry urchin who had been determined to damn and defy the world. This girl before him was broken in both heart and body. And he was the cause. She had loved him . . . once. Bitterly he recalled his own experience with love and heartbreak, and the idea that he had subjected Bonnie to that emotional upheaval disgusted him.

How easily it might have been avoided had he only looked inside himself and acknowledged the truth.

When, exactly, had he fallen in love with her?

Damien searched his mind, recalling the night she'd first turned up at Braithwaite. She'd cried out in feverish nightmares, and he'd held her, comforting her as she trembled against him. Perhaps he'd fallen a little in love with her then. Or perhaps it was the time at the stairs, him standing at the bottom looking up, her at the top gazing down, her flashing eyes and proud deportment saying far more than her bedraggled appearance ever could. She had taught him something of humility, of patience and endurance in the face of calamity. She had been a balm to his beleaguered soul, an elixir for his shattered pride. If she would only live, he would build her a kingdom fit for a princess. If only . . .

He gently laid his head on Bonnie's shoulder, feeling the heat of her body warm his face. Closing his eyes, he whispered, "Ah, God, Bonnie, don't die. I need you. I love you . . . I do love you so very, very much . . ."

Her hand touched his hair, fingertips scattering the thick black strands over his forehead. He swiftly raised his head. A faint smile curved Bonnie's mouth, and her fever-bright eyes were scarcely open. His heart turned over.

"Bloody hell," she whispered so softly he could barely make out the words. "I was dreamin' I'd married a sheep farmer."

He grinned. "Would you settle for an arrogant, ill-humored earl who's too stubborn and stupid to admit he's in love?"

Bonnie's eyes closed, but the smile remained.

Damien buried his face against her breasts and wept.

Within the week Damien began making plans for his marriage to Bonnie. He contacted the proper officials, arranged for the license. The banns, however, could not be posted until he could supply Bonnie's legal name and certificate of birth. Which presented another problem. He might not give a damn what her last name was or where she came from, but the Church of England did.

He was slumped in a chair in William's study, contemplating the problem, when Kate entered. "I've just seen Bonnie," she told him. "She's awake, if you'd care to visit."

"I will."

Kate took a chair across from him. "You've been quiet since you returned from the church."

"I'm told I can't post banns without Bonnie's certificate of birth."

"Oh. Well, that does pose a problem."

"I'll have to ask her again about her past."

"So what's keeping you?"

He frowned and left the chair. "I was hoping Investigator Bradley would turn up something."

"He hasn't, so it's up to you."

"The few times I've tried she's become upset."

Sitting back in the chair, Kate said, "Her identity may be a moot point anyway."

"What does that mean?"

"You haven't asked her to marry you yet."

He raised one brow. "She'll marry me. She's having my baby."

Kate looked a little dreamy. "A baby . . . " She sighed. "How I wish *I* were having a child. Tell me, how does it feel to know you'll soon be a parent?"

He thought for a moment, grinning. "I don't really know. I've been so concerned over Bonnie the last week I forgot to worry about the baby."

"That will change soon enough."

As Damien lit a cigar, Kate reached into her pocket and withdrew a parcel. She sat on the edge of her chair like a bird on a perch, her green eyes twinkling with humor. "Well, 'Papa,' are you ready to put your worries aside long enough to hear what I have to say?"

Damien dropped into his chair, and she handed him the velvet-covered box. He carefully opened it and gazed down at the pair of gold rings embossed with the Warwick coat of arms.

"Of course, the larger one belongs to the head of the family," Kate told him. "I'm certain you recall our grandfather and father wearing it. I'm sure you also remember mother wearing the smaller one, as did our grandmothers for generations before her. I thought you might like to present the ring to Bonnie when you propose."

He lifted the larger ring and turned it over, noting how

thin the gold had become along the base of the band. He thought of the generations who had gone before him, who had worn the ornament in battle and in peace—but always with pride.

Dare he wear it? To do so would put a final end to Vicksburg. His place would be here, in England, following in the footsteps of his illustrious forefathers. But he'd already made that choice, hadn't he? His place was with Bonnie and their child.

He slid the ring on his finger.

Kate covered his hand with hers, and smiled. "Welcome home."

Bonnie stirred and opened her eyes. As she had for the last week, she reminded herself that this was no dream. The dozens of hothouse roses surrounding her were real. The yards and yards of ribbons spilling over furniture and dangling before the window like bright banners were no figments of her imagination.

Her mind felt clear for the first time in days. When Damien moved beside the bed, she knew him immediately, and smiled. "Will you help me to sit up?" she asked.

He did, then sat down on the bed beside her. He didn't speak, just searched her face and finally placed his hand gently against her bruised cheek.

"I'm fine," she assured him.

"And the baby?"

She pressed his hand against her rounded stomach. The baby kicked hard against his palm, and Bonnie laughed.

"I wonder what he's trying to tell me," Damien said.

"Hello, I think."

"More likely it's 'bugger off y' bloody nabob.' "

"Oh. Well, in that case I'll have t' teach him better manners."

"*We'll* have to teach him," Damien corrected.

Bonnie plucked at the sheet and bit her lip, uncertain of his meaning, unwilling to allow herself to interpret the words the way she wanted to.

He caught her chin with the tip of his finger, forcing her to look directly at him. He smiled and placed a velvet box in her lap.

"Open it," he told her.

Her hands shaking, Bonnie raised the lid.

The ring looked to be a woman's, and very old. Oval and flat-faced, the gold ring bore the etched replica of a bear rearing up on its back legs. Within one paw it held a battle-worn staff.

Damien said, "This is the Warwick coat of arms. The bear symbolizes Ensign from Arthgal, who, legend has it, was the first Warwick earl and knight of King Arthur's Round Table. He holds the staff of honor for slaying his enemy in a duel. My mother wore this ring, as did my grandmothers before her." He took Bonnie's hand. "As my betrothed, then as my wife, you will wear my crest for as long as I live, and then until you remarry. At that time you will pass it to my heir."

Bonnie stared at his eyes and tried to breathe. "I—I don't understand—"

"I am asking you to marry me, Bonnie."

She lay back against the pillows and pressed the ring to her heart. "If yer doin' this because of the child—"

"I'm not."

"Oh." She closed her eyes and waited for the feeling of light-headedness to leave her. "Oh, well . . . I don't know . . ."

"Bonnie, if you still want to go away, I'll understand. I haven't exactly been the easiest man to get along with these last months. But if you stay, you'll want and need for nothing, and in turn you'll reward me with a lifetime of laughter and sunshine." He leaned nearer, holding her gaze with his. "You want to hear me say it? I love you. I didn't realize how much until they told me you were gone."

"But what about America and—"

"I had to decide what was more important to me: you or Vicksburg. I grant you, at the time the choice seemed impossible to make. I had tied up six years of my life in Bent Tree. In Vicksburg I could pour my heart and soul into the earth and reap the rewards of accomplishment. But then an old friend reminded me that those cold, inanimate possessions could not love me back. I was afraid of loving you because I was afraid of being rejected again. When I opened my eyes to that fact, it was almost too late. I'd brought you to London and watched you change from a girl who had looked at me with love, into a young woman who appeared to hate and reject me. I tried to convince myself that you meant nothing to me. Then you were gone, and I realized just how much you'd come to mean to me. I knew I couldn't continue without you. Bent Tree ceased to exist as my obsession became you, and finding you. Had it taken the rest of my life and fortune, Bonnie, I would have continued the search. I chose you above Bent Tree, then, now, and for always. Now answer me: Will you marry me?''

She closed her eyes, the rush of emotion through her more powerful than the burning fever that had debilitated her for the last days. Lying in bed, she had wondered if the memories of his holding her, whispering his love to her, had only been hallucinations brought on by her illness. Now he was admitting it. He was asking her to be his wife, and . . .

Was this real? Was it truly happening or had she tumbled into some fairy tale and . . . No, she thought, placing her hand against his cheek. He was flesh and blood, and even now his child was moving inside her. She loved him . . . oh, how she loved him. And in her heart she believed he truly loved her. There would be problems, yes, but they had survived worse than the petty issue of class separation—even her parents, who loved each other devotedly, had not been without their occasional quarrel. Love had conquered all for them. The same would hold true for her and Damien. She believed that with all her heart.

It took a moment for Bonnie to find the strength to speak. ''Aye.'' She trembled as tears filled her eyes. ''I'll marry you, my lord.''

He took her right hand and slipped the heavy gold ring onto the middle finger, then kissed her tenderly on her fever-parched lips.

Taking a deep breath of relief, Damien smiled at Bonnie and left the bed. He walked to the window and, for a moment, played with the cascading ribbons there as he considered how he should approach the problem of her identity.

''Bonnie . . .'' He glanced her way, and the desire to protect her against the dark and secret events in her past came upon him so sharply that he was forced to turn from her. ''I have contacted the church officials about posting the banns.

They cannot do so without your name and certificate of birth.''

Silence.

He gazed out the window. More quietly, he repeated, ''I have to know your name, love.''

Finally he looked at her again. She stared at him with passionate appeal, her large eyes wet with suppressed tears and panic. Her small face was white and pitifully struggling to keep some semblance of calm. ''I can't,'' she managed. ''Please, don't ask that of me, m'lord.''

He moved again to the bed and took her hands. ''Nothing is so bad—''

''No.''

''Bonnie.'' He struggled for patience. ''There can be no marriage until your identity is confirmed by the church.''

''Then we won't marry in a church.''

''It doesn't matter. There's not a magistrate or registrar in England who will marry us under these conditions.'' A little angrily, he caught her chin in his fingers and tipped her face up to his. ''It appears *you* now have a choice to make. You can continue to hide from your past without me or you can let me help you as your husband.''

She turned her head, and he watched the war she waged between fear and love march in furrows over her brow. Finally her lips parted and she whispered, ''Eden, and I'm from Gunnerside. I'm tellin' y' nothin' more than that.''

It seemed ironic that the search for Bonnie's past should bring him back to the village where his family had owned and operated one of the most productive mines in Yorkshire. The gray slate roofs of Gunnerside village were scarcely visible amid the fog as Damien urged his mount toward the White Horse Ale House and Inn. He tied his horse to a hitching post and entered.

The low ceilinged quarters had not changed since he had taken food and drink here years before. He remembered to duck his head as he passed beneath one beam after another on his way to the bar. He requested an ale and shrugged out of his wet cloak as he searched through the room pressed with men for Investigator Bradley. He had written him before leaving London, hoping that by the time he arrived here Bradley would have some information for him.

The proprietor slammed a pewter pint of ale onto the bar before Damien, sloshing foam over the sides. " 'Ere y' go, guvna. Aught else y'll be havin'? We got some lovely meat pies out back."

He dropped a coin onto the bar. "I'm looking for a man named Bradley. He was supposed to meet me here."

"I've seen him. He's gone out." The burly man grabbed up a tankard from a tub of soapy water and proceeded to dry it with a dish towel. He stared fixedly at Damien. "I know you. Y've been here before, ain't y'?"

Damien looked away.

"It's been a while, but I don't forgit faces," the man said.

Preferring to avoid the topic of the Gunnerside mine, Damien changed the subject. "I've come here looking for information regarding a man called Eden."

The man's busy hands went idle. His dark eyes pierced the room's dimness like bits of hot coals. His brows rose in question. "Now, 'at's mighty peculiar. Here's been a lot of int'rest of late in Paddy."

"Paddy?"

"Patrick Eden. 'At's who yer meanin', ain't it?"

Damien nodded and drank his ale.

"Wot's so int'restin' suddenly 'bout him?"

Placing the tankard carefully on the bar, Damien glanced around the suspiciously quiet crowd. He shrugged. "I met him several years back. He told me to look him up if I ever passed through Gunnerside."

The tavern door opened, and a man stepped in. Tall and lean, with eyes as sharp as a hawk's, the stranger approached Damien and held out his hand. He spoke quietly, a sound at odds with his fierce, angular features. "My lord, I'm Melvin Bradley."

Relieved, Damien shook his hand.

"Shall we take a table where we can speak privately?" Bradley asked.

Damien agreed and followed the inspector through the smoky room to a table tucked into a far, dimly lit corner.

"It's a pleasure to finally meet you in person," Bradley

said. "I was astonished to receive your message. May I offer you congratulations on your upcoming nuptials?"

Damien smiled his thanks. "Have you had time to check Eden out?"

"As much as possible." Elbows on the table, Bradley leaned closer and lowered his voice. "I must warn you, sir, to be very cautious in your dealings with these people. There's a great deal of animosity toward the Warwicks—"

"That's to be expected due to the shutting down of the mine. Many men lost their jobs."

"Regrettably the reasons run deeper than that, my lord. In truth, I fear you have taken your life in your hands by coming here. Should anyone recognize you, the consequences could be dire."

Damien glanced toward the tavern owner, who continued to watch from his perch by the bar.

"What the hell is going on here?" Damien asked quietly.

"Unfortunately, I can supply you with little more than you already know. The village folk are extremely closemouthed about Eden, and had I not happened upon a tavern regular who cares more for a pint than loyalty, I fear I would have nothing to disclose." Bradley took a breath. "Patrick Eden worked for you, my lord."

"At Gunnerside mine?"

Bradley nodded.

"You're certain it was—"

"He had a daughter named Bonnie, a child with coal-black hair and bright blue eyes . . . According to my source, Patrick Eden last worked for your family in 1855. He was discharged on account of taking time off his job to care for his sick child, that being Bonnie, of course. I'm told he became extremely distraught and mentioned to several miners that he intended to confront the supervisor."

"And did he?"

"I fear only Bonnie can tell us that, my lord. My source says Patrick was not seen again by his fellow miners after that day. Nor was his daughter."

"Didn't anyone think that odd?"

"Not at first. I'm told that after Eden's wife's death he became terribly grief stricken. He became obsessed with the child and her care and practically turned into a recluse. After he was dismissed from the mine, friends in the village became concerned over his absence of several days and went to the house. Of course, no one was there. There were some who questioned the supervisor of the mine, but he denied ever having seen Eden after dismissing him from his job.''

Recalling Bonnie's nightmares, cold realization shivered up Damien's spine as he stared into Bradley's features. "Is there any reason why we should believe otherwise?''

The man returned his appraisal without blinking. "My source says he *thought* he saw Eden walking down the road that evening toward the mine ranting about confronting the supervisor. But it was after dark, and he'd imbibed too much ale to be absolutely certain. He added he *thought* he saw Bonnie as well, trailing behind.''

"Who—who was the supervisor of the mine at that time?'' Damien asked the question of himself, but Bradley responded.

"My source didn't work at Gunnerside, and unless you wish to approach the touchy topic with these gentlemen''— he nodded toward the tavern patrons—"then I suggest you investigate that question back at Braithwaite.''

Feeling his anger rise, Damien stated, "Do you know what the hell you're insinuating? We may be talking murder—''

"No body was found, my lord. The man and his daughter vanished. Only Bonnie can tell us what happened, if she will.'' Bradley took a folded paper from his pocket and slid it across the table to Damien. "It's a map to Eden's house, if you care to see it. It's about three miles south of the village. You'll pass the church on your way. You can attain Bonnie's certificate of birth there, of course. Her mother, Mary, is buried there as well.'' Standing, Bradley said, "I don't envy the decision you face now, my lord. You have my most profound hopes that all this will turn out satisfactorily, not only for you, but also for Bonnie.''

Damien remained seated long after Bradley had gone. He searched his mind for any plausible reason why Eden would have turned up missing, but everything came back to one question: Who the blazes had been supervising the mine in 55? The entire year had been turbulent. He remembered that well enough because that was when he'd immigrated to

America. The fiasco with Louisa had only topped off months of confusion that had begun with striking Gunnerside miners.

Think. *Who* supervised the mine in 1855?

There had been Randolf for a time. Miles. Richard, and . . . himself.

He glanced about the silent room. Through clouds of smoke he could see the proprietor, his large hands splayed on the bar, and his gaze locked on him. Occasionally a patron's head turned and looked his way.

He reached for his cloak and slid from the bench. He strode without hesitation toward the door, unable to take a breath until stepping into the bracingly cold air. He didn't pause and, upon reaching his horse, grabbed up the reins and gracefully threw himself into the saddle. As he directed the animal south of the village, he heard the tavern door fly open. Refusing to look back, he rode off into the bleak, twilight fog.

What drove him to pass the tiny village church for the time being and continue to Bonnie's house, Damien could not guess. Having dismounted his nervously prancing horse, he stood at the bottom of the footpath and searched through the shifting mist for the cottage at the top of the hill. He could just discern its rough stone walls amid a wild and tangled lair of prickly shrubs and rose bushes. Its dark, shutterless windows stared lifelessly over the valley.

He moved up the path to a gate—a wicket. It swung on its hinges as he touched it.

Hedges raked Damien's shins as he approached the house. A movement in the bushes stopped him; a brown rabbit scurried across the path and disappeared into a burrow in some weeds. Stepping into the open doorway, he stopped and looked back. Yellowing bilberry leaves scraped against the outside wall as a gust of frigid wind swept the hill, moaning low, causing him to shiver.

He entered the dark, quiet dwelling.

Except for the thick coat of dust blanketing everything, the room remained much as it must have looked when Bonnie left it. The single room was sparsely furnished, a double bed with a now-sagging mattress shoved against one wall, a smaller cot not far from it. A chest of drawers adorned a corner, and along the distant wall a fireplace had served to warm the quarters and cook the Edens' food. Near the stone hearth was another door, its top half swinging back and forth in the wind.

Damien stood in the middle of the room, his hands clenched and a feeling of helpless fury mounting inside him. He and his reckless pride had almost destroyed Bonnie, but despite the pain he'd caused her, she still loved him. At last they had both looked forward to a life of peace and harmony and love, of his striving to make every dream come true for her and their child.

Now this.

The Warwicks had shattered her life.

They had murdered her father.

She would never forgive him for that.

He turned and drove his fist into the wall. Again, and again . . . and again.

Twenty-six

It was late as Damien sat with William and Kate in their parlor. He'd chosen to return directly to London instead of stopping in Braithwaite. There would be time later to delve into the unpleasant details of who was supervising the mine when Patrick Eden was killed—*if* he was killed.

A body was never found.

So how could he be certain?

Bonnie. She had seen it all. Her nightmares were evidence of that. She had witnessed her father's murder, and she'd run. There could be no other explanation for her turning up at Caldbergh and refusing all these years to reveal her identity. She was afraid. But if either Miles or Richard had killed her father, wouldn't she have recognized him by now?

Randolf. Randolf was dead. That could explain why she hadn't recognized his brother or uncle as her father's killer, and why the killer had not recognized her. If that was the case, there was no reason why Bonnie should ever have to know his family was in any way responsible for Patrick Eden's death.

"Damien?"

He looked at Kate. Her face was concerned.

"You haven't heard a word William and I have said in the last five minutes. Is something wrong?"

He shook his head. "It was a long journey. I'm tired."

A paper in hand, Kate left her writing desk. "We've been compiling a list of wedding guests that you should look at. I received a note from Richard only yesterday. He's recently returned home from Scotland, and he tells me Miles is at

Braithwaite as well. We'll need to send them word of your plans so they can make arrangements—"

"No."

Kate stared at him in surprise. William turned from the fire, frowning.

"No?" she repeated.

"No."

"May we ask why not?" William said.

Damien left his chair, rubbing the tight muscles in the back of his neck as he paced. Should Miles or Richard have been responsible for Eden's death, divulging Bonnie's last name would alert him to her identity. "I'm not overly inclined to invite Miles, for obvious reasons."

"But Richard—" Kate began.

"Is a drunk." He shook his head. "One toast too many and he could turn our reception into a shambles. Everything has to be perfect for Bonnie. *Everything.* I'm not willing to take the chance of anyone spoiling it for her."

"When do you intend to tell him?"

"After we're married."

Kate and William exchanged looks. "Well," she said, "it's your wedding. I wouldn't care to be in your shoes when Uncle finds out. You know he's always loved you like a son, Damien."

"I know." He took a weary breath and released it. "I've missed Bonnie. How's she been since I left?"

"Fretful," William replied.

"Much stronger, but the nightmares have returned," Kate added. "She's cried out every night. I've attempted to talk with her on the matter, but she refuses to discuss it . . . Where are you going?" she asked as he left the room. "Bonnie's been asleep for hours."

"I have to see her," he said, then climbed the stairs and strode to her room.

As he opened the door, the light from the hallway spilled over the bed. Bonnie lay on her back in the complete abandonment of deep sleep, her face turned away from him and her left arm thrown back, bent in a childlike manner. Her hair was a beautiful mess, a black spray of ebony shadows on the white pillows and sheets.

He moved silently around the bed, and upon seeing her

face, he stopped. He stood, unable to do anything but stare, overcome, as he was, by his desperate love for her. He had come so close to losing her so many times, and the agony had been torture. If she left him now . . .

Quietly, he sat in a chair, covered his face with his hands, and prayed, "God, don't let her find out."

The dream came again.

She felt so very small as she stood on tiptoe and stared through the window of the mine shack. The slow rain ran in muddy rivulets down the panes, blurring her vision. But she dared do nothing to call attention to the fact that she was there. Her da had ordered her to remain outside, and quiet. He might become angrier if he knew she had disobeyed him . . . he was so very angry already. Angrier than she had ever seen him.

"*I've worked for this company for fifteen years. Y' can't dismiss me like this.*"

"*I can do anything I bloody well please, Eden. I can't afford to keep on a man who can't be bothered to show up for work.*"

Bonnie blinked the rain from her eyes and glanced toward the sky. Thunder rumbled.

"*For God's sake, man, I worked for this company for fourteen years and never missed a day. Since m' wife died there was no one t' take care of m' daughter when she became ill, so I had no choice. Three days is all I missed. Y' can't be s' heartless as t' discharge me for that!*"

"*I can, sir. And do. I have given you your final pay. Now get out.*"

"*M' men won't stand for it. They'll walk out when they learn what y've done. They don't care for y' anyway. Since y've been in charge here, accidents in this mine have increased. Three men 've died in the last eight months, and so far y've taken no steps t' rectify the situation. There are authorities who'd be int'rested t' hear y' don't give a damn about the safety of these men.*"

Lightning turned the night into day as Bonnie strained to hear the stranger's response. Cautiously she tried rubbing the grime from the window, smearing rain and mud in streaks over the pane. The voices were louder. Angrier. There was

*movement inside, but the images were indistinct. There was
a sound, a frightening sound that shook the shack so hard
that Bonnie stumbled back from the impact . . .*

*She stood in the open door of the shack. Someone lay
sprawled on the floor. Blood. There was so much blood
on the back of his head. His eyes were open and staring
and . . .*

Bonnie groaned.

*There was movement, and for the first time she noticed the
man stooped over her father. He must have heard her for
suddenly he was jumping to his feet and turning toward the
door. She could not seem to take her eyes off his bloody
hands. He was lurching toward her. Reaching for her . . .*

Bonnie sat up in bed and screamed. Suddenly someone
was gripping her shoulders, touching her face— "Bonnie!
Bonnie, m'love, you're dreaming."

She struggled, thrashing her arms. "Let me go," she demanded hoarsely. "Let me go—"

"It's Damien. Open your eyes, Bonnie, and see me."

Slowly, consciousness came to her. She looked into Damien's face and with a relieved cry threw herself against him,
holding him close.

"Hush," he soothed. "I'm home, love, and I'll never leave
you again."

She clung to him, yet even as her body trembled with terror, she felt Damien's caressing hands and words calming her
mind's dismay. It occurred to her that no longer would she
be forced to be strong when she yearned to be weak, valiant
when she ached to be held and comforted. Damien would
protect her.

In his arms, she could put the nightmare of her father's
death behind her . . . forever.

While Bonnie rested and concentrated on recovering, Kate
was busy with plans for the wedding.

Madame Roussaue was called and new measurements were
taken, and taken again. Yet Bonnie never saw so much as a
sketch of the wedding dress, and no one would say anything
about it other than, "I think you'll be pleased."

It all seemed too wonderful to be real. But her greatest

thrill came from the changes in Damien. He courted her. Every evening he presented her with flowers or candy and oftentimes ribbons. On warm, sunny days he, along with Kate and William, took her for long rides in the park. One day, on such a stroll with Damien down Piccadilly, Bonnie spied a cradle in the window of an antique store. Like a child with her nose pressed against the glass, she imagined her baby lying in it. The next day she awoke from her nap to find it placed at the foot of her bed, a great blue ribbon wrapped around it.

Another day they had taken advantage of a break in the weather and picnicked in Hyde Park. Sitting beneath a tree, her pale blue skirts spread across the brown grass, Bonnie read aloud from a book of poems while Damien rested with his head in her lap. The day had been brilliant, steeped in azure, with a warm southwesterly breeze to stir the fallen leaves around them. He had gently taken the book from her hands and tossed it aside. He'd said nothing, but for long minutes he'd watched her with a half-fierce half-tender expression. Then he'd taken her in his arms, rolled her to the ground, and kissed her so passionately that they'd forgotten propriety, or the fact that they were surrounded by dozens of strangers who, apparently having enjoyed their performance, broke out in applause despite Kate's noisy protestations over their behavior.

It all seemed so perfect.

Her nightmares had ended with Damien's return from Yorkshire.

The secret of her identity no longer stood between them.

He'd sworn he'd only traveled to Gunnerside church, attained her certificate of birth, and returned to London.

He never again questioned her about her dreams or her father's death.

Why, then, did the feeling occasionally come over her that something was troubling him? It was nothing he did or said. In truth, his devotion had done much to assure her that his love for her was real—she never doubted that for a moment. But there were times, such as the afternoon she had looked down from her window and found him sitting alone in the rose garden, that his face belonged to a man struggling with some inner turmoil.

She told herself that it was to be expected, considering the deteriorating circumstances in America. Still, when she'd questioned him about it, he'd only shrugged the query off with the response, "My overseer is a capable man. I'm sure he'll do what he thinks is right."

"Prewedding jitters," had been William's explanation of Damien's bouts with moodiness.

So she did her best to put the negative thoughts aside. She and Damien were happy, and soon they would return to Yorkshire. She kept that notion in mind as their wedding day drew nearer, and the demands on her's and Kate's and Marianne's time grew greater. There were congratulatory teas to attend, and parties to which she and Damien were guests of honor. Bonnie watched her friends capably and graciously deal with any problem that arose, and to her own consternation she realized that, as Damien's wife—she would soon be expected to do the same. But how?

To speak correctly took all her concentration.

To glide across a floor instead of bounding seemed laborious, especially in light of her advancing state of pregnancy.

More and more she felt the strain; less and less was she able to hide it. She awoke on the day before her wedding and, as tears flowed, announced to a stunned Kate and Marianne, "I can't do it. I can't marry him. I ain't no high and mighty lord's wife. I can't hardly *read* a menu much less write one. What do I do the first time some duke or duchess decides he or she wants to drop in for tea and crumpets or to spend a week or two talkin' about the state of the bleedin' economy? What do *they* even know about it?" Jutting her chin with a touch of her old Caldbergh defiance, she added, "Maybe I'll tell 'em wot it's really like out there. How the real world is forced t' survive. That there's children livin' on the streets and starvin' cause they ain't got a ha'penny for a damned potato. That there's women livin' in whorehouses and breedin' like animals so some perverted aristocrat with his brains in his balls can someday slink int' East End under cover of darkness and buy himself a child virgin."

"Oh my." Kate gasped. "Perhaps I should send for Damien."

"A wise idea," Marianne replied.

Kate ran from the room.

Marianne smiled and, as Bonnie paced, sat in a chair with her hands folded calmly in her lap. "You're nervous, dear," she explained. "It's to be expected the day before your wedding, especially in light of the changes you'll be facing."

Bonnie scowled at Marianne.

Mari added, "And you're expecting a child. I understand women have a tendency toward emotionalism during that time."

Bonnie looked at her rounded stomach and burst into tears again. "Can y' imagine what people are thinkin' of me? They're thinkin' I trapped him. They're prob'ly pityin' him cause he has t' marry me—"

"Stop right there." Her face tight with irritation, Marianne stood and walked to Bonnie. "If you know the aristocracy so well, Bonnie, you should know that a man of Warwick's position cannot be forced into anything in which he doesn't wish to be involved. Believe me, the world is full of young women in your predicament who were whispered promises during moments of intimacy and found themselves nine months later with only a small allowance each month to tide them over or to keep them quiet . . . take Miles's mother for instance. How much easier it would have been for Damien to set you up in an apartment or send you packing back to Caldbergh, and, believe me, no one would have blinked an eye. But he didn't. He loves you. He's proud as hell of you. He's stood up before his peers and, by his actions, announced to them that he finds you worthy, despite your upbringing, to be his wife—and his countess."

"But that's just it," Bonnie cried. "I'm afraid."

"Of what?"

"Of failin' him!"

Marianne smiled and relaxed. "Dear Bonnie, you needn't be marrying an earl to have those fears. Every bride since the beginning of time has felt that way on the eve of her wedding . . . even your own mother, I imagine. Do you think it's any easier for the groom? Have you not considered that they too lie awake and wonder if they'll live up to the expectations demanded of them or if *they'll* be happy?" She turned for the door and, without looking back, added, "Think about *that* for a while."

Bonnie did. Sitting by the window, she watched rain pour

from the sky. Perhaps an hour had passed since Marianne had left the room when Damien spoke quietly behind her.

"Second thoughts?"

She glanced toward the mirror to her right and found his reflection gazing down at her. As usual, her breath rushed from her. Leaving her chair, she threw herself against him, clutching him tightly, burying her face in the crisp, starchy freshness of his shirt.

He held her, kissing the top of her head. "Bonnie, m'love, what's wrong?"

"I'm afraid."

Taking her face in his hands, he searched her features, his own lined with worry.

"It'll never work," she told him. "You're a lord and I ain't no lady. I try, but I don't like London. I don't like wearin' all these fancy clothes with horsehair petticoats—"

"Crinoline."

"Whatever. It makes me itch."

He hugged her closer.

"I owe you so much," she said quietly. "You saved my life when I was sick. You saved me from Smythe, regardless of the lie I told him about you."

Pushing her to arm's length, Damien frowned. "I don't want you to marry me because you feel obligated. You'll marry me because you love me. You *do* still love me . . . ?

For an instant Bonnie recognized the look of uncertainty Marianne had spoken of flash over Damien's features. Smiling, she returned, "Course I do, don't be daft. Why shouldn't I?"

He rubbed his hands gently up and down her arms, yet despite the smile quirking one corner of his mouth, his smoky-green eyes appeared troubled. "No reason." Releasing her, he turned away and moved about the room, indifferently studying the feminine furnishings. "I take it you don't wish to remain in London."

"No."

"You desire to return to Braithwaite?"

Bonnie chewed her lip and considered her reply.

Curious, Damien glanced at her askance. His brow rose. "Do I detect some hesitance over that as well?"

"I . . ." He faced her. His dark hair had tumbled over his

brow, and his jaw appeared tight. Taking a breath, she blurted, "I don't like Braithwaite much."

"I see."

"It's too big. And dark. And gloomy. It frightens me sometimes."

"I have a house in Wales—"

"No."

"There's another in Cornwall. It faces the sea and—"

"Bloody hell, what does a man need with so many houses?"

"In case one becomes too big and dark and gloomy, of course."

Sighing, Bonnie sat in the chair, squirming uncomfortably as the petticoats scratched her legs. "I like the moors in Yorkshire, so Yorkshire's where I'd like t' live."

She watched as he walked slowly to her. His smile seemed a little sad as he lightly touched her cheek with his fingertips. "My God, you are lovely. How could I deny you anything? If you want to live in Yorkshire, then so be it. But you'll have to be content with Braithwaite until I can come up with some reasonable alternative. Will you do that?"

She nodded.

"I'd like to kiss you," he said quietly. "I wonder if Kate will dash through the door and hit me with something if I do."

Her heartbeat quickening, Bonnie pressed her hand to his, cupping his warm palm to her face. "I'd like you to kiss me," she confessed.

He went down on one knee beside her. With his lips mere inches from hers, his voice sounded rough with emotion as he said, "I love you, girl. Never forget that, no matter what." Then he kissed her passionately, powerfully, driving all doubts from her mind until she wrapped her arms around him and kissed him back with equal desire.

Her wedding day dawned with cloudless skies and hazy yellow sunshine. Nervously, Bonnie went through the motions of attempting to eat breakfast, bathing, and sitting still while Edna brushed out her hair and plaited it with yards of pearl-white ribbon.

Madame Roussaue and her attendants arrived just past

noon. Marianne came soon after. As always she was beautiful with her fiery hair swept up and arranged in curls and
ringlets around her white shoulders. Dressed in matching
gowns the color of soft lilacs, she and Kate disappeared into
a room with Madame Roussaue for several minutes before
they appeared again, beaming with anticipation.

"Are you ready, darling?" Marianne asked.

"Aye," Bonnie said.

"Then come along," Kate told her.

She entered a bedroom and was met by scurrying attendants. One held a chemise of the finest lawn. Another gripped
pantaloons and several petticoats. Still another hurried across
the room with sheer white hose and a garter trailing from her
fingers. Layer by layer the clothes were put on Bonnie until
all that was left to don was the dress.

"Now, you must close your eyes and promise not to open
them until the dress is in place," Kate said.

Laughing with excitement, Bonnie closed her eyes. As the
dress was eased over her head, she said, "But I want to see
it!"

"Non!" Madame cried. "Not until everything is just so."

Bonnie held her breath as the gown slid over her shoulders,
her first impression that it seemed extremely heavy as she
slipped her arms into the sleeves. As it fell into place around
her hips and spilled to her feet, someone hurried to fasten
the dozens of tiny buttons up the back, then gentle hands
turned her very slowly toward a mirror.

Speechless, Bonnie stared at her reflection, unable to believe what she was seeing. The gown was of antique satin
and lace. It fell in splendid folds from just beneath her
breasts—nicely hiding her rounding stomach—to her slip-
pered feet. Across her shoulders a mantle of seed pearls
dipped to the valley between her breasts, and caressed most
of her slender neck. The sleeves were slightly full from her
shoulders to just beyond her elbow. There they joined the
deep cuffs, which were also covered in pearls. These reached
to her wrist where they formed a vee across the top of her
hand, ending in a point just above the finger emblazoned with
the Warwick crest.

Kate and an attendant moved up behind her and carefully
placed a veil of sheer lace and net on her head, just behind

the fringe of black curls framing her face. The cap was studded with pearls and silk rosettes. Kate then unfolded a length of gauzy net over Bonnie's face. Marianne placed a bouquet of white rosebuds and lilacs into Bonnie's shaking hands.

"Beautiful." Her eyes glistening with tears, Kate beamed. "Damien will be so proud."

"But—"

"Much of the dress is made from pieces of my mother's wedding dress, the pearl mantle and cuffs, for instance, which were also used on *her* mother's dress."

"But I have no right," Bonnie said softly, her voice breaking as she looked again at her image in the mirror.

Kate took Bonnie's shoulders in her hands and regarded her sternly. "You have every right. Damien has chosen to marry you because he loves you."

A movement in the mirror caught Bonnie's eye. She slowly turned to face William, who was distinguished and dashing in his formal attire.

Raising one brow, he looked Bonnie over completely, his aristocratic countenance softening with pleasure at her appearance. He said with slight amazement, "By jove, you are fetching, lass. I dare say there have been few brides so lovely on their wedding day."

"Or so pregnant," she reminded him.

"Balderdash!" With a squaring of his shoulders, he offered his arm. "It will be my honor to give you away to the groom, whom, I might add, is most eager to make you his wife. Are you ready?"

Bonnie and William boarded a shiny black Berlin coach pulled by two pair of snow-white geldings. Kate and Marianne boarded another. As they rolled slowly through the busy London streets, people along the walks stopped and stared and often waved as they noted the bride within.

She heard the bells ringing long before she arrived at Westminster Abbey. As the coach pulled up before the grand building, Bonnie looked at William in astonishment. He smiled and said, "Don't fret. It won't seem so intimidating once you're inside."

Sinking back in her seat, she whispered, "Bloody hell, I hadn't expected this."

He laughed and helped her from the coach.

Kate and Marianne, having arrived before Bonnie, proceeded her and William into Westminster's nave. Bonnie stopped and stared in awe at the soaring vaulted ceilings and the windows of stained glass that dominated the far wall.

Gripping William's arm, Bonnie followed her friends down several hallways. They showed her into a small chamber furnished with several chairs. William and Marianne excused themselves, leaving her alone with Kate. Nervously Bonnie paced the room until, laughing, Kate forced her to sit.

"You really must try to calm down," Kate said.

Bonnie peered at the colored light slanting through a stained-glass window depicting Abraham, Isaac, and Jacob.

"Would you like to be alone?" Kate asked softly.

"No." Bonnie studied the bouquet in her hands. "I was thinkin' about my parents. They wanted me to marry well and encouraged me to try for a sheep farmer."

"I'm certain if we looked hard enough we might find some sheep on one of our properties."

Bonnie laughed, then forced herself to take a breath. She did her best to swallow. "I hardly know him, Kate."

"But you love him."

"Doesn't make much sense, does it?"

"Love rarely does."

"What should I expect?"

Kate walked to the window. A streak of pink light turned her face the color of roses as she smiled to herself. "Men can be difficult. Damien will not always say what you would like him to. Men aren't good with words. Then, when you least expect it, he'll say something so beautiful and wonderful he'll take your breath away.

"Occasionally he'll be thoughtless. At times he'll hurt you. Then he will do something so considerate and caring you'll think he's a saint, and you'll forgive him.

"Damien has a million dreams that will never come true. But the important thing is that he believes in them, strives for them. You'll applaud him when he's right. You'll defend him when he's wrong. You'll tell him when he's strong and brave, and most of all, when he's magnificent, whether it be over a chess match or a battle like the one he just fought in Parliament. All because you love him."

The door opened. Marianne regarded Bonnie from the

doorway, her eyes a bit glassy and her mouth slightly thinned. Bonnie sensed what she was thinking. Leaving her chair, she joined Mari and, hesitantly, took her hand. "Thank you for being my friend."

"It is my honor and pleasure, Bonnie."

"I didn't always like you."

A flicker of a smile teased Mari's lips. "I know, but considering the circumstances your disapproval was perfectly understandable."

"I know you still love him."

"Yes, I do. I suppose I always shall."

"I love him too—very much—and promise to do my best to make him happy."

"You already have. I've just seen him, and he's . . . beaming. I'm certain I have never seen him so joyous or in love."

"Even with Louisa?"

"*Even* with Louisa." Marianne took Bonnie in her arms, and as she hugged her close, whispered, "Cherish him as much as he cherishes you, and you will be eternally happy."

She nodded.

"All right," Mari said, "Come along. He's waiting for you."

They walked the paths of kings, down the Great Cloister, through a vaulted passage which, Kate whispered, in the days of Edward the Confessor, led to the monks' infirmary. They passed the octagonal Chapter House, its vaulted roof supported by a graceful center column dating back to the thirteenth century. Kate, attempting to alleviate Bonnie's nervousness, explained that the room had been used by Parliament during the fourteenth and sixteenth centuries.

They finally arrived at a pair of closed doors. William was there to greet Bonnie and, taking her hand, placed it on his arm. "Through these doors is Henry VII's Chapel. There are approximately fifty guests in attendance. They are some of Damien's closest friends, and therefore they are your friends. I want you to feel no hesitation over presenting yourself. Earl Warwick is very proud of you."

The doors opened, and Kate and Marianne disappeared into the room. In another moment a pair of uniformed attendants stepped from the chapel and rolled out a runner of white silk to Bonnie's feet.

Somehow she moved. She wasn't certain how. Reality seemed to slip away into an image so dreamlike she thought she might be only sleeping. Entering the chapel, she became vaguely aware of people rising to their feet. They were looking at her and smiling.

And then Damien appeared at the end of the aisle, and she forgot everything except him—his smile, his eyes. As she neared him, he lifted one hand to her. She could think of only one thing to do.

She sank to her knee in obeisance.

There was a murmur throughout the chapel, and Bonnie wondered frantically if she had committed some breach of etiquette. But looking up into Damien's eyes, she found only pleasure, and gratitude. Taking her hand, he helped her stand. They moved to the chancel before the altar. The priest stepped forward to greet them. "Dearly beloved . . ." he began.

Damien held her hand throughout the service, never releasing it for a moment. The next hour passed like mere seconds, then, unbelievably, she was hearing, "By the powers vested in me by God and this Holy Church, I pronounce you husband and wife. My lord, you may kiss your bride."

As the Westminster bells began to ring out, Damien raised the veil from Bonnie's face. "My lady," he whispered, and he kissed her.

The reception went on forever, or so it seemed to Bonnie. As the orchestra played she danced about the floor in her friends' arms, smiling and laughing and wishing for all the world that she was alone with her new husband. As Philippe swept her round in a waltz, he grinned and said, "Happy?"

"Aye, more than I ever dreamed possible."

"I can collect my wager now."

"What wager?"

"The lads and I placed a rather sizable wager in the book at White's that you and Damien would marry."

"Oh? And when did y' do that?" she asked sternly.

"As soon as we returned to London after leaving Braithwaite. I knew it the moment I first saw you."

"But I was filchin' beef and puddin's."

"Exactly. I thought there is a girl who'll give ol' Dame a challenge." Smiling, Philippe added, "I became quite fond of that fiery little girl. I hope you won't change overly much."

Tipping up her chin, Bonnie grinned. "Don't be daft. I've told my lord husband that just as soon as we go back to Braithwaite I'm sheddin' these horsehair petticoats for m' breeches."

Throwing back his head, Philippe laughed. "I can imagine you and Dame having a half dozen daughters all wearing breeches. You'll set English aristocracy on its heels, by gad."

The music ended and Damien joined them, shouldering Philippe aside. "Pardon," he said, "but this last dance is mine. Then I'm taking my wife home and we're going to spend the remainder of the evening picking out names for our son."

"Daughter," Philippe argued. "I've wagered at White's that your firstborn will be a girl."

"Twins," came Freddy's voice behind them.

"A boy," Claurence chimed in. "And his name will be Asquith."

"Bloody hell if it will," Bonnie cried.

Damien laughed and kissed her, then they spun across the floor to the music, smiling into each other's eyes, forgetting their spellbound audience and losing themselves in the splendor and happiness they felt in that moment. It seemed forever before they could make their final good-byes, but at last they were running down the steps to their coach, a shower of rose petals raining on their heads and shoulders.

Damien had released the servants for the evening. As he and Bonnie stood face-to-face in his dressing room, the only sound to disturb the quiet was the crackling of the fire on the hearth. He couldn't seem to find his voice as he searched her features. Her eyes were bright, her mouth red and soft. Her hair was sprinkled with pale yellow rose petals and tumbled about her face, black and ravishingly alive where the firelight touched it. He slid his hands into it, and a single petal drifted like a snowflake to the floor.

Her lips parted in a sigh as he brushed her mouth lightly with his. "It's getting late," he said quietly. "Perhaps you should consider changing."

Bonnie offered him her back. "Will you help?"

He bent to the chore of working loose the dozens of tiny buttons down the back of her dress. Once done, he pushed aside the material and ran his fingertips admiringly down her slender spine. Then he nudged the pearl mantle off her shoulders; her skin shone gold and orange in the firelight. "Hurry," he whispered.

While Bonnie changed, Damien turned down the lights, then uncorked a bottle of champagne and poured them each a glass. He sat in a chair before the fire. Laying his head back, he closed his eyes and tried to relax, wondering at his restlessness, slightly disconcerted by his nervousness. Minutes ticked by as he waited for Bonnie, then hearing a noise, he looked around. She stood near. She wore a nightgown buttoned high at the neck and wrists. Its whiteness shimmered rose in the firelight.

"Do y' like the gown?" she asked anxiously.

"Aye." He smiled. "But there's so much of it."

"That's what Marianne said when I showed it to her. She tried t' give me some flimsy thing that was rude to look at, but I reminded her that my book, *Habits of Good Society,* which *she* gave me, says a proper young lady wears night chemises with long sleeves, and the hem of the gown must reach the feet."

He looked at her bare feet. "Ah. Well, we certainly wouldn't want to risk breaking the rules of etiquette, would we?" He left his chair, caught her hand, and tugged her closer to the fire. "Are you tired, love?"

She shook her head. Her hair, having been released from its braids and brushed, swirled around her hips, reflecting the nearby candlelight. He was suddenly struck by how childlike she appeared. The loose gown hid her curves but clung slightly to her protruding stomach. Her face seemed almost lost beneath her magnificent hair, and her hands looked like a doll's hidden within the cuffs of her sleeves. He was swept with such a fierce need to possess her in that instant, to melt into her and burn her with his body and love, that he was forced to close his eyes and take a breath. "Come and sit down," he told her.

"But I thought . . ."

"You thought what?"

A moment of indecision passed, then her white hands drifted across her stomach. Her lower lip began to tremble, and as Damien looked on, perplexed, she covered her face with her hands and burst into tears.

He grabbed her. Panicked, he asked, "Christ, what have I done now?"

Burying her face in his chest, she cried, "You don't want me!"

"What?"

"I repulse you!"

Taking her shoulders, he pushed her back and stared in disbelief at her tear-streaked face. "Don't want you?"

"Because I'm with child. I heard the servants talkin'. They say men find women in my state distasteful." She sniffed and wiped the sleeve of her gown across her nose. "I understand if you don't want me *that* way. I suppose I am rather cumbersome."

"Not nearly so cumbersome as you're going to be, my lady." Laughing, he dropped into the chair, pulling her down with him so that she perched on his lap. "Look at me," he ordered.

Reluctantly, she did so.

Watching her eyes, he said, "Yes, I want you, Bonnie. I want you like hell. But I also want your heart, and I want your soul. I want friendship from you and companionship. I want to grow old with you, and I want to die with you. I made you my wife, not just because I wanted to bed you. I married you because I love you." He closed his arms around her and pulled Bonnie up against his chest. With her head on his shoulder they watched the fire burn until her breathing became even and her body relaxed. When he was certain her earlier nervousness had subsided, he kissed the top of her head, slid one arm beneath her legs, the other around her waist, and left the chair. He carried her to the bedroom.

The room was not lit except by the faint yellow light from the street lamps outside. He walked with her carefully cradled against him, passing the ghostly white wedding gown discarded over the back of a chair. All else appeared gray within the shadows.

He gently lowered her to the bed.

How long he stood there, looking into her eyes, he could not guess. Then his arms were reaching for her, drawing her up against him with a fierceness that took their breath away. He kissed her with a wild violence stemming from passion, hunger, and need, and she kissed him back as fiercely, gripping his clothes in her hands and pressing her thin-clad body so closely to his that he could feel her heart race against his. He covered her eyes, her nose, her cheeks with light kisses, traced her lips with his tongue and slid his hands into her hair, noting the smallness of her head through its thick softness. He felt free, like a bird soaring, rising then hurtling through a fiery space. He loved her, oh, God, he loved her . . .

He managed to step away and slowly began to remove his clothes: his frock coat first, allowing it to slide off his shoulders and onto the floor. His waistcoat followed, then his diamond tiepin and silk cravat. He tugged ineffectually at the top buttons of his frilled white shirt; his fingers were shaking too badly; he could not unfasten it. On her knees on the bed, Bonnie reached and did it for him, plucking the buttons open until she could press her cool hands against the hot flesh of his chest.

He turned away and unfastened his cuffs, removed his shirt, his shoes, his socks, and finally his trousers and underdrawers. When he finally turned back to the bed, Bonnie had crawled beneath the covers, her pale face with its wide, dark eyes watching above the sheet she had pulled to her chin. He hesitated as memories of their previous moments together tumbled through his mind. He had vowed long ago that this night would be different; he had already abused her love for him intolerably; it must not happen again: no mindless passion, no lust, no madness or animality to assuage the body's hunger. Tonight they would make love. Yet— yet—the long weeks spent in frustration, imagining her beneath him filled his body with fire and pain, an ungovernable torrent of need and desire that was growing ever greater.

Easily he entered the bed, sliding beneath the counterpane.

Rolling to his side, he reached for her and drew her close. She touched his face and he seized her hand, kissing it at first leisurely, then feverishly until he felt his restraint crumbling.

He ran his hands over her flannel covered curves, her small breasts, tracing the pattern of her swollen nipple through the gown with the pad of his thumb, then down to the rounding of her stomach. There he paused and covered the swelling with his hand, felt the stirring of life against his palm. He closed his eyes, the rise of emotion inside him too powerful, too physical. He pulled her closer, pressing his body to hers while he continued to explore her, and she him. Her hands were gentle, timid, tracing each ridge, each shape of muscle and tendon and bone. Catching her wrist, he moved it down, closed her cool fingers around his erect member, and taught her the motion.

Reaching for the hem of her gown, he drew it upward, a degree at a time, allowing his fingers to trail along the silky smoothness of her inner thighs until reaching the hot nest of downy hair at the juncture of her legs. He cupped his hand against it, tenderly parting the alluring crevice with his finger until he could rub inside her, until she grew moist and slick, until her body warmed and strained against him and her legs opened, her right leg sliding over the top of his and her bare foot touching lightly against the back of his calf. Her breathing grew ragged and panting. Her fingers clawed at his naked hips as she whispered hoarsely, "Please. Please . . ."

He entered her, a slow, glorious glide into ecstasy.

Her eyes closed and she twisted her face slightly away. She groaned deep in her throat. Her body moved against him, falling into the seductive tempo that was as natural as the beating of their hearts. He kissed her mouth, her face, her shoulder, imprinting the taste and texture of her gown and skin on his lips and mind. And still he pulled and thrust, his ejaculation pounding inside him, burning, rising until his domination over mind and body became lost in their frantic coming together.

Her arms flung around him as if she would bind him to her forever. Her head fell back and her mouth opened in a wordless, soundless cry even as her body tensed against his, grew startlingly hot and tight around his, and convulsed in spasms that drove him over the edge of reason. He strained his body into hers and buried his face against her slender white throat, into the dark fan of hair strewn over the pillow and the curve of her shoulder. He burst inside her with a groan and a sob, and with words like an absolution for his body and soul.

"I love you. I love you. Oh, God, I love you, Bonnie . . ."

Twenty-seven

They rode up to the ruins of Middleham Castle twice a day. From there the view was splendid. They could easily see the farmers' meadows, purple in the late afternoon light. Yonder the river Cover sparkled like quicksilver between its heather-covered banks. Sitting in a carriage with Bonnie in his arms, Damien realized that for most of his adult life he had fought the restrictions of propriety imposed on him by his ancestry. He had rebelled against custom and tradition. He had used the fiasco with Louisa as an excuse to run away, to search for freedom among the Mississippi bogs and cotton fields worked by men whose hunger for freedom surpassed his own. He'd run a long way just to return home and discover that freedom was a short walk out Braithwaite's door, to the top of a Yorkshire fell.

Bonnie gazed out over the frozen moor and pointed to the highest rise in the distance. "That would be the perfect place t' build a home. From there y' could see all the way across the county. Y' might even be able to stand in your door and count your sheep without ever leavin' the house."

He frowned and hugged her closer. "What sheep?"

"The sheep we'll have someday." Twisting toward him, she smiled. "Y've been wonderin' what t' do with your time now that y've decided to sell Bent Tree. Instead of growin' cotton, y' can raise sheep."

He kissed the cold tip of her nose as she nestled more deeply into the folds of her ermine cloak. "Happy?" he asked her.

"Aye. I've never been happier, my lord husband. And you?"

He nodded.

"Y' haven't grown bored with me yet?"

"Bored? How could I grow bored, for God's sake? You have me traipsing over the moor the first thing in the morning and in the afternoon. I'm tutoring you in the languages, history, and literature for hours a day, not to mention our rousing games of chess—when you cheat abominably, I might add."

"You've noticed?"

"Of course."

"Then why didn't you say something? I was beginning t' think you were daft."

"I'm always amazed how you manage it. I've never known anyone who could cheat at chess. Your sleight of hand could put the deftest pickpockets in London to shame. We never have to fear becoming completely destitute, m'lady. Just turn you loose on our peers and you could lift enough money from their purses to keep us fat and content for the rest of our lives."

She laughed, then looking again over the icy landscape, she said more seriously, "The last month at Braithwaite has been wonderful, but I think at times that your mind is elsewhere, my lord. Do you miss America?"

He took her face in his hands and looked in her eyes. "Never. I have only one love now, Bonnie. You."

"Yet there are times that I wake at night and find you staring at the ceiling or sitting in a chair before the fire as if you're troubled."

"I won't deny I'm bothered about the escalating war in America. Since Madison and Slidell were taken captive by the North while sailing for England, I feel responsible. With the Queen having sent thousands of troops to Canada with a threat of retribution, we could be on the verge of an extremely bloody war between the two countries."

"But you'll not be leavin'—"

"No." Pulling her closer, he said, "When I chose you over Bent Tree, I put Vicksburg behind me forever. I'll allow nothing to come between us, Bonnie. *Nothing.*"

"Is that why, before we even returned to Braithwaite, you sent Miles off with Richard to take care of business in Cornwall?"

He looked away. "Is there some crime in wanting to be *alone* with my new wife for a while?"

"You're not still jealous of Miles, are ya?" she demanded.

"Maybe."

Bonnie slid her cold fingers around her husband's neck, forcing him to face her again. His eyes were dark as the snow-threatening clouds, yet his mouth carried the faintest hint of a smile. "I love you," she said. "I'm havin' your baby in less than two months. I can't imagine there bein' any reason on this earth why I would ever turn to another."

Their frosty breath mingled as they kissed, tongues dancing together, hands burying in the furry lining of their cloaks and clothes. With her mouth against Damien's, Bonnie whispered, "I'll be glad when this baby is born cause I miss havin' you inside me."

Damien groaned.

"There must be some way—"

"Dr. Whitman says no. You're too close to your time."

She moved on his lap, straddling his legs, while her chilled fingers darted over the hard rise in his breeches and fumbled with the buttons of the fly.

He caught her wrist. "Bonnie—"

"I want you," she told him.

"Ah, Jeez . . . "

"Right here."

"We're on the road. Anyone could happen by—"

"It's been weeks, my lord husband. I miss you."

"Bonnie . . . Bonnie!" He shoved her hand away roughly, then catching her shoulders, he pulled her closely against him—or as closely as her stomach would allow—and said, "If Dr. Whitman says you're too far along to make love, we won't make love. I'm not taking any chances with your health, sweetheart. You and this baby mean too much to me."

He planted a warm wet kiss on her mouth, then sat her back on the carriage seat. "Sit there and behave while I drive us home."

Bonnie scowled. "But—"

"No 'buts'. It's beginning to snow. I'm freezing and you're freezing. On top of that I have a stack of correspondence at home that I need to deal with if you want me to spend the remainder of the evening basking in the warm glow of your love and companionship.''

She stuck out her tongue at him.

He laughed, grabbed up the reins, and turned the carriage back toward Braithwaite.

With a smile on her face, Bonnie stood silently in the doorway of the library, watching her husband work. She didn't begrudge him this time, although she missed him terribly when he withdrew into his own world of business and finance. Since their return to Braithwaite she had tried numerous times to question him on the Warwick holdings, wanting to know everything there was to know about his life. She had learned soon enough that, while he might consider her his partner in love and marriage, their alliance did not extend into occupational pursuits.

So be it.

Sighing, she turned away and wandered toward the kitchen.

Stanley, Jewel, and Gretchen were gathered about an ancient oak table before the oven, watching Cook turn out biscuits from a flat blackened tin. They all jumped to attention as she entered the room.

"Bloody hell," she complained, "y' all look as if the bleedin' Queen just walked in." She dropped onto a red japanned armchair with cabriole legs. "I wouldn't mind some tea," she told Cook.

"Is aught wrong?" Jewel asked, hurrying to fetch a cup and saucer from a nearby cupboard.

"My lord is working." She slumped against the table and propped her cheek upon her fist. "I hate it when he works."

"He's got responsibilities, m'lady," Gretchen said.

"Aye, I know he does." She glanced about the kitchen, enjoying its smells and the cheerful fire crackling on its massive hearth. "It'll be Christmas soon. I ain't had a real Christmas since m' mum died."

Stanley measured tea into a blue and white pot. "I would imagine Christmas at Caldbergh was hardly festive."

Recalling the wretched days of despair and hunger, Bonnie shook her head, repressing her shiver. "We used to sit about and fantasize over how the aristocracy were spending *their* holiday." To Jewel, she asked, "Was it nice here?"

"Not lately. Not since the countess passed on, God rest her soul. She were more interested in doin' f' others, y' know. She were generous to charities, and all—"

"She was always encouragin' 'er peers to participate as well," Gretchen added.

The back door opened and the footman entered, a whirlwind of snowflakes and crisp brown leaves swirling about his feet. Seeing Bonnie, he dragged off his hat, exposing ears bright red from the cold. He bowed, and in a breathless voice said, "Might I see his lordship?"

"His lordship is occupied with business," Bonnie responded.

"Well, we've got a problem—"

"What is it?"

"His lordship—"

"Is busy," she repeated. Leaving her chair, she asked, "Perhaps I can help?"

The footman glanced worriedly toward the others. Wringing his hat in his hands, he shrugged. "We've just caught ourselves a thief. He was attemptin' to steal a couple of chickens. Caught him with a bird under each arm as he was crawlin' from beneath the coop."

In that moment another man entered, holding a boy no older than ten years by the scruff of his threadbare coat. Upon seeing Bonnie, the lad's mouth dropped open and he squirmed even harder.

She recognized him immediately: an urchin from Caldbergh.

"Let him go," she ordered the servant.

"But, ma'am, he were—"

"Stealin' chickens," she interrupted. "That ain't no reason to string him from a damned gibbet."

The servant released the boy as if he'd burned him. As Stanley hurried to close the door, Bonnie crossed her arms and eyed the young thief sternly. "Kyle Leeland, what the blazes did y' think y' were doin'?"

His amazed gaze locked on her face; he sneered. "Starvin'. In case y've forgotten what *that* is, it means I'm hungry."

"What's that supposed to mean?"

"Well, you ain't doing too badly, are ya?" He looked at

her stomach and laughed. "So it's true. Smythe tol' us y'd decided it was better t' whore for the gentry than t' come back t' Caldbergh."

Gretchen and Jewel gasped. The footman cuffed Kyle across the mouth and said, "Watch yer tongue! You be speakin' t' the countess, y' young idiot."

Bonnie watched Kyle's face go from an angry red to a shocked white in a matter of seconds. She felt her own spurt of anger dwindle to a cold realization that just a few short months ago she might well have been the freezing, starving child, hating the aristocracy for their ignorance and indifference. How could she have forgotten so easily?

"Give 'im the chickens," she told the servants.

Silence.

Finally Stanley stepped forward, and in a quiet voice said, "I don't think his lordship would approve, ma'am. To do so would be the same as inviting every poacher in Yorkshire to traipse over Braithwaite and take what they will."

"I'll deal with his lordship on the matter should he question my decision."

"Very well." Stanley spoke quietly to the footman and the servant who had dragged Kyle into the kitchen. She watched their eyes shift questioningly to her then back to the boy. Then they both grabbed his arms and ushered him out the door.

"He'll get his chickens, ma'am," Stanley informed her.

Bonnie turned away. Standing before the hearth, she stared down into the flames. "I almost forgot. I ain't—haven't—been away from that bloody, wretched place for a year, and already I've forgotten how awful it was. I ought t' be ashamed. I should be usin' my experience and knowledge of those awful memories t' better their lives. I'm worse than the aristocracy. They're just too damned ignorant t' know any better. But I *do* know. And what am I doin' about it? I'm mopin' about and whinin' cause I'm bored and don't have enough t' do t' occupy my time."

She half turned and addressed Jewel. "You mentioned earlier that my husband's mother was generous t' charities. What exactly did she do?"

"She collected money, food, and clothes from her peers and distributed 'em t' the needy."

Bonnie chewed her bottom lip as she contemplated the information. "I reckon that means I'd have t' contact those people myself." The very idea made her flush with nervousness. "Course, m' mum used t' say charity begins at home. What exactly do we have planned for Christmas?"

The servants exchanged glances. Finally Stanley replied, "Nothing."

"Nothing?"

They shook their heads.

"Bloody hell, what did you *use* t' do for Christmas? I mean when the countess was alive."

Eyes twinkling, Jewel rubbed her hands together. "We used t' cook f' days."

"Ooh, aye," Gretchen added. "We baked birds—"

"Pheasants and hens and quail," Stanley said.

"And pasties and plum puddin's," Cook joined in.

"Breads and cakes and biscuits—and mince pie, too!" Jewel squealed with excitement.

Stanley smiled and his face became dreamy. "The house was covered with holly and berries and wreaths made of mistletoe. There were candles burning constantly. On Christmas Eve the family and servants would all gather 'round the great room hearth, burn the Yule log, and drink wassail."

"Then we'd do it all again on boxing day," Gretchen exclaimed.

"Boxing day?" Bonnie asked.

"It's the day after Christmas when the gentry does for the servants."

"Y' mean they cook?"

They all nodded.

Feeling her mood lighten with the aspect of participating in the festivities, Bonnie clapped her hands. "What are we waitin' for?"

Damien rubbed his eyes and sat back in his chair. He'd spent more time than he'd wanted on the books, but things were looking better. At least the problems had stabilized. Richard had managed to sell his properties in Scotland and Wales, and had paid back the money in full that he'd pilfered from the businesses. There was only the selling of Bent Tree to contend with now . . .

Damien left his chair. He was lying to himself again. There wasn't *only* Bent Tree. His inability to sell his Vicksburg plantation was the least of his worries. By sending Richard to Cornwall and convincing Miles to go with him, he'd managed to dismiss the problem of Bonnie's father for the time being. And for a while he'd put the thought from his own mind. He and Bonnie had been so happy during the last weeks. He could spend the rest of his life being nothing but husband and father to her and their children, but the unresolved past loomed larger every day.

He couldn't contrive problems on the other side of England forever. Soon his uncle and brother would be returning. How was he going to explain to Richard why he had not informed him about his marriage to Bonnie?

Damien took a long, slow breath and released it. Not for the first time he thought of confronting his wife with the truth. He couldn't do it. He couldn't take the chance of spoiling the happiness and love they'd found together.

He walked to a shelf lined with the Warwick business ledgers. How many times had he stared at the Gunnerside account book, unable to force himself into taking it down and opening it up, knowing the awful truth it would reveal. Could he live with the secret any easier by knowing who had struck Patrick Eden down?

It wasn't so much his dread of facing the murderer that stopped him. It was the thought of Bonnie finding out—it was her turning from him, unable to forgive the fact that his family had destroyed her—that consistently forced him to leave the ledger where it rested.

He exited the study and wandered down the gallery. Stanley and a stable man were descending the stairs, carrying a trunk between them. "What's that?" Damien asked.

"A trunk," Stanley replied smugly.

He grinned.

Stanley plunked the chest at Damien's feet and raised the lid. "I realize the great state of bliss in which you have been existing, my lord. However, I feel it behooves me to inform you that the holiday is practically upon us. Bonnie—the countess, I do beg your pardon—has decided to celebrate accordingly."

Damien bent to one knee and retrieved the small china

image of Mary holding the baby Jesus in her arms. "Where is my wife?"

"The attic, sir."

"What the blazes is she doing there?"

"On a mission of mercy, I believe."

He replaced the statue and stood. Without speaking again, he climbed the stairs to the attic, meeting numerous servants, their arms loaded with decorations and their dusty faces beaming with anticipation.

A scattering of glowing lanterns sparsely illuminated the cavernous room. He found Bonnie on the far side of the drafty chamber, perched on a large rocking horse, rolling to and fro. Sliding his hands in his pockets, he watched her for some time. Finally he said, "And here I thought you were pining away for my company."

She threw back her head and laughed, a sweet, clear sound like music that tugged at his heart. A nearby lamp brightened her face, and she looked exceptionally beautiful, exquisitely happy, full of an inner as well as outer light that spoke of her contentment more than mere words ever could. He found himself staring, as if engraving the picture on his mind forever. He realized that life without her would be no life at all. He'd rather be dead.

She slid from the colorful wooden horse and walked to him. He could not help but smile. Pregnancy had done much to hamper her ability to move gracefully; she was beginning to waddle.

He closed his arms around her as she nestled against him. "My lord," came her voice. "There are dozens of trunks of clothes and toys here, and I was thinking . . . How do you feel about our giving them to the needy? They ain't—aren't—doing us any good. There are plenty at Caldbergh who could use the shoes and coats and clothing. I'm certain there are children in the village who would love the books and toys . . . all except the horse. I think I'd like to keep that for *our* child. Does that seem too selfish?"

He smiled down at the top of her head. "I don't think that sounds selfish at all." Catching her chin with one finger, he tipped up her face and kissed her. "I love you," he said.

She smiled in return. Her cloud of black hair, her twinkling impish eyes gave her an elfin appearance as she spoke.

"I have something to confess. I released a Caldbergh waif today after he'd stolen two chickens."

He frowned in an attempt to hide his amusement.

"You aren't angry?" she asked.

"No."

"Even if I told you I gave him the chickens?"

"What's a chicken or two?"

She grasped his hand and raised it, pressing it to her lips in adoring zeal. At last she said, "I love you, too."

Twenty-eight

Bonnie sat on the stairs and frowned at her husband. Damien scowled back as he donned his cloak and gloves.

"Out of the question," he told her. "You're seven months pregnant, Bonnie. You are not riding to Caldbergh and facing Smythe in your condition. I'll deliver the goods myself, if I must."

She looked beyond him, out the open front door toward the wagon loaded with trunks and bundles of clothes. "Y'll make certain the children receive 'em? Smythe's bound to make off with the lot and turn a profit before the others ever get 'em."

"I'll stand there until every boy and girl receives his or her share. I swear it."

"Y'll tell 'em there's more where that came from. Christmas Day there will be roasted hens and puddin's and pies."

"I'll tell them."

Stanley entered the foyer, his face red from cold and exertion. In his arms he hefted a log. Walking to Bonnie, he grimaced and lowered the timber to the floor. "My lady . . . your Yule log."

"That's nice, Stanley."

"I wandered half of Middleham before I found one of appropriate size. Where shall I lug it now?"

"The great room hearth, please."

He nodded, took a breath, and lifted it again. He struggled down the gallery.

Damien briefly quit the vestibule, then returned, joining Bonnie at the stairs. He held a wrapped parcel out to her.

Her face brightened. "What's this?"

"A Christmas present, of course."

"But it ain't Christmas yet."

"You look as if you could use some cheering up." As she started to open it, he placed his hand on hers and grinned. "Not until I get back. We'll unwrap it together."

"But I haven't got anything for you."

"No?" He glanced at her stomach. "So mine will be a little late."

She stood and planted a kiss on his cheek. "Hurry home, my lord."

Smiling, Damien turned for the door. "While I occupy my time with Smythe, how will you spend your afternoon, m'lady?"

"I was thinkin' of writin' a few letters. Instead of travelin' all about the county pleadin' my cause for charity, I thought of invitin' the people here."

"On the pretense of celebrating the holiday, I suppose."

Bonnie batted her lashes. As Damien laughed, she said, "You mentioned that your mother kept a book of contributors."

"Aye. It'll be buried in the library somewhere, if it still exists. You're welcome to search for it, if you want."

"Give m' best t' Smythe!" she called jokingly as her husband, joined by Stanley, left the house.

"I'll give him my boot up his butt," he yelled back.

She hurried to the door and watched as Stanley and several more servants boarded the wagon. Her husband mounted his horse, then all headed down the road toward Caldbergh. She waved and thought, I'll miss you . . . I love you . . .

Shivering with cold, she closed the door and stood for a long moment studying the present Damien had given her. She shook it gently, and unable to contain her curiosity, sat again on the steps and unwrapped it. Her vision blurred with tears as she tugged back the tissue paper to reveal a music box identical to the one he had given her before—the one she had destroyed in a fit of anger. Carefully, she lifted the porcelain lovers and wound the stem.

They danced round and round to the music.

Closing her eyes, she imagined herself and Damien waltzing on their wedding day, as beautiful, as in love, as blissfully happy.

She found the card where it had spilled in her lap. Opening it, she read: *Kate tells me the other box was* accidentally *broken. Merry Christmas. I love you. Damien.*

Sighing, she stood and, as the song played, she spun across the floor, gripping the present to her breast as if it was her partner.

The music stopped.

Bonnie gathered up the discarded wrappings. If she allowed herself, she could lag about for the remainder of the afternoon daydreaming about her husband, but there were invitations to address. But before she could do that she needed Damien's mother's book. She would find that in the library.

She rarely visited the grand room now. Standing inside the doorway, she gazed about the towering walls at the hundreds of books lining the shelves. The atmosphere felt warm and masculine. A hint of tobacco hung in the air. She could easily imagine Damien sitting behind the massive desk, his face stern with concentration as he took care of business.

"Where to begin?" she asked aloud.

Crossing the floor, she carefully placed the china piece on the desk, then walked to the shelves directly behind Damien's chair. These were his account books. Some were very old and worn, the leather bindings cracked and peeling with age. Others were newer. She ran her hand over them all, smiling.

"M'lady?"

Bonnie turned to face Jewel.

"Cook has prepared yer lunch, m'lady."

"I'll be right there."

Jewel bobbed a curtsy and departed. Bonnie returned to the desk and gathered up her gift, hugging it closely as she followed the servant from the room.

The Caldbergh waifs pushed close to the wagon as Stanley proceeded to distribute the bundles of clothing to each outstretched hand. Damien stood near, the fur collar of his coat turned up around his ears as he watched the children's blank, gaunt faces. Their eyes seemed lifeless, their bodies wasted. A shiver of anger and disgust washed through him as he saw Smythe peruse each parcel with calculating interest.

"Very nice," Birdie said, rubbing his hands together to

warm them. "My lord, this is most generous. How very kind of you to remember us."

"I can hardly forget you," he drawled.

Smythe chuckled. "And how is our little troublemaker—Bonnie, wasn't it?"

Glaring down into the man's face, Damien smiled coldly. "I assume you mean the *countess.*"

Smythe's mouth dropped open, but before he could respond, Damien added, "My wife is well and happy, Mr. Smythe. I'll be certain to tell her you asked on her behalf. She'll be thrilled."

Turning to the wagon, he grasped a bundle of clothing and tossed it to Stanley. "That was the most profitable five hundred pound investment I ever made, Smythe. I have you to thank for it."

He laughed as the man pivoted on his heels and marched, shoulders hunched and fists swinging, back to his office. "Slimy bastard," Damien said under his breath. He flung another batch of dresses to his butler before forcing his mind off the Caldbergh manager and back to the children.

As he searched their features, another image emerged. Bonnie's. He recognized her earlier hunger, her hopelessness, her despair reflected in all their faces, and although he'd done his best to force those memories from his mind, they all tumbled in on him now. He recalled the joy she'd received over his gift of kittens, and over something so simple as a tiny rosebud. The vision of her laughing face, shining with contentment and happiness as she rode his childhood rocking horse, made him catch his breath, and for a moment he was forced to turn away to collect his emotions.

He gazed down the road to Braithwaite.

No doubt the little imp had already unwrapped her Christmas present.

She was probably plowing through the study in search of his mother's book and . . .

He blinked.

Jesus.

Oh, Jesus.

She would find the Gunnerside ledger.

Cold fear washing over him, he ran for his horse.

* * *

Bonnie tugged hard on the needlepoint book wedged firmly between two others. With one last yank, it tumbled to the floor, spilling several more at her feet.

Bloody hell. It was bad enough walking these days, considering how cumbersome she had grown. Crawling about the floor was no picnic. She briefly considered calling for Jewel to collect the books, but she knew the servants were all busily preparing the house for the holiday. Carefully, she went down on both knees, first retrieving the bound text she hoped would be the countess's. She flipped open the cover and ran her fingers over the yellowing pages. This appeared to be the one. She placed it next to her music box on the desk, then glanced about the floor at the larger volumes.

Her eye caught on a scrawled heading, and she hesitated.

She reached and straightened the book.

Gunnerside Mine.

Gunnerside . . . ?

Forgetting to breathe, Bonnie slowly opened the leather cover and allowed her eyes to study the columns of names and numbers, noting the months and years heading each section. Her gaze skimmed the entries.

Patrick Eden.

Oh, no.

Da?

Oh, no.

She slammed closed the book and clutched it to her chest. "It can't be. God, it can't be."

Clumsily, Bonnie climbed to her feet, her mind spinning with shock, her heart breaking. For a moment she stood with her eyes closed, leaning against the desk, feeling as if her life was crumbling, as if she was dying.

She shoved away from the desk and stumbled toward the door, her pain giving way to anger as her mind grasped the realization that the Warwicks had owned Gunnerside mine, that the man supervising the operation of that mine had killed her father. And that man was . . . who?

Oh, God, who?

Slowly, she climbed the stairs to the bedroom she shared with her husband. She sat on the bed and placed the ledger before her. Her hands trembling, she leafed through the pages, unable to make sense of the often haphazard entries. She searched until she found the final entry for Patrick Eden.

"Terminated," she read.

She flung the book across the room and fell to the mattress, her sobs tearing at her chest and throat. Finally, when she lay spent from crying, she rolled to her back and stared at the ceiling.

Someone living in this house had murdered her father.

With tears rolling down her cheeks, she closed her eyes, frantically remembering the conversations she had had with Kate. The Warwick businesses had been passed from one person to another so many times . . . any one of them could have been in charge of Gunnerside at that time, including her husband.

Bonnie left the bed.

Standing at the window, she looked out over Braithwaite's gardens to the frost-covered moor beyond.

Not Damien. Oh, please, not my husband.

She covered her face with her hands and swayed against the windowsill, pressed her cheek against the cold glass as tears slid from her eyes.

Not my husband.

My lord husband.

She whirled back toward the bed as the memory of that awful night flashed before her. How many times had she attempted to remember the murderer's face? But she'd never seen it. Her eyes had been locked on his bloody hands as he came after her.

If the murderer lived in this house, why hadn't he recognized her?

The night had been rainy. She had been much younger. She'd been wrapped in layers of clothes and wearing a heavy scarf around her head. She'd stood in the doorway for only seconds before bolting into the dark and escaping over the moor.

Hurrying to the wardrobe, Bonnie grabbed her cloak and threw it over her shoulders as she ran from the room and down the stairs, vaguely hearing Jewel's cry of alarm as she threw open the front door and fled the house.

"M'lady, what's wrong?" came the servant's plea.

"Please, m'lady, y'll freeze out there. Come back! F' the love of God, come back!"

Bonnie hastily made her way down the path that had led her to Braithwaite that stormy night, sliding occasionally on the freezing earth, remotely feeling the bite of sleet upon her face. She ran until her lungs burned from the cold and the effort to hold in her grief. She felt her father's death as keenly as she had six years ago, the wound lay open as painfully because her mind told her she might well have married his killer . . . Her heart didn't want to believe it—wouldn't believe it. Yet . . .

The ruins of Middleham Castle loomed up before her, shrouded in mist, the crumbling walls towering toward the bleak sky. She collapsed upon the keep steps, exhausted, weakened, heartbroken . . . angry. Only days before she had sat yonder with her husband and they had daydreamed of their future together.

Was there the remotest possibility that Damien had no knowledge of how her father died?

She had never told anyone. She'd been too afraid.

But the people of the village had known. She'd hidden in the dark and listened to the Gunnerside workers talk among themselves of hers and Patrick's disappearance. They all thought her dead as well—murdered by the mine supervisor— but when she'd considered revealing the truth to them, she'd overheard one man say, "The law won't prosecute the bloody nabob. He's practically bleedin' royalty. Best keep yer mouth closed or yer liable to find yerself buried at the bottom of some mine shaft like the lass and her father."

Damien must know. There had been something different about him since his return from Gunnerside that she had attributed to worry over his plantation. She should have guessed he wouldn't be content with just riding to the church to collect her birth documents. Of course he would want to know everything he could about her.

He knew, and he'd said nothing. He'd married her with the knowledge that he, or a member of his family, had killed her father.

He either loved her desperately.

Or he intended to keep her quiet . . . forever.

* * *

Miles tossed his coat over the stair rail and blew into his hands to warm them. He glanced about the decorated vestibule, noting the holly and berries, the red candles and velvet bows adorning every possible fixture. Turning to Richard, who was more slowly removing his wrap, he said, "Well, you were right. Seems Damien has settled at Braithwaite for good."

Richard removed his hat. "So it seems. Where the blazes is all the help when you need them? Where's Damien?"

"Lording over his realm, no doubt."

Richard walked partway down the gallery before returning. Miles smiled coldly. "Still in a tiff, aren't you, because your beloved nephew conveniently dropped your name from his wedding list. Seems you rate no better than I. No doubt he thought you'd propose one too many toasts to the bride and groom."

"I haven't taken a drink in months," Richard replied gruffly.

"Apparently Dame doesn't store much faith in your abstinence."

"I wonder where the lady of the house is?" Richard frowned.

"Ah, the *lady*. Imagine addressing Bonnie as *lady*. The last time I saw her she was begging money from my mistress."

Jewel entered the foyer just then, wringing her hands in worry. Seeing Miles, she stopped and puffed out her cheeks in obvious disapproval. Then she spied Richard. "Sir!" she cried. "Thank God, y've arrived. His lordship is out and I fear somethin' dreadful 'as 'appened t' m'lady."

"Indeed," Richard replied. "Why so?"

"M'lady went t' her room a short while ago. The next thing I know she was runnin' out the door weepin', and she ain't come back."

"No doubt my brother's been an ass again," Miles said.

Jewel squinted her eyes at him. "They've been happy as two lovebirds. His lordship left early t' deliver some goods t' Caldbergh and Bonnie—m'lady—went searchin' for the old countess's address book in the library. The next I seen her she was dashin' out the door in a state of distress. I found the address book where she'd left it in the library and some ledgers strewn about the floor.''

"I see.'' Richard looked concerned. "Have you any idea when my nephew will be home?''

"No, sir.''

Richard looked at Miles. "Perhaps you should have a look.''

"Perhaps I should.'' He reached for his cloak and swung it around his shoulders. He tugged on his gloves. His mouth curling in a smile, he said, "I'll do Dame this last favor before I inform him I'm moving to Paris permanently. Have you any idea where Bonnie might have gone?'' he asked Jewel.

"She were headed toward the castle. Her and his lordship walk or ride up there every day.''

"Then I'll begin looking there.'' Pivoting on his heels, he started for the door. Richard called out behind him. "Careful of this damned fog and ice, Miles. The path could be slippery. I'll be along just as soon as I change into something warmer.''

Without responding, Miles left the house. Turning his collar up against the cold, he searched the horizon, spying the distant ruin of Middleham Castle as it appeared and disappeared behind intermittent clouds of mist.

"*Countess,* is it?'' he said aloud.

Shoving his hands in his pockets, he strode toward the castle.

Bonnie stood on the steps of the keep, her face in the wind. She felt numb with cold and despair. How could she return to Braithwaite? How could she face her husband? She could hardly pretend she knew nothing of the Warwick involvement with Gunnerside.

Snow drifted soundlessly across the rising and falling moor, collected in the crevices of the ancient stone walls, and lightly dusted her hair. She held out her hand, and the flakes momentarily danced upon her palm before disappearing completely.

"Y' didn't kill him, my lord husband,'' she said aloud. "I know in m' heart y' didn't.''

But if he hadn't, why had he not confronted her with the

truth? Why had he married her with this terrible secret between them?

She heard a noise and turned. A movement at the far edge of the crumbled castle wall caught her eye. Through the thickening fog a figure moved toward her, his cape fluttering about his legs in the wind. Bonnie backed further up the steps, scattering loose stones that bounced to the ground.

"So there you are," came Miles's voice.

He moved silently through the mist, stopping at the foot of the stairs. His face looked ashen in the cold and twilight. His eyes were dark.

She couldn't speak.

"What the devil are you doing up there, Bonnie? Come down before you're hurt. Let me help you." He moved forward, raising his hand toward her.

"No!" She stumbled, sliding on gravel and ice, unable to take her gaze off his hands. "D-don't touch me."

He appeared momentarily surprised; he lowered his arm. The corners of his mouth turned up coldly as he said, "I take this show of hostility to mean we aren't friends any longer. That's too bad. I had grown quite fond of you, you know." He moved closer, and his eyes looked angry. Bonnie felt her heart freeze as he said, "That's really quite a shame . . ."

Twenty-nine

The cold wind slashed Damien's face as he drove his lathered horse toward Braithwaite. The gray stone house loomed through the fog as he approached, its windows casting dim yellow light into the fog.

Before the animal could stop completely, Damien hit the ground, running, tearing off his cloak as he entered the doorway. Casting the garment to the floor, he purposefully slowed his steps as he moved down the gallery to the library. He told himself there was no reason yet to panic. Perhaps he would find Bonnie curled in a chair with a book or struggling over some needlepoint or making a nuisance of herself in the kitchen by attempting to tell Cook how to do his business.

He entered the library and stopped, his eyes drawn immediately to the scattered ledgers on the floor. Slowly, his gaze shifted to the desk, to the china music box, and beside it, his mother's address book. He closed his eyes, the cold fear inside him like a blade in his heart. He felt staggered by it. He stood and stared at the floor, numb, disembodied, lost in that moment more profoundly than he had ever been in Vicksburg, no longer simply a man wrenched from his home by silly pride but an entity robbed of its soul. He was more of a dream than a reality—there, yet not there; though his body remained, his life had ended.

Slowly, he turned and left the room, woodenly climbed the stairs, his sights set straight ahead, the peripheral world a confusion of images and memories tumbling through his mind as if he were a drowning man clutching at life. He moved into his and Bonnie's bedroom, preparing to face her one last time.

What would he say?

I'm sorry.

Forgive me.

I love you.

He would go down on his knees, if he must. Such an act seemed a small compromise to make in order to keep Bonnie.

Yet, she was not there. Only the ledger lay open on the floor, proof positive. He bent and picked it up, placed it on the bed.

Lost. Lost.

His life swept over him like a black avalanche as he quit the room. With Bonnie he had been reborn—rather, born for the first time, alive for the first time in his thirty-three years. Living without her meant returning to America, struggling to forget, existing one day to the next in an emotionless vacuum.

He stared straight ahead, as if the portraits of his ancestors on the walls that he passed were silently watching, judging. He crossed the hallway obliquely, blindly, refusing to look again at their room. It was as deserted as if he had not slept with her there the last month. As if he had never held her and made love with her or felt their child move . . .

A hand on his arm stopped him. He turned to Jewel without really seeing, vaguely noting her look of shock at his appearance. Her lips moved, yet he could not hear her. He tried to pull away. She grabbed him again and shook him.

"What?" he asked. "What are you saying?" He tried to concentrate.

"M'lady . . . she went out . . . upset . . . gone a long time."

Then she said something that lurched him from his suffering. His hands came up and clamped onto her arms. "What did you say?"

"I said yer brother and uncle have come home. I told 'em about m'lady and they went huntin' her at the castle, but they ain't come back."

He shoved her away, hearing her cry out in surprise as she tumbled to the floor. He took the stairs two at a time, knocking aside Gretchen, who was hurrying to assist her friend. He flung open the door and ran into the encroaching night.

Mist and sleet converged upon him as he forged his way over the moor, along the frozen footpath to the ruins. He slipped and fell, cursing violently, pounding the earth with his fist before struggling to his feet and continuing onward. He felt like a man possessed, all former anguish vanquished by a greater anger toward the fiend who had murdered Bonnie's father, who, even now, might be holding her life, as well as the life of his child, in his hands.

Bonnie stared fixedly into Miles's empty face, her heart racing. Seconds ticked by like an eternity as she awaited his next move. She dared say or do nothing to further aggravate him. The servants' warnings about him rushed through her mind, gossip of violence toward her husband, rumors she had ignored because she had felt sorry for him.

"Come down from there," he ordered.

She pressed back against the wall.

Then some movement beyond him caught her eye. The vague image drew nearer, emerging soundlessly through the mist until she could make out Richard's face. He held one finger to his lips to silence her, yet some voice, some warning, some instinct made her cry, "No!"

Miles spun a moment too late. Richard brought the rock against his head with a sickening crack.

Miles collapsed into Richard's arms, and as Bonnie watched, horrified, Richard lowered him to the ground, huddling over him before turning back to her. She stared at his bloody hands, the old terror clawing up her throat. She heard herself groan. Suddenly the past and present were yawning before her like bottomless caverns. She tried fiercely to hang onto reason, to reality, yet the nearer Richard came, the more that fine line of rationality frayed.

"You. It was you," she said in a raw voice. "You killed my father."

Richard walked toward her. His face appeared at first angry, then troubled. "It was an accident, Bonnie. I'd been drinking, then he showed up making threats and my temper got the better of me. I didn't mean to strike out."

"Oh, God." She wept. The memories were a physical as well as a mental torture. She had tried so long to refuse them, to deny them, surrendering to them only in her nightmares.

Now they rained upon her like a man's fists. She trembled. Her legs weakened. She braced herself against the rough wall and tried to keep from collapsing.

"I have suffered, lass. I've truly regretted the act. If there was any way I could bring him back, I would. But I can't, Bonnie."

"Murderer! When Damien learns of this—"

"He won't. I can't let that happen. Don't you see? I've worked hard these last months to get my life in order. Damien gave me one last chance to do that. I won't let him down. You see, he's been like a son to me. The others treated me like a peasant, but not Damien. We've always been close, and I simply cannot let some foolish mistake I made in the past destroy all that."

"You—you're insane."

"No, my dear, just determined."

Bonnie backed up the stairs—there was nowhere else to run. She slid on the stones and fell hard on her back. "He'll never forgive you if you kill me," she cried.

"He won't know it was me. He'll think it was Miles. Miles was always the black sheep, the troublemaker. Damien will find your bodies at the foot of the keep. It'll appear as if you both struggled and fell to your deaths. He'll suffer unbearably, but in time he'll recover."

Closing her fingers on a stone, she hurled it at Richard. It missed him by inches. She tried scrambling up the steps, then realizing that was exactly where Richard would want her, she looked frantically toward the ground. She was already too high to jump.

"Imagine my chagrin when I arrived in London and learned Damien had married and had not even bothered to tell me," Richard said, his voice oddly flat. "Naturally, I questioned how you managed to marry, considering your lack of documentation. Then when I learned your last name, I couldn't believe it. I prayed it was some terrible coincidence. Upon returning to Braithwaite and finding the Gunnerside ledger, I was deeply saddened. But you see, I simply cannot risk losing everything I've attained. For so many years I was Joseph's whipping boy, forced to endure his ridicule. Then it was Randolf—just like his father—looking down his nose at me, mocking me, deriding me for my shortcomings. It was no wonder I drank and gambled. I lived in fear that any day I would be called up before the bastard and informed I was no longer employed. Randolf threatened to do just that the day he died. But as fate would have it, he shot himself while hunting. Clumsy idiot. I suppose I could have saved him. I saw the entire thing from across the river. But as I stood there, watching him crawl toward me, pleading for my help, my only thoughts were, 'I'm free at last. Now it can all be Damien's. Damien will have to come home now.' ''

Richard lurched toward her, his bloodstained fingers hooked like claws, the face she'd grown so fond of now that of a stranger. He was mad. Truly mad. She did her best to hold onto her own sanity, refusing to let it shatter. She screamed as his hands gripped her clothing, and desperately she informed him: "Damien knows, Richard. He already knows you killed my father!"

He hesitated, shock turning his face to a mask of indecision.

"If he finds me dead, he's going to know you killed me. He'll—he'll never forgive you. Never!"

"Liar!" His hand struck her across the face, and pain and blackness splintered her mind. Her arms flailed uselessly as she felt herself being lifted and dragged further up the stairs.

"No!" she cried again and again. "He knows! He knows! He'll never let you get away with this!"

A blast of frigid wind hit Bonnie full force, driving pellets of sleet into her face as they reached the top of the narrow, primitive staircase. She gasped for breath as she fell onto the disintegrating balcony that had once been the floor of the castle keep. Wind howled over the parapets, tearing at her, soaking her hair, and ripping her clothing as fiercely as Richard's hands struggled to send her flying into the roiling mist beneath her.

Gathering her strength, she drove her fists into his chest, his arms, bracing her legs against the stone walls, yet feeling the stone, little by little, give way to the stress and tumble and fall to the rock-strewn floor below. She was sliding nearer and nearer the precipice; her legs dangled uselessly over the edge. She vowed if she went she would take him too. She locked her hands in his coat and—

A howl of rage rent the air, and suddenly Damien's face

loomed over her, contorted in fury as he gripped Richard's shoulders and dragged him off her. She seized a jagged ledge for a handhold and pulled herself away from the edge. She rolled to her knees and huddled near the floor as Damien and Richard struggled for a foothold at the top of the stairs.

His arms gripped from behind, Richard drove backward, propelling Damien against the wall so forcefully that he was momentarily stunned. Bonnie cried out as Richard whirled and slammed Damien upon the wall a second time and wrapped his fingers around his throat.

Damien clawed ineffectually at his uncle's hands. He tried to speak.

Richard, his eyes wild, shoved him again and again against the wall. Damien planted his hand on Richard's face and tried to shove him back. He could not breathe. His vision came and went like flashes of lightning. He could feel the life slowly draining from him, yet there was nothing he could do to break Richard's hold. His uncle's mind had snapped completely, and with it all reason.

One last time he threw his weight onto Richard, ramming his elbow into his neck, momentarily dislodging the grip his uncle had on his throat. They tumbled to the floor, rolling, fighting for dominance on the icy precipice. Then Bonnie was there, throwing herself on Richard's back, sinking her nails into his face and dragging him away as he yowled in pain and fury. Before Damien could regroup, Richard had turned on Bonnie with his fist raised, stumbling toward her as she backed toward the black abyss in an attempt to escape him. "No!" Damien rasped between breaths. "For the love of God, Uncle—"

Miles plowed up the stairs through the shifting mist, his face streaked with blood and his teeth bared in pain. He stumbled over Damien and fell upon Richard, dragging him down and spinning him around. For an instant they tottered on the keep's top step, flailing for a handhold, poised like dancers frozen in mid stride.

Damien lunged for Miles.

Their hands touched, grasped.

A frightened moan escaped Richard in that last instant. A fleeting moment of sanity passed over his features, then was gone as he hurtled down through the darkness. A despairing cry echoed back before his body struck the ground below with a thud. Overwhelming relief swept through Damien, even as his heart acknowledged the grief of losing Richard. He felt liberated from a turbulent black pressure, confusion, and boiling rage. He was too numb for tears, too weakened for elation. As Miles dropped to the floor beside him, Damien looked around for Bonnie.

She sat on her heels, her fists pressed to her mouth. Her long hair blew in the wind, and her face was as pale as a moon.

He could not think of what to say.

He raised his hands and let them fall. He sat and drew his knees up to his chest, buried his face against them as if he could hide. In that moment he felt slightly insane himself. But he could not face her condemnation. Better that he fling himself down the steps after Richard than suffer one instant of her rejection.

There was a movement beside him, a touch on his arm; he raised his head. Bonnie's face was close to his, her fingers light on his shoulder. Her expression was intense, frightened but not hostile. She seemed uncertain what she should do.

"Y' knew," came the words, a soft vapor from her lips.

"Yes."

Something of her old anger flashed in her eyes. Her breasts rose, as if she were out of breath. "Why didn't y' tell me?"

"I was afraid of losing you."

Her long lashes lowered. A long, tormenting moment of irresolution passed. When they lifted again, there was the faintest smile about her eyes. She said quietly, "I was hopin' that was the reason."

He began to shake, whether with relief or from cold, he could not guess. Bonnie opened her cloak and did her best to close it around him. She kissed his cheek, then whispered, "My lord husband, I'd like t' go home now."

The half door of her parent's house swung unsteadily on its hinges, creaking quietly as an icy wind wedged through the roof and windows and gusted through the empty rooms. Bonnie stood in the center of the dwelling and viewed her surroundings.

"It's much smaller than I remember," she said.

Damien hunched his shoulders against the cold. He wasn't altogether certain he should have brought Bonnie here. She was too near her time. But she had insisted.

The front door squeaked shrilly, causing both of them to jump. A stoop-shouldered old man peeked his head around the door and eyed them. ''Thought someone was nosin' about up here.'' He considered Bonnie for a time, then shook his head. ''For a minute there I thought I was lookin' at Mary. She lived 'ere, y' know, some six, seven year ago. That was before she died, o' course.'' He shuffled into the room, rubbing his arthritic hands together for warmth. ''Entire family's gone now. Been gone for near that long. The village folk figure they're all dead.''

Damien turned away and stood alone, facing the blackened fireplace.

The old man frowned. ''Just vanished, did Patrick and the lass. I forget the girl's name now.'' He studied Bonnie speculatively as she walked past him and stopped at the door, gazing down the overgrown path, beyond the front gate to the road winding in the distance.

''Aye, it were a pleasant place when Patrick and Mary lived 'ere,'' he said. ''They made a fine couple for certain. Ever'one figured Paddy would never settle down, but Mary managed to win him over. They both had tempers hotter'n a cauldron, and when they fought y' could hear 'em all way down t' the village. The next y' know they're standing in that rose garden carryin' on like a pair o' lovebirds.''

Bonnie smiled at the memory.

The old man moved up behind her, and like Bonnie, peered down the valley. ''Some say they've seen 'em, y' know. Usually it's in the late spring when the sun plays tricks with the light as it sets behind the dales. They say they see Mary standin' in this door, watchin' down that lane for Paddy t' return home from the mines, just like she did when she was livin'. She waits until he nearly reaches the gate, then she runs t' meet him. Folks say he picks her high in the air and spins her 'round and 'round.''

The stranger stepped past Bonnie and walked several paces before stopping. Squinting, he threw up his hand to shield his eyes from the setting sun, and said, ''That kind o' love happens only once in a lifetime, I figure. Always did wonder what it was that Mary said t' Patrick t' make him laugh so hardy when he was holdin' her so high and spinnin' her around. Reckon we'll never know.''

Without another word he ambled down the path. He looked back once, as Damien moved up behind Bonnie and wrapped his arms around her, then he shook his head and walked on.

They stood in silence for a long while, listening to the wind moan over the moor, watching until the old man had disappeared down the lane. Finally Bonnie turned in her husband's arms. Regret had been a constant companion to them since that dreadful day at the castle. He had refused to speak of the incident; so had she. It was time to confront the past and bury it for good.

"Do y' suppose Richard is well taken care of in that sanitarium?''

"Yes.''

"Does he know y' yet?''

"No.'' He shook his head.

She continued to regard him. His features, indeed his entire being, were like the tenuous walls of a crumbling dam. She felt him shake against her and knew it was not from the cold. Raising her gloved hands, she took his face in them and smiled.

He swallowed, and closing his fingers around her wrists, he spoke. "I'm ashamed that my family destroyed yours. I wish I could bring your father back, but I can't.''

"But y' have.'' She placed his hands on her stomach. "What Richard took from me, y've given me back.''

His eyes burned upon hers, and for a moment it appeared as if the damn would break. Then, little by little, the cataclysm passed. His face warmed and, to her relief and pleasure, she saw that there was in his eyes, if not on his lips, a suggestion of a smile, a touch of his old arrogance, and a spark of fire that blazed ever brighter as their babe moved against his palms.

"I love you,'' he said.

Without looking back, they left the cottage.

Epilogue

The threat of a summer storm having ended, Bonnie shoved back the shutters on the house and stood at the window with her face in the breeze, breathing in the heady scent of moorland peat and fragrant roses.

Patrick William Philippe Asquith Warwick sneezed in his cradle, and Bonnie looked around. The baby lay on his back, his feet in the air and his pudgy fingers gripping his toes. His green eyes twinkled back at Bonnie, and he smiled.

Scooping the lad up in her arms, Bonnie said, "Come and see what a lovely view your father's given us, Patrick."

Bonnie moved back to the window. Mother and son gazed out over the moor, enjoying the breeze that stirred their thick black hair and cooled the heat from their brows. Bonnie pointed to the distant village. "Someday you'll be earl of that village, and the lands as far as you can see will belong to you." She shifted him to the other hip and pointed in the opposite direction. "Just beyond that fell is Braithwaite Hall. If you so desire you may live there, but if you're half the gentleman your father is, you'll build your spoiled wife a house wherever she desires and live there whether you want to or not." She giggled and buried her face against the child's chubby neck. Patrick squealed with delight.

"Wot's this?" Jewel asked from the door. "Is his young lordship Patrick ready for his bath, m'lady?"

"Aye." Bonnie laughed. "It certainly sounds like it."

Jewel chucked the babe under the chin. "Best get him while he's happy or there'll be hell t' pay. He be blessed with yours and his lordship's temper, I vow."

Handing her son over to Jewel, Bonnie asked, "Has Cook started dinner?"

"Aye. It's beef and puddin's f' certain."

"Puddin's!" she cried. "Bloody hell, he'll be makin' 'em with water again, I wager."

She ran from the room and down the stairs, hesitating as a burst of laughter sounded from the drawing room. She walked to the door and looked in. Philippe, Claurence, and Freddy sat around a table staring at Marianne as she considered what wager to place on her cards.

"I'm out of coins," Marianne announced. "Who will lend me some?"

"I have a better idea," Philippe said.

"What's that?" she asked.

He leaned toward her and whispered something behind his hand.

"Animal!" Marianne snapped. Then, smiling wickedly, she added, "You're on."

"We'll have none of *that,*" Bonnie said, and the foursome looked around.

"I say," Claurence said, "when is Damien to return from this sheep-buying expedition?"

"Sheep." Freddy snickered. "Imagine Warwick raising sheep. He hated bloody sheep all his life. Said sheep were good for only one thing and that was—"

Philippe cleared his throat and flashed Bonnie a smile. "Is that pudding I smell?"

"Oh!" she cried. Spinning, she ran to the kitchen just as Cook shoved his tins of puddings into the oven. "Too late," she said.

"I beg your pardon?" he asked with a tip of his chin.

"Y've gone and made 'em with water."

"I haven't."

"Y' bloody well have and I know it."

Cook sniffed and turned away. "Won't rise anyway," he said. "That oven is simply unacceptable. I could prepare better meals over a heap of peat."

"It was good enough for *my* mother."

"Pre-cise-ly."

Bonnie grinned and walked to the half door at the rear of the kitchen. Lovingly she ran her hands up and down the aged wood before turning back to study the comfortably warm room.

She recalled her surprise when Damien had sauntered into Braithwaite and informed her that they were moving. She recalled her joy upon seeing the house he'd built her. He called it slightly larger than cramped and only minutely smaller than spacious, though Bonnie called it grand. Half the size of Braithwaite, it was still an imposing structure perched atop the highest hill overlooking Middleham. She recalled the love she'd felt when he informed her that he'd moved her parent's house, stone by stone, to the site, that its walls now made up the kitchen of Bonnie's new home. The remainder of the house had been built of Middleham Castle stones.

Now he was off somewhere buying sheep.

Stanley walked in, his arms full of cut wood. He stacked it neatly near the stove before straightening to face Bonnie, a strained expression on his face. "My lady. Had I wanted to be so involved with wood, I would have become a carpenter. This"—he pointed to the wood—"is the footman's job."

"But we don't have a footman any longer," she reasoned.

"If you are not very careful, you will not have a butler either." He turned toward the door, stopped, and looked back. His eyes were twinkling as he said fondly, "I do believe I heard the unmistakable *baa*ing of sheep somewhere down the lane."

With a squeal of excitement Bonnie dashed past him. She paused at the drawing room and announced, "Damien's home!" then ran down the hall, stopping just long enough to check her appearance in the mirror. She secured the bow tightly in her hair and smoothed her hands over her skirt, deciding to leave her apron in place.

The front door was open. Philippe stood on one side, laughing. Jewel stood on the other, cradling Patrick in her arms. Bonnie joined them.

"Would you look at that," Philippe said. "He's done it. He's actually done it."

The sheep topped the first rise, jostling and leaping, the bells around their necks ringing out in the afternoon air. And then Damien was there, his long strides eating up the lane as he rushed home to Bonnie. Seeing her standing in the doorway, he waved.

"What are y' waitin' for?" Jewel whispered.

Bonnie hurried down the path, her skirts brushing the top-heavy roses that crowded the walk and filled the air with perfume. She shoved open the wicket and ran down the road, her dark hair and ribbons flying like a banner behind her, her approach scattering the *baa*ing lambs and ewes.

Smiling, Damien stopped and opened his arms, grabbing her up against him, spinning her around and around above him. His face was dusty and streaked with sweat, but it didn't matter to Bonnie as he said, "Careful, darlin', or you'll spoil your pretty clothes."

"So I'll wash 'em." She laughed. "Just kiss me, m'love!"

He did, of course, right there in the lane for all the world and God to see. They laughed then, as he spun her again—

And their laughter echoed all the way down the moor.

Dear Readers,

Over the last four years, since the publication of my first book, you have continued to support me and to show your support by writing me such wonderful, heartwarming letters that I am occasionally moved to tears. You cannot know how much those words of encouragement and congratulation mean to me. I have saved every one and reread them often—some I have framed and hung on my office wall. They are there to remind me, when I'm feeling very tired and lonely and occasionally discouraged, that there is a reason to continue this often frustrating business. That reason is you.

I hope you have enjoyed reading Damien and Bonnie's love story as much as I enjoyed creating it for you. This book is very special to me for reasons too complicated to go into, but it serves to remind us all that out of the merest spark of fantasy—of hopes—of dreams—fairy tales *can* come true, if you only dare to aspire.

Readers, thank you for making my dreams come true and please continue to write me.

Katherine Sutcliffe
P.O. Box 866363
Plano, Texas 75086-6363

The Timeless Romances
of New York Times Bestselling Author
JOHANNA LINDSEY

DEFY NOT THE HEART 75299-9/$4.50 US/$5.50 Can
To save herself from the union being forced upon her, Reina offered to become her kidnapper's bride, but the nuptial bed was not part of the bargain.

SILVER ANGEL 75294-8/$4.50 US/$5.95 Can
Kidnapped and sold into slavery, Chantelle Burke swore she'd never surrender to her ruthless master. Yet the mysterious stranger ignited the fires of her very soul.

TENDER REBEL 75086-4/$4.50 US/$5.95 Can
Insisting on a marriage in name only was something Roslyn quickly grew to regret as she dared to trust her new husband with her life...and her love.

SECRET FIRE 75087-2/$4.50 US/$5.95 Can
From the tempestuous passion at their first meeting, theirs was a fever that carried them to the power of undeniable love.

HEARTS AFLAME	89982-5/$4.95 US/$5.95 Can
A HEART SO WILD	75084-8/$4.50 US/$5.95 Can
WHEN LOVE AWAITS	89739-3/$4.50 US/$5.50 Can
LOVE ONLY ONCE	89953-1/$4.50 US/$5.50 Can
TENDER IS THE STORM	89693-1/$4.50 US/$5.50 Can
BRAVE THE WILD WIND	89284-7/$4.50 US/$5.95 Can
A GENTLE FEUDING	87155-6/$4.50 US/$5.50 Can
HEART OF THUNDER	85118-0/$4.95 US/$5.95 Can
SO SPEAKS THE HEART	81471-4/$4.50 US/$5.95 Can
GLORIOUS ANGEL	84947-X/$4.50 US/$5.50 Can
PARADISE WILD	77651-0/$4.50 US/$5.50 Can
FIRES OF WINTER	75747-8/$4.50 US/$5.50 Can
A PIRATE'S LOVE	40048-0/$4.95 US/$5.95 Can
CAPTIVE BRIDE	01697-4/$4.50 US/$5.50 Can

AVON BOOKS